SUN TOUCHED

SUN TOUCHED

A TOUCH OF VAMPIRE

BECKY MOYNIHAN

BROKEN
BOOKS

Published by Broken Books
www.beckymoynihan.com

ISBN-13: 978-1-7327330-9-1

Cover design by Becky Moynihan
Cover model by Ravven
www.depositphotos.com

To anyone courageous enough to start over,

I'm rooting for you.

PROLOGUE

KADE

The call came when I was minutes away from the castle.

I fished the phone from my pocket, expecting it to be my drothen's pregnant—*very* pregnant—mate. She'd run out of cookie dough ice cream, and I'd volunteered to pick some up from Sanctum Isle's sole grocery store. It was nearing dinner time though, so I wasn't surprised that she was calling me again.

She was almost seven months along and eating for *three*, after all.

Smirking, I answered the call without checking the number. "Don't tell me you have another craving, little Kenna. Your ice cream will be soup if I head back out again."

I waited for her response, but when none came, I pulled the phone away from my ear to check the connection.

What I glimpsed on the screen—the *name* I saw—nearly shorted out my heart.

My Mustang fishtailed on the narrow road and I quickly slammed on the brakes. Several pints of cookie dough ice cream tumbled from the backseat and onto the floor. Even after the car came to a screeching stop, I stared at the phone screen, utterly frozen.

She *never* called me. Not in almost five years.

And now that she had . . .

I couldn't move. Could barely even breathe.

Precious seconds passed before I regained some common sense.

Before I was finally able to press the phone to my ear again and say, "Isla?"

There was too much hope in the word, and I silently cursed myself. She'd probably butt-dialed me, nothing more.

When she didn't reply, I smothered all traces of hope. Yup. Butt dial. But I didn't hang up. Like the pathetic sod I was, I strained to catch even the slightest hint of her voice. I'd even settle for the sound of her breathing at this point.

It didn't matter that she could barely stand me. That the very sight of me caused her to run the other way.

I'd waited five long years for her to contact me. I didn't care that it was an accident. Just knowing that she was on the other end quickened my pulse.

A minute of silence went by. A minute of pretending that she too simply wanted to hear me breathe. To know that I was *there*, despite the distance between us.

Then . . .

"Help. Help me."

A second later, the line went dead.

CHAPTER 1

ISLA — 20 Hours Earlier

"I'm so sorry, Mrs. Bateman," I said as the middle-aged woman's face crumpled. She gripped the photos with trembling hands, her expression one of stupefied shock.

I loved my job, but this part sucked. My victory in these situations would always mean my client's loss.

I tracked the bob of her throat as she swallowed once. Twice. Three times. I tore my gaze away, digging my nails into my palms to center myself.

"I-I just . . . I *knew*, but I'd hoped I was wrong," she weakly stammered. I nodded sympathetically, but kept quiet. It wasn't professional to share my personal feelings. To say that her husband was a cheating douchebag and she was better off without him. No matter how much it pained me, I never voiced my opinion to my clients.

My job was to *oust* scumbags, nothing more. What others thought about them wasn't my business.

"Right, well," Mrs. Bateman said with a heavy sigh, tucking the incriminating photos back into their manilla envelope. "Guess I'll be needing a divorce lawyer."

I remained perfectly poised, even as I did an inward jig of celebration. *Good call, Mrs. Bateman.*

"I have a reference, if you need one," I replied, pulling a business card from my purse.

Not surprisingly, the woman blinked up at me in surprise. I ignored the look, completely used to them by now. It didn't matter that I had my very own *reputable* private investigator practice, or that I was twenty-three years old.

I still looked eighteen, barely old enough to graduate highschool, let alone have lawyer contacts at the ready.

Sure, I refused to stop dyeing the tips of my blonde hair a soft pink, but I'd let it grow out a little, at least. I'd also swapped my frilly skirts and short dresses for sensible jeans and pencil skirts. I'd even given up my sparkly lipgloss and nail polish.

But they still stared. Still questioned my expertise, despite my near flawless case-solving record within the Knox County area.

I simply stared back with unwavering confidence.

In the end, they usually came around. Perhaps out of desperation. And maybe a little fear.

I didn't try to intimidate them, but vampires kind of had that effect on humans, intentionally or not. I might still look like a human, but there was a predator lurking just beneath my skin, begging to be unleashed.

My nails mercilessly bit into my palms once again.

After a moment's hesitation, Mrs. Bateman accepted the offered card with a wane smile. "Thank you, Miss Andrews. You've been most helpful. I'll be sure to recommend you if anyone I know should need your . . . services."

"I'd appreciate that," I said, standing from the table a little too eagerly when she moved to do so.

I could have left then. I *should* have. Our business was concluded. She had no more use for me. But I paused, watching as she tightly clutched the thin envelope that had turned her world upside down.

I'd done that. Irrevocably changed her life.

Sure, I'd been paid to do it. She'd *wanted* me to. But I still felt . . . Responsible.

Like I owed her something.

"Mrs. Bateman?" I said, feeling my stomach clench when she lifted tear-filled eyes to mine. "I just wanted to say . . . make sure you have a plan in place before confronting your husband. You know, in case he doesn't take it well. Don't do this alone. You need a support team, even if it's just one person. And contact that divorce lawyer as soon as possible."

At my words, her chin began to wobble. I should have seen the signs and hightailed it out of there, but I paused again. Paused like the glutton for punishment I was. With tears streaming down her face, the middle-aged woman stepped around the table and pulled me into a hug.

I went poker straight as every cell in my body sprang awake. I stopped breathing. Stopped breathing as her neck came within inches of my mouth.

She said something to me, but I was suddenly deaf. Deaf to everything but the sound of her blood rushing through her veins and the strong heartbeat pounding in her throat.

Don't breathe, don't breathe, don't breathe, I inwardly chanted, squeezing my eyes shut. At the same time, I cursed myself for my stupidity. For my *youngling* mistake.

I hadn't fed earlier today, too preoccupied with wrapping up this case. I never should have come here. Not without feeding first.

I knew better. *I knew better.* And yet, I'd let my ego get in the way. Let my latest victory cloud my judgment.

I gouged my nails into my palms, realizing too late that they were no longer nails, but *claws.*

The sharp points pierced my skin. Blood warmed my palms.

I jerked away from the woman in a flash, quickly ducking my head. "I have to go, Mrs. Bateman," I blurted, panicking when my fangs began to painfully descend. Stiffly whirling around, I threw over my shoulder, "Best of luck to you," and dashed out the restaurant door.

Despite how dark the moonless, late autumn evening was, I forced myself to walk slowly toward my car. To act like the human I was pretending to be. Rain lightly drizzled down, soaking through my silk top, but I paid it no heed. I passed too close to a man on the sidewalk and the pain in my gums increased.

Don't breathe, don't breathe, don't breathe.

When I neared my white Mini Cooper, my hands shook so badly that I dropped my keys. Before they could hit the ground, I snatched them up again midair, thanks to my inhuman reflexes. The moment the engine started, I peeled onto Main Street to the sound of squealing rubber.

As I drove, I silently called myself every name in the book. Not only had I gone out on an empty stomach, I hadn't brought a thermos with me. Not that I had anything to put in it. My blood supply had run out last night, and I'd been too busy to get more. There was a vampire-owned store in Bangor that supplied blood to the surrounding vampire populace, but I hadn't taken the necessary time to make a trip there. It was only forty-five minutes from my apartment in Rosewood, and I'd thought I could hold out until tonight.

I'd thought wrong.

My throat burned fiercely with *need*, a need that had plagued me every day for the past five years. I'd learned fairly quickly that my bloodlust was stronger than most vampires. I could control it, but it grew unbearable if I waited too long to feed. Up until now, I'd managed to avoid attacking anyone. Well, I'd tried to attack my best friend once, but that had been days after I'd first been turned.

I could barely remember that time. Only that I'd been insatiable. And terrified.

Refocusing on the road, I made a beeline for the closest blood bar. The addition had been built shortly after I'd become a vampire, thanks to my brother's suggestion. Several more had recently cropped up along Maine's coastline, serving the denser vampire-populated areas. The establishments doubled as regular bars, welcoming both humans and vampires alike. But the clientele weren't allowed to mix, unlike feeding dens.

I shivered, recalling my time trapped in a den five years ago. It had also been a nightclub, but I hadn't spent my time on the dance floor. I'd been held upstairs, where I was eventually drained of all my blood. Where I'd been *killed*.

And when I had woken up . . .

I was an entirely different being.

Undead. An immortal creature of the night. A created Feltore.

My knuckles bled white as I strangled the steering wheel. Realizing I was going sixty in a thirty-five zone, I eased off the accelerator.

When the sign for Mike's Tavern flashed in my peripheral, I breathed easier. Steeling myself for what was to come, I pulled into the already packed parking lot. I rarely frequented blood bars, and for good reason. Too many humans hung out there in an enclosed tight space. Sure, I only passed through their section on my way to the back room where vampires were served, but having them all lined up at the bar—their bloodstreams fizzing with alcohol—was hard to resist.

The moment the engine shut off, I was out of the car, walking at a fast clip toward the front entrance. A handful of bikers were loitering under the roof's awning, puffing on cigarettes. At my approach, all five of their gazes snapped to me. Or, more accurately, to the white blouse sticking to my chest.

I was used to men checking out my body. Even women. Curves had a way of drawing attention and I had plenty of them. It was the double D's they saw first though. Couldn't really blame them. I'd stare at them too if they weren't attached to me.

My heels clicked smartly against the wet asphalt as I ignored their looks, focused on my destination. As long as they didn't try to cop a feel, they could gawk to their heart's content.

"Looking for a ride, sweet thing?" one of them had the balls to say as I passed.

"Not with any of you, sugar plum," I tartly responded with a fake southern twang. His cohorts chortled and guffawed, which was a good sign. When I reached for the door handle and none of them made a move toward me, some of my tension eased. The second I entered the crowded interior though, fear shivered up my spine.

Not for myself, but for *them*.

The dozens of clueless, drunken humans ripe for the taking.

It would be so easy. With a little thrall, I could have anyone in this room at my mercy. They wouldn't resist. Wouldn't *want* to. Not if I told them not to.

I cursed under my breath, pausing just inside the entrance. Coming here was a bad idea. I was too hungry. Too *starved*. Despite the chill rain sliding down my skin, my body broke out in a hot sweat.

"Not *now*," I quietly groaned, trembling in my effort to hold still.

The shivering heat—combined with an increased heart rate and shortness of breath—could only mean one thing.

I was losing control.

And if I stepped one more foot inside this place, someone was going to get hurt.

My heart thundered with excitement at the thought of slaking my thirst on warm blood. *Fresh* blood. Straight from the source. I'd always wanted to. *Craved* to.

I was also afraid to. Terrified of what it would do to me. What I would become.

But the longer I stood there, breathing in the intoxicating scents surrounding me, the less I cared. The less *human* I felt.

A woman brushed past me on her way out the door and my fangs dropped to their full length.

A growl of need pushed at my throat and I turned. Turned to follow her. To stalk her into the night. To *prey* like the predator I was.

The moment I did, a hand firmly gripped my elbow.

"Let me buy you a drink," a deep, slightly-accented voice— British, maybe—said in my ear, causing me to stiffen. "Looks like you need one."

I tried to yank my arm away, but the grip only tightened.

"Let go of me," I hissed, instinctively baring my fangs.

"I'd put those away if I were you," he responded, refusing to budge. "We wouldn't want to cause a scene and get kicked out for breaking the house rules."

My breath caught.

He was a vampire.

"Let me find you a seat. It's a bit crowded in here tonight," he went on, smoothly steering me forward. Every instinct demanded I dig my heels in and tell this guy off, but it finally dawned on me what he was trying to do.

Help me.

Somehow, in the short amount of time I'd been here, he'd realized I was in trouble and had come to my rescue.

My stomach soured.

Despite my annoyance at his unwanted gallantry, I let him guide me toward the back room without resistance, keeping my gaze firmly trained on our destination. Before we could enter, a vampire blocked our way. One whiff of our scent and he let us through.

The stranger at my back continued to usher me forward, leading me directly toward the bar. When I claimed an empty stool, I stiffly waited for him to drop my arm. His touch lingered a few seconds too long, then slipped away.

"Thanks," I tightly said, barely able to speak past my burning throat, "but I've got it from here." I made eye contact with the bartender and he headed my way.

"It's no trouble at all," the vampire smoothly replied, sliding onto the stool next to mine. I inwardly cringed as he swiveled on his seat to face me. "I couldn't leave a lady in distress now, could I?"

I snorted, reaching up to unstick wet hair plastered to my cheek. "Look, I'm not the damsel in distress type. I also don't feel like being hit on tonight, so thanks, but no thanks. I can get my own—"

I chose that moment to finally glance at him. The second I did, the words froze on my tongue. Good goddess, he was *hot*. Not conventionally, but in a rakish sort of way. As with all vampires, there was no guessing his true age, but he looked to be in his late twenties. His skin was pale, almost as pale as mine. Hints of crimson shone in his slicked-back dark hair. His sharp cheekbones and jawline were just short of severe, and an expensive-looking suit covered his lithe frame.

But what caught my attention were his eyes. They were a light hazel brown. So light that they were almost gold. The color drew me in, causing me to pause and stare far longer than I'd intended.

As the silence stretched, a slight smile pulled at his full lips.

8

"Forgive my rudeness. I'm Samuel Quinn, rescuer of beautiful women and harmless flirt."

I snorted again but couldn't suppress a small smile of my own. "I doubt there's anything *harmless* about you, Samuel Quinn," I said in reply, gratified when his grin broadened. If there was one language I understood, it was flirting. Most men sucked at it, which was why I rarely engaged, especially with strangers at bars. But there was something about this guy. Something . . .

Alluring.

When the bartender placed my drink before me, I did something then that I never did. "I'm Isla," I said to Samuel, giving up my name with only the slightest hesitation.

"Pretty name for a pretty woman," he replied, picking up his drink.

Instead of responding to the shameless compliment, I reached for my own glass. My fingers noticeably shook as they raised the drink to my lips. Samuel saw, but didn't comment. He watched while I took a sip, then another and another until I'd drained the whole thing in a matter of seconds.

A relieved sigh shuddered through me and I set the glass down.

Without taking his eyes off mine, Samuel motioned the bartender over and said, "The lady needs another."

It was on the tip of my tongue to protest, to settle my bill and leave before *this*—whatever this was—could continue. But I didn't. A part of me wanted to see where this would go. To flirt with this intriguing man just a little while longer.

But he's not a man, I warned myself. *He's a dangerous predator. A vampire. You're playing with fire.*

I didn't have many rules when it came to men, but fraternizing with vampires was the one rule I never broke. They weren't for me. I might be one of them, but that didn't mean I had to settle for one, no matter how easy it would be. I'd much rather cozy up to a warlock, human, or werewolf—even if their mortal blood drove me crazy with need.

I'd rather endure the cravings than be at the mercy of a vampire.

Yet, here I was, accepting a drink from a perfect stranger. A *vampire*. Allowing him to engage me in flirtatious banter.

"So tell me about yourself, Isla," he said, nudging the offered drink toward me. "What are your hobbies? Likes and dislikes?"

His gaze and voice were so mesmerizing that I felt my guard lower. Felt my muscles relax as I reached for the drink. Then I did something else that I never did.

I told a vampire about my personal life. First my job as a private investigator, then details about my friends and family. It felt good to share. It fed my extroverted nature, supplying me with a heady dose of serotonin. We talked for hours, ordering drink after drink until my mind grew hazy from the blood overindulgence.

I knew I had to stop soon. I'd become blood drunk several times in the past, and it always made me horny as hell. Thankfully, I'd always been in my apartment when it happened. I'd simply turn on my trusty vibrator and pass out soon afterward.

When I felt my core warm, tingling with need, I set down my glass and stood. Or tried to. My legs wobbled gracelessly before giving out completely. Arms were suddenly around me, keeping me from falling.

"I think you've had enough to drink," Samuel said with amusement, setting me back on my feet. "Maybe you should sit a while longer until the effects wear off."

I shook my head, which only made me sway against him. "No. I need to pee like a racehorse." When I took a teetering step toward the bathrooms, he slid an arm around my waist.

"I'll make sure you get there safely."

I wanted to protest, but it felt nice having his arm around me. It was warm and solid. So was his body pressed to my side. The close contact made my lady parts tingle even more.

Good goddess, it had been *way* too long since I'd last been with a man. Over a year, in fact. My last relationship—if one could even call it that—had only lasted a week due to my insatiable bloodlust. Sex wasn't worth killing a man over. I had morals, thank you very much.

But Samuel was a vampire. I didn't lust after his blood like I did every other being's. I could have a little fun with him without wanting to rip his throat out. What would the harm be?

Everything. It would harm everything, I tried to warn myself, but the warning felt weak. The usual conviction wasn't there. So, instead of pulling away, I let Samuel guide me toward the back right corner of the building.

When we reached the women's bathroom at the far end of the dimly-lit hallway, he let go of me. "Safe and sound, as promised," he said, but his voice sounded deeper than usual, his accent thicker.

I glanced up at his face and saw the unmistakable desire there.

That was all it took.

One heated look.

We were suddenly in the bathroom together. He slammed the door shut behind us and pressed me up against it, his body flush with mine. I moaned breathlessly as need exploded in my core, leaving me pliant and trembling. His lips found mine, firm and unyielding. They ravenously pillaged my mouth, until my head was swimming in sensation.

No, drowning.

Drowning in sensation.

He ground his hard cock against my core, and I whimpered, wanting more, yet *not* wanting more.

"Samuel," I managed to get out, grabbing onto his shoulders. "I think . . . I think we should—"

He darted his tongue into my mouth before I could finish. As our tongues tangled, I moaned again, forgetting what I was going to say. Forgetting everything but the pleasure pounding through me.

His hands slid down my body and grasped my skirt, tugging up the material with one swift yank. "I want to touch you, Isla," he breathed against my lips, slipping his fingers between my thighs. "Touch and *bite* you."

My eyes flew open and I choked out, "No biting."

His eyes slid open to half mast, still clouded with desire. I shook as I felt his fingers come within a hair's breadth of my aching center. "Then let me at least touch you. Let me pleasure you, Isla."

When I didn't immediately respond, he slowly slid his fingers inside my panties. Excitement charged through me. Excitement and . . .

Panic.

"Too fast," I gasped, struggling to close my legs. To stop him before I no longer could. "This is happening too fast."

His fingers stilled.

After a moment, he pulled them from my panties, studying me closely. "Are you sure?"

No. Yes.

Ah! Why couldn't I *think* straight?

Finally, I blurted, "Yes," ignoring the way my body whimpered in protest. It wanted him, no doubt about it. But this . . .

It didn't feel right.

"Sorry," I said as he slowly straightened and stepped back. "I didn't mean to—"

"No need to apologize, Isla," Samuel said, tugging on his suit jacket. "I came on too strong."

That I could agree with. It wasn't all his fault though. I hadn't exactly discouraged him—or communicated that I didn't hook up with vampires.

And yet . . . I almost had.

Resituating my skirt, I struggled to clear my head. To remember why we'd come here. My full bladder reminded me a second later. I gave him a sheepish look. "Maybe you should go now. I still need to pee."

He blinked at that, but quickly recovered. "Understood. Can I at least give you my number before I go? You know, in case you need rescuing again."

When he smiled charmingly, I only hesitated a moment before smiling back. Before I heard myself say, "Sure."

CHAPTER 2

ISLA

Everywhere I looked, the world was red.

Rain dripped from the crimson sky.

Red rain.

It dripped and dripped, forming a ruby puddle at my bare feet. Feet covered in . . . red. I lifted one bare leg. Then the other. Both were covered in red. I held out my hands. Red. My arms. Red. I glanced down at my naked body . . .

Red.

The rain dripped faster. And faster.

I tried to wipe it off me, only for more to take its place.

The more I wiped, the faster the rain came down. Until I could no longer see my body. Only red. Red everywhere. Blinding me. *Choking* me.

It poured into my mouth. Drowning me. Making me realize with horror . . .

It wasn't rain after all.

It was blood.

"Help me!" I screamed, but the words were swallowed by the sea of blood.

My heart was pounding, pounding, pounding.

So loud that I thought it would burst.

I thrashed against the red sea, desperate for air. Desperate to consume something besides blood.

"Help," I tried to scream, but only a whimper emerged.

"Isla!" someone shouted, the deep voice muffled as if my ears were clogged.

Clogged with blood.

More pounding. *Thud, thud, thud.*

I struggled some more, gasping for breath.

"Isla, open the door or I'm going to *break* it down!" the voice roared, this time closer. Clearer.

Wait. I recognized that voice.

Before I could place a name with the voice, a splintering *crash* destroyed my red world.

I was suddenly falling, falling . . .

Ooph!

When I hit the ground, the impact didn't hurt like I thought it would. I was more startled than anything. Peeling my eyes open, the first thing I saw was . . .

The very *last* person I thought I would see.

Kade Carmichael, the vampire who'd turned me five years ago.

Uncertain if I was still dreaming, I simply gawked at him. Gawked at the hulking six-foot-five-inch golden god framing my apartment doorway. Seriously though, he looked like *Thor*—the short-haired, beardless version of him. Add in some caramel-colored waves and that was Kade Carmichael. He probably had a big *hammer* too.

Don't go there, I scolded myself. *Do* not *go there. Not with him.*

He was breathing heavily, like he'd just run across the entire state of Maine or something. His sky blue eyes, brilliant even in the curtained-off darkness of my apartment, frantically tore up and down my body. Without taking my gaze off him, I quickly touched my thigh, relieved when I felt clothing.

Wait, why was I still wearing yesterday's outfit?

At least I wasn't naked. Maybe this wasn't a dream after all.

Before I could find my voice, before I could ask what he was doing here, Kade said, "Would it hurt you to pick up your phone?"

I blinked, caught off guard by the question and his heated tone.

Then I noticed my front door. It was split down the middle, desperately hanging on by one hinge. I pointed at it. "Did *you* do that?"

"*Isla*," Kade said, a slight growl rumbling in his chest. "This is serious. Why didn't you answer my calls? Why did I hear you whimpering? And why are you on the floor?"

I finally glanced down at myself and, sure enough, I was sprawled on my shaggy white living room rug. "Huh," I murmured, slowly sitting up. "I must have fallen off the couch." I shot an accusatory glare at the door. "After you broke down my door."

A buzzing sound came from the coffee table beside me, and I glanced over to find my phone. The screen lit up and I caught sight of several missed phone calls and texts. Blowing out a silent whistle, I reached for the device. Couldn't a girl get a little undisturbed sleep?

"Isla, you can't just blow me off. Not this time. It's too important," Kade said, striding into my apartment uninvited. I bristled at his bossy tone, at the way he entered my private domain like he *owned* the place.

"I'm not," I curtly replied, forcing my gaze to remain glued to the phone screen. "You're the one who woke me up by busting down my door and demanding answers. I have no idea what you want."

"What *I* want?" The incredulousness in his voice finally made me look up. He was towering over me, which immediately raised my hackles. I shoved down the urge to jump up and stand my ground. "You're the one who called me first, Isla."

I froze, my thumb hovering over the lock screen. "Excuse me?"

"You *called* me," he repeated, still looking at me far too intensely. "An hour ago, you called and said, 'Help. Help me.' I nearly wrecked my car getting here. I thought you were dying, trapped out in the sun or something."

I felt my eyes start to bug out and couldn't do a thing about it.

Before I could deny the ridiculous accusation, my phone vibrated again. *Saved* by the bell. Thank the goddess.

"Hello?" I quickly answered, picking myself off the floor to escape Kade's looming shadow. He still towered over me by more than a foot though, leaving my eyes level with his chest. The moment I stood, blood rushed to my head. To cover up my sudden dizziness, I plopped onto the couch.

Kade made an exasperated sound, but I ignored him as I heard my dad say, "Isla, where have you been? I've been trying to reach you for over an hour."

I frowned. "Uh, sleeping? What time is it?"

"Almost six."

Crap. I never slept that late. I was usually home a couple hours before the sun came up and in bed no later than eight. Most of the afternoon was gone by the time I woke up, but I still had to wait until sundown before going outside. I used that time to phone clients, check emails, and do online research for my cases. But with winter fast approaching, the nights were becoming longer and longer, which I was extremely grateful for.

"Sorry," I said to my dad, pushing a clump of tangled hair behind my ear. "I must have forgotten to set my alarm."

"It's fine. But we need you here as soon as possible."

"We?"

"The SCA."

Despite my spinning head, I sat up straighter. "What's the case?"

Ever since the Supernatural Containment Agency had put me on permanent retainer two years ago, I never lacked for work. I still had my regular human clients, but I now had supernatural cases as well. Most weren't too dangerous, but sometimes I got a little action. I was hoping for some now. *Needed* some. The adrenaline would help distract me from the giant vampire who'd randomly crashed back into my life.

"I'll debrief you when you arrive," my dad replied. "Meet me at Rosewood Inn off Highway sixty-four. There's blood at the crime scene, so be prepared."

Crime scene? I silently mouthed, doing a little jig on the couch.

This was a juicy one. With my heightened sense of smell and sleuthing expertise, I was often called in to track people down. Mostly supernaturals who'd recklessly exposed themselves to humans and needed disciplinary action. I never brought them in though. The SCA usually paired me up with my brother Noah, who'd been specially trained to handle supernatural confrontations.

The second the call ended, Kade plucked my phone from my hand.

"*Kade*," I snapped, jumping up to retrieve it. "Give me my—"

Whoa.

The room abruptly tilted, and I nearly crashed back onto the couch. Silencing a groan, I focused on remaining upright. On not passing out. Or throwing up.

When the room finally stopped moving, I looked up to find Kade's gaze on me. *Severe* gaze. A muscle was popping in his jaw like crazy, and the hand not holding my phone was balled into a tight fist.

I swallowed the nausea down and held out my hand. "Give me back my phone, please."

See? I could be nice. Even when he was being a *dick*.

"Have you been overfeeding again?"

The blunt, probing question immediately killed my efforts to be civil.

"*Excuse* me?" I shot back, making a fruitless swipe for my phone. Why did the men in my life have to be so freakishly *tall*? Not that Kade was in my life, unless you counted life *crashers*. Realizing he wasn't going to leave me alone unless I gave him what he wanted, I said with a huff, "No, I haven't been overfeeding. Not that it's any of your business. Even if I was, it's still none of your business. Now give me my phone. I have somewhere important to be."

"I heard."

I narrowed my eyes. "Didn't your mother ever teach you that eavesdropping is rude?"

He shrugged. "Is it really eavesdropping if you already know the person is listening?"

"That's . . ." I curled my lip back in a silent snarl, totally done with him. "Give it to me, Kade. I won't ask again."

"Or what?" he said, lowering the phone to within my reach. "What will you do?"

Don't engage. It's a trap, I warned myself, closely watching his face. Sure enough, a smirk slowly twisted his mouth. A *wicked* one. One that I knew well. One that used to draw me in like a moth to a flame, that used to incite all sorts of illicit fantasies inside my brain.

Not anymore. I wouldn't let it.

"I'm not playing this game, Kade," I deadpanned, and his smirk began to fade. "I have a job to do. Sorry you thought I called you, but I most definitely did not. I've been sleeping all afternoon like I always do."

On my *couch*. Which was odd. I never slept on my couch.

He was silent for a moment, long enough that I almost gave up. Almost stormed off to my bedroom in a huff, hoping that would make him leave. I couldn't take much more of this. Having him here, larger than life, in my *sanctuary*.

It would take *weeks* to air his sun-kissed citrus scent from my apartment.

When he suddenly stepped forward, I wasn't ready. My heart leapt into my throat as he grasped my still outstretched hand and placed my phone in it. "Maybe this will convince you," he murmured, letting go before I could yank my hand away from his branding touch.

I glanced down at my phone and what I saw nearly made me drop it.

My gaze flew back up to Kade's in a panic. "But I *didn't*. I didn't call you."

"But you did," he said, nodding at my phone. At the indisputable evidence there. At the *proof*. "You called me and asked for my help, and I'm not leaving until I know why."

CHAPTER 3

ISLA

Something was off. *Really* off.

Now that I'd had a few minutes to myself, I could finally think clearly. Finally remember that my evening last night hadn't exactly been . . . innocent.

I *had* fed too much. And with a perfect stranger as company. A rakishly handsome *vampire*, at that.

But that wasn't all.

I'd almost had sex with him. A vampire. In a dirty public *bathroom*, of all places. I'd almost broken my number one rule, all because he was charming and hot.

And that wasn't me.

That wasn't me at *all*.

I flirted like the act gave me oxygen, but sex was different. Sex was intimate. Sex was passion and tenderness and vulnerability. I didn't open up that deeply to just anyone—my vibrating dildo didn't count.

In fact, I'd never truly been in a serious relationship before. Sure, I'd had a few flings over the years. I'd experimented with my sexuality, quickly discovering that I had an exceptionally high libido. But after a week or two, I always cut ties. Always realized they weren't for me. Weren't *right*. I craved more. *Much* more.

But not with a vampire. Never with a vampire.

Which was why my actions last night troubled me. Even if I'd intended for my short time with Samuel to be a quick fling, I'd sworn never to let a vampire hurt me again. And having *sex* with one was a sure-fire way of getting hurt.

And then there was that mysterious phone call I'd made while *sleeping*. Kade was the last person I'd call for help if I needed it. Maybe at one time, he would have been the first, but those days were long over. All ties had been severed between us, except for a polite friendliness when our paths crossed. Kade knew that.

So why was he trying so hard to make me admit to that phone call?

If only I could erase what had happened in the last twenty-four hours. It would be so much easier than facing last night's rashness and this afternoon's oops call. But both were a mystery, and I could never pass up the opportunity to solve a case.

They'd have to wait though. The sun had set and my dad was expecting me. I'd already taken a quick shower, blow-dried my hair, and hurriedly applied some mascara and lipgloss. I wasn't meeting any clients this evening, so I chose to wear black jeans and an emerald green top, my hair swept back in a loose braid. Grabbing a tan leather jacket from my closet, I opened my bedroom door.

The first thing I saw was Kade. More like his *backside*, on prominent display with his head buried inside my fridge. My gaze lingered far too long on the way his low-slung jeans perfectly cupped his butt. By the time I tore my gaze away, it was already too late.

He'd spotted me ogling him.

Even from here, I could see the mischievous glint in his eyes. Any second now, that wicked mouth would open. Would do its utmost to send a blush rising to my cheeks.

Good thing I didn't easily blush. Or get embarrassed.

Still, I beat him to it, saying crisply, "I thought I told you to leave."

My words didn't cow him in the least. He closed the fridge with a snap and leaned against it, crossing his arms over his broad chest. "You're out of blood."

"I know," I said with a shrug, even as I inwardly cringed. I'd meant to restock my supply today before work. Now I wouldn't have time. *Again.* And I didn't want to revisit the bar again tonight. Not after what happened last night.

Oh the joys of being a bloodsucker, my brother would sarcastically—yet affectionately—say.

"I'll pick some up for you," Kade said, watching as I grabbed my keys from the entryway table. "And a new front door."

I paused, then dug my phone from my pocket. "Don't bother. I can handle both myself." At the same time, I hurriedly sent a text to Kenna. *Can you tell Kade to go home? Please?!?*

When Kade didn't persist like I thought he would, I chanced a peek at him. He looked . . . pensive. The muscles in his jaw were ticking again. I suppressed a sigh, wishing things weren't so *tense* between us.

They didn't used to be.

But that was a long time ago. There was no changing the past. What happened between us happened. I went my way and he went his. It was better like this. *Safer.*

Trying to fix what used to be was impossible. There was no reclaiming that innocence. That trust. He'd betrayed me and I wouldn't let him do it again, plain and simple.

When the silence stretched between us, I turned toward the exit. "Look, I have to go. Which means there's not much point in you hanging around here."

Which means, get your butt out of my apartment.

I kept that last part to myself, still trying to be nice. He must have gotten the gist though. His lips thinned as he pushed off the fridge and ambled around the kitchen island toward me. Relieved that he was finally leaving, I reached for the door handle to see him out. Before I could grasp it, a large hand slid into view and gripped the metal. I quickly pulled back, barely avoiding a finger collision with him. If he noticed my hasty retreat, he didn't comment.

The moment he opened the wobbly door, I slipped into the hallway, not bothering with the busted lock when he closed it behind him.

"Aren't you worried someone will break in?" Kade commented as I made for the building's exit.

"Nope. Just you," I sardonically sang.

Kade's phone chimed. Seconds later: "Did you just sic a *pregnant* woman on me?"

Ugh, I should have known Kenna couldn't play referee for her two best friends.

Huffing, I checked my phone for the time. I could still grab a bite on my way to the crime scene. The food wouldn't curb the slight ache in my throat, but it would at least fill my growling belly. I really needed to prioritize restocking my blood supply though, no matter how exciting this new case proved to be. I couldn't go more than twenty-four hours without feeding. Not unless I wanted to be in a world of pain.

"Stupid bloodlust," I grumbled under my breath, then wished I hadn't a second later when Kade came up beside me.

"When's the last time you fed?"

I reached for the door handle, but he beat me to it again, pulling the door wide so I could exit first. I used the moment to avoid answering his question, pausing a split second to glance at the sky before stepping outside. A Feltore could never be too careful. One slight miscalculation and—*poof!*—instant barbeque.

"Isla."

Biting back a groan, I finally said, "Last night."

"How much?"

"Enough." More than enough, but I wasn't going to tell *him* that.

"How much is enough?"

"Kade," I ground out, my patience wearing thin. "I know how to take care of myself. I've known how to for a long time now. I don't need any of your lectures. *Please.*"

It was true that I'd needed his constant reminders for a short time, that I'd probably be long dead without them—or at least feral. But I hadn't needed his help for almost five years. I wasn't going to start now.

Thankfully, he honored my request and fell silent.

Until I stopped dead in my tracks to gape at my empty parking space.

"Where's your car?"

Ignoring his question, I pressed the unlock button on my key fob. Nothing. Not a single clicking sound in the entire parking lot. What the—? "Someone stole my car. Someone stole my flipping *car.*"

I quickly racked my brain, trying to recall how I'd come home last night.

But there was nothing. No memory. Just a blank space, like my empty parking spot.

"Did you lock it when you got home?" Kade oh-so-helpfully asked, stepping from the sidewalk to inspect my parking spot.

"Of course I did," I snapped, more at myself than him. Still, his entire back stiffened at my brusque tone. I didn't bother with an apology though, knowing that I'd do it again if he kept questioning me.

My head was already whirling out of control with unanswered questions. This part of Rosewood, Maine was exceptionally safe. Car break-ins rarely happened. Even then, I *always* remembered to lock my car.

"I don't have time for this," I grumbled, turning on my phone. At least my car had a GPS tracking device. Having a sheriff as a dad definitely had its perks.

Right when I'd narrowed down my car's location, Kade straightened from his crouched position and said, "The exhaust scent is faint. At least a day old. Are you sure you parked it here when you got home?"

"No," I distractedly said, staring in confusion at my phone screen that showed my car several miles from here.

Parked in front of Mike's Tavern.

Uh oh.

I suddenly became aware of Kade's presence. *Acutely* aware. If he found out where my car currently was, he'd put two-and-two together. He'd figure out that I'd been feeding at a *blood* bar last night. That I'd apparently consumed so much blood, I hadn't been able to drive home. That was the only explanation I could think of. The only reason why I couldn't remember walking home. Or getting inside my apartment.

I'd been blood drunk. In *public*. Something I never did. Something that Kade would lecture me for. Maybe worse. Maybe *much* worse. And no way was I letting that happen.

"Oh, *duh*. I forgot," I said with a fake depreciating snort, turning off my phone before he could see. "I drove it to the shop this morning, right before I came home. The engine sounded funny."

He didn't say anything. Not good. *So* not good. I turned on my phone again to avoid eye contact, searching for a cab.

Before I could dial the number, Kade said, "I'll drive you."

Every muscle in my body tensed.

"Thanks, but—" I began, immediately ready to turn him down.

"It's just a car ride, Isla. Don't be stubborn," he interrupted before I could finish.

I bristled, snapping my gaze to his. And, once again, immediately wishing I hadn't. Challenge darkened his eyes. When his mouth slowly curved into a smile, I itched to smack it off.

He was *enjoying* this predicament. Enjoying backing me into a corner.

My eyes narrowed to slits. "I'm not the stubborn one, Kade Carmichael." I made sure he heard the *threat* in my voice. "I've told you to leave several times now, and yet, here you are. You've just about worn out my patience."

He studied me for several moments, undeterred by my words. So undeterred that he abruptly stepped forward, right into my personal space. I held my ground, even as a tremble worked its way up my body at his nearness. At his warmth. At his *scent*.

"You want to talk about patience, Isla Andrews?" he said, coming so close that I had to crane my neck back to maintain eye contact. "I've been waiting five years for you to knock that chip off your shoulder. How long are you going to make me suffer? I've apologized countless times, but you won't let me get within ten feet of you. This right here is the closest we've been since . . ."

No. No, don't say it! I silently pleaded, squeezing my phone until the case creaked.

But there was no stopping him. Once Kade Carmichael set his mind on saying something, there was nothing anyone could do. Nothing short of bodily shutting him up, and I had no intention of putting my hands anywhere near his mouth. Or any other body part, for that matter.

". . . you kissed me," he finished, not sounding the least bit apologetic for dredging up the memory. He simply thrust it out into the open, forcing me to see it. To *face* it. When all I wanted to do was run from it. Run and run and run like I'd never run before. Like a *coward*, which wasn't me at all. I faced everything, always willing to confront, to unravel, to get to the bottom of something, no matter how difficult.

I'd faced learning about the supernatural world. Discovering that my entire family were witches. That they'd kept the fact a secret from me my whole life. I'd faced my new reality as a vampire, the immortality and sun aversion and bloodlust. My *death*. I'd faced lies and betrayals, challenges and hardships, forcing myself to move past them. To forgive. To adapt.

But when it came to Kade . . .

I was stuck.

Stuck in an endless loop of uncertainty and what-ifs and *fear*. So much debilitating fear.

So, when staring into his relentless gaze became too much—when the warmth of his closeness made me think of that *kiss*—I chickened out. I stepped back and broke eye contact, running from the subject. Running from *him*.

"I'm calling an Uber," I said, my words barely discernible. It was safer this way. Safer and smarter. Maybe some things weren't worth solving. Maybe some things were just too dangerous.

But as I raised my phone to my ear, determined to keep that wedge between us firmly in place, Kade said, "I won't say a word."

Ring. Ring.

Pick up!

"If you let me drive you, my lips are sealed. Not a peep. No more questions the entire trip."

Ring.

"Please, Isla."

Aaah!

Ring.

Don't do it, don't do it, don't do it.

Despite my screaming instincts, I felt my arm lower. Felt my thumb end the call. Felt my lips part and words spill out. Words that I wanted to take back the second I said them. "Fine. You can drive me. But not a *single* word, Kade. I mean it."

What was *wrong* with me?

I opened my mouth to tell him I'd changed my mind, but made the mistake of looking up at him. The moment I saw the huge grin on his face, I froze. Utterly froze and gawked at his grinning fool face like I'd never seen a smile before. Seen *him* smile.

But I'd seen Kade smile hundreds of times. He was always smiling, always teasing and flirting and joking. Kade wasn't Kade without a smirk on his lips and an innuendo dancing on his tongue.

And yet, I couldn't stop staring. Because he hadn't smiled that way at *me* in a very long time.

"You won't regret it," he said, snapping me out of my stupor.

I quickly blinked and looked away, muttering, "I already am."

He chuckled, easily catching the words.

"No laughing either," I warned, falling into step beside him as he headed for the guest parking spots to the left of the three-story building.

"I can't really control that," Kade said with another chuckle, shortening his long strides to match mine. "It comes out when it wants to. Kind of like when I breathe. That pesky air always comes right back out, even when I try to hold it in."

I rolled my eyes, regretting my decision more and more with each step. "Not my problem. You said 'not a peep.' That includes laughter."

"Well, if you feel *that* strongly about it."

"I do."

Because his smiles weren't the only thing that messed with my brain. His laughter was just as bad, if not worse. The easygoing sound had a way of sliding under my skin and loosening my tense muscles.

And that was bad. *Really* bad. I couldn't let him in like that.

Ever.

CHAPTER 4

KADE

"This doesn't mean I need your help, by the way. I'm perfectly capable of getting myself from point A to point B. This'll just save me some time."

I listened to Isla as I drove, obediently keeping my mouth shut. It wasn't easy, but I managed. Not a sound left my lips. I couldn't keep the smirk off them though.

Despite her many protests, I'd won this round. It had only taken five years of constant defeat to claim this one small victory, but it was worth every single painful rejection.

"And don't even think about hanging around the crime scene," she went on, gesturing at me to take a left. "This is strictly SCA business. There are some laws even *you* have to follow."

I pressed my lips together to keep a chuckle at bay.

"What?"

I glanced over to find her watching me, her stormy blue eyes narrowed suspiciously. I wordlessly raised both brows, the perfect picture of innocence.

"I'm serious, Kade," she said, settling against her leather seat with a huff. "Drop me off, then go home. Well, after getting rid of *those*." She jabbed a thumb at the spoiled pints of ice cream still in the back seat. "Kenna craving?"

I nodded, smirking again when Isla snorted.

A minute later, she pointed at a fast food restaurant up ahead.

"Pull in there real quick. I'm starving."

I did as instructed, sneaking glances at her while I swung my Mustang into the drive-thru lane. Discovering her fridge empty of blood earlier had put me on high alert. I knew, probably more than anyone, how dangerous that was for her. How foolish. Vampires with exceptionally strong bloodlust like Isla often went feral. She knew this. I'd drilled her for hours after first discovering this about her. Warned her of the consequences should she fail to keep herself in check.

Not only would the SCA target her, so would Ambrose D'angelo. The vampire king didn't tolerate wanton bloodlust in his kingdom, not if it threatened our anonymity. No one was exempt, not even his sons. Troy, his youngest, was still locked away in a high security SCA prison for trying to expose the entire vampire race to humans in order to gain dominion over them.

There would only be one outcome if that happened. *War.* None of us wanted that. Thankfully, neither did the SCA. Protecting the human populace from dangerous supernaturals would always be their main objective, and after we gave them Troy, there'd been a tentative truce between the two previously-opposing sides.

They no longer fired on all vampires first and asked questions later. In return, we enforced stricter rules. If a vampire broke them, we were authorized to turn them in to face the proper punishment.

Knowing this, and knowing how important this fledgling alliance was, I keenly watched the female beside me. Watched for the warning signs. Dilated pupils. Sweating. Shortness of breath. Trembling hands. Fixation.

It didn't matter that she'd been a vampire for five years now. That she was no longer considered an unpredictable youngling. A vampire like Isla Andrews would always struggle with blood dependency. It was her curse, one that a witch couldn't cure. One that she would bear for eternity.

I'd done that to her.

Turned her. Cursed her. Doomed her to a life of darkness and bloodlust.

But that wasn't why she hated me. That wasn't why she ran every time I got too close.

"Roll down your window," she impatiently said, jostling me from my thoughts. When the employee asked for our order, Isla leaned over the middle console and ordered for herself, making it clear she didn't want *me* to.

A smile of wicked amusement danced on my lips, then froze as her vanilla scent invaded my personal space. This close, I had no choice but to breathe it in. To inhale the sweet aroma not only on her skin, but flowing through her veins as well. It wasn't a secret that I had a sweet tooth, but I'd never told anyone just how deeply it affected me. That the scent and taste of sweet things was often more intoxicating to me than blood itself.

Unless the blood was *sweet*. And Isla's had always smelled exceptionally sweet, even as a vampire. My thoughts immediately went to a forbidden place, conjuring image after image in a matter of seconds. Just as quickly, my cock hardened, uncomfortably tightening my pants.

"Want anything?"

At the question that fell from her sensuous lips—at the inopportune *timing* of it—I almost opened my mouth and spilled my guts out. Almost told her *exactly* what I wanted. But, after a lengthy beat, I managed to stiffly shake my head no. She gave me an odd look, but I kept my gaze straight ahead. I could only hope she wouldn't look down and notice the sizable bulge in my pants that refused to go away.

After another torturous beat, she finished her order and we silently pulled forward to the pickup window.

"I gave you the opportunity to speak and you didn't take it," she mused, once again leaning over to hand the employee some cash. If I wasn't still fighting a major boner, I would have stayed her hand and paid for the order myself. But drawing *any* attention to my pants was a bad idea. The last thing I wanted to do was freak her out. To send her running again.

I shrugged in reply, which kept her gaze safely upward.

"Wow. I didn't think you had it in you," she sarcastically said, leaning even closer to accept her change.

I squeezed my eyes shut for a moment, forcing my breathing to remain even. To not give me away. If I had to endure much more of this, there would be no masking the scent of my arousal. Her pert little nose would instantly detect the scent and I would be screwed.

But I was determined not to let that happen. This short car trip was going better than I'd hoped. I hadn't failed to notice how chatty she'd been for the last ten minutes. How relaxed. Just like how she *used* to be around me, before I'd ruined everything with my big mouth. Before a few short words had destroyed her trust in me.

If keeping silent helped her relax around me again, then I'd gladly give her that—even if it was slowly killing me. Even if the missed opportunity to banter with her was the worst kind of torture.

By the time we reached our destination, I was desperate for relief—in more ways than one. Needing to cool off, I almost honored her request then. Almost left to run some errands while she did her private investigator thing. But the minute she stepped from the car, I changed my mind.

Something wasn't right.

Her posture was too stiff. And her hands . . .
They were trembling.

CHAPTER 5

ISLA

When I stepped from Kade's car, the first thing I smelled was blood.

Human blood.

Which wasn't abnormal, considering I was standing in front of a motel. Plus, my nose was especially sensitive to humans. I could catch a scent from miles away, better than most predators in the animal kingdom.

But the blood that had immediately snagged my attention wasn't safely encased in a warm body. This blood was exposed. And cold. And . . .

Oddly familiar.

"Isla," a booming voice announced, startling me. My claws instinctively shot out as I whirled toward the blond-haired, barrel-of-a-man striding toward me. Immediately recognizing him, I scrambled to retract my claws before he noticed, before he saw how on edge I was. But something behind me caught his attention, drawing his gaze upward. His dusky blue eyes, nearly identical to mine, blinked in surprise. "Kade. What brings you into town?"

I went poker straight as fingers materialized beside me and clasped my dad's outstretched hand.

"Sheriff Andrews," Kade greeted him, easing into the space next to me like he belonged there. "I was just visiting your daughter, actually. She needed a ride, so here I am."

"Oh?" My dad swung his surprised look my way, a million

questions burning in his gaze.

Heat rushed to my face. Angry heat. *Raging* heat. My dad could misconstrue those words in so many ways, especially since he hadn't been able to reach me earlier. Knowing Kade, he'd done it on purpose.

I dug my claws into my palms before I could put them to good use, forcing myself to laugh off Kade's words. The sound was tight. Strained. But at least it didn't come out as a scream. "He arrived right before I took your call, Daddy. A simple misunderstanding, really. In fact, he was just leaving. Right, Kade?"

I didn't dare look at him, not when I was this mad. Not when my dad was looking between us with interest. Ever since he'd found out that Kade had brought his baby girl back to life—had *saved* me—my dad had softened toward the hulking vampire who he'd once tried to kill. Kade being Kade had put their sordid past behind him and readily accepted the olive branch.

Now, on the rare occasions their paths crossed, *this* happened. Friendly exchanges that grew friendlier with each visit. If I didn't nip it in the bud post haste, we would end up invited over for family dinner.

Before Kade could answer me, my dad waved his hand dismissively. "Nonsense. Kade can stay. We could use his help, actually. That is, if you don't already have plans."

"He *does*," I spoke up, my voice rising an octave as I desperately tried to stop this train wreck. "He has *things* to pick up. Don't you, Kade?" I finally looked up at him, smiling sweetly. My face probably looked constipated, but whatever.

He easily held my gaze, meeting my fake smile with a lazy, lopsided grin. "I'm not in a rush. I can get those things for you later. Unless you're trying to get rid of me . . ." His grin grew downright evil, that sneaky *rat*.

"Not at all," I said between clenched teeth. "Don't be silly."

"Perfect," my dad said, clapping his hands together. "Then let's get you two caught up to speed."

Silently fuming, I followed my dad toward the crime scene, trying to listen, catalog the situation, and ignore Kade all at once.

"Based on the blood loss, we believe this was a vampire attack," my dad was saying as he led us toward the weather-beaten motel located on the poorer side of town. I noted the shiny black Harley parked right outside the ground floor room we were heading into.

When he pulled the door open wide, motioning for me to precede him inside, I froze.

The smell.

The *blood*.

It was coming from inside the room.

My throat clamped shut, viciously cutting off my air. A thudding sound filled my ears, growing louder and louder and louder. It was my heart, thundering out of control as *need* ripped through me. My gums began to fiercely ache, my fangs moments away from emerging. A tremble worked its way through me, one I couldn't suppress.

Every muscle in my body locked, every instinct firing off rapid commands.

Hunt. Feed. *Kill.*

A whimper pushed at my raw, burning throat. A whimper of need. Of *fear*.

I was going to lose it, right here in front of my dad. In front of *Kade*.

Just as saliva filled my mouth, a large hand warmed my lower back. Immediately knowing whose hand it was, I tried to jerk away. But I didn't have the strength. Kade firmly guided me through the door, keeping his hand on me even when we were both inside. If my dad noticed, he didn't comment, already striding into the small space.

Straight toward a still form sprawled across the queen-sized bed.

"The victim's name is Gunner Landry. Male. Human. Late twenties," my dad said without preamble. "A housekeeper found him two hours ago and immediately called it in. Once I saw the bite marks, I contacted the SCA."

I could tell, even from here, that the man was dead. Which meant that this was a homicide case.

I'd never been asked to investigate a murder before, supernatural or otherwise. Up until now, my clients and targets had always been very much alive.

"You okay?" Kade quietly said in my ear, his warm breath stirring my hair.

We were still standing just inside the entrance, drawing more than a few glances. A handful of SCA operatives were busily doing their jobs, dusting for fingerprints and securing evidence into plastic bags. Most of them knew me by name, even though we barely crossed paths in the field.

At the sight of not one but *two* vampires entering the room, they stiffened. I knew they couldn't help their fight or flight response to the two predators in their midst. I usually tried to smile and put them at ease, but this time . . . I couldn't manage it.

Struggling and failing to swallow, I rasped out, "I'm fine," before forcing my legs to carry me forward. Kade let me go, but stayed close as he followed in my wake.

When I paused at the foot of the bed, a pretty black-haired woman in her mid twenties glanced up at me. She was bent over the dead man, not the least bit squeamish. "Hey, Isla," she said, greeting me with a small smile. When she spotted Kade behind me, her smile turned shy. Knowing him, he'd probably just winked at her. Most of the operatives had never personally met Kade, but they all knew *of* him.

Loyal drothen and best friend to Prince Lochlan D'angelo. And, most notably, the vampire who'd turned Sheriff Andrews' daughter.

He was a curiosity to them, especially now that the SCA and vampires were no longer actively gunning for each other. I'd heard the tittering whispers among the female operatives, that the renowned vampire bachelor flirted with anything on two legs. That Kade and I must have hooked up and separated at some point. That the fun-loving Feltore must have had dozens of lovers since then.

I didn't bother squashing their talk. No matter what species they hailed from, females would always gossip, especially about relationships. Or sex, more accurately.

Thankfully, the woman currently eyeing me was a rare exception. The *last* thing she wanted to do was talk about her nonexistent love life. Or mine.

"Hey, Saanvi," I brightly replied, trying my utmost to sound normal. If anyone could read my moods, it was Saanvi Patel. As the SCA's forensic scientist, it was her job to examine the smallest of miniscule details. She may be quiet, but she was thorough and extremely good at what she did. Her job was her life, which was something we had in common.

"The smell is strong, I know," she said, giving me a sympathetic look. "It must be *really* bad for you."

My throat constricted. "Yeah. The blood is a bit strong."

She blinked. "Oh, I meant the vinegar smell. The entire room and victim are doused in it. I'm assuming the murderer used it to mask their scent."

Vinegar? I hadn't even noticed. I'd been too fixated on the dead guy's *blood*.

Frantically trying to cover up my mistake, I said, "Oh, *that*. Yes, it's awful." When her brow pinched and what looked like suspicion entered her insightful gaze, I quickly added, "Have you seen Noah?"

It was a dirty trick, mentioning my brother's name. I didn't know her well, but I'd seen the way she looked at him on several occasions when his back was turned. Knowing my brother, he'd probably flirted with the poor girl at some point, and now, she carried a secret torch for him.

Yuck.

It was my *brother*, after all. The guy still slept with mounds of dirty laundry on his bed. He really should settle down one of these days, or at least hire a housekeeper. The dude was almost twenty-seven.

Sure enough, the moment I mentioned Noah's name, Saanvi's warm brown cheeks darkened. She fixed her large, doe-brown eyes on the Sony camera in her hands. "Not for a few days. I think he's on another case."

"Noah's scouting out a situation in Fairfax," my dad supplied, drawing my attention back up to him. Saanvi immediately started snapping pictures of the victim again. "We have several people out there right now, actually, which is why I called you here today. I know homicide cases aren't technically your jurisdiction, but we're a little short-staffed right now."

"Th-that's fine," I said, covering up my excited stutter with a quick, "I can handle it."

Wow. Short-staffed or not, I couldn't believe my dad was allowing me to take on this case. And *alone*. Ever since I'd been exposed to the supernatural world, he'd been uber protective. My job often had me working alone, but my dad and brother were never too far away. Any hint of danger and they were there.

Not surprisingly, my dad studied me a little too closely, clearly having caught the slight stutter. "You sure? I can call in a detective from Bangor if this is too much for you."

"No need, I've got this," I immediately replied, getting down to business before he could change his mind. "So, when do we think the murder took place?" I approached the head of the bed opposite Saanvi, carefully holding my breath as I took my first good look at the victim.

When I saw his face, I nearly choked on the lungful of air.

I knew him.

He was the biker who'd propositioned me outside Mike's Tavern last night.

Right then and there, I should have spoken. Should have shared the information I already knew about this man. But, against my better judgment, I hesitated. Hesitated, because I didn't want anyone to know about my drunken bender last night. Then they'd know that I'd slipped up. That perhaps I wasn't the best person for this job.

But I *wanted* this case. So badly. Something about it fiercely beckoned to me. *Tugged* at me. I needed to solve it. So I kept my mouth shut. Pretended that the victim before me was a complete stranger.

"Sometime late last night or early this morning, judging by the rigor mortis," Saanvi replied, oblivious to my inner turmoil. "His body was stiff and cold when we got here."

I'd seen death before. Even though I'd been lied to about the cause of my mother's death nine years ago, I'd seen her body laid out in the casket. Felt her skin devoid of warmth as I'd kissed her cold cheek.

Death didn't scare me. The *cause* of death did.

My mom had been murdered, and so had this man.

Callously. Viciously. Unforgivably.

Vindictive witches had killed my mom, and—judging by the bite marks clearly visible on Gunner Landry's neck—a vampire had bled him dry. I didn't hate supernaturals, not all of them anyway. Only the violent ones. The users and abusers. The ones who preyed on the weak and took lives for their own gain. Humans could be just as bad, but they didn't have supernatural abilities like we did. They most often needed protection from supernaturals, not the other way around.

It felt like fate had called me here today. And even though it freaked me out that I *knew* this victim—that I'd seen him very much alive less than twenty-four hours ago—I was determined to solve this case.

And when I did, I was going to take his bloodsucking murderer *down.*

Just when the adrenaline high from discovering a new unsolved mystery kicked in, my dad spoke again. "Before you take on this case, Isla, there's one thing we need to address. The matter of your partner."

I scrunched up my nose. "Partner? You know I work alone. My hours don't mesh with most of the operative's."

"I know, but this is your first homicide. I'd feel better if you had someone watching your back."

I blinked up at him. "Then I'll call Noah when the case gets hot."

"Not good enough. I want someone with you every step of the way. There's only one other person besides Noah I trust to watch over you, and he just happens to be here today. Which is why I'm going to ask"—No. *No!* But he was already turning. Already lifting his gaze to—"Kade if he can help you."

All pretense gone, I argued, "But he's not a part of the SCA. They—"

"Will gladly accept his assistance on this case," my dad interrupted. "Two vampires working to bring in one of their own will go a long way toward strengthening the alliance."

"Yes, but I—"

"Have been a huge asset toward that cause, but Kade is practically a member of the royal family. Having his support with this case would speak volumes. The SCA might even employ more vampires after this, which would benefit us all."

"But—"

"Do you want this case or not, Isla?"

"Of course I do. But—"

"Then that's the stipulation. It's nonnegotiable."

He noticeably widened his stance, a clear sign that he wasn't going to budge. I opened my mouth to argue some more anyway, *needing* him to reconsider. I couldn't work with Kade Carmichael. I just *couldn't*.

But as much as my dad had spoiled me over the years, he always got the last word. He was in charge here, not me, and he made that known by turning to Kade once again. "What say you, Kade?" he said, done arguing with me. "Can I count on you to work this case with my daughter?"

When Kade's eyes locked with mine, I didn't hide my fury. I let him feel it all. Let him see just how angry I would be if he agreed to this. He unflinchingly held my burning gaze, his expression unreadable. I threw everything at him. *Everything*. I knew he felt it. Knew he could tell I didn't want him on this case. But . . .

He broke our staredown and firmly replied to my dad, "You can count on me, sir. It would be my honor to help your daughter."

CHAPTER 6

ISLA

The moment we left the motel, I lapsed into icy silence.

I'd managed to keep a tight lid on my emotions for our remaining time at the crime scene, accepting my dad's orders without further complaint. I'd even managed to keep my growing thirst under control, scouring the room and surrounding area with laser-sharp focus so I couldn't obsess over how *starved* I was.

But the second it was just me and Kade, ensconced in his car where my colleagues couldn't hear, I dropped the act. Any minute now, I was going to explode. I knew it. Kade knew it. Which was probably why he'd kept so quiet at the crime scene. Why he was so quiet now. But that was the problem. He *knew* I didn't want him here. *Knew* I didn't want to work this case with him.

Then why? *Why?*

"Why are you doing this, Kade?" My words cut through the silence like a hot knife, sharp and to the point. "*Why?*"

His response was immediate. Rehearsed, even. Like he was expecting the question. "Because you called me for help."

"That was a mistake."

His knuckles whitened on the steering wheel. "I heard your voice, Isla. You were scared."

I snorted. "I wasn't fully awake. I was having a nightmare."

"You could have called anyone, but you called me. Something isn't right, whether you admit it or not. And I don't buy your car in the shop story. You're hiding something from me."

"I'm not hiding anything," I said through clenched teeth. "My personal life is just none of your business."

"Well, it is now. I'm staying here to help you with this homicide case. And until you come clean about earlier, I'm not leaving your side."

"I was *drunk*, okay?" I yelled, so forcefully that he slammed on the brakes. A car horn blared behind us and Kade quickly swerved off the road.

When we came to a jarring stop, he turned in his seat to face me. "What do you mean drunk? Drunk *how?*"

Oh, he was angry. *Really* angry. Well, that just made things easier. I was itching for a fight, and now I had it.

"*Blood* drunk. At a *blood* bar," I said, watching as his eyes brightened to twin flames of blue fire. "I got so drunk that I had to walk home. So *hammered* that I don't even remember getting into my apartment. So *wasted* that I drunk-dialed you."

A rumble sounded deep in his throat. Every inch of him tensed, his muscles so stiff that a tremor shook him. "Was anyone there with you?"

I scowled at the quiet threat in his voice. "Of course there was. The bar was packed."

"I mean, did you *drink* with anyone?"

"So what if I did? I'm single and available. Guys approach me all the time."

Oh, *that* got a reaction.

With a sharp hiss, he faced the road and stomped on the gas. The car jolted forward, making my head whip back. I bit out a curse, but didn't comment on the reckless driving.

After a moment of tense silence, Kade said, "That was stupid,

Isla. Stupid and dangerous."

"I *know*," I snapped, hating that he was lecturing me. Hating that he was right. "I left before things could go too far. No one was hurt."

Kade continued to drive twice the speed limit, his jaw set like granite.

When it became clear he was done with the fight, I faced forward with a sigh. "Take a left at the light."

He flicked a glance at me. "Why? Your apartment's the other way."

Steeling myself for more of his disappointment, I replied, "My car's parked in front of Mike's Tavern."

He didn't say a word, which was almost worse. I'd rather *hear* how disappointed he was than feel it emanating from him in heated waves.

By the time we arrived at the bar, I was physically aching with the need to put space between us. The second the car rolled to a stop, I flung my door open and jumped out. Before I could slam the door shut, Kade was there, reaching around me to close it a lot more gently. His nearness forced me to retreat until my back thumped against the side of his car.

When he didn't move—when he continued to invade my personal space, making it hard for me to breathe—I glared up at him and snapped, "Do you mind? I need to get to my car."

"And then what?" he said, leaning toward me. I stopped breathing as he deliberately placed his hand on the car's hood beside my head, bringing his body *way* too close to mine.

I dug my nails into my palms, forcing them to remain at my sides. "And *then* what?" I parroted, my voice far too breathy. "And then none of your business. I told you what happened last night and why I called you. There's no reason for you to follow me around any longer. Call my dad and say you changed your mind. He can assign a *trained* field operative to help me."

He made a soft tsking noise and leaned even closer. "You're not getting rid of me that easily. Not this time. We have a job to do and the night is young. Where to first, partner?"

Every inch of me stiffened. "We're not partners. I'm a private investigator. Private investigators work alone."

He hiked an eyebrow. "Partner. Bodyguard. Male escort. Whatever you want to call me, we're working this case together."

I clenched my teeth. "I despise you."

He studied me impassively for a moment, then brought his other hand down on the hood, trapping me between his arms. "You're not scaring me off, Isla. We either work this case together, or I'm informing your dad of last night's drunken activities."

I was too shocked at his words to react to his nearness. To his face mere inches from mine. "You wouldn't," I whispered, searching his determined expression for any sign of teasing. I found none.

"Try me," he whispered back, dipping his head so that all I could see, all I could feel, all I could *smell* was him.

I was suddenly drowning. Drowning in *panic*.

I lashed out, saying the first hurtful thing I could think of. "Why blackmail me when you could easily command me? You're my sire, after all. My *master*. So go ahead and force me into submission. Go ahead and *make* me. I know you want to."

Kade jerked back as if I'd slapped him. The hurt on his face immediately sobered me, making me regret the spiteful words. I'd unfairly gone for the jugular, painting him as the villain when he'd tried countless times in the past to apologize for what he'd done.

"Kade," I whispered, my throat tight with remorse. "I . . . I'm—"

"It's fine, Isla," he said, shoving a hand through his hair and retreating another step. "I shouldn't have pushed you so hard. I'll go now. Call if you need me."

Not knowing what to say, I watched in silence as he got into his car. When he took off, I stood in the parking lot and listened to the Mustang's growling engine until it faded.

I'd really done it this time. I'd pushed him away so hard that he was never coming back. I should feel relieved, *ecstatic* even. I'd wanted the wedge between us to remain firmly in place, and it was.

Then why did I feel so . . . awful?

The sound of a door opening and raucous laughter reminded me of why I'd *really* come here. I hadn't told Kade that I already had a lead, that I already knew far more about the case than I'd let on. I'd been hoping to run him off first so I wouldn't have to. So that I could work on this case solo until my dad caught wind of it.

He'd no doubt be upset with me, but this was my chance to show him that I didn't need a babysitter. I could handle the supernatural cases without help. I was ready to be solely independent and self reliant in all areas of my life.

This was my chance. My chance to prove to myself and everyone else just how strong I'd become. I didn't need a partner or bodyguard. And I most definitely didn't need Kade Carmichael.

So I shoved aside any lingering guilt and went into PI mode. I had a job to do, one that I was itching to get started. Adjusting my top, I strode toward the once again packed bar.

The first thing I searched for was the bikers who'd been loitering outside last night. They no doubt knew the victim personally. Maybe they saw him leave with someone last night. A *vampire* someone— even if they didn't know that. As far as I could tell, they were all human. Unless they had a blood kink, they were probably clueless about their supernatural neighbors.

But when I neared the building, the space under the awning was empty. I hadn't spotted any motorcycles in the lot either. Not so easily deterred, I squared my shoulders and entered the tavern.

The scent of blood immediately blasted me, nearly bowling me over. It was even stronger than last night. *Much* stronger. If I wasn't so focused on my task, it would have driven me outside again. Worry that my lust for blood was amplifying poked at me. Soon, waltzing inside a room filled with humans might no longer be safe.

I wasn't dense. I knew not to push myself. Knew that my control would eventually snap if I stretched it too thin.

But I also wanted to solve this case. No matter how starved for blood I became, I wouldn't jeopardize my job. It meant too much to me. My investigative work was everything. It kept my energetic self busy, which was key. Without that, I was afraid of what would happen. Afraid that my need for blood would dominate my every thought. Would *enslave* me. Would turn me into something I hated. Burying myself in unsolved cases was the only way to prevent that.

So, clenching my already aching jaw, I zeroed in on the far side of the room and plowed forward. I only needed to reach that spot and I'd be safe. One drink to take the edge off and I'd be set to go. A human patron abruptly stood from his barstool, cutting off my path. My gaze snapped to his neck, to the artery pulsing with what I desperately craved. A familiar burn filled my mouth as my fangs dropped. I walked faster.

At the last second, I swerved around him, swallowing a disappointed hiss. Every instinct in my body screamed at me to go back, to take what I wanted. *Needed.* He was prey. It was only natural for me to hunt, to capture, to slake my thirst. That's who I was now. An apex predator. A vampire. I was *meant* to feed on humans.

NO, I inwardly yelled at myself, forcing my feet to keep moving. That wasn't me. I wouldn't let myself become that.

Only three steps to go. Two. One.

You're safe. It's over. You can relax now.

The vampire barring the way to the back room took one whiff of me and stepped aside. I hurried to the bar and ordered, trembling as I claimed a stool. One quick drink and I could get back to business. One quick drink and I could *focus.*

Just as the bartender slid my drink toward me, a deep, accented voice purred in my ear, "I was hoping you'd show up again tonight."

A shiver raced up my spine and I felt myself stiffen as the vampire from last night took a seat beside me. "Samuel," I said, noticing that the hand gripping my drink started to tremble even harder. I faced him with a tight-lipped smile, making sure to keep my fangs safely hidden.

Samuel motioned to the bartender before fixing his golden brown eyes on me. He took in my stiff posture and forced smile without comment before saying, "I'll be honest, I was hoping to hear from you before this. I thought maybe you'd reconsider and call me."

I blinked. Oh. *Oh.* I'd almost forgotten he gave me his number. Probably hoping I'd booty call him. Pausing a moment to collect my thoughts and composure, I took a sip of my drink. I waited for the blood to soothe my aching throat, to ease the hunger burning through my insides. When nothing happened, I hurriedly took another sip. Then another.

A small smile curved Samuel's lips. "Thirsty?"

"Yes. Sorry," I managed to say, gesturing for the bartender to refill my glass. "It's been a stressful day."

Samuel leaned an elbow against the steel counter, interest flickering in his gaze. "Do tell."

I huffed a laugh, reaching for my drink again. "I'm actually here on business tonight. I don't really have time to chat."

"Oh?" He tilted his head, disappointment clear in his expression. "Maybe next time then."

I fiddled with my glass a moment before charging ahead. "Look, you're a nice guy. Charming and extremely good-looking." He grinned at that. "But I don't date vampires. Sorry, I should have told you that last night. I was just . . . I don't know. Lonely, I guess."

He stared at me, long enough that I took a sip of my drink. Then another. Finally, he raised his own glass, slowly downing a large mouthful before saying, "You fascinate me, Isla. You're a strong, independent woman who knows her mind. I like that about you. Too bad I'm not your type."

I shrugged with a slight grimace. "Sorry again."

"No need to apologize. We can still be friends, right?"

At the hopeful look he gave me, I managed to smile and say, "Sure."

I rose to resume my investigative work soon after, barely satiated, even after two drinks. The stress of seeing Kade again must have really gotten to me. After work tonight, I'd restock my blood supply and down just enough to get drunk. As long as I was in my apartment, I would be safe—and so would everyone else. I could drink until thoughts of Kade became a hazy memory, then sleep off the effects.

After a quick roll in the sheets with my vibrator, of course.

Planning to ask the main room bartender if the bikers under the awning last night were regulars, I faced the human horde again. So far, everyone in this establishment with fangs was on my suspect list. I'd question the humans first, then go from there. It was important to tread carefully when dealing with supernaturals. I was strong, but so were they. If I confronted the wrong one, they could very well try to rip my head off. I'd much rather interrogate humans first and hope they could give me more leads.

I was just about to flag down the bartender when I heard a thundering rumble from outside. Motorcycle engines. Several of them. I switched course, heading straight for the exit. When I left the building, the bikers from last night were getting off their bikes. There were four of them, and I took a moment to study them. Although the parking lot was dimly lit, I could easily make out their forms with my night vision. They all wore bandanas wrapped around their heads and black leather jackets. A skull with fiery eyes was emblazoned on their bandanas and jackets, including the name "Highway Demons."

Biker gang then. One that my case victim had been a part of. He'd been wearing the exact same jacket at the crime scene.

Perfect.

Interrogating this group could go a long way toward helping me find the murderer.

I approached them without hesitation, a greeting on the tip of my tongue. But when one of them saw me, he straightened and barked, "*You*. What did you do to Gunner?"

All four of them were suddenly staring at me. More like *glaring*.

I paused, completely caught off guard.

Before I could say a word, all four of the burly bikers stalked toward me.

CHAPTER 7

ISLA

Holy goddess, I'd been hoping for a little action, but not *this* much.

"Whoa," I said, holding up my hands at their fast approach. "Slow down there, boys. I didn't do anything to your friend."

"Cut the crap, lady," the first one growled, getting so close that his chest pushed against my hands. "We just got a call that he's dead and *you* were the last one who saw him. What happened? Did he play a little too rough? That's no reason to *kill* a man over."

"Wait a second," I said with more force, shoving him back a step. When I easily made him move, his eyes widened. Then narrowed to slits. Before he could think too long on how someone my size had done that, I added, "Are you talking about last night? I didn't go anywhere near him. You were all there. After he spoke to me, I went into the bar."

"Are you *daft*, girl?" another of the bikers said, crowding in close. "When you left the bar a few hours later, you were all over Gunner. You told him to take you somewhere *quiet*, so he did. We watched you leave with him on his hog."

The blood drained from my face. "But I—"

"Why did you kill him?" the first guy spat. Spittle hit my cheek. "Gunner was a good guy. He didn't deserve to go down like that. Especially not by a little tart like you."

"Hey, I'm not a tart," I sputtered, then snapped my mouth shut, suddenly realizing the danger I was in. These guys were piping *mad*.

And, judging by their livid expressions, they weren't going to leave here peaceably. They wanted revenge for their friend's murder, and it just so happened they thought *I* had killed him.

"Let's take her back to our place," a third biker said, muscling his way toward me. "Teach her what happens to whores who mess with the Highway Demons."

When he reached for my arm, I knocked his hand aside and took a step back. "Look, you don't want to do this," I hurriedly said, wishing someone would exit the tavern and draw their attention. That way, I could give them the slip without using my abilities. No such luck.

"Oh, but we do. We really really do," sneered the second guy, stepping into my personal space. "I suggest you come quietly or we'll have to bruise that pretty face of yours."

Laughter bubbled up before I could suppress it. "My face isn't the one that's going to be bruised if you don't step the hell back."

The fourth biker guffawed, which only incensed the second. His nostrils flared as he reached inside his jacket and pulled out what looked like brass knuckles. Yup. Brass frickin' knuckles. He slipped his fingers inside them and clenched his fist. "I'm going to enjoy this," he gritted out, winding his arm back. "Just a little."

His fist streaked toward my face.

Before it could connect, I ducked under his arm and shoved him. He flew back several feet, smacking right into a motorcycle. All four of the bikes tipped over like dominoes, crashing against the asphalt.

Oops.

The three bikers still standing shouted curses, fixing me with looks that could kill. Well, if I were *mortal*. They had no idea who they were dealing with. No idea that, instead of my body flooding with fear, excitement thrummed through me at the thought of fighting these men. Of winning. Of proving who the dominant species was.

"Fellas, let's talk this misunderstanding out," I said, once again holding up my hands. "There's no need for violence. I'll only end up handing your butts to you."

Okay, probably not the best thing to say. Hey, I'd never been in a gang fight before.

The guy who'd called me a tart yanked a wicked-looking knife from his belt and brandished it in the air. "We're done talking. This is for Gunner."

Then he lunged at me.

He was surprisingly fast, angling his blade for my midsection. What a dirtbag. Trying my hardest to react like a human, I whirled to the side. Not fast enough. The blade sliced through my right jacket sleeve, leaving a jagged tear.

Okay, I'd had enough of these losers.

"This is my favorite jacket, you jerkwad!" I snapped, whirling again at inhuman speed to catch his extended wrist. With a savage twist, I broke the bone. He screamed and dropped the knife.

I thought that would scare them off, but the douchebags were relentless.

One of them slipped behind me and grabbed my braid. When he yanked my head back, an unearthly growl tore from my throat. He made the mistake of getting too close then. I whipped my head back and heard the crack of bone, probably a nose. Another scream lit up the night.

As I shoved the man away from me, I caught the scent of blood. *Warm* blood. Instinct grabbed hold of me like a vise, forcing me to search out the source. I jerked around, my body on autopilot as I set my sights on the man behind me. A hiss slipped past my teeth when I saw the blood pouring from his busted nose.

Don't breathe, don't breathe, don't breathe.

Too late.

A powerful need flooded my body as I inhaled the intoxicating aroma. My fangs dropped to their full length in preparation, aching to pierce the man's flesh. Aching to *feed*.

Focused on him and only him, I didn't see the blow coming. Metal pounded into my jaw, snapping my head sideways. Blood, my *own* blood, filled my mouth. Fury ripped through me. Fury at the idiot dumb enough to distract me from my prey.

Ignoring the screaming pain in my jaw, I faced the biker with the brass knuckles. His fist was already cocked back, ready to hit me again. Ready to knock me out or bludgeon in my skull. I bared my bloody fangs and snarled.

At the sight, he cursed and stumbled back. Just as he did, a car came out of nowhere and rammed him. The man went flying for the second time tonight, striking the car's windshield before rolling off with a meaty thud.

Not wasting any time, I once again whirled toward my target. Warm blood still dripped from the man's broken nose. Before I could step toward him, hands gripped my upper arms from behind. I growled and jerked away, but the hands held fast.

"Get in the car, Isla. *Now*," a familiar voice barked, knocking some sense into me. When the hands forcibly steered me toward the idling car, I didn't resist. When they ripped the passenger door open and shoved me inside, I didn't put up a fight.

Tires squealed as the car recklessly reversed out of the parking lot. I braced myself against the dashboard, keeping silent when the car whipped around and shifted gears. It peeled onto the road, leaving a trail of smoking rubber in its wake.

Less than five seconds later, Kade lit into me. "A *bar* fight, Isla? *Really?*"

"They started it," I defensively garbled out, still trying to retract my fangs. "And it was a biker gang fight, actually."

"Oh, that's *much* better. And you thought exposing yourself to them right out in the open was a good idea?"

I touched my still aching jaw with a wince. "I didn't mean to. Only one of them saw me. And he's probably dead anyway after you hit him with your car."

"Don't put this on me. You recklessly exposed yourself in a very public way. People were starting to come out of the bar when I got there. Who knows what they saw or if they managed to snap a picture or two."

At his raised voice, I finally lost it. "Why are you always so *hard* on me?"

"Because I don't want something *bad* to happen to you," he thundered back.

"Fine. I get it. I screwed up. But I don't need you to—Ah!" When I cradled my jaw with a pained whimper, Kade swore and swerved onto the shoulder.

"You should have told me you were still hurt," he said, shifting to face me. "Let me see."

"Kade, no," I said, leaning away from him. "I just need to—"

His hand shot forward and cupped the back of my head, halting my retreat. "Hold still." Every muscle in my body locked as Kade leaned toward me, frowning at my aching jaw. "It's dislocated. I need to pop it back into place."

My eyes widened at his prognosis. Adrenaline must have kept me from feeling how bad the pain was. Well, I could definitely feel it *now*. After the hurtful words I'd spewed at him not an hour earlier, I expected his hands to be rough. Expected him to get his revenge by popping my jaw back into place with brute force.

But, for once, I didn't pull away. Didn't stop him from placing his thumb over the injury. A part of me felt like I deserved the pain. I'd been mean to him. Why shouldn't he be mean back? As I stared at him though, he didn't look angry. Only concerned.

He continued to hold my head still while his thumb gently probed my jaw. When I winced, I could have sworn he winced too.

"Kade . . ."

"Don't speak. It'll only make the pain worse."

"I—"

"Shh, it'll be over soon."

"I'm sorry."

His eyes snapped up to mine. A tremor shook me at how close we were. I'd never been this close to him before. Not like this. Not with his hands on my face. Not with an apology on my lips and vulnerability in my voice.

He could easily ignore or reject the words. I'd spent the last five years doing just that to him. It was only fair that I suffer in return.

But his expression only softened. "I'm sorry too," he quietly said, feathering his thumb across my jaw.

Relief shivered through me. The apology didn't fix what was broken between us, but it felt good to have said it. I felt . . . lighter.

"Brace yourself. This will hurt a bit," he murmured, continuing to stroke my jaw. The pressure slowly increased, firm yet gentle. Tears of pain filled my eyes, but I held still. A second later, I felt my jaw pop back into place. The relief was immediate, my fast healing abilities taking care of the rest.

"Thanks," I sighed, tentatively flexing my jaw.

"Anytime," he whispered. When he made no move to release me, when he continued to slowly run his thumb along my jaw, I looked up at him.

My breath caught.

His eyes weren't on mine. They were on my mouth.

As my heart skipped several beats, his gaze finally lifted to mine.

Good goddess, this wasn't good. This wasn't good at *all*.

And then he spoke. Confessing words that froze me solid. "I've thought about that kiss every day. Every. Single. Day."

Oh, gods. I knew exactly which kiss he was referring to. *The* kiss. The only kiss we'd ever shared.

"Kade," I breathed. I'd meant the word as a warning. Instead, his name came out as a prayer.

This wasn't happening. This wasn't *happening*.

I didn't move, *couldn't* move, as he skated his thumb over my skin. As he slowly—ever so slowly—brushed the pad across my bottom lip.

The featherlight touch immediately kindled awake a want, a *desire* I'd tried so hard to suppress. I felt myself leaning into the touch, aching for more.

"How long, Isla?" he softly rasped. I felt the sound to the tips of my toes. "How long must I suffer?"

Moon and stars, I couldn't do this any longer.

With a shuddering gasp, I leaned back and broke his hold on me. His hands fell away and I immediately felt cold without them. Swallowing with difficulty, I looked away and inhaled several calming breaths. He didn't utter a sound, but I could still feel his gaze on me, warming the side of my face.

"Why did you come back?" I finally said, relieved when my voice held steady. "I thought you'd be halfway to Sanctum Isle by now."

He took awhile to respond, staring at me a moment more before saying, "I meant what I said earlier, Isla. I'm going to help you solve this case. I just needed to clear my head. I was doing loops around the block, waiting for you to leave the tavern."

I blinked at him in surprise. "You knew I was in there this whole time?"

A slight smirk tilted his lips and he shrugged, dispelling the intense moment we'd just shared. "I knew you were up to something. You don't have a good poker face."

I scowled, but it wasn't a serious scowl.

As easily as we got into fights, Kade knew how to squash them. With a few words and a smile, he could make the tensest of moments fade away.

It was one of his superpowers.

"Now," he said, facing forward in his seat to resume driving. "Are you going to tell me why you were attacked by a *biker* gang?"

Then again, he was awfully *nosy* sometimes. Not that I had room to complain, since I was too.

Blowing out a sigh, I quickly said, "They-think-I-killed-their-friend."

The car fishtailed on the road as Kade shot me an incredulous look. "*What?*"

I groaned, wishing I didn't have to tell him, but knowing he wouldn't stop questioning me until I did. "They think I whored myself out to Gunner Landry last night and killed him for playing too rough."

Kade nearly swerved off the road, and I grabbed the wheel before we ended up in the ditch. He didn't even seem to notice, too busy *gaping* at me. "And is it true?" he said, with enough accusation that I bristled.

"Of course not. I like it rough."

My vindictive jab worked a little *too* well. Kade looked ready to explode.

I rolled my eyes. "I'm not a *hooker*, Kade. No one has ever paid for my goods."

He made a sharp hissing noise and focused on the road again, gripping the wheel so hard that I worried he would tear it in half.

"I *mean*," he said, his voice little more than a growl, "did you kill him?"

I pursed my lips. "Do you really have to ask? I struggle with bloodlust, but I'm not a *murderer*, Kade."

A muscle jumped in his jaw. "I didn't say you were."

"But you *think—*"

"I don't think you are either. But I think you're not telling me everything. I think you're worried, maybe even scared about something. What is it?"

I opened my mouth and promptly closed it. More than I wanted to admit, it felt good to talk about the case with him. But how could I tell him that last night's memory loss didn't quite add up? That I couldn't remember drinking enough to get drunk? That I couldn't recall how I'd left the tavern? That my bloodlust had been harder to control than usual?

Worst of all . . .

What if I hadn't gone straight home last night?

CHAPTER 8

KADE

"I have to go back."

I glanced at Isla, noting that she hadn't answered my question. I didn't push her though. She was spooked about something. Pushing her would only make her run. Make her shut me out, right when we'd finally had a breakthrough.

I'd felt her tremble. Heard her heart flutter as I'd touched her mouth.

She didn't despise me. Not completely. She'd even apologized for her harsh words. A first for her.

My reaction to the apology had been instantaneous. I'd wanted to express my gratitude by taking her mouth. By showing her just how much I'd forgiven her. How much I wanted to put the past behind us and begin anew.

But desire couldn't mend what was broken between us. She had to want this. Had to want *me*. If she didn't, then she'd never allow me to get close enough to fix this. To fix *us*. In the meantime, the only thing I could do was burn from afar and wait for the day when she'd let me in. And if that day never came, I would still burn. That I knew with absolute certainty.

Isla Andrews was my kryptonite. My achilles heel. Her continued rejection had weakened me.

But not exactly in a bad way.

I wasn't the same male I'd been five years ago. Before she'd sashayed into my life with her frilly skirts and bubbly personality, I'd never actively pursued females. I hadn't needed to. They'd eagerly flocked to me, drawn to my confidence and easygoing nature.

Relationships with them had been about casual fun and sex, nothing serious. I hadn't *wanted* serious. Not with them. None of them had felt right. I couldn't envision spending the rest of my long immortal life with one of them by my side. But Isla . . .

Isla was different.

Isla was a challenge. An intoxicating one. One that kept me on my toes. She made me work for even the tiniest scrap of her affection.

Not only that, she was tied to me, in a way no one else was—or ever would be. She was the first human I'd ever turned into a vampire. And she would be the last. I didn't want a sire bond with anyone else but her. She might hate the bond we shared, but I sure didn't.

"Earth to Kade," she sarcastically sang, pulling me from my thoughts. "Did you hear me? I need to go back to Mike's Tavern."

Focusing on the road again, I replied, "Can it wait a few hours? Those biker thugs might still be there."

She began nibbling on her thumbnail, a distracted look on her face. "No, it can't wait. Hopefully they left to seek medical attention."

"If not, I could thrall them into forgetting you."

"*No*," she said, a little too quickly. A little too forcefully. She flicked a glance at me, then said in a calmer tone, "I still need to interrogate them about last night. Tampering with their memories could affect their testimonies."

I cocked an eyebrow. "You think they're going to speak with you after the altercation you just had?"

"Well, maybe not *willingly*, but I can be persuasive when I want to be."

A smirk tugged at my mouth.

"What?" she said, eyeing me suspiciously.

The smirk grew. "Nothing."

"Kade, just tell me. I'm going to weasel it out of you one way or the other."

See? A challenge. One that often made me hard, kind of like right now.

"Fine," I gave in, taking the exit that would lead us back to the bar. "I was envisioning you beating the crap out of those bikers, twisting their arms behind their backs until they sang like canaries for you."

Isla harrumphed, not the least bit amused. Did I mention she was a challenge? "I can make them sing without violence."

"I'm sure you can, shortcake."

She turned in her seat toward me, a look of affront stamped across her face. "I'll have you know, I deal with ornery witnesses and targets all the time, mister. I hardly ever have to use brute force to get the information I want. And—" She abruptly stopped to owlishly blink at me. "Did you just call me *shortcake?*"

I shrugged. "Maybe."

"But why? We've known each other for five years and never once did you give me a nickname."

"The moment to give you one finally feels right."

"But why shortcake?"

"Because you're short and smell like vanilla cake."

And cake is my favorite. Throw in a few strawberries and I'd devour you whole, I silently added, growing even harder at the mental image.

After a lengthy pause, she said, "No. Absolutely not."

"People don't get to choose their nicknames, Isla."

"They do too. Noah used to call me *Whyla* because I was always asking questions, but I made him stop—"

"With brute force?"

When her lips thinned, I barked a laugh. "Tell you what. Let me partner with you on this case and I'll let you pick your own nickname."

She stared at me for a long moment. Outwardly, I kept up the appearance of looking calm, like the request I'd just made wasn't a big deal. Inwardly, I was begging her to agree. To give me this one chance. I wouldn't command or blackmail her into letting me stay. I wouldn't force her hand into accepting my help.

I wanted her to want this.

To want *me*.

When the silence stretched, my calm facade began to waver. She wasn't going to agree. She—

"Okay. Deal."

CHAPTER 9

ISLA

What was *wrong* with me?

A little bout of teasing banter and I'd caved like a cheap deck of cards. I'd seriously lost my ever-loving mind this time. And I wasn't the only one in shock that I'd agreed. Kade hadn't spoken for a solid five minutes. His mouth had opened and closed several times, but nothing had come out.

He was probably as mystified as I was by my hot-and-cold act. I told myself that it wasn't like I had a choice anyway. My dad had ordered me to partner with him, and disregarding his orders wasn't in my best interest at this time.

But this was more than that. I'd just agreed to partner with Kade of my own *free will*. I couldn't so easily explain that away.

Thankfully, we arrived back at Mike's Tavern then, which allowed me to once again focus on my job and not my messed-up feelings for the man beside me.

"I'll just be a minute," I said, hopping out of the car the second he swerved into a parking spot. Not waiting for his reply, I booked it toward the tavern.

When the Mustang's engine died and the driver door opened, I grimaced. I'd only made it a few steps before Kade joined me, easily keeping pace.

"Really, I don't need you to—" I began, but he cut me off before I could finish.

"You agreed, Isla. Partners, remember?"

"I know, but—"

"That means we watch each other's backs."

"I *know*, but—"

"I'm not letting you walk into a potentially dangerous situation alone. Kenna would have my hide if I did, not to mention your father and brother."

"*Kade.*" I grabbed his arm, forcing him to a halt. He turned toward me, his face set in determined lines. Crap, what had I done? Why had I *agreed* to this? "I don't want you to . . . I need you to wait out here. In case the bikers come back."

He frowned and scanned the parking lot—now devoid of motorcycles—before fixing me with a suspicious look. "You don't want me to go in there. Why?"

I sighed impatiently. "Look, I agreed to let you work with me, but I'm the boss here. Which means that you need to listen when I tell you to do something. No questions asked."

His frown deepened. "I don't think it works that way."

"Well, it does for us," I firmly said, widening my stance. "Take it or leave it."

He was silent for a long moment, a muscle thrumming in his jaw as he searched my face. Then, "Partners shouldn't keep secrets from each other. One or both are bound to get hurt if there's no open communication."

A scream built in my chest. "Fine. There's someone inside I don't want you to see. Happy?"

"No. Who?"

"Ugh, can we drop this already? He's just a guy I had drinks with last night. No big deal. But I don't want you to—Kade!" I screeched, swiping for his arm again and missing as he abruptly stormed toward the building. "Don't you dare open that—" He wrenched the door open. "Don't you dare enter the—" Cursing, I took off after him as he stalked inside the tavern.

When he suddenly stopped just inside the entrance, I had to use my vampire reflexes to avoid colliding with his back. "Where is he?" Kade said, scanning the room. His height allowed him to easily see over the crowd, something that I secretly envied. Being short sucked most of the time.

"I'm not telling you, Kade, so you might as well—" The scents in the room finally hit me. *Really* hit me. I snapped my mouth shut and stopped talking. Stopped breathing. Need trembled through me anyway.

"What's wrong, shortcake?"

Gah, that stupid *nickname* again! At any other time, I would have lit into Kade for continuing to use it. But I was frozen solid, and I *hated* it. Hated that Kade could so easily waltz into a room full of humans and I couldn't. He didn't even seem to *notice* that the air was saturated with the tantalizing aroma of fresh blood. How could he be so unaffected?

After a moment that felt like an eternity, Kade quietly swore and grabbed my upper arm. "Why didn't you tell me you were struggling? Let's get out of here."

When he moved toward the exit, I stubbornly dug my heels in. "No," I managed to croak, shaking my head. "I'll be fine. I just . . . need a moment."

His hold on my arm tightened as he leaned down and hissed in my ear, "This is *dangerous*, Isla. For them *and* you."

"I'm *fine*," I said again through gritted teeth, not bothering to yank my arm free. He was stronger than me by far. "I don't need your help with this."

When he flinched, I almost felt bad. Until he said, "Is this the real reason why you didn't want me to come in here? So I wouldn't see how weak your control is?"

"My control is *fine*, Kade Carmichael," I snarled in his face, barely suppressing the need to flash my fangs. "I'll show you just how fine it is if you'll let go of my *arm*."

"Isla," he warned, but his grip loosened.

I jerked my arm free and shrugged out of my jacket in one swift move. Shoving the jacket into his hands, I whirled without another word, marching toward the bar. On the *human* side. Flagging the bartender down, I slid in between two patrons who unconsciously gave me some space. Not enough though. I needed more. *Much* more. I could practically hear the alcohol fizzling in their bloodstreams.

Before I could fixate too hard on their tantalizing blood, I strategically leaned against the counter, giving the bartender an ample view down my deep v-neck shirt. He took the bait—most guys did—letting his gaze linger on my cleavage before meeting my stare. I flashed him a beaming smile. "Hi. I was wondering if you could do me a favor."

He flicked a glance at my cleavage again before answering, "What do you need?"

"Well . . ." I bit my lip demurely, fluttering my lashes a bit for added effect. "It's kind of an embarrassing request. Can I whisper it to you?"

I leaned over the counter even more, giving him a very generous eyeful. Drawn to the boobs like a bee to honey, he bent forward, lending me his ear. This close, his scent was overwhelming. Unable to contain them, my fangs started to descend.

Before I lost my chance, I quickly whispered, "I was wondering if I could see your security footage. I'm pretty sure my boyfriend is cheating on me and came here with the bimbo last night. I just want confirmation before I dump the sorry loser."

He pulled back with a dubious expression.

Time for the waterworks.

On command, tears filled my eyes. I let them dampen my lashes, blinking fiercely. "I know it's a big request . . ." I swiped at my cheek with a watery laugh. "Sorry. Forget I asked. I don't want you to get into trouble."

I started to pull back. Slowly. When I turned, robbing him of his *view*, he finally spoke.

"Hold on a sec, miss."

As he disappeared through a door behind the counter, I slowly grinned.

"Did you seriously just use your breasts to get that guy's cooperation?" a deep voice rumbled in my ear, causing my heart to skip a few beats. I knew without looking who it was. I also knew that he wasn't amused.

I shrugged, keeping my eyes trained on the door the bartender had gone through. "'Play to your strengths,' my dad always taught me. My boobs just happen to be one of my best assets."

"They are," Kade bluntly agreed, catching me off guard. The admission—the knowledge that he'd *noticed*—made my body heat up in all the wrong places. I quickly clamped my thighs shut, desperately trying to contain a certain scent. A scent that would betray me in the worst way possible. "But why didn't you just tell him you're investigating a murder?" he continued, standing close enough to warm my back.

"Humans aren't supposed to know about this case. You know how they like to share everything on social media. And the *other* bartender is supernatural. Until I can see that footage, he and everyone else in the back room are on my suspect list. Playing as a harmless civilian will get me the best results, hence the boob display and cheating boyfriend act."

Over the loud music and voices, I heard Kade say, "Well, you shouldn't show your best assets to someone undeserving."

I snorted, keeping my gaze locked on the door when all I wanted to do was see his expression. "And who, pray tell, deserves to view my assets?"

A pause. Then, "Someone who cares about you. Someone who respects you enough to keep their eyes on your face and not your chest during a conversation."

I squeezed my thighs together, so hard that they trembled. "Kenna respects me. Should I let her see them?"

Kade placed a hand on the counter beside me, drawing so close that his chest brushed against my shoulder blades. "It should be someone you *want* to show them to. Someone who makes you feel beautiful and cherished when they look upon them. Someone who will worship them with their eyes, hands, lips . . . and tongue."

All the air whooshed out of me. I had to lean against the counter again as my legs threatened to give out. Unable to hide it any longer, my arousal coiled into the air. Kade's chest expanded against my back as he deeply inhaled. His hand on the counter formed a tight fist. So tight that it shook.

Seconds later, *I* was the one deeply inhaling. Recognizing the scent of his arousal, my body had a visceral reaction. My nipples painfully hardened and my panties dampened. My breathing grew labored as I waited. Waited for him to move. To act. To do anything other than torture me by remaining so close without touching me.

"Isla," he finally breathed against the shell of my ear, making my eyes flutter shut. I tried to respond. Tried to move. But I suddenly forgot how. My brain could only focus on one thing. *Him.* His warmth. His scent. His body.

So close. So unbearably *close.*

A door suddenly opened, yanking me out of my stupor. I jerked my eyes open and straightened as the bartender returned. Thankfully, Kade got the hint and pulled back. Not fast enough though. The bartender eyed him shrewdly before refocusing on me. More specifically, my boobs. Instead of thrusting them out and giving him a better view, I found myself crossing my arms over my chest.

His gaze finally lifted to mine. Without a word, he gestured for me to step aside. I followed his lead, relieved when Kade remained where he was. The guy *definitely* wouldn't cooperate with an alpha male breathing down his neck. The second I slipped behind the counter and through the employee door with him at my heels, he said, "That the boyfriend?"

Caught off guard by the abrupt question, I nearly missed the first stair leading up to what I hoped was an office. "Who? The guy standing behind me?"

"Yeah. If that's him, then I don't think you have anything to worry about."

"Oh?"

"I see it all the time. That guy isn't interested in anyone but you."

My stomach took a swan dive. For a second, I almost forgot what I was doing. Forgot my mission and everything else as my mind latched onto the bartender's words, replaying them over and over. I nearly blew my cover with my silence, but I hurriedly recovered with a dismissive wave. "Well, he's definitely not my boyfriend. I'm not really into the over-muscled Norse god type. Lean builds and curly brown hair are more my thing."

As I ascended the stairs, I threw a winning smile at the bartender whose description I'd just described, only to find his gaze glued to my butt. I turned around with an eye roll. Maybe if he wasn't so skeevy, I'd almost feel bad for leading him on.

When I reached the top, the guy thankfully stopped ogling me and headed for a desk. "We keep all the security footage on external servers," the bartender said, bending over a keyboard. His face glowed blue as the computer monitor turned on, highlighting his semi-nervous expression. "Give me a sec while I pull up last night's recordings. Do you need indoor or outdoor footage?"

"Both, if that's all right." I joined him at the desk, hiding a grimace as I sidled up beside him. His wayward eyeballs were annoying, but I could put up with them if it meant getting the information I sought. It was his *scent* I was currently struggling with. The two drinks I had earlier might as well have been water, for all they helped. I needed to see the footage and get out of this place as quickly as possible.

"There," he said after a few torturous minutes, sliding the computer chair out for me to sit on. When I accepted the seat, he needlessly leaned over the chair back to point at the computer screen. "That's the play and pause button. There's hours of footage, so you might have to fast forward through most of it."

His arm intentionally brushed against my shoulder. Knowing him, he was probably looking down my shirt right this very second. Grabbing the mouse with a little too much force, I gushed, "Thank you *so* much. You're a doll. Are you sure you won't get into trouble for letting me up here?" Gritting my teeth, I forced myself to look up at him with a fake worried look.

"Oh," he said with a nervous laugh, gripping the chair on either side of my head. "My manager's on a break. He knows I sometimes bring girls up here though, so it's okay. We can just pretend to fool around if anyone shows."

It was then that my nose picked up a different scent. His arousal. YUCK.

I was liking this guy less and less. First off, I looked barely old enough to drink. That and he was probably in his late thirties. The guy was seriously giving off child predator vibes. He was probably planning on hitting on me the second I "dumped" my nonexistent boyfriend.

What was with people lately thinking I was a *tart*?

If I wasn't so desperate for this footage, I would've kneed him in the balls already.

"Good idea," I responded with another bright smile, when what I really wanted to do was puke on his face. As he continued to invade my personal space, I frantically searched for a way to get rid of him. Casting an anxious look at the stairs, I murmured, "Maybe you should keep watch though, just in case. I really don't want you to get fired."

Although, that would be a perk of this mission, especially if he had a habit of propositioning girls half his age.

"Sure," he said, slowly moving around me toward the stairs, even though his heart wasn't into it.

Too bad, dude. Your balls are safer over there anyway.

The second he wasn't behind me, I got to work, hitting play on the recorded footage. When a black screen greeted me, I checked the time stamp. Noting that it was a little before the time I'd arrived last night, I started to fast forward. More black greeted me. Confused, I switched to another recording, this one from outside the bar. More black.

"Um, is something wrong with your computer screen?" I asked the bartender, wishing I didn't need to get him involved again. I was pretty good with electronics, considering my line of work, but fixing a dead computer screen wasn't exactly my area of expertise.

He immediately rushed over, all too eager to "help." Double yuck. "It was working fine earlier today," he said, reaching across me to fiddle with the mouse and keyboard. "Maybe a cord got disconnected or—"

My phone suddenly buzzed. I fished it out of my pocket and accepted the call without taking my eyes off the computer screen. "Hello?"

Silence.

I checked the caller ID, frowning when I saw an unknown number.

Just when I was about to hang up, a gravelly voice spoke. "Found what you're looking for, Miss Andrews?"

A cold shiver worked its way up my spine. "Who is this?"

"I could be your friend, or I could be your worst enemy. It all depends on you."

My frown deepened. "I'm hanging up now."

"Wait," the voice spoke in that same gravelly tone. "I have something you're looking for."

"And what's that?"

A pause. Then, "Footage of what you did last night."

CHAPTER 10

ISLA

I didn't think my heart could pound any faster. "Who is this?" I asked again.

"Wrong question," came the gravelly reply.

"What do you want?"

An equally gravelly chuckle came through the phone. "Better. As I'm sure you've discovered, the security footage you're seeking is missing. I left a blank dud in its place. If you want the real footage—and trust me, you do—then all you have to do is feed off the human beside you."

"*What?*" I hissed, flicking a glance at the bartender. Thankfully, he didn't seem to have picked up on the conversation. He was still oblivious, tinkering with the computer. Not bothering with pretense, I said, "I can't do that."

"Why not?"

"Because it's *wrong*. I won't do it."

"Then I can't give you the footage. I'm sure your *father* would like to see it though. Goodbye, Miss Andrews."

"*Wait.* Wait. There has to be another way. I've got money. How much in exchange for the footage?"

"I'm not interested in money, Miss Andrews. I want to see you act on your true nature. Do that for me and I'll give you anything you want."

A chill skated down my spine. They said "see you." Could they see me right *now?*

"I'm sorry, but—" I said, pushing back from the desk and standing in one fluid motion. Without getting too close, I peered out the closest window onto the street below. "—I don't negotiate with psychopaths."

For all I knew, there was nothing incriminating on that footage. I wouldn't so easily let someone blackmail me. Maybe they were recording me right *now*, hoping to catch me in a compromising situation so they truly had something to hold over my head.

Yeah, no.

"I'm sorry to hear that," came the gravelly reply.

"Me too."

"Until you come to your senses, we must be enemies then."

I rolled my eyes. "How unfortunate."

"Yes. Especially for the human you're with."

The line went dead.

A moment later, a phone on the desk rang. The bartender reached over and picked it up. "Mike's Tavern. How can I—?" He suddenly went poker straight. "Of course. Right away."

Alarm flared through me when he mechanically set the phone down to pull open a desk drawer. With my heightened hearing, I'd managed to catch the short conversation he'd just had, but it didn't make any sense. *"Open the top desk drawer,"* the person on the other end had said. *"Use it on yourself."*

Use what?

I was just about to question the bartender when he suddenly reached inside the drawer and pulled out a handgun. Without the slightest bit of hesitation, he cocked back the hammer and raised it to his head.

Horrified, I screamed, "No!" and dashed toward him. Not even caring if he saw, I put on an extra burst of inhuman speed and grabbed for the gun. The second my fingers touched the weapon, white hot pain seared my skin. *Silver.* The shock of pain was enough to weaken my grip. Before I could stop it, a shot fired.

The noise blasted my sensitive eardrums, and I stumbled back a step, clutching my head. Through the sharp ringing, I heard a distant boom of thunder. No, the splintering of *wood*, like a door being blown off its hinges. I looked up at the bartender again to see him frozen in place, blankly staring at the gun in his hand. But when a familiar hulking form suddenly materialized at the top of the stairs, he flinched.

That's all it took.

One little flinch.

The silver gun discharged again and I reacted on instinct. Kade bellowed as I intercepted the bullet heading directly toward him. He moved, but not fast enough. I'd already placed myself in its path.

The bullet struck me in the chest.

My insides immediately burst into flames. Strong arms banded around me before I could hit the floor, but I barely felt them. Barely felt myself being lifted and cradled against a hard body. Barely felt anything but *fire*.

"Why would you *do* that, Isla?" Kade's frantic voice washed over me. "*Why?*"

The room suddenly moved. Spun. As he swiftly carried me down the stairs.

My world was fire and brimstone. Everything burned and burned and burned, like I'd been dropped into the pits of hell.

I shook uncontrollably, reaching for the cause of my agony.

"Don't touch it," Kade commanded, so forcefully that I felt my will slip away. Felt my body obey his words.

Through the tears blurring my vision, I threw him the most scathing look I could muster. One that said, *I'm going to rip your balls off and feed them to my nonexistent dog.*

As he shouldered through a crowd of panicking humans, he caught my look and grimaced. "I'm sorry," he said, clear remorse in his voice. "I spoke without thinking. Just . . . please don't touch it. You'll only make it worse."

I listened. Not that I had much choice. The sire bond was still in effect, wrapping its invisible fingers around me. Bending me to its will.

As we burst outside, a smattering of rain struck my face. The cold drops did nothing to soothe the fire raging throughout my body.

Willing my fingers to move, I fisted them into Kade's shirt. I'd never been injured by silver before, never experienced the agony both vampires and werewolves felt by even the slightest bit of contact with the element. And now, an entire silver bullet was lodged inside my chest, eating away at my sanity.

The pain. The *pain.*

It was slowly driving me mad. If it didn't stop soon, I was going to lose control. Instinct would take over and force me to reveal my true form. Only when I felt truly threatened, truly *helpless*, did my vampire form fight to emerge. It was like a defensive reaction to danger, a warning that I shouldn't be messed with.

Shadow-like skin, blood red eyes, sharp claws, and a wicked set of fangs would scare off most threats. But revealing myself to all these people would ruin everything. For one, I could kiss my career goodbye. For another, the SCA would probably lock me up.

I couldn't let either of those things happen. It would destroy me.

Good thing the tavern was butted up to a stretch of woods. Kade stalked toward them, barely managing to control his speed. The second we were deep enough inside the trees though, he took off at lightning speed.

I must have passed out then.

When I came to, he was lowering me to the ground. It almost felt soft, like he'd placed me on a patch of moss. I blinked my vision into focus, noting the crude rock walls surrounding us. With how dark it was in here, he must have found a small cave.

When he felt my eyes on him, he quietly swore. "I was hoping you'd stay asleep for this."

I didn't respond, too busy trying not to cry as the pain came rushing back to greet me. Instead of laying me flat on the ground, Kade propped me up against the cave wall. In all the chaos, he'd miraculously held onto my jacket, which he placed behind my head to use as a pillow. The second I was situated, he peeled the top of my bloody shirt back to expose the wound.

He swore again.

"W-what?" I finally managed to stutter, trying to see the wound for myself. "Is it . . . is it in my heart?"

"No, but the entrance healed over. I'll have to reopen it to extract the bullet."

My stomach gave a nauseating swoop.

"Whoa, wait a second," I said, my voice trembling like crazy as he shucked off his jacket. "It's too dark in here. Maybe we should—"

He fished his phone out of his pocket and turned on the flashlight.

"Okay, but what if you can't find it? Maybe we should—"

"I dug a bullet out of Loch's *heart*, Isla. I can find it."

When he reached for me again, true panic set in.

"I-need-something-for-the-pain," I blurted, cringing away from his hand.

Only my wheezing breaths filled the silence as he paused to stare

81

at me. I didn't bother hiding how freaked I was, silently pleading with him not to do this.

His expression grew pained. "Isla, you're a vampire now. Human medicine won't help you. The bullet has to come out as quickly as possible. Waiting will only prolong your agony."

I panted for a moment before admitting, "I don't handle pain well."

He studied me a moment more. "Then why did you intercept the shot? Why not let the bullet hit me instead? You know I can handle pain."

A memory flashed before my eyes. Of Kade, roaring in agony as Loch's younger brother ripped off his arm. Red obscured my vision. *Rage.* It didn't matter that five years had passed since then. That Kade's arm was fully healed now. The memory would always haunt me. Would always plague me with guilt.

"Isla," he pressed.

"Because I can't stand seeing you *hurt*," I snapped, then immediately regretted it as the bullet shifted, burning a fresh path through my insides. "Kade," I whimpered, my eyes welling with more tears. "Please get it out. *Please.*"

He suddenly cupped my face, gently wiping the tears away. "I'll get it out. I swear on my life, you're going to be okay."

Inhaling a ragged breath, I blinked the tears away and nodded. "Then do it. Before I lose my ever-loving mind."

"That's my girl," he said, catching another tear. Before I could react, he leaned forward and kissed my forehead. I barely had time to register the slight pressure, the warmth of his mouth, before it was gone.

Despite the terrible pain I was in, butterflies tumbled in my stomach. There was no controlling my reaction to the affectionate gesture. I silently watched Kade, whose attention was now on my closed wound. As far as I could tell, the bullet was lodged several inches to the right of my heart. I hadn't noticed before, but he was trying *really* hard not to expose my chest while examining me.

"Take it off," I blurted.

His eyes jerked up to mine.

"My shirt," I explained. "It's in the way."

He paused for only a second. Then his hands were on my waist, lifting the hem. I shifted to help him and fresh pain shot through me. When I slumped against the cave wall with a groan, he stopped.

"Rip it," I said through gritted teeth.

"Isla . . ."

"*Rip* it, Kade."

A second later, the cave echoed with the sound of tearing material. I glanced down at my bare stomach, then up at him again. "I hadn't meant my *entire* shirt."

He made a sound of exasperation.

"I was kidding, Kade. Lighten up. Just don't get distracted by my assets."

I thought for sure that would get a reaction out of him. At least a *smile*. But I got nothing. He looked more serious than I'd ever seen him before. His gaze didn't even dip to my exposed skin like I thought it would. He remained focused on his task, so focused that my humor died a sudden death.

"Maybe we should—"

"No more stalling, Isla," he sternly said, carefully tugging my severed shirt off. My eyes widened as his claws suddenly lengthened. He used them to cut off a clean section of the shirt, tightly rolling the material before lifting it to my mouth. "Bite down on this."

My throat constricted. "I don't need it."

"Yes, you do. This is going to hurt like hell, shortcake."

Every inch of me began to tremble. I threw him a panicked look, not bothering to hide how scared I was. "Make it quick."

His expression softened, yet still managed to remain firm. "I promise. Now open."

I did, allowing him to wedge the fabric between my teeth.

"Here are the rules," he said, grasping one of my bare shoulders. *Anchoring* me in place. "Scream all you want. Curse me. Claw at me. But *don't* interfere. Understand?"

Swallowing around the gag in my mouth, I frantically nodded. My eyes tracked his every move, fearfully watching as he straddled my legs. The position gave him even better leverage, not that he needed it. We were both Feltore, but he was bonded to a powerful Venturi. His drothen's strength amplified his, and there was no way I could best that.

Still, the urge to fight my way out of this helpless situation was overwhelming. I dug my fingers into the damp moss beneath me, unable to stop trembling. When he positioned a clawed hand over my closed wound, the last of my strength failed me.

"Wait," I garbled out, but it was too late.

The second his claws punctured my flesh, I threw my head back and screamed. The pain was *sharp*. Breath-stealing. My body bucked away from it, but Kade was relentless. His legs and free hand mercilessly squeezed me, forcing me to remain still. I hooked my claws into his waist and dug in for dear life. He didn't utter a sound. Didn't even flinch. He was too busy torturing me. Too busy burrowing a *hole* through my chest.

I screamed and screamed and screamed. Screamed until my throat was raw.

Still, he didn't stop.

I bit into my makeshift gag until my sore jaw trembled with fatigue. My breaths sawed in and out of my nose. Just when I thought I couldn't stand a second more of this hellish agony, Kade withdrew his bloodied fingers from my chest. With a hiss, he threw the silver bullet toward the cave entrance.

Within seconds, the pain began to slowly fade as my blood rapidly healed the injury. My relief was so great that a loud sob heaved from my chest.

"It's over," Kade said in soothing tones, gently prying the gag free. His grip on my shoulder and legs fell away. I continued to sob, unable to stop. When I heard him whisper, "I'm so sorry, Isla," like this was *his* fault, I retracted my claws from his waist and threw myself at him.

My arms snaked around his neck like twin boas, squeezing him impossibly tight. He audibly sucked in a breath, clearly caught off guard. So was I. We'd hugged before, but not like this. Except for one fleeting moment five years ago. I remembered the day like it was yesterday. The day he'd been seriously injured because of me. The day I'd kissed him and realized my true feelings.

The day I'd run away from him.

And now, here I was, hugging him. *Torturing* myself again. But it felt so good. So comforting to be this close to him. And when he finally responded, embracing me equally as tight, I allowed myself to melt against him. Just for a moment. Just for one blissful moment where I could pretend we belonged together. Where I could pretend he was mine.

And I was his.

I didn't mean to prolong the hug. But, before I knew it, a minute had passed. I was about to make myself pull away when he suddenly burrowed his face in the crook of my neck and deeply inhaled. "Sweet mother of Moses, you smell so good," he groaned on an exhale, fitting me even tighter against him. At the feel of his hot breath on my skin, a shiver of pleasure trembled through me. I melted even more.

Gods, I was in so much trouble.

He continued to inhale my scent, lightly brushing his lips over my sensitive skin. The more he did, the more I *wanted* him to. My mind went rogue and thought of where *else* it wanted those full lips to roam. The second it did, hot desire rushed through my body.

Crap.

I tensed, preparing to rip myself away before he could smell my arousal. But he suddenly moved again, shifting the hug into something more.

"Don't run," he murmured, sitting on the cave floor with me straddling his hips. "Please, Isla."

Just like that, I hesitated. Not because he commanded me, but because I was curious. Curious to know where this was heading. Curious, because apparently I was a cat with a death wish.

When I remained where I was, one of his hands slowly slid down my bare spine to press my lower half against him. Against his rock hard *length*. My body immediately lit up like the sun, burning hotter and hotter out of control. He caught my head as it fell back. A breathy moan pushed at my throat, and I let it roll out.

Even through our jeans, I could feel how huge he was. Bigger than I'd imagined, and I could imagine quite a lot. My mind could be a dirty place sometimes. Most of the time, actually. Right now, it was imagining how he would feel without our jeans in the way. The mental image was almost enough to make me orgasm.

"I can hear your heart racing," Kade breathed, keeping me flush against him. "I can smell your desire. Sense how much you want this. You can stop running, Isla. Stop fighting what's between us."

Every inch of me shook, thrumming with powerful need. My

heart pounded faster and faster, urging me to give in. To accept his words as truth and allow the flames between us to soar. To *consume*. What would the harm be? We were two consenting adults with high sexual drives. Having sex with him in this cave wouldn't be the end of the world. Yes, he was a vampire, but this was Kade. *Kade*. Not some random guy in a bar.

Wait a minute. This was *Kade*.

My eyes flew open and I gasped, "I can't."

Not ready to let this go, he pressed, "Why not, Isla?"

"B-because . . . because you're my *sire*."

That did the trick. Or so I thought.

He stiffened, but after a moment said, "So? We share a bond. All the more reason why we should be together."

I loosened my grip on his neck, pulling back so I could look him in the eye. "A sire bond is nothing like a soulmate bond. A soulmate bond is rare and beautiful and sacred. But a sire bond is . . . well, it's *toxic*. The two halves aren't equal. One is the master and the other is—"

"Don't say it," Kade said with a quiet warning growl.

"The slave."

Kade hissed a curse. He abruptly stood, bringing me with. The second I was on my feet, he let go and stepped back.

I felt the absence of his warmth like a bucket of ice water. When I wrapped my arms around my naked torso and hugged myself, Kade swore again. Yanking his shirt over his head, he handed it to me. "Here. Put this on."

I accepted the shirt, trying not to stare at his sculpted golden chest. Or chiseled abs. I was pretty sure he had an eight pack. I stopped my eyes from traveling lower, to the bulge that was probably still in his pants.

Slipping on the shirt without comment, I shuffled my feet in the moss for a lengthy moment before saying, "I didn't mean to upset you. I'll admit that there's chemistry between us." A *lot*. "But if we go down that road, we'll end up crashing and burning. We'll only hurt each other more. Things are already awkward enough during the holidays and get-togethers with your family and mine. Adding sex to the mix will make it ten times worse."

He didn't bat an eye at my blunt choice of words. He and I had that in common, which oftentimes got us into trouble.

Shoving a hand through his hair, he paused before replying, "Then I'll wait."

I blinked at him. "Wait for what?"

"Wait for you to accept us."

I sighed in exasperation. "Haven't you been listening to me, Kade? We're not *meant* for each other. We would only—"

"End up hurting each other. Yes, I heard you. But I think you're wrong," he said, slowly stepping toward me again. I stiffened at the determined glint in his eyes. "I think there's so much more between us than lust and a sire bond. I think you'd learn to trust me again if you'd give me another chance. I think you'd see that I have no desire to let the bond between us become toxic. That I would fight with every breath in my body to make you feel safe around me. To convince you that we can be equals, that we can have what soulmates have. I've waited this long, Isla, and I'll continue to wait for as long as it takes."

He stopped in front of me, so close that I had to tip my head back. "I'll wait until you can see what I see. That, through pain and heartache, fate brought us together. I don't want a casual hookup with you. We are *destined* for each other, Isla Andrews. Today. Tomorrow. A thousand years from now. Nothing you say will make me think otherwise."

My chest tightened to the point of pain. I hadn't expected him to say all that. Hadn't even known he felt that way. I was speechless, which pretty much never happened. Still, I managed to whisper, "You're a stubborn fool, Kade Carmichael."

A faint smile graced his lips. "Never pretended otherwise."

CHAPTER 11

ISLA

It was almost midnight when we trekked back to Mike's Tavern.

Kade had allowed me my silence, not saying a peep the entire trip back. Good thing too. My brain was firing on all cylinders. One second, it was stewing over the case and the crazy turns it had taken. The next, on my time in the cave with Kade and his bold admission.

Once words were spoken, they couldn't be unsaid. Or unheard. I couldn't stop *thinking* about them. How long had he felt this way about me?

I wanted to ask him but didn't dare. The less attention I put toward his admission, the better. Besides, it didn't change anything. I still felt the same about dating vampires. About *him*. Especially him. I had meant what I said. The sire bond spoiled any chance we could have possibly had. Once I'd figured out the hold he had over me— once he had *used* it on me—everything had changed.

Never again. Never again would I be at the mercy of a vampire. Never again would I let one destroy my life. They'd taken my humanity. I wouldn't let them take what was left of me.

When we rounded the side of the bar, red and blue flashing lights caught my eye. Panic fluttered in my chest and I bit back a curse. Kade didn't seem to notice, a step away from waltzing into the parking lot. Before he could reveal himself, I grabbed his arm and yanked him back. He stumbled but caught himself as I dragged him into the building's shadows, stopping only when we were safely hidden.

"Isla, what—?"

"Shh!" I hissed, slapping a hand over his mouth. Tilting my head, I let my sensitive hearing do its thing. Seconds later, my dad's deep baritone reached me. Cursing aloud this time, I let go of Kade and crept along the building's side. One peek around the corner was all I needed to know that I was screwed.

I jerked my head back and clenched my hands into fists.

"What's wrong?" Kade quietly rumbled in my ear. He was so close that I could feel his warmth seeping into my back. The need to pull away was overwhelming, but doing so would expose me to the parking lot's lights.

"They've seen our cars. They know we're here," I replied, forcing myself to stay where I was.

"So? Someone probably called in the shooting. We can tell your dad to arrest that bastard bartender for attempted murder."

I whirled on Kade. "*No.* We can't do that." When both his eyebrows raised at my frantic tone, I quickly added, "Just let me handle this, okay?"

Ignoring his skeptical look, I hurriedly tucked in my borrowed shirt and zipped up my jacket. Thankfully, there weren't any bloodstains on the outside of my jacket, and my jeans were dark enough to hide any stains. I fixed my attention on Kade next, cringing at his bare chest.

"Here," I said, reaching out to button his jacket. He remained perfectly still, silently watching me. When my fingers accidentally brushed his bare torso, he jerked, the muscles in his stomach contracting. I froze, painfully aware that both our hearts sped up at the small slip. Just like that, cloying heat simmered between us. Desperate to snuff it out, I grabbed the last button and quickly secured it.

While my gaze searched the rest of him for signs of blood, I willed my galloping heart to slow. If only he hadn't expressed his true feelings. Now that I knew, even the slightest bit of contact with him felt . . . intimate. Every part of me knew that I needed distance from him, that I needed to clear my head before I gave in to the lust pulsing beneath my skin.

It would be so easy. *So* easy to give in.

But I'd have to endure his presence for a little while longer. At least until we were in the clear. My inspection finally led me to Kade's face, where I tried my hardest to avoid his eyes. Eyes that were fixed on me a little too intensely. Eyes that were no doubt bright with blue fire.

Spotting a smear of dried blood on his neck, I wet my thumb without thinking and rubbed at his skin. When his pulse beneath my thumb soared, I froze again. Crap, I shouldn't have done that. I yanked my hands away from him and cleared my suddenly dry throat. "Okay, you're good. Maybe just put your hands in your pockets. You still have some blood visible beneath your fingernails."

I was about to turn and expose our position when he quietly said, "Wait."

Still not looking him in the eye, I said a tad impatiently, "We really need to go. My dad is—"

"Just wait," he said again and reached for my face.

When his fingers caught my chin, I could no longer keep my eyes downcast. They jumped up to his face, wide as saucers. I gulped as, sure enough, twin pools of fire flickered in his gaze. He rubbed his thumb over my chin several times, never once breaking our stare. Just when I thought I would either drown or burn alive—maybe both—he dropped his hand and murmured, "There. Good to go."

I swallowed again, uttering a tight, "Thanks." My legs wobbled a bit, but I managed to turn and finally step into the light. While I scanned the nearly empty lot, I focused on my breathing. On calming my thundering heart.

Spotting my dad just outside the bar near the entrance, talking to who appeared to be the manager, I hurried over. The only way out of this was a heaping dose of confidence and quick talking. The moment my dad saw my approach, he waved me over.

"Isla. Thank God you're okay," he said, giving me a once over before doing the same with Kade, who wasn't far behind. "I tried calling when I saw both your cars parked in the lot."

I stopped farther away from him than I normally would as a gust of wind carried his scent toward me. Although I'd smelled his rich blood hundreds of times since becoming a vampire, I wasn't immune to it. I craved witch and warlock blood just as much as human blood. Which was why I'd limited my visits with my best friend the last several months. Kenna's pregnancy had amplified her Syphon side, making her blood that much harder to resist. I wouldn't risk her safety, especially now that she was carrying precious cargo.

"Sorry, I must have missed it. I've been running around like crazy tonight," I explained, then quickly steered the conversation away from my whereabouts. "What happened here?"

"There's been another death. Male. Late thirties. This one a suicide, by the looks of it. Bullet right to the head. Mike here was heading up the stairs when it happened. Two seconds earlier and he could have stopped it."

Bile rushed up my already raw throat. I nearly choked on it, barely able to swallow before saying, "Was he a bartender? Slim build, curly brown hair?"

My heart began to pound again as my dad blinked at me in surprise. I should have kept my mouth shut. Should have backed out of the conversation while I could. But I had to know.

"Yeah. How did you know?"

I cast old Mike a quick look. He was human, but he knew vampires existed. He was tight-lipped about it, all too willing to expand his clientele for his silence. Still, I didn't want him to know about my case.

"I talked to him about an hour ago. He was trying to help me find something." I glanced at Mike again, hoping my dad would get the hint.

Nodding his understanding, my dad said, "And did you find what you were looking for?"

"No. I don't think it's here."

"Too bad."

"Yeah. You sure it was suicide?" I casually segued. "He didn't seem like the type."

"They never do. But all evidence points that direction. Saanvi is pretty sure of it."

Evidence. Saanvi!

I was so *screwed.*

I heard Kade shift on his feet, like he wanted to say something. Like he wanted *me* to say something. Before he could ruin everything, I blurted, "Do you need another set of eyes? Since I'm here, I could give the scene a quick once-over."

Please say yes, please say yes.

"Oh, that's okay. I know you're really busy trying to find that *thing* you were looking for. Plus, it's getting late. I wouldn't want to keep you."

I inwardly screamed every curse word I could think of.

Before I could come up with a solid reason why he should let me view the crime scene, my phone buzzed with an incoming text. I pulled it from my pocket, frowning at the sight of another unknown number.

Don't worry, Miss Andrews, the text read. *Your prints and blood have been wiped clean. No one saw you with the bartender right before his death. No one but me.*

The night was young compared to how late I usually stayed out, but I couldn't wait any longer.

I needed space to think, and I needed blood. *Lots* of it.

The second I'd picked up my blood supply in Bangor, I'd hurried to my car and greedily downed an entire bag.

It hadn't been enough.

Still, I'd forced myself to drive back home without reaching for another. For a vampire, drinking too much blood while driving was similar to a human's alcohol consumption. I *never* drank and drove, no matter how thirsty I was.

When I'd left Mike's Tavern shortly after receiving that creepy text, I'd barely managed to avoid Kade's probing questions. He knew something was up. Knew I was hiding something. To his credit, he hadn't said a word to my dad though. After telling him I was done for the night, that I needed to grab my blood supply, he'd allowed me to leave.

I didn't for one minute think he was going to give up though. At the first available opportunity, he was going to pressure me into telling him. Or at least try. Which was why I'd so desperately needed time away from him and copious amounts of blood. Without those two things, I'd cave.

Because I seriously needed to talk to someone about my phone stalker. A gazillion questions were buzzing around my tired brain and I needed answers *now*. My overprotective dad and brother weren't an option. They'd have me off this case faster than I could down a pint of blood. I could talk to my best friend, of course. Kenna was calm and supportive and a great listener. But I already knew what she'd say: "You need to tell your dad." Or worse: "You should let Kade help you."

I loved her like a sister, but I knew she wanted me to give Kade another chance. She'd never directly said it, but she didn't have to. She and Noah had both witnessed the kiss I'd given Kade five years ago. Since then, I'd received more than one suggestive look whenever Kade was near. Plus, she was pregnant. I didn't want to stress her out. My other friends weren't an option either. This case was becoming more than a little dangerous, and I didn't want them involved.

Which left me with only one person I could talk to . . .

Kade.

Groaning, I pulled into my parking spot and killed the engine. It was nearly three in the morning now. I still had a couple hours before I needed to be inside for the day. Not wanting to waste my precious outside time, I rummaged in my cooler for another blood bag and popped the top. With my tinted car windows, no one should be able to see me. If they did, they'd probably just think I was guzzling a bag o' wine. Most humans were like that. Rationally trying to explain away odd things.

I had the nozzle pressed to my lips when someone knocked on my window. Startled, I nearly dumped the blood all over me. Hissing a curse, I quickly hid the bag from view and glanced up at the intruder. I cursed again.

"What are you doing here?" I said, knowing he could easily hear me through the closed window.

"Fixing something I broke," Kade drawled. I stiffened, until I realized he wasn't talking about *us*, but my apartment door. He had a new one slung over his shoulder like it weighed nothing more than a cardboard box.

I sighed and put the blood bag away. "I told you I could handle that."

"I know, but I'm not letting you sleep alone in an apartment with a busted door."

At the slight insinuation, I threw him an irritated look. "You're not staying in my apartment."

"Let me fix your door and I won't."

Ugh! He was so *relentless*.

"Fine," I grumbled, shooing him away so I could open my door. When I emerged with the cooler, he glanced at it without comment. Worried that this was the calm before the storm of questions, I started walking and talking. "Have you been here long?"

He fell into step beside me. "No. Just got here. It took me a while to find a place open at this hour that sold doors. I got a few odd looks."

Despite myself, a small smile pushed at my lips.

Then, "We need to talk about what happened at the bar, Isla."

My smile died.

When I didn't respond, he pressed, "Why did that bartender pull out a gun?"

Grinding my teeth, I finally answered, "I don't know."

"Why didn't you want your dad to know you got shot?"

I grabbed the entrance handle and yanked it open. "Because old Mike was there. I'll tell him eventually."

"I call bull," Kade said, motioning for me to precede him. Huffing, I marched inside, leaving him to awkwardly rangle his cargo through the doorway. Except that he wasn't awkward at all, smoothly handling the situation with preternatural grace. I bristled when he added, "Your dad needs to know how dangerous this case is."

"He can't know. Not yet. I need to figure something out first."

"And what's that?"

Silence.

"Isla, we're partners, remember? It's not safe for you to hide things from me."

More silence.

"Isla."

"*Kade.* For heaven's sake, if you keep pushing me, I'm going to—"

He suddenly lunged forward. In the blink of an eye, he was in front of me, a low growl rumbling in his chest. The door on his shoulder thumped against the wall, leaving a small dent.

"What the crap, Kade?" I snapped, jerking the cooler back before his legs could knock into it.

"Something doesn't smell right," he said, the growl still edging his voice.

"*Smell* right?" Rolling my eyes, I ducked under his arm still holding the door and beelined for my apartment. "It's probably the curry. I have Indian neighbors."

"Isla, *stop*," he barked, loud enough that I tensed all over, expecting my limbs to immediately obey the command. When they didn't, relief trembled through me. Then anger. Because he *could* have commanded me, and I would have listened like his obedient little slave.

Something heavy crashed to the floor behind me, but I didn't turn. Not when I was determined to prove Kade wrong. There was nothing weird about the smell of my—

It hit me then. *Slapped* me. So hard that I stumbled to a halt just shy of my apartment door, nearly losing my grip on the cooler.

"Isla, don't—"

"Vinegar," I whispered, then shoved open the broken door.

The second I saw my living room, Kade hauled me back against him. I didn't pull away, my usual fiery resistance petering out. Instead, a wave of numbing shock washed over me at the sight of my apartment.

It was destroyed.

CHAPTER 12

ISLA

Nothing was missing. Not a single thing. But every square inch of my apartment had been ransacked.

My suede couch was overturned, the cushions gouged in several places, like a knife had been slashed through them. My tv was on its face, glass from the broken plasma screen scattered around it. My round dining table was in pieces. So were the chairs. Broken kitchen plates and cups were littered across the floor. Even my bedroom had been destroyed, clothing and shoes and jewelry dumped all over the carpet.

My laptop had been snapped in half like cheap plastic. My computer screen was smashed to smithereens.

But nothing had been taken.

Why? Who would destroy someone's life simply for the pleasure of it? What sick prick could do something like this?

You know who, my mind nagged at me. *Follow the clues. This is all connected somehow.*

I hadn't said a word since entering the apartment. Kade hadn't either. I knew he wanted to though. After searching every nook and cranny, making sure the perp wasn't still here, he'd taken up pacing the length of my living room. Back and forth. Back and forth. Every line of his body was taut with fury, his jaw set like granite.

Crouching in the kitchen, I picked up a "world's best sister" mug Noah had gifted me a few years ago. The handle was snapped off, and a huge chunk was missing from the cup.

"Okay, that's it," Kade abruptly said. "You're coming with me. Pack your bags."

I slowly stood, gingerly setting the broken pieces of the mug on the counter before facing him. "I'm not leaving Rosewood," I said with eerie calmness. "I still have an open case to solve."

He stared at me like I'd lost my mind. "Can't you smell the vinegar? The *murderer* was in here, Isla. There's no other explanation. They know you're on the case and are trying to scare you off. Next time, they might destroy more than your apartment."

I winced from hearing the words out loud. I was usually so careful with my cases. My targets never knew I was on their tails. How had this one gone so horribly wrong?

Still, I raised my chin a notch, saying more firmly, "I won't be scared off. This is my job and I'm going to see it through."

Determination flashed in his eyes. "Then I'm calling your dad. He needs to know what we're up against."

Every inch of me stiffened when he pulled out his phone. *Don't you dare*, I silently warned him with narrowed eyes.

One of his eyebrows slowly lifted, as did his phone. *Try to stop me*, he said in return, his thumb hovering just above the screen. It inched closer, and closer, and . . .

"Okay, *fine*," I snapped, slapping my palms on the counter hard enough to make the island shudder. "I'll go with you." Victory brightened the blue of his irises. "But only if we stay in Rosewood."

"Deal."

"And only if you swear not to tell my dad about my apartment break-in."

His brows slammed down over his eyes.

"Swear it, Kade. I'll tell him when I've had a chance to puzzle all

101

of this out first."

A muscle thrummed in his jaw. Then, "I swear. But only so long as you're not in immediate danger."

"Okay, then." I pushed off the counter, already cataloging in my head what I'd need to pack.

"And only if you tell me everything you know so far."

My gaze shot up to his again. At the knowing look in his eyes, my chest tightened.

"I know you haven't told me everything, Isla," he quietly said. "I know you're keeping secrets. That ends now."

"Fine," I said after a tense moment, then quickly averted my gaze and began gathering supplies.

But it was a lie.

I had no intention of telling him everything. Of letting him know just how confused, how *scared* I was. This case was way more than I'd bargained for, and I was terrified of what I had yet to discover. Of what *evidence* I'd find that would link me to these deaths.

By the time I was done packing, salvaging what little I could from the wreckage, it was nearing four o'clock. Still enough time for me to be outside, but the clock was ticking. Kade seemed to sense it too, hurriedly removing my busted door and installing the new one in record time. I barely had time to glance at it before he was ushering me into the hallway, making sure the door was firmly locked behind us.

We didn't say a word on the walk to the parking lot, both lost in our own thoughts. But we smelled it at the same time. The *blood*. My heart nearly gave out, then started up again with a frantic jolt. I recognized that blood. Before Kade could stop me, I sped up, following my nose to the source.

"Isla," he sharply said, hot on my heels.

I ignored him, passing car after car until . . .

Startled, I stopped dead in my tracks, right in front of my Mini Cooper. Because there, spelled out on the windshield in capital letters, was the word MURDERER. And the letters . . . they were painted with blood. Not just any blood. The blood of the bartender.

My insides turned to ice.

Behind me, Kade released a low growl. When he grabbed my shoulder and pulled me back against him, I was tempted to stay there. To melt into his protection and mentally check out. Because I was done. My brain couldn't handle anymore right now. But it didn't matter what I wanted. What I *needed*. I couldn't let anyone see this message.

Shrugging off Kade's hand, I set down my packed belongings and stepped toward my car. He growled again but remained where he was, silently watching as I unzipped my jacket and tugged it off. With trembling fingers, I balled my favorite jacket up and began scrubbing the blood from my windshield.

It was slow-going and painful, my throat spasming from being this close to so much human blood. Kade tried to help me, but I stopped him with a warning look. Whatever he saw in my eyes made him back off. By the time I was finished, my jacket was covered in blood and my body uncontrollably shook.

It was only then that I allowed Kade to approach, to take the jacket from me and gently steer me toward his Mustang. He managed to gather all my belongings in one hand, using the other to keep me from curling into a ball on the sidewalk. When we were in his car, he wordlessly passed me a blood bag from my cooler.

I could have cried, but I didn't, accepting the blood without a sound.

He kept silent while I drank, starting the engine and slowly pulling out of the lot. I finished the entire bag off in less than a minute, still aching with need. My fingers itched to pull another bag from the cooler, but I dug my nails into my palms instead. When my phone buzzed, I quickly fished it from my pocket, hoping it was Kenna. I could really use a distraction right about now.

But the incoming text wasn't from Kenna. Or from anyone else I knew.

It read: *I helped you hide evidence twice now, but I could just as easily reveal it. Are you sure you want to be my enemy?*

My fingers shook so hard that I nearly dropped my phone. Shoving it back into my pocket, I reached for another blood bag.

By the time we arrived at our destination, I was blood drunk and didn't even care. It was so much easier this way. *So* much easier. And I really needed easy right now. The last twenty-four hours had majorly sucked.

"Oh, I like this place," I slurred, jabbing a finger at the gorgeous, three-story lakehouse we'd just pulled up to, the one belonging to Loch and Kenna. Kade too, I guessed. "It's big."

Probably bigger than Kade's dick.

I started cackling like a hyena, slapping my thigh. Oh, it felt good to laugh. I hadn't laughed in what felt like forever.

Kade didn't laugh with me, the sour puss. He was too busy being all serious, throwing me concerned looks every so often. Screw that. I *deserved* to be drunk right now. The stress of the past day had been overwhelming.

Grabbing the door handle, I practically fell out of the car. Kade was there in a flash, pulling me to my feet. "So chivalrous," I purred, not sure if I said the word right. Oh well. I patted his chest, letting my hand linger far too long. It was just so *firm*, and my hand liked being there. I swerved toward the stairs, promptly getting my feet tangled. Before I could go down, Kade caught me again. I doubled over with more laughter.

The world suddenly spun as he scooped me up, carrying me into the house. I let my head fall against his chest, enjoying the feel of his firm pec and the sound of his steady heartbeats. Lights flicked on as he continued to carry me across the large foyer and up a flight of stairs. Shouldering open a bedroom door, he crossed the space and entered a bathroom. The moment we were inside, he set me on my feet.

Grasping my shoulders when I swayed, he said, "Take a shower. I'll bring in your stuff."

"Aren't you worried I'll pass out and drown?" I drunkenly crooned, then giggled at my own joke. Vampires couldn't drown. I could definitely pass out though and probably would soon enough. But right now, I was enjoying being blood-high. It *never* took this much blood to get me drunk. I'd almost downed half my blood supply before the buzz finally kicked in. I was surprised Kade hadn't tried to stop me.

"You'll be fine," Kade replied, letting go of me. At the sight of him leaving, a sliver of fear poked through my drunken bubble.

"But what if the . . . what if the murderer followed us here?"

At the tremor in my voice, he paused in the doorway. "No one followed us here," he softly reassured me. When I continued to stare at him with uncertainty, he added, "I won't let anyone get you, Isla. I swear it."

Just like that, his words whisked my fear away. We'd been in enough scrapes together for me to believe him.

"Don't let the sun get me either," I said, untucking my borrowed shirt. *His* shirt. "I don't want to go poof."

"You won't. I'll start closing the blinds and curtains."

I whipped the shirt off and held it out to him. "This is yours." When I felt him take it, I got to work on my jeans. "Ugh, these are so *tight*," I groaned, shimmying them down my hips. "It's a good thing I'm wearing a thong or I'd have a permanent wedgie."

Realizing Kade had fallen silent, I glanced up to find him watching me. Like *really* watching me. Whoa, baby, was it hot in here? Because my skin was suddenly burning under his intense gaze. When he realized I'd caught him staring, he jerked his eyes up to mine. The look he gave me then was enough to make me snicker.

Kade frickin' Carmichael was *embarrassed*. I didn't think such a thing was possible.

Deciding to put him out of his misery, I crooned, "You can look. All the men do. It's no big deal." Slightly wobbling, I managed to peel the jeans off my legs until I was standing in nothing but my hot pink satin underwear.

His nostrils flared, yet his gaze remained firmly on my face. "It's a big deal to me."

I shrugged. "Your loss." Whirling toward the shower and nearly falling over, I presented my curvaceous backside to him. When I heard his sharp inhale, I grinned. He could leave at any moment, but he didn't, which meant that he *wanted* to look. And that made my body all sorts of hot and horny. Unhooking my bra, I slowly let it fall to the floor.

Even from across the room, I could hear Kade's heart begin to race. Which made *mine* race. I suddenly wanted nothing more than to have him look at me. *All* of me. Every single inch. I reached for my panties, bracing myself against the glass shower door as I slid them off my legs. When they joined my bra on the floor, I turned to face him.

But he was no longer there.

I desperately needed my vibrator. The horniness that always came with being blood drunk had hit me *hard*.

"Where is it, where *is* it?" I moaned, riffling through the stack of belongings Kade had placed on my bed. I could have sworn I packed it. After another few minutes of fruitless searching, I huffed and marched toward the door. Yanking it open, I traipsed into the hallway in nothing but a white bath towel. I paused for a moment to inhale, then followed Kade's scent to the bedroom adjacent mine.

Not bothering to knock, I shoved his door open. "I can't find my vibrator. Have you seen—?"

My brain emptied at the sight of him. He was standing in the middle of the room, towel-drying his damp hair. Completely. Utterly. *Naked*. Every square inch of his godlike body was on display, and my eyes greedily feasted upon it. Water still glistened on his golden skin, further accentuating his muscular physique. My gaze followed a droplet as it slipped down each of his abs. Down, down, down it went, trailing past his navel to slide over the final expanse of taut flesh above his waist.

I should have looked away then, but I didn't. I was too curious. Too hypnotized. Too *horny*. When my eyes finally landed on his manhood, I actually swooned. *Swooned*. I grabbed onto the doorframe for physical, emotional, and spiritual support as I continued to stare. Under my bold perusal, his semi-erect shaft noticeably twitched. My core heated in response, immediately growing wet. As my heavy arousal saturated the air, I watched in abject fascination as his shaft engorged with blood, swelling bigger and bigger and bigger.

"Good goddess," I breathed, clinging to the door for dear life. I'd never seen a penis that big before. I didn't even know they could *get* that big. Someone needed to redo the *David* statue with Kade as the model.

"Isla. You can't be in here right now," he said, in a tone I'd never heard before. Strained. Guttural. When he wrapped the towel around his waist, cutting off my view, I stuck out my bottom lip.

"Why not?" I said, not hiding my disappointment.

"Because you're clearly still drunk, and you don't have any clothes on."

I snorted. "I'm *barely* drunk, and I have a towel on, see?" I waved at the towel wrapped around me and it chose that moment to unravel. Before I could catch it, the material plopped to the floor. Whelp, guess I didn't have any clothes on after all. Not even underwear. I blinked up at him innocently, a smirk tugging at my lips. "Oops."

His nostrils flared, and this time, he looked. Oh *boy* did he look. Not a single inch of my skin was safe from his hungry gaze as it burned hotly over my flesh. I leaned against the doorframe, basking in the warmth. Loving the feel of his eyes on me. They lingered the longest on my breasts, brightening to blue fire when my nipples hardened.

"Like what you see?" I purred, my voice lowering seductively.

Kade released a harsh, shuddering breath before forcing his eyes to mine. "You know I do. I think you're beautiful. Every last curvaceous inch of you."

The warmth lapping at my skin grew fiery hot. "Then look at me. I want you to."

His chest rose and fell. "You're drunk, Isla. You should leave. Go sleep it off."

I cocked my head to the side, not the least bit deterred. Not when I could *smell* him. I pushed off the doorframe and swayed toward him, twirling a damp strand of pink and blonde hair around my finger. He clenched his fists as I approached. His entire body trembled with the effort of holding still. When I reached him, I brazenly placed my hand on his chest, whispering, "I can't sleep it off. Not when I'm this horny. I need relief first."

At my barely-hidden suggestion, Kade bit out a curse and squeezed his eyes shut. Reacting to the fresh wave of his arousal, I slid my hand down his chest. Lower, lower, lower. His breathing came in short spurts as I trailed my finger all the way down to the towel wrapped around his waist. But when I grasped the material, prepared to rip it off, he finally moved.

Faster than I could blink, he had me against the nearest wall, both hands pinned above my head. The position only inflamed my need, sending sharp desire coiling into the air. Desperate for relief, I arched my body into his, only for him to jerk back out of reach. I stuck my bottom lip out again. "You're no fun."

Breathing heavily, he replied, "Oh, I'm more fun than you'd know how to handle, shortcake. But I've already told you that casual sex is off the table for me. Come to me when you're serious and we'll have all the fun you could possibly desire."

"But you *want* me," I said, trying to reach him again. "If we have sex, I'll probably forget about it in the morning anyway. See? Win-win for both of us."

He stiffened at that. Hurt crossed his expression, then his gaze hardened. "Please leave, Isla. Get some rest. I'm going to take another shower."

In the next instant, he pushed off the wall and closed himself in the bathroom. I listened as he turned on the shower and stepped inside. I stayed where I was, continuing to listen. My body still ached with unmet need, and I couldn't seem to pry myself away. Just knowing Kade was a few feet away, naked and wet, kept me glued to the spot.

Running water was the only sound for several minutes until a quiet groan reached my ears. Holding my breath, I inched closer to the bathroom like a perv. But I couldn't seem to help myself. I wanted to be closer to him. Wanted to be in the shower *with* him.

I almost did it then. Almost entered the bathroom. He wouldn't be able to resist me all hot and wet and pressed against him in the shower. I knew he wanted my body as much as I wanted his. Having sex with him one time wouldn't destroy me. I just had to convince him that we could—

At the sudden sound of low panting, I froze. The panting grew louder and louder with each passing second until he released a breathless groan. And at the end of the groan, his lips expelled my name. I slapped a hand over my mouth when I realized what he'd just done.

Jerked off in the shower. With *me* in the forefront of his mind.

My stomach tightened. Not with disgust, but with excitement. He was no doubt picturing me naked right now, and that made me hornier than ever. My mind made up, I wrapped my fingers around the doorknob. But before I could turn the handle, another sound reached my ears.

A shuddering exhale. One that sounded a lot like a sob.

"Isla," Kade groaned again, with such longing, such *pain*, that my throat clamped shut. He started panting again, but for a different reason this time. He was crying.

Kade Carmichael was *crying* . . .

Because of me.

CHAPTER 13

ISLA

I ran from his room as fast as my unsteady legs could carry me.

Grabbing my towel on the way out, I wrapped it around me tightly and hid my nakedness. Not good enough. I still felt exposed. Still felt *dirty*.

Hearing Kade's misery in the shower had slapped me awake, enough to make me painfully aware of my recent actions. I'd never felt such guilt, such *shame* than I did right now.

I'd hurt him. I'd hurt him *badly*.

Slamming my bedroom door shut, I barely made it to the bathroom before my stomach violently heaved. I crouched over the toilet, throwing up everything I'd just consumed. Blood gushed from me. The toilet grew red with it.

The sight drove me to my knees. Fear and panic washed over me. I choked and gagged, trying to rid myself of the blood. I flushed the toilet, but I still saw red. I saw it *everywhere*. I couldn't escape it. I could *never* escape it.

"I hate you, I hate you, I hate you."

I didn't know if I threw the words at the blood or at myself. Probably both.

Curling into a ball on the floor, I clutched my empty stomach and sobbed.

I didn't remember falling asleep, but when I awoke, I was in bed.

Not in my apartment, but somewhere else.

Before I could panic, a phone buzzed near my head. I peered at the white nightstand and found my phone plugged in on top. Fumbling for the device, I picked it up and squinted at the screen. Wow. It wasn't even noon yet. When had I fallen asleep? The phone buzzed again with an incoming call. When I saw who it was, I quickly answered.

"Hey, girl," I groggily greeted, pushing wild strands of pink and blonde hair off my face.

"Isla, are you okay?" came my best friend's concerned voice.

"Of course," I replied, pushing into a sitting position. When I did, the white towel wrapped around me slipped, pooling at my waist. "Err, except that I'm naked and sleeping in a strange bed."

I scrubbed a hand over my face, trying to fully wake up. Trying to remember where I was and why I was frickin' *naked*.

"Kade said you had a rough day yesterday," Kenna said. My spine immediately snapped straight at the mention of Kade's name. Oh, right. I'd been with Kade all evening. Then why was I *naked*? "He didn't give me any details though. Want to talk about it?"

Memories of last night slowly revealed themselves, pushing back my brain fog. The murder, the biker gang attack, the shooting, the suicide, the break-in, the bloody message, the creepy texts and phone calls. In between all those moments was Kade. Standing by my side, helping me, *saving* me.

And then I'd gotten drunk. *Again.*

And Kade had patiently carried my sorry drunken butt into the lakehouse. And then I'd . . . then I'd . . .

The blood slowly drained from my face.

"Oh no. Kenna, I did something really really stupid. I'll explain what happened later, but I really need to find Kade right now."

"Okay, but at least let me know if you're safe."

"I am. Perfectly safe," I said, meaning it. Because Kade had kept me safe all night. Even from *myself*, when I'd drunkenly thrown myself at him. When I'd tried to *seduce* him. *I* was the only unsafe person here. What I'd done . . . what I'd done to him was . . .

Wrapping up my phone call with Kenna, I scrambled out of bed in search of clothes. I found them neatly tucked away in a dresser, along with my makeup, hair, and toiletry supplies carefully placed on the dresser's surface. I paused, blankly staring at my stuff. Had Kade put these away for me? I couldn't remember doing it. I couldn't remember how I'd gotten into bed either. Everything before that was fuzzy, but I remembered what happened.

I remembered what I'd done to him.

Pursing my lips, I pulled the baggiest outfit I could find from the drawer and slipped it on. Not bothering to apply makeup or brush my hair, I left the room without even looking at myself. I couldn't. Not after what I had done.

Kade wasn't in his room when I checked. The door was open, the bed unmade. It didn't even look like he'd slept there. The curtains were carefully drawn though, safely protecting me from the sun. So were the ones in my room. As I went in search of him, every window I passed either had blinds or curtains on them, all closed. I could still tell the sun shone brightly outside though, even if I couldn't see or feel it. It was light enough inside that my night vision hadn't kicked in.

As I made my way downstairs, I finally heard it. The soft strains of music. Of a guitar, actually. I paused to listen, captivated by the sound. The longer I listened, the clearer it became that the sound wasn't coming from a device.

Quietly padding down the remaining stairs, I crossed the foyer on silent feet. Still, Kade heard my approach. As I entered the living room, he'd already stopped playing, his hand splayed across the guitar strings. I halted just inside the room, an unfamiliar awkwardness stealing over me when he straightened on the couch and raised his eyes to mine.

"Did I wake you?" he said, before the silence could become uncomfortable. It was like he knew how unsure I suddenly felt. How strange I felt in my own skin.

"No," I quickly reassured him, tugging the sleeves of my gray hoodie over my hands. Before I could hightail it out of the room like I desperately wanted to do, I forced my legs to carry me farther into the room. Just like in the foyer, I noticed the tall windows overlooking the picturesque lake were now darkly tinted. "I didn't know they could do that," I lamely said, gesturing to them.

He briefly glanced at them. "They're new. Smart windows that tint with a switch of a button. Guaranteed full protection from UV rays."

"Cool." I inched closer, edging around the leather couch across from him. "Whose idea was it to install them?"

He studied me for a moment, then looked down at his guitar. "Mine."

A lump formed in my throat. There was no denying his reason for putting tintable windows in this house. I was the only Feltore allergic to the sun who sometimes came here. I was the only one who would have a need for it during the daytime.

Kenna's parents were Feltore, but now that she'd graduated college and was pregnant, they rarely left Sanctum Isle. In fact, both the D'angelo and Belmont families resided at the island's castle more often than not, including Kade. This was the first time I'd seen him in

Rosewood for almost half a year.

No, I couldn't deny why he'd had these windows installed.

He'd done it for me.

Suddenly feeling lightheaded, I perched on the couch across from him. He flicked a glance at me again, but when it became painfully obvious that I was tongue-tied, he started strumming his guitar. Not knowing what else to do, I tucked my hands between my legs and listened. His large fingers confidently plucked the strings, with a fluid grace that made my breath catch.

"You're good," I blurted after a moment, then winced, wishing I'd kept my mouth shut. He didn't need my stupid *praise* right now. Flustered, I spoke again without thinking. "When did you learn how to play?"

A small smile tugged at his lips. It was equal parts serene and melancholy. Sad, even, as if the memory was bittersweet. Without looking at me, he replied, "About a hundred and forty-five years ago, give or take a few years. My dad taught me."

I stopped my mouth from falling open, always forgetting how old he really was. It was easy to believe that he was barely older than twenty since that's how he still looked. It was easy to forget that he grew up in a different era, that he'd once been human, just like me.

"Were you close with your dad?" I hedged, nervously squeezing my thighs together. I shouldn't pry, especially not right now, but I couldn't seem to help it. He'd never told me about his past before becoming a vampire, and I'd never asked.

Still softly playing, Kade replied without missing a beat, "When I was younger, yes. But when I refused to join the family business, we had a huge argument and I left. I did my own thing for a few years, not speaking to my family the entire time. I racked up some major debt and got into trouble with the law."

He gave a self-deprecating snort. "I was a different person back then. Always drinking and partying, shirking all responsibility. By the time I saw the error of my ways, it was too late. The family estate caught on fire one night, killing my dad, mom, and baby brother while they lay asleep in their beds."

Horrified, I placed both hands over my mouth. "Oh, Kade, I'm so sorry." An errant tear slipped down my cheek.

"Me too," he said, his voice heavy with regret. "I spiraled after that. Lost all will to live. Or so I thought. When a vampire attacked me one night, I fought back. Little did I know that it was a test. Apparently, I passed, because I was whisked away to Sanctum Isle and offered a deal I couldn't pass up."

I dropped my hands. "A deal to become Loch's drothen?"

"Yes. Everett had been tasked with finding a suitable candidate to protect his brother, and I was just what they were looking for. With the only people I truly cared about dead, I jumped at the chance. I didn't even care that I had to die first. I felt like I deserved it anyway."

"Kade," I said, my heart turning over for him.

"It's okay," he said with another small smile. "It all worked out in the end. My drothen responsibilities gave me a reason to live, and I gained a new family—even if Loch hated me at first. The rejection was good for me though. It let me properly feel the pain I'd inflicted on my own family when I left. It changed my view on life."

Tears clogged my throat. Tears of guilt and shame. So much shame. Because he was feeling the sting of rejection once more. After our kiss five years ago, I'd left without talking it through. Without giving him a second chance. And now, he was in pain again, and I was the cause. "How?" I said after a moment, my voice barely more than a whisper. "How did your view change?"

He looked up at me then, and my breath caught at the depth of emotion in his eyes. It was too much. Too heavy and all-consuming. I could almost feel what he was feeling. The sadness, the hope, the regret, the determination. I could hardly bear the weight of it all. At the same time, I couldn't look away. Wouldn't. I deserved to carry some of his burden. *Needed* to. I'd put him through so much. This was the least I could do.

"I learned that life is fleeting," he finally said, still quietly strumming his guitar. "That holding a grudge against someone you care about isn't worth it. At the same time, that patience is *always* worth it. Life is fragile, and filling it with laughter and love will make it stronger. I no longer only wish for happiness, but to make *others* happy. To make a difference, even as a vampire. To make my life count, no matter how long or short that may be."

The words tipped me over the edge. No, *shoved* me. I could no longer keep my tears at bay. I choked on a sob, gasping, "Oh, Kade, I'm sorry. I'm so sorry for what I did." He stopped playing. "I wish I could take it all back. *Everything*. I hate myself for how I treated you."

I heaved another sob, then another, burying my face in my hands. I didn't see his approach. Didn't feel him until his hands were cupping mine, gently peeling them off my face. I knew I looked terrible. I was an ugly crier, even as a vampire. My eyes were no doubt swollen and my nose bright red. But I didn't cover my face again, letting him see how wretched I felt.

Through my tears, I saw him crouch before me, his gaze filled with sorrow yet also sympathy. When he reached up to wipe my tears away, I let him, continuing to hiccup and sob. When my crying had somewhat lessened, he tucked some pink-tipped hair behind my ear and said, "That's another thing I learned, shortcake. Hating yourself never fixes anything. All we can do is move forward and do better next time."

I hiccuped again, then nodded. "I will. I promise I will. I want to make up for what I've done."

He regarded me for a moment, then rocked back on his heels and stuck out his hand. "Then how about we start over? Hi, I'm Kade Carmichael. I love everything sweet, making people laugh, and taking long walks on the beach."

A devilish grin curled his mouth when I sputtered out a surprised laugh. "Fine," I said with a sniffle, placing my hand in his. "I'm Isla Andrews. I love pineapple on my pizza, hanging out with friends, and anything pink and sparkly."

His grin widened, stretching across his face. Firmly shaking my hand, he said, "Nice to meet you, Isla. Maybe we can hang out sometime. You know, as friends."

I returned his smile, even as my heart twisted a little at the word friends. Still, I shook his hand just as firmly and replied, "I'd really like that."

CHAPTER 14

KADE

I turned my phone on. Then immediately turned it off.

With her heightened senses, Isla could still overhear any conversation I had if she tried to. I walked farther down the crude path leading toward the neighboring lakehouse a couple miles away. Not too far though. Whoever had broken into her apartment was still at large. It had to be the murderer, and the psycho was playing a sick mindgame with her.

She was shaken. Scared, even. And that put me on edge. I hadn't slept a wink all morning, worried that she was right. That the murderer knew she was here. I'd wanted to pry her with questions about last night's events. Like why I'd found her grappling with the bartender for a silver gun. Like what had happened to the footage she'd been seeking. Like why someone would leave that message on her car.

But I hadn't. I'd left shortly after our conversation in the living room, needing to clear my head. Needing to fully process what had transpired between us.

Friends. She'd agreed to be my friend.

The word felt so small. So insignificant. But we were starting fresh, and that was a huge step in the right direction. I could be her friend. If it meant I could remain close to her, I'd be anything she wanted me to be. I could contain the burgeoning fire that threatened to consume me whole every time she was near.

I'd done it last night, after all. Cock-blocked myself when she'd thrown herself at me, something I hadn't been prepared for in the least. I almost hadn't been able to, though. Seeing her naked before me, her many luscious curves on full display, I'd almost caved. Almost taken her with all the fiery passion bottled up inside me.

But my willpower was strong. It was a skill I'd honed for over a century out of necessity. Out of duty. Being a drothen to a powerful Venturi prince required many sacrifices. My needs always came second. My wants and desires were never to jeopardize my drothen's safety. Without my undying loyalty to the royal vampire family, I had no purpose. I'd sworn an eternal oath to serve another, to lend my strength when needed and obey without question.

Fleshly desire, including bloodlust, was never to supersede my duties. Even though my sexual drive was strong, I'd learned how to contain it, to deny myself when needed. Loch didn't care who I bedded or how often, but the king certainly did. I'd been specially chosen to boost his son's morale. To share my fiery passion for life with him through our drothen bond. Focusing solely on myself was akin to treason.

Which was why I'd been able to rebuff Isla's advances. One hundred years of conditioning had kicked in. Plus, she'd been blood drunk. It was no secret that too much blood equaled a powerful need for sex, which was why I had an ironclad grip on my own blood cravings. I hadn't struggled in decades . . .

Until last night.

Last night had almost broken me. The pain of resisting her had been unbearable, and I'd eased the ache the only way I could. After I'd finished, I'd gone in search of her, needing to make sure she was okay. I'd found her passed out on the bathroom floor, curled up in a tight ball.

She'd been crying.

The sight had torn my heart to shreds. I knew she regretted her advances on me. Knew that having sex with me wasn't really what she wanted. Her body might want it out of desperation for release, but her heart didn't. Despite my wounded pride, I'd carefully picked her up and tucked her in bed. Then made a vow to never bring up what happened between us, to pretend that my chest hadn't been ripped wide open knowing she didn't really want *me*.

I could do that for her. Sacrifice what I wanted. What I *needed*. I could be her friend, because that's what *she* needed right now. A friend who would stand by her side while she solved this case. Someone who would allow her to shine while she struggled with the darker side of her vampire nature. And struggling she was. This was the second night in a row she'd become blood drunk. The second night of making unwise decisions.

She might not want me, but she needed me, even if she refused to admit it. And I'd continue to support her, no matter the outcome. No matter how much it hurt me. All the pain in the world wouldn't stop me from remaining by her side, for as long as she'd let me.

But the decision wasn't solely my own. I still had a duty to my drothen, even though he'd healed from his past scars, no longer needing me as he once did. His soulmate now cared for him, in a way I never could. Their bond was stronger than ours was. Fuller. Richer. More complete. I could feel how happy they were together, how utterly content. They never made me feel like a third wheel, but I still tried to give them their space yet remain available at the same time.

I turned my phone on again, blankly staring at the screen until it darkened.

I'd already called Kenna and profusely apologized for not delivering the ice cream yesterday. She'd been more than understanding when I'd explained what happened though. She hadn't pried for details, but I knew she wanted to. Having access to my emotions through her bond with Loch, she knew how I felt about her best friend. Knew that I hadn't given up hope, even after all these years. I could tell she wanted there to be more between us, almost as much as I did.

I knew I had her blessing in helping Isla with this murder case, no matter how long it took, but my drothen might not be so understanding. I'd sworn to protect Kenna with my life, and now that she was pregnant, Loch expected me to uphold my oath all the more. To him, his wife's safety was my first priority, not Isla's. Even though witches and rogues hadn't targeted Kenna in years, his overprotectiveness never dimmed.

Because of that, he might not tolerate my absence much longer.

Heaving a sigh, I turned my phone on once more and dialed Loch's number. He picked up on the second ring, answering in his usual perfunctory way. "Everything okay?"

"Not exactly," I hedged, rubbing at the back of my neck. "Someone's after Isla."

"Explain," Loch immediately replied, his tone brooking no argument.

I sighed again, feeling guilty for betraying Isla's trust. But I consoled myself with the fact that I hadn't told her dad or Kenna. Loch was different though. He was more than my drothen. More than my best friend. He was the brother I never got to meet. My *family*. As much as I was there for him, he was there for me. Telling him the goings on of my life was second nature. Anything less was an insult to our bond.

So I told him everything I knew, starting with the call for help I'd received from Isla. He listened without interruption, letting me get my thoughts out. When I was finished, he simply said, "Do you need backup?"

"Not at the moment. Thanks, though. But . . ."

When I hesitated, uncertain how he'd respond to my request, Loch said, "Spit it out, Kade."

I cracked a smile. "So articulate, as always."

"You're welcome. Now say what you need to say."

Inhaling a bolstering breath, I plowed ahead. "I'd like your permission to stay out here for as long as Isla needs my help."

"You have it."

"Wait, really? Just like that?"

"Just like that."

"I . . . wow. I just thought—"

"That I would put my needs above yours? It's time you pursued your own happiness, Kade. You have my blessing. Just be back in time for the twins' birth. Both of you. McKenna's orders, not mine."

I barked a laugh, quickly blinking the moisture from my eyes. "We will, I promise. And, Loch?"

"Hmm?"

"Thank you. I appreciate this more than you know."

"Oh, I know. Just don't screw it up. Also McKenna's orders."

My roar of laughter shook the trees.

CHAPTER 15

ISLA

I felt his eyes on the side of my face like a hot brand.

His stare was insistent. Expectant.

I'd kept him in the dark for as long as I could, but he wasn't going to allow it a second more.

"You need help, Isla," Kade quietly said, killing the ignition. I kept my gaze straight ahead, blindly focusing on the rundown motel through the Mustang's front windshield. "But I can't help if you continue to keep things from me."

Mule-headed stubbornness reared up, making my lips purse. I didn't need his help. I *didn't*. But when he continued to stare at me, firm yet patient, I leaned back against the headrest with a sigh. "I'm missing several hours' worth of memories."

He shifted in the driver's seat to better face me. "What do you mean?"

"I'm not sure, but I've been thinking about it all afternoon and things don't add up. The night of the murder, I saw the victim. He made a pass at me and I rejected him. It happens often enough, no big deal. But the next evening, his biker friends said I left with him. I didn't believe them, of course. He's not even my type. But . . ." I swallowed with difficulty, then forced myself to say, "But I don't remember leaving the bar. Everything from that point to the moment you broke into my apartment is just . . . blank."

When Kade remained silent, I conjured up the nerve to look at him. The muscles in his jaw were jumping like crazy as he ground his teeth together. After a tense-filled moment, he slowly exhaled and raked his fingers through his caramel locks. "You were drunk. Maybe—"

"But that's just it. I don't think I drank enough to get plastered that night. Even then, I always remember most of what happened afterward. Blood isn't like alcohol. I get high, reckless, and super horny, but I always retain my memories to some capacity. I don't even get hangovers, but I was extremely woozy when I woke up after that night. Something's off, Kade. It's like I was roofied."

"Vampires can't get roofied. Human drugs don't work on us."

"Well *something* happened," I insisted, my voice rising as panic kicked in.

Kade's expression suddenly softened. "Isla, you didn't kill that guy."

But what if I did? I almost asked, but didn't. I was too scared to. Too terrified to think that I'd somehow lost all control and drained a human, then blocked out the memories.

What if *I* was the murderer?

"What about that guy you were with?" Kade continued, his expression turning pensive. "The one you drank with that night. Did he see you leave the bar?"

"Samuel? No, I don't think so. We were in the bath—" Oooh, crap. I hadn't meant to share that.

I quickly looked away to hide my wince, but not before I caught the dangerous flash in Kade's eyes. Crap, crap, crap.

"You were in the *bathroom* with him?" Kade seethed, the words half growl.

"Only for a few minutes." *I think.* I winced again.

"Doing what?"

"None of your business."

"Doing *what*, Isla?"

At the barked question, just short of a sire command, I shot him a warning glare. "Don't use that tone with me, Kade Carmichael. You have no right."

We stared each other down, the silence between us deafening. When it became clear I wasn't going to share the sordid details with him, he exhaled through his nose and softly growled, "You vex me more than anyone I've ever known, Isla Andrews."

"The feeling's mutual," I replied with a huff, fighting back a full-body shiver as his growled words sank beneath my skin.

So much for starting over. We were still at each other's throats like cats and dogs.

Before either of us could say anything else we'd later regret, I opened my door and jumped out. The cool night air nipped at my face and I greedily gulped it in. When had the car become so *hot*?

As I shut the door and veered toward the motel lobby, Kade quietly fell into step beside me. I didn't bother telling him to stay in the car. Not this time. He was in a serious mood and I had no intention of making it worse.

"You're worried the motel's security footage will show you with the victim," he finally spoke as I reached for the lobby door. It wasn't a question.

I paused for a second, then grasped the handle and pulled. "Yes."

No point in denying it. He practically knew everything now anyway. Well, except for the threats from my phone stalker.

Thankfully, he let me take the lead again as I approached the receptionist. It was a young woman, and this time, I didn't think a boob show would gain her favor. In fact, she looked right past me and fixed her sights on Kade. Her bored expression immediately disappeared and she shot up from her seat, tugging on her top. The action pulled down the material, revealing a hint of cleavage.

"Good evening," she said in a simpering voice, flashing a megawatt smile at him. "Are you here to check in?" I stifled an eyeroll when she ignored me completely.

"Yes, my girlfriend and I would like to book a room," Kade smoothly replied, wrapping an arm around me. I went poker straight, but he didn't drop his arm, squeezing me lightly before adding, "Actually, do you have a restroom? Millie here is about to burst."

What the crap?

Still not looking at me, the receptionist smiled again and gestured to the right. "Just around the corner."

"Thanks. I'll check us in, sweetie," Kade said, bending down to quickly peck my cheek. "Take your time."

Shocked, I didn't react when he gently nudged me toward the bathroom. But when I hesitated, still flabbergasted, he slapped my butt. *Hard.* At the sharp sting, I gasped and whirled around, only to find him smirking at me. Before I could yell at him, he blatantly winked and purred, "That's just a prelude, pumpkin. I know how rough you like it."

My mouth fell open. Good goddess, what had gotten into him? Before I could nip whatever this was in the bud and regain control, he ambled toward the check-in counter and leaned against it. *Exactly* how I had last night. I watched, stupefied, as he made a show of sniffing the air.

"Mmm, your perfume smells divine. Honeysuckle?" he asked the receptionist, shamelessly flirting with her right in front of his *girlfriend.*

Gah. Correction. *Fake* girlfriend.

She tittered a bit, basking in his attention. "Why, yes. How did you guess?"

"I never have to guess when it comes to sweet things," he crooned, making me want to gag. Then peel off the woman's honeysuckle-scented skin. Then toss her through the window for good measure.

When I continued to hover in the background like an abandoned puppy, Kade subtly motioned for me to leave, all while chatting it up with the overzealous receptionist. I bared my teeth at his back, then balled my hands into fists and stormed toward the bathroom.

The *nerve* of him. Stealing my thunder, all so he could get back at me. Pssh, not that I cared if he flirted with desperate women. I only cared that he was trying to do *my* job. Using *my* tactics. Yes, that's what was bothering me. Not the blatant flirting. Kade wasn't mine. He could flirt with whoever he wanted.

Still, I caught myself straining to overhear them, managing to catch random snippets of conversation. Good grief, he was laying it on *thick*. The woman was probably salivating, and not just from her mouth. I waited in the bathroom for what felt like hours, digging my nails into my palms until the skin broke. The wounds immediately healed, but I washed my hands anyway, making sure no traces of blood remained.

When his boisterous laughter suddenly reached my ears, my patience snapped. Stalking to the bathroom door, I shoved it open, letting it thwack loudly against the wall. As I rounded the corner, Kade and the woman stopped talking, clearly surprised by my whirlwind return. I fixed the brunette with a death glare and her face blanched of all color.

"Come on, *honey*, we're leaving," I said in clipped tones, marching up to Kade and grabbing his arm. "The service here *sucks*."

He didn't resist as I dragged him from the lobby and through the door, slamming it so hard that the window cracked. At least it wasn't the woman's *head*. Throwing her through a window still sounded therapeutic.

"What was *that*?" I gritted out, dropping Kade's arm as we hit the parking lot.

When he had the gall to snicker, I fixed my death glare on *him*. He raised his hands placatingly and drawled, "Easy there, shortcake. I was only playing to my strengths. Besides, she wasn't interested in you. A little harmless flirting was all it took for her to give me what I wanted."

I snorted incredulously. "*Harmless?* Are you sure you didn't *promise* her something while you were at it? Maybe a little finger action later on while poor oblivious *Millie* slept? Or maybe you went big and offered to eat her out."

He choked on laughter, which only incensed me further. With a growl, I stormed toward the car. Before I could wrench the door open, he slapped his palm on the window. I whirled with a hiss, placing both hands on his chest to shove him back. But even with my vampire strength, I couldn't make him budge. He slapped his other palm on the window, trapping me between his arms.

Unwilling to be dominated, I whipped out my claws and aimed them for his groin. He jerked when the sharp tips made contact with his jeans, but otherwise didn't move. He had balls of steel, I'd give him that.

"Move or I'll castrate you," I quietly snarled, digging my claws into the material for good measure. In response, his cock hardened, filling the space between my claws.

When my breath hitched, a devilish grin stole across Kade's face. "Were you jealous, Millie?" he breathed, close enough to stir the hair by my ear. My claws spasmed around his erection, and he didn't even jerk this time.

"Stop calling me that. And, no, of course I wasn't jealous."

"Because, if you were, that would make you kind of *serious* about me."

I gulped. "I'm not . . . I'm not jealous."

"I think you were," he pressed, lightly brushing his lips over the shell of my ear.

My eyes fluttered shut, and I briefly lost the ability to speak.

"Brunettes aren't my type though," he continued, his lips still feathering across my sensitive skin.

"Then what is?" I managed to rasp, curiosity overriding my common sense.

"Short, curvy blondes who smell like sweet, sweet vanilla."

Oh, gods.

Warning, warning. Exiting the friend zone and entering off-limits territory.

"Well, whatever your type is, you can flirt with whoever you want," I breathlessly insisted, feeling my claws retract without my permission. "It's not like I have a claim on you."

"Feels like it to me," he whispered, firmly pressing his rock-hard length against my palm.

Good goddess, that felt *amazing*. Even more amazing if it was pressed between my thighs. At the thought, arousal soaked my panties within seconds. Sharp desire pierced the air, a heady mixture of mine and his. I leaned fully against the car as my legs threatened to give out. When I did, he eased forward, aligning his pelvis with mine.

It was like he knew. Knew exactly what I was thinking. The second I dropped my hand, he slowly erased the space between us. Giving me ample time to move. To stop him. But I didn't. Heaven help me, I couldn't. Weakness stole through my body, leaving me pliant and trembling with anticipation. My heart began to race. So did his. They thundered so hard that it was all I could hear.

I met his blue eyes, so bright, even in the shadows. The hunger in them stole my breath away, making me tremble even harder. He most definitely did *not* want to be my friend. Unless he was interested in friends with benefits. It was a step up from casual sex, but not exactly serious. I suddenly didn't care though. The lines were blurring between us again and I couldn't pull away. Apparently, neither could he.

I thought I'd shake right out of my skin, unable to bear the tension a moment longer. Just as it became painful, he pressed against me. Fully. Completely. Aligning his hardness with my core.

The sensation splintered my vision. I lost the ability to see. To breathe. To think.

All I could do was feel his thick shaft between my legs and how it affected my entire body. Any twitch, any movement, sent pleasure racing through my veins. When he grabbed my butt with both hands and ground himself against me, sharp bliss exploded through every inch of me. A breathless moan rolled up my throat and I curled my fingers into his shirt, spreading my thighs to better accommodate him.

At the submissive move, a growl rumbled deep in his chest. The sound sent exquisite pain straight to my core and I couldn't hold back a whimper. "You feel like heaven," he groaned, slowly rocking against me. "Sweet, sweet paradise."

I opened my mouth to speak, but no words came out. The ability was lost to me. All I could focus on was how amazing I felt. How amazing *he* felt. Why had I resisted this for so long? It felt so *good*. Better than any sex or blood-high I'd ever experienced. Definitely better than my vibrator. I never wanted it to stop.

"Faster," I managed to whisper, looking up at him through

lowered lashes.

Whatever he saw in my eyes made his brighten even more. His breathing grew ragged. Frantic. A violent tremor shook his body. "Are you sure?" he said, the words almost too guttural to understand.

Before I could respond, the phone trapped beneath his hand buzzed. I almost ignored it, desperately wanting the release Kade was offering me, but it buzzed again. And again.

Huffing, I reached for my back pocket to turn it off, but when it buzzed again, I made the mistake of checking the screen.

Ditch the guy you're with.

If you don't . . .

I'll release the motel footage to your father.

Your choice.

Chills snaked up my spine, making my hair stand on end. I jerked my head left, then right, trying to spot anything out of the ordinary. Trying to spot *them*. My stalker. They were here. Watching me. Watching *us*.

"Isla, what's wrong?" Kade said when I wrenched myself away from him. The heady buzz from seconds ago was now completely gone, my thoughts whirring a mile a minute.

"Did you see the footage?" I asked him, peering into cars as I strode across the parking lot.

"Actually, no. The camera must have been faulty because nothing was recorded. What's this about? Isla. Isla, slow down."

"Shoot," I hissed, searching at an even more frantic pace. "Shoot, shoot, *shoot*."

"Isla, talk to me." Kade's hand came down on my shoulder and I jerked to a stop, suddenly realizing how crazy I must seem to him right now.

Casting one last look at the dense treeline beyond the parking lot, I inhaled a calming breath and turned to Kade. "Sorry about that. I suddenly remembered what we came here for and freaked out a little. Camera footage is really turning out to be a dead end, sheesh."

I quickly stuffed my phone in my back pocket to hide my trembling hands from him, but I couldn't hide my erratic heartbeats. Kade looked at me a little too closely, no doubt seeing right through my words.

"We should go," I hurriedly said, desperately trying to distract him. "I need to talk to those bikers again."

But it didn't work. He ignored my words and continued to stare at me. Continued to riffle through the emotions no doubt plastered to my face. Unable to bear his gaze a moment longer, I glanced away, only for him to grasp my chin. Startled, I jerked my eyes back up to his.

"Kade, what—?"

"I pushed you too far again, didn't I," he said. Not a question.

My eyes started to burn with the need to look away, but his fingers still held my chin and it felt cruel to pull away. Especially when I forced myself to say, "We're just friends, right? Friends with benefits wouldn't be much better than a casual hookup." Even though it felt amazing. And *perfect*.

When undeniable pain darkened his gaze, my heart twisted miserably. "Right. Just friends," he agreed, dropping his hand. "Sorry about the dead lead."

I inhaled an uneven breath. "Yeah. Me too."

When he shoved his hands into his pockets and turned toward the car, my stomach cramped with guilt. With *shame*. I'd hurt him *again*. I couldn't keep doing this. Couldn't keep caving to desire. Couldn't keep stringing him along. It wasn't fair. It wasn't *right*. But I couldn't control myself around him. Couldn't *think* properly.

Which was why I'd kept my distance all these years.

I craved him like I did blood, no matter how much I tried not to. No matter how screwed up that was. The moment I'd woken up in his arms five years ago, freshly turned into a vampire, my body had been drawn to him. I'd found him attractive before then, and even harbored a secret crush, but I hadn't yearned for him.

Not like I did now.

Which was seriously twisted, since it was probably just my body's response to the sire bond. His blood had given me life again, and in a messed up way, I felt like I belonged to him. Felt like I *owed* him. The first time he'd used the sire bond to command me, my body had actually *wanted* to obey. It had felt good to serve him, to listen to my master's orders. He owned my body and my body was all too willing to be owned by him.

But that was the problem. I needed the freedom to be *me*. Ever since my mom had died, I'd been given a heaping dose of independence. I'd learned who I was at a younger age than most. Learned what I wanted. My plan had always been to graduate from Rosewood High and move somewhere more exciting. Maybe Boston or New York City. Anywhere but here. I craved fun and adventure. The world was bursting with potential and I wanted to explore every inch of it.

Then I'd become a vampire and everything had changed. Suddenly, the thought of meeting new people and forming fresh connections wasn't so appealing. Not when most of the people in the world were human. I wanted to bite them more than I wanted to befriend them now.

So I'd poured myself into becoming the best private investigator in the Knox County area, forging a new way of life for myself. The steady work kept me from pining over the life I'd originally wanted.

Kept me focused on the here and now, not the past where I'd left my broken heart. I lived in a strange limbo, not quite in the supernatural or the human world. Neither of them fully suited me, so I kept my toes dipped in both.

At least this life was *my* choice. I called the shots and no one told me what to do. Well, except for my dad, since he was kind of my boss.

But now Kade was here, and his presence threatened my new reality. Everything I'd tried to bury and everything I was *working* toward were colliding. And I didn't know what to do. Didn't know what to frickin' *do*.

Pulling my phone out again, I stared at the text messages demanding I ditch him. I'd never felt so torn. So *lost*. A few days ago, I would have had no problem ditching Kade if it meant protecting myself. But now?

I didn't know what to do.

CHAPTER 16

ISLA

I want to meet with you.

I stared at the words for several minutes, erasing them, then retyping them. Kade silently drove beside me, his gaze firmly fixed on the road. He'd been distant ever since I'd dropped the friend bomb on him. Couldn't blame him. I knew he was still hurt, and I had no one to blame but myself. At the same time, I didn't know how to fix it. Words were inadequate. And a hug would only lead to . . . *other* things.

No, the best solution was to focus on solving this case so Kade and I could go our separate ways. I needed to meet up with my blackmailing, creep-bag stalker and end this stalemate once and for all.

If they were human, I'd have the upper hand. If they were supernatural . . . Well, I'd go prepared. This wasn't the first time I'd put myself in a dangerous situation to solve a case. Usually, my dad or Noah were there to help if things went south, but I'd have to handle this one alone. If I *was* on that footage, I'd need time to figure out what to do next.

Staring at my phone a moment longer, I finally hit send. There. I'd taken the first step toward righting my life again. Blackmailing *sucked*.

When my phone buzzed a couple minutes later, I nearly jumped out of my skin. Kade flicked a glance at me but didn't comment.

Angling the phone away from him, I checked the screen and frowned. The incoming call wasn't from an unknown number. Still, I debated answering it, knowing Kade would easily overhear the conversation. On the fourth ring, I threw caution to the wind and answered.

"Hello?"

"Isla? Is that you?"

"Um, yes. Who is this?"

"Oh, it's Saanvi. Sorry to call you like this, but your dad gave me your number and I really need to talk to you."

I blinked, uncertain how to react. Best to keep it casual, like everything was cool and I had nothing whatsoever to hide. "Okay. What's up?"

"Oh, could we talk in person, please? This isn't a phone call kind of conversation."

Right. Now I was freaking out a little. Or a lot. Then again, what were the chances she simply wanted to chat about her secret crush on my brother?

Probably none.

"Sure. I'm working right now, but I can meet up real quick. Where at?"

"Your apartment?"

I cringed. "Uuuh, it's super messy right now."

"That's fine. We can meet at mine."

She relayed her address and ended the call soon after, leaving me a bit dazed and confused. We'd never met up outside of work before, so this was definitely unexpected. Before my thoughts could go haywire, I cleared my throat and focused on Kade. "Mind dropping me off? I'm sure I won't be long, but maybe you could go run an errand or something while I'm in there."

Yes, I was totally kicking him to the curb. Might as well go for broke.

"Sure," he said, his voice calm and steady. "I could use some alone time anyway."

Ouch. The words *sounded* harmless, but they sure didn't feel like it. I was pretty certain they'd punched a hole straight through my chest. He needed a break from me, was what he meant but was too nice to say. He needed time away. Distance. Because I was a sucky person who treated him like dirt.

Yeah, I deserved that.

"Cool," was all I said, because my throat was too tight for anything more.

It was a relief when we finally reached Saanvi's apartment building. I practically dove out of the car, desperate for air untainted by tension and hurt feelings.

"Call if you need me," were Kade's parting words before he took off. I watched him go, feeling worse and worse by the second. He must be *really* hurt if he was willing to leave me alone like this. Well, not really alone, but he didn't exactly know Saanvi. Yup. He was in pain. Which made me feel like utter crap. My need to please him was riding me hard, flooding me with self-loathing.

See, this was why we couldn't be together. *Toxic*. The sire bond was nothing but pain and torment for both of us. It made me want to give up everything for him and made him want something broken. No good. It was *no good*.

Heaving a dejected sigh, I turned toward Saanvi's apartment complex and climbed the stairs. She readily buzzed me in and I made my way to the third floor.

The moment she opened her apartment door for me, I knew something was wrong. Nervous energy came off her in waves. It didn't matter that her face looked serene as she ushered me inside with a small smile. Being a vampire meant that I could sense certain emotions. There was no hiding her anxiousness and little flashes of fear.

Fear of me?

I tried to put her at ease, giving her a megawatt smile despite how thirsty I'd suddenly become. Her apartment smelled *amazing*. Or rather, *she* smelled amazing. The space was saturated with her spicy tangerine scent. I kept my smile close-lipped so I wouldn't accidentally drool.

"Hey, Isla," she greeted, swiftly closing the door behind me. "Sorry again for bothering you like this."

"It's no bother," I once again tried to reassure her, relieved when my voice didn't crack. "So what's up?"

"Well . . ." Her heart began to race. "Maybe you should see for yourself." She hurried over to what looked like a mini personal lab stationed in her dining area. "I ran numerous tests, but they all had the same results. I . . . well, have a look."

When she gestured me over to a microscope, encouraging me to peer through the lens, I hid my confusion and did as instructed. After a moment, I said, "Err, what am I looking for exactly? All I see are squiggly lines."

"Oh, it's a sample of your DNA. Your saliva, actually."

I straightened to look at her, no longer hiding my confused frown. "How did you get my spit? And why?"

"Remember the cheek swab you received when you first started working for the SCA? It's a mandatory precaution for them to have every employee's DNA on file. The CIA does it too."

As she explained, she could barely look me in the eye. A new scent invaded my senses. Guilt, maybe. "What's going on, Saanvi? Why are you showing me this?"

She took a few steadying breaths, which did nothing to decrease her heart rate, then finally looked me square in the eye. "I found your DNA on the murder victim, Gunner Landry."

My jaw slackened at the news. All I could do was stare at her, my eyes growing rounder and rounder.

"I extracted your saliva from the bite wound on his neck," she plowed on, flicking a nervous glance at my mouth. "But I haven't shown my findings with anyone yet, not even your dad. I wanted . . . I wanted to give you the chance to explain yourself first. I'm sure it was only self defense, right? He tried to hurt you and you got a little carried away?"

My mouth fell open at this point. Numb shock spread down my entire body, making it impossible to respond.

"I know how much your job means to you," Saanvi continued, "which is why I want to help you, Isla. Your work is your life, just like mine is, and I don't want to see you get punished for this. I don't think you deserve to be locked up in a supernatural containment cell. Your dad and brother would be devastated."

My throat closed. The beginnings of fear stole through my limbs, making them shake. "What . . ." I managed to croak. "What are you trying to say, Saanvi? What are you saying I *did?*"

At the panic in my voice, Saanvi's expression softened. "I'm so sorry, Isla."

I shook my head, saying louder than I intended, "Just *tell* me. Tell me what you think I did."

She noticeably flinched, fear bleeding into her eyes. "I-I think you killed a man, Isla. I think you drained him, then left him for dead."

I sucked in a sharp breath, nearly losing my balance as horror struck me. I slumped against the lab table, my mind reeling. I'd been right then. I'd lost control and blocked out the memory for my own self-preservation.

I was the murderer.

It made sense. My increased thirst could only be from drinking warm blood for the first time. Now that I'd consumed blood straight from the source, I was struggling with the need to do it again, dissatisfied with anything else. Which explained why it had taken me so long to become satiated recently. My body only wanted fresh blood now.

And the vinegar at the crime scene. What if it had been used to mask *my* scent? What if my phone stalker had been telling the truth this whole time and really had been helping me hide evidence? What if they really did know everything? What if they'd *seen* me murder someone?

"Isla, are you okay?"

The question dimly echoed inside my whirring brain, barely registering. All I could think about was how screwed I was. My life was over. It deserved to be over. I'd *killed* someone.

My phone buzzed and I pulled it out on autopilot, answering with a dull, "Hello?"

"You believe me now?"

The scratchy voice was unmistakable. My phone stalker had found me at my weakest once again.

"Yes," I said in a barely audible whisper.

"Good. Then we can be friends now. This can all go away, Isla. No one has to know about this evidence."

"H-how? Saanvi knows."

"Put her on. Let me speak with her."

Still too shell-shocked to think clearly, I did as instructed, passing the phone over without comment. Saanvi's forehead wrinkled as she took the phone from me and pressed it to her ear. The second she did, the wrinkles disappeared. "Of course," she woodenly said, handing the phone back to me.

If I'd been in the right state of mind, I would have realized what was about to happen and stopped her. But I watched like an idiot as she stepped toward the microscope and grabbed the glass square containing my DNA sample. Then, without the slightest bit of hesitation, she dragged the glass up the inside of her wrist.

As her blood spurted into the air, I gasped and scrambled back, knocking several beakers over. They crashed to the floor, but all I heard was Saanvi's thundering pulse as it forced more and more blood to leave her body. The scent of it invaded my senses. My gaze locked onto her arm with predatory focus.

Distantly, I heard someone call my name. Again and again until I finally lifted the phone to my ear again. "Drain her," my stalker said.

"What?" I weakly whispered, unable to tear my gaze from her spurting blood.

"She knows too much. She's a loose end. The only way out is to drain her and make it look like a suicide."

"What?" I squeaked again, desperately trying to look away. To stop breathing. To stop *thinking* about her blood. Why wasn't she trying to staunch the blood flow? Why was she just *standing* there? "I-I won't do that. I won't kill someone else."

"Then you're giving me no choice."

"What? Look, I can handle this myself. I don't want you to—"

"Listen very carefully, Isla," my stalker interrupted. "This is exactly what is going to happen . . ."

Blood suddenly rushed into my ears. Into my mind. Into my mouth. All I saw was *blood*. Thick and red. It drowned my senses, consuming my every thought. I helplessly flailed against the powerful deluge, desperate for air. Desperate to clear my head.

I thought it was simply a dream, like the one I'd had a couple days ago. Thought I'd wake up and find myself in my apartment, safely tucked in bed. But when I finally peeled my eyes open, I discovered how wrong I was.

I was living in a waking nightmare of my own making.

I was *draining* Saanvi!

My fangs were embedded in her arm. My mouth filled with her hot blood. I held her upright as she listed sideways like a limp rag doll.

The moment I realized what I was doing, I jerked away from her, so fast that she fell to the floor with a meaty *thump*. When her head struck the hardwood, I rushed toward her, only to pull back with a whimper. In the next instant, I was across the room, wedged into the farthest corner.

I curled into a tight ball, every inch of me trembling as I fought the urge to go to her. To continue *feeding* from her. My veins were engorged with her blood, racing impossibly fast, making me feel strong and invincible. I squeezed my legs together, forcing them to hold still, so hard that the bones threatened to snap.

For what felt like hours, I stared at Saanvi's inert form, unable to hear her heartbeat. Unable to tell if she was still alive. Not when her blood continued to gush through my veins like boiling hot lava, drowning out everything else. I shook and shook and shook, not knowing what to do. I was helpless, terrified to move an inch lest I attack her again. She needed help. *I* needed help. This wasn't something I could handle by myself, not with bloodlust raging through my system.

I needed my dad. My brother. My best friend. But I didn't want any of them near me right now. I could attack them too in this state.

I could drain them. *Kill* them.

I whimpered again, feeling utterly wretched and alone.

Until a name suddenly filled my head, pushing aside my desolation.

Kade, Kade, Kade.

My heart beat even faster, fueled by a hope so powerful that I sobbed and fumbled for my phone. Not finding it, I panicked and sobbed harder. And then I saw it. Through the hot tears obscuring my vision, I spotted my phone on the floor near Saanvi's feet.

Shaking violently, I clenched my jaw and forced myself to move. To crawl. To drag myself inch by inch toward my latest victim. I focused on my phone, refusing to look anywhere else. Afraid what would happen if my concentration broke, even for a second.

Minutes. Hours crawled by. Until I finally reached my phone. The moment my fingers wrapped around the case, I shot toward the far corner again. My back struck the wall hard enough to dent the sheetrock. It took several tries, my breath coming in harsh pants, but I eventually dialed his number.

And then I waited for what felt like an eternity. Waited for him to pick up, terrified that he wouldn't. That I'd hurt him too badly this time. That he'd finally washed his hands of me. I wouldn't blame him. I wouldn't blame him one bit.

Just when despair threatened to drag me under, I heard him pick up. Heard his beautiful, beautiful voice say my name.

I lost it then. All composure vanished. My words were gasps. Sobs of anguish and fear. I poured all of my emotions into saying, "Kade, I n-need you. I need you so badly."

He arrived minutes later, busting through the door like he had the first time I'd called him. But this time was different. This time, I knew just how desperately I needed his help. He frantically searched the room, taking in the shattered glass, spilled blood, and the lifeless girl on the floor. But when he found me curled into a ball, hidden away in the shadows, he strode forward.

There was no hesitation in his steps. No disgust or disappointment in his eyes. And I just stared and stared, convinced this wasn't real. He couldn't possibly be here. Not after all the terrible things I'd done.

He reached me in three long strides, immediately crouching to my level. Scanning every inch of my face, he tracked the tears that wouldn't stop falling. When his gaze landed on my mouth, he slowly reached up and gently swept his thumb across my lower lip. "Oh, Isla," he whispered, with so much compassion that I burst into fresh tears.

"Y-you came," I whimpered, still not quite believing it.

But when he said, "Of course I did. I'll always come when you need me," it finally sank in.

He came. He *came*.

Overcome with gratitude and relief, I listened to my screaming instincts and lunged at him. My arms and legs wrapped around his body, clinging to him with every ounce of strength they possessed. He rose with me still wrapped around him, securing me tightly in one of his signature bear hugs.

"I'm here now, shortcake," he murmured against my neck. "I've got you."

CHAPTER 17

ISLA

"She's still alive," I heard Kade say, but I wasn't convinced. Not when Saanvi's warm brown skin looked so ashen. "She just needs a little vampire blood."

I tensed at the mention of blood, pushing myself even farther into the corner, which only dented the plaster more. Kade propped Saanvi's head up before biting into his wrist and bringing his blood to her lips. A violent shiver racked my body, the sight painfully reminding me of what I'd done to her mere minutes ago. I tried to look away, but couldn't, riveted by how careful Kade treated her frail mortal body.

Was this how he'd treated me when I'd died? When he'd coaxed me back to life with his blood? Had I fed from his wrist, just like this?

My throat closed at the thought. I couldn't remember feeding on him. Couldn't remember how his blood tasted.

I only remembered waking up in his arms. Confused. Afraid. But I'd also felt safe. So safe that I could have stayed there forever.

Seeing him now, cradling someone else in his arms, squeezed my heart. Not because I was jealous. That would be messed up. I simply wanted to feel his arms around *me* again. To feel safe, in a way only he made me feel.

A few moments of silence passed before I heard a faint moan. My back snapped straight. As Saanvi struggled to open her eyes, relief flooded me. But something else did too. A powerful need to finish what I'd started.

Don't breathe, don't breathe! I inwardly screamed at myself, covering my mouth and nose for good measure.

Kade slowly propped Saanvi into a sitting position, lending his support when she swayed. "You're okay," he quietly reassured her, brushing long strands of black hair from her face. "This will all go away in a moment. Look at me."

My heart tumbled in my chest at the soft, albeit firm command.

She did, her eyes fluttering open and fixing on his.

Kade's voice took on a persuasive tone as he said, "I want you to forget—"

"No," I interrupted, scrambling to my feet. "Don't thrall her."

Kade looked at me in surprise. "But what if she remembers everything?"

"Then I'll deal with it. Just . . . don't take her memories away. Please. No one should have that done to them."

His expression turned compassionate again, which threatened to unravel my weak grasp on composure. He knew how strongly I felt about the subject. How some of my own memories had been erased when my mother died. How Loch's younger brother had cruelly tampered with Kenna's memories. Even if it was meant for protection, stealing someone's memories was a terrible thing to do.

And it left scars. Deep ones. I'd already hurt Saanvi enough. She deserved to remember, even if it cost me everything.

"Just lay her on the couch," I said, keeping my distance. She'd probably panic at the sight of me, and I was still parched for more of her blood. Kade did as I asked, carefully depositing her on the living room sofa. The moment he let go of her, she passed out again. But this time, I could see her chest rise and fall evenly. And her rich brown coloring had returned.

Kade began cleaning up the mess I'd made of her lab, barely making a sound. When he was finished, he approached me on silent feet, casting his gaze over every inch of me. "Are you sure about this?" he said in hushed tones, stopping close enough that I caught myself leaning toward his warmth. "She could report you to the SCA. They'll lock you up. Or worse. And I doubt even your dad could stop them."

"I know," I whispered back, wrapping my arms around myself. "But that's a risk I have to take."

His lips thinned. "Well, I don't."

I blinked up at him in confusion.

"Come on, we're leaving," he continued, sliding his arm behind my back to urge me forward.

"But what about Saanvi?" I protested, glancing over my shoulder at her as he ushered me toward the exit.

"She'll be fine. My blood will replenish what she lost."

"But . . . where are we going?"

"To Sanctum Isle."

"*What?* Why?" I tried slowing down, but Kade tucked me firmly against his side, practically carrying me.

"You need immunity, and King Ambrose might be the only one who can give it."

By the time we reached the castle, I was a complete wreck.

Kade hadn't pressured me for details about what happened, but I almost wished he had. Spending the past hour remembering the nightmare I'd just gone through only made me feel more and more unhinged. Until, as we parked in the roundabout in front of the six-story stone dwelling, I sputtered, "I-I can't go in there."

"Why not?" Kade said, turning off the ignition.

"Because too many humans are in there. And I still crave Kenna's hybrid blood. I would die. *Die.* If I did anything to hurt her and the babies."

"Isla."

Tears sprung to my eyes at the renewed compassion in his voice. I shook my head. "No. I won't risk her safety."

"You won't. Isla, look at me." I did, struggling to breathe past the panic squeezing my throat. When a tear slipped down my cheek, Kade reached over and wiped it away before saying, "I swear on my life, I won't let you hurt anyone."

His words only made the tears flow faster. "If I lose control," I whispered, my mouth quivering like crazy, "lock me up."

Pain contorted Kade's face.

"*Promise* me, Kade."

"I promise," he said, using his thumb to capture more of my tears. "But I won't let it come to that."

Something loosened inside my chest at the resolve in his voice. I knew I could count on him. Knew that Kade's promises were gold. There wasn't a more loyal, dependable soul in the universe than Kade.

Unable to verbally express my gratitude, I grabbed his hand and tightly squeezed it. As if startled by the action, he looked at our joined hands. The longer he stared, the warmer his skin felt against mine. The warmth was comforting, seeping through my palm to further reduce my panic.

After a long moment, he slowly ran his thumb over the back of my hand. "So small, yet so strong," he whispered, before lifting his gaze to mine and squeezing my fingers in return.

The comment was innocent enough, but I felt it to the tips of my toes. I was suddenly hyperaware of our joined hands, of the heat building beneath my skin and spreading up my arm. I should pull away. I should *really* pull away. The longer our skin touched, the more I wanted it to remain that way. The closeness was making the last of my panic fade.

It was as if, with a single touch, Kade could share his energy with me. Calm stole through my limbs, making me feel comforted and safe.

When I continued to hold his hand, greedy for more of his calming energy, his gaze drifted to my mouth. I parted my lips, knowing that I needed to speak, to end this moment. It was going somewhere I hadn't intended. But when he gently tugged on my hand, urging me toward him, I didn't resist. Didn't pull away when he lifted his other hand to cup my face.

Just like that, I wasn't calm anymore.

My pulse jumped skyhigh as his fingers slid into my hair, urging me closer still. I knew where this was headed. Knew without words what he wanted to do. And I didn't stop him, even though I knew I should. We were both in a vulnerable state. Both needing comfort and reassurance. I'd called him. I'd called for his help. He'd come without hesitation, believing I needed him.

And I did. I desperately needed him. But I didn't want to hurt him again. Didn't want to encourage something that might end in heartbreak for us both.

At the same time, I. Wanted. This. With a fierceness that terrified me.

I ached with the need to have his lips on mine. To *taste* him again.

As he lowered his head, erasing the space between our mouths, I could barely breathe. He paused, inches away. His ragged breaths warmed my lips, but he made no move to kiss me.

Just when the waiting grew painful, he said, "Show me this can be something more." I sucked in a gasp when he leaned forward an inch, just enough for our lips to briefly touch. Fresh energy charged through me, white hot and electric. "Show me, Isla," he continued to whisper in the scant inch separating our mouths. "Show me and I'm yours."

A whimper lodged in my throat when it became clear what he wanted. He wanted me to make the first move. To seal the kiss. To *prove* that I wanted this with him. That I wasn't simply caught up in the moment. That I wanted *more*.

Apparently, my "just friends" speech hadn't deterred him in the least. He still believed we had a chance. Still believed we were meant to be together. But how could he? How could he still feel that way after I'd just attacked a human and almost *killed* her?

Maybe the truth was the only way to dispel this moment. To stop myself from further hurting him. From hurting *myself*. We couldn't go down this road, no matter how *right* it felt. A rightness that was making it harder and harder for me to remember why this couldn't happen. So I blurted out the truth before I could lose my nerve.

"I killed Gunner Landry." At my confession, Kade went deathly still. "I drained him like I tried to drain Saanvi. I'm the murderer in my own murder case."

He finally pulled back to look at me, his expression unreadable as he searched my face. I let go of his hand and my panic immediately returned. After a long moment, he shook his head and firmly said, "I don't believe it."

I gaped at him. "How can you say that? You just saw me drain Saanvi."

He shook his head again. "You didn't drain her. You *fed* on her. And you still haven't told me why."

I scoffed. "I don't know, maybe because I'm going *feral?*"

His expression hardened. "This isn't the time for sarcasm, Isla."

"I'm not being sarcastic, *Kade*."

"You didn't kill anyone. That's not who you are. Case closed."

I threw my hands in the air. "Why are you so *stubborn?* All evidence points to me being the killer. Even Saanvi thinks so. The case is only closed when I'm behind silver bars."

Kade released a low growl. "I won't let that happen."

"Well, you might not get a say in the matter. Ever since the vampire kingdom allied with the SCA, the rules have changed. I'm not jeopardizing that alliance by hiding what I've done."

"We're not hiding it," Kade said and opened his door. "We're simply going to make an appeal for immunity until this misunderstanding gets resolved."

I exited the car too, slamming the door a little too hard. "I don't need special treatment, Kade. I broke alliance rules and am prepared to face the consequences. I'm not going to use my personal connections to get out of this."

Even though it was still dark out, sometime past midnight, I saw Kade bare his teeth in a silent snarl. "So that's it then? You're going to believe the worst about yourself, just like that, without a fight?"

Some of my resolve wavered as I caught a sliver of fear in his eyes. "What's there to fight? The biker gang can testify to me leaving with my victim. The security footage also caught me with him. My *DNA* is on the bite mark I left on his neck. Saanvi can confirm that, along with the DNA I left on her. And then there's my phone stalker who's seen it all from start to finish."

Kade's brows slammed over his eyes. "What phone stalker?"

I opened my mouth to finally tell him everything, my reasons for not doing so no longer valid, when a sound caught my attention. I whirled toward the castle. At the sight of a girl with long chestnut hair standing just outside the front doors, the blood drained from my face.

"Kade," my best friend called, a smile in her voice. When she spotted me, surprised delight brightened her silver eyes. "Isla? Oh, I'm so happy you're here!"

At the pure joy in her words, misery sat on my chest like a two-ton boulder.

"Little Kenna," Kade called back affectionately, lightening his tone by several degrees. "Where's Loch? You know better than to come out here by yourself in the middle of the night."

With an eye roll, she started waddling toward the stairs. "I'm not a prisoner, you know. And it's not like I'm helpless. Besides, I'm not alone." She gestured at her feet, and it was then that I saw her fox familiar emerge from behind her. Silver's ice blue eyes fixed on me, seeing far too much in a matter of seconds.

"Kade," I quietly pleaded, unable to say more with my pregnant best friend descending the stairs toward us. Without a word, he rounded the car to stand by my side. But when my panic noticeably grew the closer she came, he slipped an arm around my waist and drew me against him. Despite how it looked, I buried my trembling fist in his shirt and clung to his side.

Kenna hit the bottom stair and promptly stopped dead in her tracks. At the sight of me clinging to her husband's best friend, her jaw dropped. She blinked rapidly, as if doing so would change the image before her. When it didn't, her eyes misted with tears. *Happy* tears. My stomach dropped.

"I-it's not what you think," I hurriedly said, feeling like the worst person in the world when Kade stiffened and Kenna's expression fell. "I just need his help for a little while."

Okay, could I get any more cruel? What was flipping *wrong* with me?

"What's wrong?" Kenna said, looking between us with a worried frown.

"We should wake the others first," Kade said, his voice not as light as before. "Here, let me help you back up the stairs."

"Hands off my wife, drothen," a new voice said from above, and we all looked up to see Loch at the top of the stairs. The words were only half serious, but his dark penetrating gaze made me want to retreat all the same. He took in the sight below, noting the way Kade and I were attached at the hip. When Kade didn't wisecrack like he usually would, the formidable Venturi prince swooped down.

Kenna yelped in protest as Loch picked her up and protectively held her against his chest. "I'm not an invalid," she grumbled, yet twined her arms around his neck as if it were the most natural thing in the world. Seeing them so effortless together made my heart hurt all the more. Would I ever have what they had? Especially when a prison cell was calling my name?

"Explain," Loch said, cutting right to the chase.

"Isla's in trouble. She needs immunity," Kade spoke without preamble, which I was secretly grateful for. I couldn't stand here much longer, pretending that my world hadn't just shattered. I felt like I was going to break into a million pieces at any second.

"Come inside," was all Loch said, turning with Kenna in his arms. Silver followed in their wake as they climbed the stairs, peering over her shoulder at me a few times. My throat closed. She knew. Somehow, I just knew she did.

When I hesitated, Kade whispered for my ears only, "You okay?"

I should be asking *him* that. He was the one risking his drothen's wrath by bringing an unstable vampire near his pregnant wife. He was the one who kept getting hurt by my repeated rejections. He shouldn't even be helping me, yet I couldn't seem to push him away. Not this time. Not when his arms were the only thing keeping me from curling up on the ground in the fetal position.

"I'm scared," I eventually whispered back, leaning against him a little bit more.

With a sigh, he gave me a comforting squeeze and said, "Whatever happens, I won't let you handle this alone. Not even for a second. We'll get through this together."

Emotion clogged my throat, but I managed to choke out, "Okay." Then, "Kade?" When he glanced down at me, I moved before I could chicken out. Rising on tiptoe, I quickly kissed his cheek and said, "Thank you for helping me."

He swallowed roughly and whispered back, "Always."

CHAPTER 18

KADE

The emotions in the room ran the gamut, but Kenna's reaction was the strongest.

"I don't believe it," she passionately said, jumping up from her chair. When she teetered sideways a step, Loch was instantly there to lend his support. "I know my best friend. She wouldn't kill someone."

"Exactly what I said," I replied, giving Isla's fingers a reassuring squeeze. She hadn't left my side ever since we'd entered the castle, allowing me to either hold her hand or wrap an arm around her. Even under the dire circumstances, I drank up her nearness like a man dying of thirst.

It didn't matter that she continued to play with my heartstrings until they were stretched beyond their snapping point. I wasn't going to give up on her. On *us*. Especially now that she finally admitted to needing me. Her walls were crumbling, and she was ever-so-slowly letting me in.

"Be that as it may," King Ambrose said from the head of the table in his soundproofed office, "the SCA won't look kindly on me granting her immunity. They might not have jurisdiction on Sanctum Isle, but protecting Isla from their justice system will be a significant breach of trust. They could end our alliance and treat all vampires as threats again if we so flippantly disregard their rules."

"Not even Troy was given special treatment," Everett, the eldest D'angelo brother, said.

At the mention of Troy's name, Isla sat up straighter. We didn't speak his name often, but she always reacted when it did pop up. The youngest brother had been responsible for her human death, after all. We'd all been scarred by his selfish deeds in one way or another, and we were all healing at our own pace. I swept my thumb over her knuckles, feeling her gradually relax against her seat the longer I did.

"We're not sending her to an SCA high security prison," Loch said, coaxing Kenna onto his lap as he reclaimed his seat. "If the SCA seeks retribution, we'll bargain with them to let Isla remain here."

Everett lifted a dark brow. "In a dungeon cell meant for uncontrollable younglings?"

A growl pushed at my throat, one I barely managed to suppress.

"Absolutely *not*," Kenna snapped, trying to rise again. Loch laid a comforting hand on her swollen belly, and she settled against him, still fuming.

"I was thinking more of a house arrest situation," Loch replied, which made his father lean forward with interest. "She won't be able to step foot outside this castle until they deem appropriate, and we agree to any in-house terms they set."

Isla's hand began to tremble. I glanced at her, watching as she struggled to swallow. Panic was written across every inch of her face.

"Can we reconvene in the morning?" I spoke up, leaving the rest of my thoughts unsaid. That Isla was starting to freak out and I wanted to take her somewhere she'd feel safe.

The king eyed us both thoughtfully before saying, "Only if she stays with you at all times. No exceptions."

"You have my word."

"Good." His garnet gaze returned to Isla. "You won't try to escape?"

She quickly shook her head.

157

"Then I'll allow you temporary freedom within my house. But if you harm any of my wives or the female who carries my unborn grandchildren, I'll punish you myself."

At the clear threat, I bristled, saying more harshly than I intended, "She won't, sir. I'll make sure of it."

He blinked at me in surprise. That made two of us. I'd *never* spoken harshly to him before. I valued my head too much. "See that you do," he said after a moment, once again turning to Isla. "And I'll be contacting your father first thing in the morning."

"My . . . my dad?" she weakly whispered, trembling harder.

Seeing her clear distress, the king gentled his tone a bit. "Better him than an SCA superior who doesn't care about you. I'm sure he'll support you through this, Isla."

By her expression, I could tell she wasn't so sure.

But the king had made his decision, rising from his chair to dismiss us all. Kenna scooted off Loch's lap, aiming a sympathetic look at her friend. I knew that look. It always came with a heartfelt hug attached to it. Before she could lift a single foot in Isla's direction, I stopped her with a warning shake of my head.

When tears filled her eyes, Loch stood and gently pulled her back against him. "She's in good hands, love," he quietly reassured his wife, throwing me a look over her head. I knew that look too. *Don't let Isla anywhere near my mate and unborn children*, it said.

I nodded, letting him feel through our bond how serious I was about this. Isla was going nowhere without me. And if she tried to, I'd do everything in my power to stop her, even if that meant commanding her against her will. Even if that meant destroying any possible chance I had with her once and for all.

CHAPTER 19

ISLA

"You should get some sleep," Kade said, finally breaking the silence. "There's a spare toothbrush in the bathroom. If there's anything else you need, let me know. I'm sure Kenna has some stuff you can borrow."

I nodded, but continued to stare at the only bed in the room. *Kade's* bed. I'd never been in his bedroom before. Not the official one on the fifth floor. I'd only seen his temporary room when he'd moved across the hall from me during my brief stay here five years ago.

This room was lived in. His sun-kissed citrus scent completely filled the space. There was a small kitchenette and dining table to the left, and the entire right wall contained shelf after shelf of stacked CDs and record albums. There were even some cassette tapes. A guitar was propped up in the corner, similar to the one he'd played at the lakehouse.

My gaze returned to the king-sized bed, covered in luxurious cobalt blue sheets and a plush comforter. *I wonder how many women he's had in this bed*, my mind abruptly thought.

Frowning, I headed for the bathroom and quietly shut myself inside. My movements were methodical as I found the spare toothbrush and readied myself for bed. Since I didn't have my usual nightly routine supplies, it was quick. And then I made the mistake of glancing at my reflection in the mirror. To the human eye, there was nothing to see but a pale-faced teenage girl. The miniscule smudge on her light gray shirt wouldn't have garnered any attention. But my vampire sight led me straight to it.

To the speck of blood on the collar.

Saanvi's blood.

In a flash, I ripped the shirt off and flung it in the farthest corner, then stared at it as if it would come to life and bite me. I yanked off my dark-washed jeans next, searching the fabric for any signs of blood. Suddenly, it was all I could think about. All I could *smell.*

A knock came at the door, jerking me from my frenzied thoughts. "Isla?"

I didn't reply, too busy trying not to hyperventilate.

"Isla, what's going on? I can hear your racing heart. I'm coming in if you don't answer me."

"I'm fine," I managed to croak. "Don't come in, I'm naked."

Silence. Then, "Do you need anything?"

"No. I'm going to take a shower."

"Okay," Kade said after another beat of silence. "I'm here if you need me."

My throat closed at the words. If only things were different between us. If only I could ask him to join me in the shower, to help me wash away the guilt and shame staining my skin. But I kept my mouth firmly shut, cranking on the shower to scalding and removing my underwear.

The second I stepped under the hot spray, pain lit up my skin. I instinctively recoiled, barely able to tolerate the heat. Pain would always be my weakness, but I forced myself back under the water. I deserved this pain. Deserved to feel miserable.

As fast as the burns reddened my skin, they vanished, healed by my vampire blood. But the water was relentless, pounding against my body, scouring any trace of Saanvi's scent from my pores. If only it

SUN TOUCHED

could burn away her blood still simmering in my veins.

Another idea came to me. One that required more pain.

Gritting my teeth, I shoved aside my pitiful inner whimpering and swiftly gouged my nails into my forearm, deep enough to break the skin. When blood started to freely flow down my arm, dripping off my elbow to swirl down the drain, I gagged. Within seconds, the wound started to heal, so I willed my claws to emerge and dug them deep into my flesh. At the sharp, biting pain, my body betrayed me and whimpered.

The moment the sound left me, the bathroom door burst open. With a startled gasp, I retracted my claws and hid my injury. But not fast enough.

"*Isla*," Kade said, so sharply that I winced. I looked up to find his gaze pinned to my arm, to the blood still seeping through my fingers.

"Kade, no," I weakly said, shaking my head when fury contorted his features. "Let me do this. I can't have her blood inside me."

His angry gaze shot to mine. "Stop this *now*."

My bottom lip began to quiver. "Don't do it, Kade. Don't command me."

His expression was unyielding. There was no compassion. Only firm resolve. "I will if it'll keep you safe. If it'll *protect* you. Even from yourself."

Tears blurred my vision. Tears of frustration and humiliation. "Just let me do this. It'll only take a few more minutes."

When my claws extended again, prepared to reopen my skin, a warning growl cleaved the air. "Don't push me, Isla."

"Don't push *me*, Kade," I cried, desperate to finish what I started. "This is *my* problem. *My* pain. I'm not yours to *protect*."

"To *hell* you aren't!" he roared, storming toward me. He whipped the glass door open and grabbed my uninjured arm before I could

161

stop him.

"Let go!" I screamed as he dragged me out of my self-induced torture chamber and turned off the scalding water. When he ignored me, I kicked and scratched him like a crazed feline, hissing through my bared fangs. I was suddenly airborne, hoisted over his shoulder in all my naked glory. I continued to flail with all my might, taking out my pain on him.

He silently endured my blows, stalking from the bathroom toward his bed. He threw me onto the mattress with force, hard enough to knock the wind out of me. Stunned, I didn't move while he began to wrap a towel around my body. His hands were rough, his face set like stone. But when he was finished, he knelt on the mattress and gingerly picked up my arm. His fingers examined my skin with infinite care, checking that all my wounds were fully healed.

My desperate need to purge the blood from my veins slowly faded as I watched the anger bleed from his eyes. As sorrow filled them instead.

His voice was hoarse when he spoke next. "Please don't do that ever again. I can't . . . I can't bear it."

At the agony I heard, remorse hit me hard. "I'm sorry," I said in a broken whisper. "I'm so sorry I hurt you again."

"Oh, shortcake, come here," he groaned, then gathered me into his arms. I immediately melted against him, pressing my cheek to his chest. As I listened to the steady rhythm of his heart, my muscles began to relax. He continued to hold me, for so long that I drifted in and out of consciousness.

I could have stayed there forever, safely wrapped in the cocoon of his embrace. But he suddenly shifted, dragging the comforter and sheets down. When I made a sound of protest, he pulled away enough to look at me. "You should sleep. Knowing Ambrose, he'll want to see us both at the crack of dawn."

"Windows," I sleepily yawned, sticking my feet under the covers.

"Already took care of them," he said, pulling the comforter up to my chin when I settled back against the pillows.

I was already drifting off again when I felt a featherlight pressure to my forehead. Just in time, I cracked my eyes open to see Kade's strong jawline impossibly close as he softly kissed me. When he pulled away, I murmured, "Where will you sleep?"

"I'm not."

"What?"

"I'm not sleeping."

My eyes came fully open. "When's the last time you slept?"

He shrugged. "Doesn't matter. I promised to watch over you and that's what I'll do."

A frown tugged at my mouth. "Kade, you need sleep. Even vampires have to recharge to maintain their strength."

"I'll make do," he stubbornly persisted, making my frown deepen.

"Well, at least lie down for a little while. I'm not going anywhere." As soon as the words were out, I realized my mistake. There was only one place he could comfortably lie down in this room, and that was on his bed. Beside *me*. Too late. I wasn't going to take the words back. I wouldn't let him suffer anymore because of me. I patted the spot to my right. "Here. There's plenty of room."

He zeroed in on my hand, on the invitation I was offering. His Adam's apple sharply bobbed. "Are you sure?"

I rolled my eyes. "Just get in. I'm not going to bite."

Crap. Mistake number two.

I expected him to call me out on my words, or at least *say* something, but he was as silent as a tomb. His eyes weren't though. They glowed with a blue fire hotter and brighter than I'd ever seen before. At the unspoken words brewing inside them, my heart jumped into my throat.

It felt like a century dragged by before he finally moved. The first thing he did was remove his shirt, which I wasn't expecting. I nearly swallowed my tongue at the sight of all that glorious skin. When he turned to flick off the light, I enjoyed ogling the rippling muscles in his back just as much.

The room plunged into darkness, but my night vision quickly kicked in. Still, the darkness made the room feel smaller. More intimate. If I hadn't already committed to letting Kade share the bed with me, I would have scurried to the bathroom and locked the door like a yellow-bellied chicken.

He approached the bed on soundless feet, having removed his boots at some point. I let my eyelids fall to half mast, pretending that I was already on my way back to la-la-land. That the sight of him heading toward the bed half naked wasn't affecting me in the least. But I couldn't pretend away my racing pulse. Or my uneven breathing. And when he rounded the bed and slid onto the mattress, I almost leapt out of my skin.

He settled on top of the covers, as if *that* made a difference. When silence filled the room, I closed my eyes, willing myself to relax. To fall asleep. Seconds ticked by. Minutes. I remained perfectly still. So did Kade. Neither of us made a peep.

"This isn't going to work," he suddenly spoke, startling my eyes open. "I can't relax for fear of falling asleep. And I can't sleep for fear of you sneaking off."

I huffed. "I won't sneak off." At his silence, I flicked a sideways glance at him. "What will ease your mind so we can both get some sleep?"

He was silent for several more moments, then, "I have to be

touching you."

I gulped. "Okay, fine. Then touch me."

Good goddess, that did *not* come out right.

Before he could exploit the comment, I added, "What do you want to do? Hold my hand?"

"Roll over."

I blinked. "Huh?"

"Roll toward the wall." He shifted onto his side to face me. The second I rolled away from him, he draped an arm over my waist and pulled me back against him. The action dislodged the towel wrapped around me, leaving me stark naked beneath the sheets. I went stiff as a board, barely daring to breathe. If he decided to sleep beneath the sheets after all, he'd find my bare skin in no time.

With his arm still around me, I couldn't move though. Couldn't reclaim the towel. But maybe he'd stay like this for the rest of the night. As long as the sheets remained between us, he wouldn't know.

"What's wrong?"

"What?" I said, cringing when my voice squeaked.

"You're super tense."

"I'm fine." I squeezed my eyes shut, trying to relax. No such luck.

"Isla." Silence. "Isla, I can leave if this is too—"

"I'm naked."

Crap! I'd totally blurted that out loud. I held my breath, hoping he hadn't heard the words. Yeah, right. Of *course* he had. It was only a matter of waiting now. Painfully waiting to find out what he'd—

He slowly lifted his arm off my waist, then slipped his hand beneath the covers. As his fingers grazed my bare stomach, I flinched and sucked in a gasp. Not because they were cold, but because they were warm. So blissfully warm.

"So you are," his voice rumbled near my ear, causing my stomach to flip. "Guess I didn't wrap that towel tight enough."

"Guess you didn't," I agreed, a little too breathlessly.

When his fingers found my stomach again, all the air left me in a rush. I held perfectly still as they lazily traced a circle around my belly button, slowly stirring the sensitive skin awake. Goosebumps erupted over my flesh, drawing a full-body shiver from me. The fingers paused, then continued their lazy exploration, traveling up the length of my ribs.

I double-fisted the comforter and squeezed, forcing myself to remain still so he wouldn't stop. So I could bask in the pleasure of his touch a little while longer. I wouldn't let it go too far. I'd end it before anything serious could happen. Before I lost the ability to pull away.

"You can stop me whenever you want," his voice rumbled again. "Just say the word."

When I didn't utter a sound, he gently scraped his nails down the length of my stomach. Pleasure zipped through me, shooting straight to my core. My back arched and I squeezed my thighs together as heat pooled between my legs. Okay, that was intense. More intense than I bargained for. If he did much more than that, I wouldn't be able to stop him. My resolve was already embarrassingly weak.

He circled my navel again, this time with a fingernail. No, a *claw*. My eyes popped open just as he scraped all five of his claws up my stomach. Unable to control my reaction, my eyes rolled back and a moan burst from me. The claws didn't stop there. They continued to scrape a path upward, lightly digging into the flesh of my right breast.

When one nicked my nipple, I cried out from the pleasure pain it brought me. He paused again, as though worried he'd hurt me. "Don't stop," I gasped.

He started to pull away anyway and I grabbed his hand, guiding it back down. As I placed his fingers over the swell of my breast and arched into them, he growled, so deep that the bed shook.

I was suddenly on my back, blinking up at him as he shoved the sheets down to expose my upper half. He greedily took in my naked form, breathing heavily before dipping his head.

I wasn't prepared. Not in the least.

His hot mouth landed on my right breast, sucking the hard nipple inside.

"*Kade*," I cried out, my back nearly bowing off the bed as pure bliss shot through me. I grabbed onto his shoulders, his head, his hair, desperate to anchor myself before I floated away. He continued to suck on my nipple, harder and harder until I saw stars. His tongue rolled over the sensitive peak, flicking, teasing. I trembled, clenching my fingers in his hair for dear life.

I'd officially lost control. I couldn't pull away now even if I wanted to. But that was the problem. I didn't *want* to. Not when he was worshiping my breasts exactly the way he'd described the day before. One of his hands landed on my other breast, kneading the flesh with deft fingers. I squirmed beneath his thorough ministrations, which only made my arousal saturate the air.

He pulled back, deeply inhaling my scent. A groan rolled up his throat, and he opened his eyes to look at me. Desire burned in his gaze, so hot that I could barely stand it. He paused for a moment, as if giving me a chance to put an end to this. But I was too far gone. Too frantic for his hot hands and mouth and tongue on my flesh.

I dragged his head back down, this time to my left breast. He readily captured the nipple, making me quiver uncontrollably.

When it was thoroughly licked and sucked, his mouth left my breast and traveled south, blazing a path down my stomach. I panted as he kissed and licked my sensitive skin, pausing to dip his tongue into my navel. I threw my head back and moaned as my core heated to the point of pain.

"I can't . . . take . . . much more," I gasped, desperately needing release.

He lifted his head once again to look at me, his voice little more than a growl as he said, "Do you want me between your legs? Because there's no place I'd rather be."

Good *goddess*. His words alone nearly tipped me over the edge into oblivion. A whimper escaped me and I weakly nodded.

Gods, yes. I wanted his sinful mouth between my thighs. I wanted his tongue to pleasure me until I came so hard that I screamed his name. Yes, yes, *yes*, I wanted that.

At my consent, his eyes brightened even more, burning white hot. "You don't know how long I've waited for this, Isla," he huskily said. "You don't know how much I've yearned to taste you, to coat my tongue with your arousal."

Oh gods, he was a *dirty* talker. Nothing turned me on more.

"Then taste me," I urged him, tightly gripping the sheets on either side of me in anticipation. "Please, Kade. Make me come."

A chuckle rumbled from him. "Only if you tell me how good it is afterward."

I blinked at the wicked smirk on his face, barely able to think straight, let alone understand him. "What?"

"You heard me. Rate how good your orgasm is. I want to know how I measure up to your past lovers."

My eyes widened in shock. "That's twisted."

"Maybe. But I think you like it." His smirk widened.

Okay, maybe I did. Playing games in the bedroom sounded kind of . . . erotic. It appealed to my competitive side.

"I hope you never compare *me* to your past lovers," I said in reply, nearly losing my ability to speak when he grasped my thighs and slowly spread them apart. "It wouldn't be fair. You've lived over a hundred years, which means you've probably had at least a hundred women in your bed."

His eyebrows climbed toward his hairline. "At least?"

"And I'm a little rusty," I started to ramble, suddenly realizing how out of my league he was. He had a lifetime—*two* lifetimes—of bedroom experience. "I haven't had sex in over a year, whereas you probably had some last week—and with *multiple* partners."

He froze and I inwardly panicked, realizing I'd blathered like an idiot. But before I could hide my face in abject humiliation, he quietly said, "I haven't taken a female to bed in over five years, Isla. Not since I first laid eyes on you."

My jaw dropped at his open admission. Reality suddenly slammed some sense back into me. Gods, what was I doing? This wasn't a game to him. This was *real*. I knew that but had somehow forgotten again. One touch from his warm fingers and I'd forgotten *everything*. Forgotten to see how *permanent* he wanted this to be. I wasn't a quick roll in the sheets to him. I wasn't one more name to add to his long list of lovers.

He thought we were destined. *Fated* to be together.

What was I doing, telling him to pleasure me senseless, when I was too afraid to truly commit to this? To *him?*

He seemed to realize where my thoughts had gone, because the fire suddenly dimmed in his eyes. He straightened from his bent position with a gut-wrenching sigh. "You're not ready for this."

It wasn't a question. He knew. He knew that I'd reached the same conclusion I always did: I wasn't ready for a serious relationship with him. Maybe never would.

He looked away, but not before I saw the hurt in his eyes. I could have died then. Died from all the self-loathing I felt.

"Don't do that," he said, still not looking at me. "This one's on me. I wanted it to happen too badly and missed the signs. You were in a vulnerable state and simply wanted comfort. Don't blame yourself."

As he abruptly stood from the bed, I drew my legs together and covered my nakedness. His words did nothing to ease my shame. I knew better. I *knew* better. Yet, I'd allowed it to happen anyway.

"Kade," I whispered, needing to ease his pain somehow. Pain that I continually caused with my selfish actions.

He shook his head and backed away. "Forget it, Isla. I already have. Try to get some sleep." With that, he retreated across the room, slumping into a seat at his dining table.

I watched him for a long time. Watched until my eyes would no longer stay open. But his words continued to echo through my head.

He'd waited for me. For five long years, he'd waited in hopes that I'd return his feelings.

He may have said that he'd forgotten what just happened between us, but I knew that couldn't be further from the truth.

CHAPTER 20

ISLA

I woke up screaming.

The nightmare clung to my subconscious like a vicious leech, bleeding into my reality. It coated the bed and room around me in thick red paint. In *blood*. I raised my arms and screamed even louder, frantically scrubbing and scratching at the blood there.

"Isla. *Isla!*" a voice boomed, cutting through my screams. Hands grabbed my flailing arms, stopping me from further hurting myself. "It's just a *dream*."

"No. *NO*," I shrieked, fighting to break free. "I have to *go*. I can't *be* here. It's too dangerous."

"Isla, stop. STOP." The command was so forceful that I went limp against the mattress, breathing heavily like I'd just climbed a mountain. But the images were still there. Still forcing me to *see*. To face what I'd done. There was no escaping the horror.

I began to shake as sobs racked my body.

The hands suddenly lifted me. I didn't resist. Couldn't, even if I tried. They wrapped a bedsheet around me before depositing me on a lap. Strong arms, *familiar* arms, pressed me tightly to a hard, bare chest. I leaned my cheek against it, frantically soaking up his warmth and scent. "I didn't mean to hurt them," I choked out. "Please don't hate me. I'm so so sorry."

"I could never in a million years hate you, Isla Andrews," Kade's comforting voice washed over me. He ran his thumb over my bare shoulder in soothing circles. The touch slowly pulled me from the nightmare, dissipating the last of the haunting images.

I still remembered though. Every last detail of that terrifying reality.

"Want to talk about it?" Kade said, continuing to stroke my shoulder.

I blankly stared at a spot across the room, a room no longer covered in blood. "What time is it?"

"Almost dawn."

My heart sank. "I should . . . I should get ready then."

"We have time, Isla. I want to make sure you're alright first."

Another tear slipped down my cheek, further dampening his chest. "I'm a monster."

He was silent for a moment, then, "You're a vampire, Isla. Not a monster. They aren't one and the same."

"But I've given in to the dark side of my nature. Who knows when I'll do it again, or who I'll hurt next. Even my dreams paint me as the villain. I'm always covered in blood. *Their* blood. My victim's. It's what I was dreaming about when you broke into my apartment a few days ago. I was dreaming about Gunner Landry's *blood*."

"Is that what you were dreaming about just now?"

"Yes. His blood. The bartender's. Saanvi's. I'm responsible for all of them. But I saw their faces too this time. Their fear when they saw me. And that's not all. My dad and Noah were there. So were you and Loch and Kenna. And you were all . . . *staring* at me. With such horror and loathing that I just . . ." I heaved a defeated sigh. "I can't do this anymore. I'm dangerous and need to be locked up."

He stiffened against me. "There's no way I'm allowing you to be put in a cell."

I lifted my head to look at him. "What other option is there? Even if the SCA lets me stay here under house arrest, I'm a liability. There are too many humans here. I could lose control again at any moment."

"I won't let that happen."

"You can't watch me *forever*, Kade. I appreciate your help, truly, but I'm not your responsibility. You have a duty to Loch as his drothen. To *Kenna*. You can't protect them if you're always having to watch me. And soon, there will be two more responsibilities. Two helpless little babies who may or may not have their hybrid mother's blood. What if I lose control around them? What if I *hurt* them?" My voice rose in panic, my heart galloping like a runaway horse. "No, I can't risk that. I'm unstable, and unstable supernaturals need to be locked up. I won't jeopardize everyone else's safety for my own selfish wants."

When I scooted off his lap and stood, determined to tell the others what I'd just told him, Kade rose as well. I whirled toward him, holding the sheet tightly to my chest.

When he opened his mouth to speak, I beat him to it, firmly saying, "You can't fix this, Kade. I'm not like a busted door. You can't replace me with a new version of myself. I am who I am, scars, splinters, and all."

His lips thinned. Before he could say anything, a soft knock came at the door. He was next to me in an instant, securing me to his side like a human-sized barnacle.

"Isla?" Kenna said through the door. "I have some stuff for you. Can I come in?"

I was pretty sure my heart caved in. This was it then. No more girl's nights with my best friend. No more family dinners with my dad and brother. My career was over. I'd be spending the rest of my days alone in a reinforced cell with nothing but my regrets as company.

When I didn't reply, too distraught for words, Kade sighed and turned to me. I stared straight ahead, unable to look at him. The second I did, I would burst into tears. I was going to regret how things ended with him the most. How we were never able to fix all that lay between us.

When my bottom lip began to quiver, he reached up and gently touched it. "This isn't over, shortcake," he quietly said. "I won't give up. I'm *going* to fix this."

I shook my head, but he was already turning and striding toward the door. "Don't—" I said, but it was too late. He opened the door, revealing my best friend in the hallway. She wasn't alone though. Of course she wasn't. Silver hovered beside her while Loch shadowed her back, one hand resting protectively on her belly. And . . .

My eyes widened at the sight of two more familiar faces. "Daddy?" I whispered in disbelief. Next to him was an equally tall, broad-shouldered man, one with blond hair tied back in a messy bun. When he suddenly strode into the room, heading right for me, my mouth opened in horror. "Noah, *no!*"

Completely ignoring my frantic warning, he scooped me into a bone-crushing hug, bedsheets and all. "We're here for you, baby sis," he murmured against my hair, unmindful of my mouth mere inches from his vulnerable *neck*.

I tried to stop breathing, but this close, his scent was everywhere. Before I could full-blown panic, he set me back on my feet, leaning away just enough to look at me.

Something he saw on my face made him scowl, and the sight of his disapproval made me want to weep. This was what I'd been afraid of. "Okay, first off, you're not a monster. So get that out of your head right now, Isla. Also, we could never loathe you, no matter what you do."

I didn't blush often, but shame burned my cheeks when I realized what had happened. "You overheard? *All* of you?"

His look turned sheepish. "We didn't mean to. Dad and I immediately portaled here when King Ambrose called. We spotted Kenna heading this direction and joined her. I'm so glad I got back last night when I did. Just in time to bail my kid sister out of a little trouble."

"A little? Noah, I messed up. *Big* time. You can't make this all disappear with your magic and sarcastic wit."

"Hey, sarcasm has helped me out of many tough scrapes, so don't knock it."

"I'm not. I just know that talking my way out of this won't solve the bigger issue." The issue that was still *very* much a problem. With Noah so close, and Kenna and my dad not far away, I was struggling to focus. I shouldn't be this thirsty so soon after feeding, but things were different now. My craving for fresh warm blood was only growing stronger, and I suddenly had a major hankering for the witch and warlock variety.

No sooner did I begin to struggle that Kade was beside me again. He casually draped an arm over my shoulders, subtly shifting me back a step to place himself between me and my brother.

Noah caught the move, but his attention was suddenly diverted to my *apparel*. Or lack thereof. His eyes widened, then narrowed on Kade. "Are you banging my sister?"

I flicked a horrified glance at the door, at my dad who could hear *everything*. "*Gods*, Noah, you're such a dick sometimes." He danced out of reach when I tried to kick him. "And, no, we aren't having sex. I just didn't have anything clean to wear."

"So you decided to parade around the room naked? Classy."

"I'm not naked, you immature *brat*," I snapped, swinging a fist this time. He snickered when Kade easily stopped me from hitting him, tucking me more fully against his side.

"Stop fighting, you two," my dad said, taking in the scene rather calmly. *Too* calmly. He eyed my makeshift clothing as well, observing how close Kade and I were standing before seemingly dismissing it for more important matters. "I found security footage on my doorstep this morning from an anonymous sender. You were seen in both of the videos with Gunner Landry shortly before he was killed."

Oh. Oh crap.

My stalker had been telling the truth then.

I really was guilty of murder.

"I'm not here to discuss that right now, though," he continued before I could fall apart. "I'm here to place you in protective custody before the SCA finds you."

I gaped at him. That was the *last* thing I'd expected him to say. He'd loyally worked with the SCA for decades. "Can you even do that?"

"You're my only daughter. I'll do whatever the hell I want to keep you safe."

"Go, Dad," Noah chimed in with a devil-may-care smirk, clearly on board with this crazy plan.

"I'm not saying I'm okay with this," my dad said, ever the diplomat, "but I'm on your side. The evidence against you doesn't look good, but I've dealt with cases like this before. With a little time, we can build your case and present it to the SCA."

I blinked, not fully understanding. "What are you saying? That you don't think I'm guilty?"

He harrumphed, looking more than a little affronted by the question. "Of course you aren't."

"Dad. I know you don't want to believe it, but I hurt Saanvi. *Seriously* hurt her."

"And she's not pressing charges."

"What? Really? But I—"

"She's shaken and confused by your actions, but she still doesn't think you deserve to be locked up. She even said she wouldn't testify against you if the SCA asked her to."

Shocked, I struggled to hold back fresh tears.

"I raised you, Isla," he continued, his voice softening. "I know my little girl. Your mother wouldn't have thought you were guilty either, no matter how damning the evidence was."

Pain squeezed my chest at the mention of my mom. It took several moments before I was able to say, "Then what do you suggest? I still have to be contained somehow. My bloodthirst has gotten out of control, that part is true."

He stared at me for a long moment, then at Kade, seeming to take his measure. Finally, he looked back at me and said, "I know the perfect place where you can stay, but before I bring you to it, there's one stipulation. One thing I'm asking you to agree to."

I nodded, even though my gut told me I was going to hate this stipulation. It was the look he gave me. One that said, *I'm only doing this because I care.* But I agreed anyway, because he was *helping* me. They all were. Which was a miracle, considering the terrible dream I'd just had.

Approval shone in his eyes at my decision, and I could have basked in it all day. But then he turned to Kade and opened his mouth, blowing my reality to pieces.

It started to rain in sheets, which more than suited my somber mood. The boat violently rocked as the ocean churned with the angry storm. Wind whipped strands of blonde, pink-tipped hair across my face. I barely felt it. Barely felt anything.

I was too busy pretending this was all a bad dream. That I hadn't woken up yet.

"I vow to take full responsibility for her. To protect her with my life. To make her safety my number one priority. I, Kade Carmichael, swear this solemn oath."

Those were Kade's words to my dad when he agreed to this impossible situation twelve hours ago. A part of me understood why my dad had suggested this, that I was never going to get better otherwise.

But why *here* of all places?

And with *Kade.*

Why him? *Why?*

Why did he have to agree so readily? Why did he have to make a vow so sacrificial in front of everyone I cared about? Why had Loch and Kenna nodded their approval? And why oh *why* had my dad seemed so pleased by it?

The universe must hate me. That was the only explanation.

Before I could stop them, my eyes found him on the far side of the boat, standing at the bow with Loch. They'd been in deep conversation for the past hour, one even I couldn't overhear past the wind and pounding waves.

"I still trust him, you know," my dad said from the covered helm where he manned the steering wheel. I tore my gaze from Kade to find him watching me. "I believe he would have stopped every bad thing from happening if he could."

Of course he would have. If I'd been more honest with him. If I'd been more honest with *myself*. If I'd admitted days ago that I didn't have everything under control. But Gunner Landry would still be dead. I'd still be a murderer.

I didn't reply, not knowing what to say. I might agree with him, but that didn't make this any less painful.

An hour later, a small dark splotch smudged the night's horizon. At the sight of it, panic tightened my chest. I gripped my seat cushion to keep from jumping overboard. It was too late for that anyway. We were miles from any other land source, approaching the farthest known uninhabited island off the coast of Maine.

It showed up as little more than a white blob on the Maps app, only a mile long and half a mile wide. The sole dwelling on the island was a safehouse, electrically self-sustained by wind and water. But there was no internet. And my phone had been taken from me—for my own protection, of course.

My dad had ensured every precaution to make certain the SCA couldn't track me down. He'd left his phone behind. Even Kade's phone had been confiscated. To avoid suspicion, Noah had returned to Rosewood after retrieving my things from the lakehouse. He'd been able to quickly portal back and forth, but portalling to the island was too dangerous. It only worked if you knew where you were going, and neither my dad nor Noah had ever personally visited the tiny island. There wasn't much room for error, and portalling with me and Kade, plus all of our supplies, was too risky.

King Ambrose had allowed us to use one of his boats, assuring us he was on board with the plan if the SCA should question him about my whereabouts. No one had seen or heard from me. I'd vanished the second Saanvi had confronted me with the DNA evidence.

Which officially made me a fugitive. Kade too, if they considered him my accomplice.

"You can do this," Kenna had said before I left, unable to join us due to her pregnancy. "Never forget that you're my best friend and that I love you. I'll talk to Tess when you're all better. I know she'll listen to me." She still kept in touch with her ex-guardian, and Tess Walker had always liked me. With her high status in the SCA, there was a chance she would fight for me.

Unless she found me guilty. In that case, maybe she'd convince them all to turn me in.

"Isla." A hand gripped my shoulder, jerking me from my thoughts. I released a startled hiss, but the hand's owner didn't retreat in fear. I threw an apologetic look at my dad, but he seemed unfazed by my reaction, giving my shoulder a light squeeze. "It's time."

My throat closed at the words. Only then did I realize we'd stopped. Loch had already hopped out of the boat onto a narrow dock, catching the rope Kade tossed him. I stood on wooden legs, grabbing a backpack near my feet. For the next few minutes, I busied myself with removing our supplies from the boat and onto the dock.

Despite my raincoat, cold water slithered down my face and neck, sticking wet hair to my cheeks. When the last of the supplies were deposited on the dock, Kade said, "Thanks, guys, but we got it from here. You should go before the SCA gets suspicious."

"You know how to contact me if there's an emergency," my dad said, reaching out to shake his hand. "I can portal here in seconds if need be."

When Kade nodded, my dad faced me one last time. I knew my eyes were wide. Knew he saw the panic in them. The fear. *Don't go,* they begged him. *Please don't leave me here.*

Compassion stirred in his stormcloud gaze, but he simply took me by the shoulders and said, "Stay strong, Isla. You're an Andrews, and Andrews always pull through."

Not giving me a chance to respond, he turned and climbed back into the boat. Loch embraced Kade before hopping into the boat as well. As the engine started, I suddenly had a million things to say. But the boat was pulling away. They were *leaving*. I didn't have enough time.

The boat was several feet from the dock when I finally found my voice. "I love you, Dad," I shouted, scared that I'd already blown my chance. That the words were lost to the wind and waves.

But he lifted his head and found me. Opened his mouth and shouted back, "I love you too, sweetheart."

It was all I needed to hear. Tears streamed down my face, hidden by the buffeting rain as the boat slowly faded away, disappearing from view.

CHAPTER 21

ISLA

The safehouse was a frickin' shanty.

It barely had a kitchen and living room. Worst of all, there was only one bedroom. Ergo, one *bed*.

To top it off, the electricity was out.

"I'll check the breaker," Kade said, heading for the hall closet masquerading as a laundry room. "Maybe it just needs a reset."

I cast another glance over our new crackerjack box living quarters, then backed toward the front door. "I'm just gonna go . . . get some fresh air."

The second I touched the doorknob, Kade whipped his head out of the closet. "Where are you going?"

"I don't know. To check out the sights?"

"In the *rain?*"

"Why not?" I said, feeling hysteria bubble up. "I'm sure it looks the same, dry or wet."

"Isla," he said, his expression softening. "Why don't you unpack your things and get settled in? We can explore the island together when the storm passes."

Something about what he said tipped me over the edge. Or maybe it was his voice. How *calm* he sounded, when I was unraveling at the seams.

"This isn't a *vacation*, Kade," I said too sharply. "I'm here to lay low so I don't end up in a supernatural prison. Oh, and let's not forget that I have to *detox* so I don't go *feral*. So, no, I'm not going to *settle in*. I'm going to frickin' let off some steam. *Alone*. And do it however or wherever I *want*."

With that, I whipped the door open and slammed it shut behind me, so hard that it nearly rattled off its hinges. Too late, I realized I'd left my raincoat inside. My shirt was already soaking through. No way was I going back inside though. I probably only had seconds before Kade came after me. He'd been so flipping *protective* lately. I worried he'd use his sire abilities and command me to stay, which made me desperate for space. *Lots* of it.

Picking a random direction, I took off at top speed. With the wind and the rain masking my scent, Kade should have trouble tracking me down right away. I at least had a few minutes to myself. The terrain was rocky, interspersed with tall pale grass and black spruce trees. The closer I got to shore though, the flatter it became. In under a minute, I was at the edge. Angry waves pounded over the rocks, reaching for my waterlogged shoes. I stared out across the ocean, at the endless expanse of . . . nothing.

It was so huge and powerful, and I was so insignificant and . . . and *weak*.

I was completely and utterly helpless here.

The realization made so much panic well up inside me that I tipped back my head and screamed. Screamed and screamed and screamed until my throat burned with more than bloodthirst for once.

I felt a presence soon after, and knew it was him. There was no one else on this godforsaken spit of land. But I wasn't ready yet. Wasn't ready to face him. To accept this harsh new reality.

"I want to be alone, Kade," I called, knowing he could hear despite the whistling wind and crashing waves. "Please leave."

He was silent for a beat. Then, "I can't."

Digging my nails into my palms, I whirled around to glare at him. "Leave before I say something I'll later regret."

"Go ahead," he said, crossing his arms over his chest. "I'm not going anywhere."

My vision bled red. With a shriek of rage, I charged toward him at top vampire speed. The impact hurt as I collided with his middle and nearly knocked him over. He skidded back several feet, but didn't go down. "Gods, what is *wrong* with you?" I yelled, planting both hands on his chest to shove him back another step. "How can you be *okay* with this?"

"I'm not," he said, grabbing my wrists when I tried to shove him again. "I'm not okay with this at all."

"Well, you could have fooled *me*," I continued to rail at him, yanking my hands free. "You seem perfectly okay with trapping me on an island and taking away all my control. Are you happy now? *Are you?*"

His expression fell. "No, Isla. I'm not happy."

A sob built in my chest. Before I could break down in front of him, I took off again. A minute later, I was on the far side of the island, skidding to a stop at the edge. This time, it ended at a steep cliff. The waves pounded even harder here, frothing and leaping over the jagged rocks far below.

Kade joined me again seconds later, standing several yards behind me in silence. And I couldn't stand it any longer. Couldn't stand *any* of it.

So I jumped.

"ISLA!" he bellowed as I went down, down, down. The water rose up and grabbed me, plunging me deep into its cold dark depths. It stole my breath, but only for a brief second. The cold couldn't penetrate me like it had when I was human. But I wished it could. I wished it could completely numb my body so I wouldn't feel this overwhelming powerlessness anymore.

I wanted to be nothing. *Nothing.*

Arms wrapped around me from behind and lifted me. Higher and higher. My head broke the surface and I obligingly sucked in air.

"You could have been *hurt*," Kade thundered in my ear, treading water for us both when I went limp against him.

A wave washed over me and I choked on a mouthful of saltwater. "So what?" I sputtered, spitting out water. "I'd heal like I always do. Like I will for my miserably long life."

"Is that what this is about?" he said incredulously. "Because you hate being a vampire?"

"*Yes*," I yelled, finally starting to tread water. "I hate how much I crave blood. Hate how scared I am of the sun. Hate that I still haven't willingly traveled anywhere outside Maine because I'm too *afraid.* I'm supposed to be this strong, immortal creature, yet I've never felt more lost. More *broken.* Even on my worst day as a human, I was never this pathetic. I knew what I wanted. Nothing could stop me. And now I'm just . . . *this!*"

"You're not broken, Isla. You're trying to *find* yourself."

I twisted around to face him. "That's crap. I can't find myself because I'm *dead*, Kade, remember? I died. Isla Andrews *died.* I'm something else now. Something dark and *ugly.*"

Kade grabbed me as a wave pounded down on our heads, forcing us beneath the water. Seconds later, he lifted me to the surface again and growled, "You are not *dead*, Isla. You were brought back to life and given another chance. Don't *waste* it."

"I'm *not*," I shouted, jerking away from his hold. "I was trying to help others. To make a *difference.* But look where it got me. Stuck

185

going nowhere. I'm *nothing* now. I never should have become a PI. All I did was screw it all up."

"You didn't screw it all up and you aren't nothing," he fiercely said. "You're still you. You're funny and caring and passionate, not to mention smart and sexy as hell."

"*Stop*," I screamed, my voice cracking. "I'm none of those things now. I'm a lost cause, admit it."

"*Never.*"

"You're a bloody *fool*, Kade. Why did you have to make that vow? Why won't you give *up* on me? All I do is hurt you. I'm *toxic*. You should leave me here alone to rot like I deserve."

"I can't do that," he shouted. "I could *never* do that."

"But why, Kade? Just tell me *why?*"

"Because I'm in *love* with you!" he roared, latching onto my arms to shake me. "Ever since you came to Kenna's rescue in the cafeteria wearing one of those frilly little skirts, I've been falling. I didn't know what it was at first. I never imagined something like this would happen to me. But it has. Once I had a taste of you, I wanted more. More than I've ever wanted anything. You're *it* for me, Isla. So don't ask me to give up on you because I won't. You're my forever, even if I'm not yours."

I stopped treading water, struck dumb by his confession. He wrapped an arm around me before I could sink, taking my silence as a sign that the conversation was over. He started swimming with me in tow, making for the jagged rocks. When he snagged one with his claws and dragged us both on top, I was still too shell-shocked to move. Lifting me into his arms, he crouched and sprang into the air.

I knew he was strong, but not "scale a cliff in one jump" strong. In the next blink, his feet were firmly planted on solid land. Still holding me, he began walking toward the safehouse, his expression unreadable. I didn't make him let me down. Didn't resist as he carried me all the way back.

All I could do was replay his words in my head.

Because I'm in love with you. I'm in love with you. In love with you.

I tossed and turned for hours, unable to fall asleep. Not only because of Kade's profession of love, but because I hadn't fed in over twenty-four hours. It now hurt to swallow, the action like shards of glass against my esophagus.

I knew what I was supposed to do. Knew that I had no other option. But guilt and copious amounts of stubbornness kept me firmly glued to the bed. I could endure the pain longer than this. Not that I ever had in the past. But I had a reason for denying myself this time. A big, *complicated* one who was currently occupying a chair in the next room, trying to stay awake so he could guard the door.

But he hadn't slept in days. He couldn't stay vigilant forever. Even his powerful stamina would wear out eventually.

Blinking up at the ceiling, I strained to hear any sound from him. When a few minutes passed without a peep, I inhaled a fortifying breath and rose from the bed. My bare feet were silent against the rough floorboards as I crept across the room. I even managed to crack open the squeaky door and slip through without a sound.

The moment I stepped into the short hallway, I saw him, propped against the front door in an uncomfortable-looking chair. Fast asleep. Even though I knew he was taking precautions in case the SCA somehow tracked me here, a part of me couldn't help but wonder if he barred the door to keep me in. As soon as I had the thought, fresh guilt assailed me.

Was that all he was to me? My *prison* master?

He'd done nothing but help and protect me all week, and here I was, clinging to the past. Letting bitterness taint my vision of him. I could be such a selfish, ungrateful brat sometimes.

Quietly sighing, I resumed my trek, aiming for the kitchen. I was almost there when Kade's breathing suddenly sped up. I froze, certain that I'd woken him. But when I turned, his eyes were still closed. Changing directions, I slowly approached him, noting the way he held something with both hands. Hands that were now tucked into leather gloves. The long object was balanced across his lap, silver and thin like a . . .

My own breathing quickened when I realized what it was.

His sword.

The same sword he'd been holding five years ago when his arm had been ripped off. I hadn't seen the sword since then. I'd hoped to never see it again. Just the sight of it forced me to relive the horrible memory of his arm being severed. To hear his agonized screams. To smell his burnt flesh as the sword reopened his wound. As my brother reattached his limb.

I hadn't been able to stand it. Seeing him in pain had gutted me.

So I had kissed him.

Not a quick kiss, but a passionate one that I'd poured my soul into. I'd wanted to ease his suffering. Distract him from the pain. And all these years, I'd desperately tried to convince myself that the kiss was just that. A simple distraction. Nothing more. It hadn't actually *meant* anything. But now, seeing him like this, recalling his heartfelt confession from a few hours ago . . .

"Isla?"

I jumped, emitting a short scream. Kade was up in a flash, sword at the ready as he sought out the threat.

"I'm sorry," I rushed to say, feeling even more guilty that I'd woken him. "No one's here. You just startled me."

He gave me a thorough inspection, taking in my pink t-shirt and polka dot pajama bottoms before lowering his sword. "Why are you up?" he groggily said, using his free hand to rub his eyes.

"Couldn't sleep. I was just getting a snack." Even the mention of food soured my stomach, but I hid my grimace. The *last* thing I wanted him to know was how thirsty I was. Quickly changing the subject, I said, "I didn't know you brought your sword with you."

This time, I *did* grimace, and he quickly caught it.

"You don't like Betty?"

My eyes jumped back up to his. "Your sword is named *Betty?*"

"Well, this one is," he said, gesturing at the weapon with the faintest of smirks.

Just like that, the terrible tension between us broke. It felt like a great weight had been removed from my chest.

"You'd better not be one of those guys who names their dick," I said with an eye roll, and his smirk grew.

"Wanna hold it?"

At the question, I gave him a deer-in-headlights look.

"*Betty*, Isla," he said, still smirking unapologetically. "I'm talking about Betty. Not my dick."

I swallowed past the glass shards in my throat. What a dirty, dirty trick. One I enjoyed a little too much. "Maybe another time. I didn't bring gloves."

"I have an extra pair. You could—"

"No," I said, a little too quickly. A little too *panicked.* "I mean, no thanks. I'm good."

The second his brow furrowed, I wanted to kick myself. "You're afraid of her."

Crap. Why did he have to be so *observant?*

"No, I just . . . don't like silver."

"And Betty."

"Ugh, *fine.* I don't like Betty."

He took a step toward me and I immediately backpedaled, staring at him with wide eyes. "Why don't you like Betty, Isla?"

He took another step and I gritted my teeth, forcing myself to stop. To hold my ground. "Because she's dangerous. She can hurt people."

He paused a foot away from me, his sword held loosely at his side. "I don't think that's the only reason," he said, searching my face. "Why else don't you like her?"

This conversation had become serious *way* too quickly. I wanted to end it and flee back to the bedroom. At the same time, I wanted him to know. Wanted him to understand why I loathed the sword at his side. "Because she wasn't there when you needed her," I said, my voice slightly trembling. "Because she brought you pain. Because she *hurt* you."

It took me a moment, but it suddenly hit me that I wasn't just talking about the sword. I was talking about *myself.*

Kade's expression softened, and I knew he'd come to the same conclusion. "It doesn't matter," he replied. "I still want her by my side. And I always will."

A tear slid down my cheek. When he lifted his free hand, I didn't pull away. Didn't stop him from cupping my face, from gently running his gloved thumb over my skin. Everything felt different now that I knew the extent of his feelings for me. Every look. Every touch. Every gesture was infused with love.

How had I not seen it before? How had I not *felt* it? But I could now. And the scary thing was . . . I had no desire to run away.

CHAPTER 22

ISLA

I watched Kade through the narrow slit between the curtains, my body racked with pain. Focusing on his sweat-slicked chest and back while he practiced swordplay with Betty did wonders for my eyes, but even his sun-kissed skin couldn't distract me from my agony.

Thirty-six hours since I'd last fed. I'd never gone this long before.

Sweat beaded my brow, and I'd barely moved a muscle all morning. Kade knew. He'd seen my fatigue. Seen through my pathetic attempts at pretending to eat food. Then there was my rapid pulse and dilated pupils. I couldn't formulate clear sentences, too busy daydreaming about blood. Warm blood. *Fresh* blood. Not the cold, bottled stuff.

I was struggling *hard*, and Kade hadn't said a word. For whatever reason, that made some of my stubborn resistance fade. Maybe because he wasn't threatening to command me into giving in. He was letting me do this on my own. I could tell my pain and resistance bothered him though. Hence why he was working himself into a lather outside. Plus, we'd both been avoiding the elephant in the room all day—his admission during our little swim last night. Things were currently super awkward between us.

I made it until sundown.

Then, I broke.

Kade had gone outside again—this time to scout the island's perimeter for any sign of the SCA—when I couldn't stand the bloodthirst any longer. Furious at my weakness, I took it out on the living room, throwing chairs, shattering lamps, and punching holes in the walls. Kade found me half an hour later, curled up on the floor of the destroyed room, clutching my blazing throat.

He approached cautiously as if he knew. Knew how far gone I was. A switch had flipped and I was no longer in control.

"It's just me," he said, as if he wasn't sure I recognized him. I did. I wasn't *that* far gone. But I was gone enough that I could no longer hold back my true form. My skin was now pitch black, my eyes no doubt red. And my claws and fangs were fully extended, poised to rip into anything they deemed a threat.

He was still several feet away when I raised my head and loudly hissed at him, baring my aching fangs. He slowly crouched so as to appear less threatening, showing no fear. Still, my raging instincts demanded I test him. I scrambled toward him and lunged, bringing him to the floor. A small, rational part of me was aware that he'd *let* me plow him over, that he was far stronger than I'd ever be, even in my feral state.

But I didn't care. I had him exactly where I wanted him.

Pinned beneath me.

I was in control, the vampire side of me that acted purely on instinct. His blood was *mine*.

"Easy, shortcake," he said in soothing tones, remaining calm when I sank my claws into his shoulders. "I'm yours to feed from, but you need to fight your instincts. Push through the pain and cravings. My blood will only satiate you. It'll take time to adjust to this way of feeding, but it's the fastest way to get your bloodlust under control. You'll only get worse if you panic and try to drain me."

I knew what he was saying, but the wild side of me currently holding the reins didn't want to listen. "Feed," I growled, digging my claws in deeper. "I need to *feed*."

He raised one of his arms, making sure I saw. When he opened his mouth to reveal his fangs, poised to puncture his skin, I grabbed his arm and slammed it back to the floor.

"I want to *bite!*"

He seemed more shocked than I was at my words, stilling beneath me. That small, rational part of me recoiled, horrified that I'd admitted to such a thing. I'd never bitten or been bitten before. Not consciously anyway. Not since a vampire had viciously drained and killed me five years ago. The thought of being bitten again filled me with fear. As did biting someone else.

And yet, I wanted nothing more than to bite Kade right now.

When I whimpered, struggling with myself, Kade's face relaxed. "Do what you need to do, Isla," he said. "I won't stop you."

I whimpered again, this time with excitement. His eyes brightened at the sound, yet he held perfectly still. I didn't know what possessed me then, but certainly not common sense. Instead of reaching for his arm, I lowered myself on top of him and set my sights on the pulsing artery in his neck. It was engorged with blood, roping down the length of his golden skin.

And I. Wanted. It.

With my heart thundering in my chest, I grabbed a chunk of his hair and pulled his head back. The vein bulged even more and saliva filled my mouth. Need pounded through me, an incessant drum I couldn't ignore. I pressed my nose to his neck, nuzzling the artery, preparing it for my bite.

His chest rose and fell sharply beneath me. I clenched his hair tighter and growled. When he made no further movement, I opened my mouth and licked the vein, all the way up to his jaw. He shuddered violently, but I was too enthralled by his taste to chastise him. His skin was both salty and sweet, and deliciously *male*. I licked him again, letting my tongue linger against his throbbing vein. The longer I tasted him, the stronger my thirst became.

My fangs suddenly went rogue and sank deeply into his neck. He jerked against me and released a groan, one that sounded a lot like my name. His hands came up and grabbed my waist, but I paid them no heed, too focused on drawing his blood into my mouth.

The second I tasted his rich, sweet and savory blood, I latched onto his neck and greedily fed like a thing possessed. Releasing his hair, I gripped the nape of his neck and pressed him more fully against my mouth, allowing my fangs to sink in as deep as they would go.

"Sweet mother of Moses, Isla," Kade breathlessly said and shuddered again, squeezing my waist. When he did, I felt his hard arousal between my legs. Reacting instinctively, I pressed against it and slowly began to rock. As bliss coiled through me, I did something I'd never done before. I let venom bleed from my fangs. Let it flow into Kade and mix with his blood. His back bowed off the ground and he bit out a curse.

I should have stopped then. Should have realized I'd crossed a forbidden line. But I didn't. Because what I was doing felt natural. Biting him. Tasting him. Sharing my venom with him. Seeking pleasure from him. It all felt perfectly natural and *right*.

And when he flipped me over onto my back, settling his hard length between my legs again . . . that felt right too. It was my turn to arch against him as he took the lead, grinding his erection against my throbbing core.

"Good girl," he crooned, shifting his position until he hit the perfect spot. "Take what you need from me."

The unexpected praise crumbled the last of my resistance. Without restraint, I rode the high he gave me, continuing to draw from his neck. My throat still burned a little, but the blood was slowly satiating me. Slowly bringing me back to myself. The wild need was lessening, making me more aware of my surroundings. And my actions.

Like the fact that Kade and I were frantically dry humping.

And I was so close. *So* close to orgasming.

Instead of pushing him away, I wrapped my legs around his waist and held on for dear life. Held on while he drove me closer and closer to the brink. When the orgasm exploded through me, I instinctively wrenched my fangs from his neck, throwing my head back to scream.

Kade joined me a second later, roaring so loudly that he shook the floorboards.

Quivering from the pleasurable aftershocks, I panted, trying to catch my breath. After a moment, I lifted my head toward Kade's neck again, ready to puncture his skin a second time.

Before I could, he gently captured the nape of my neck. "No, baby," he huskily said, still trying to catch his breath. "You need to fight this. You've had enough for now."

The urge to growl at him, to *defy* him, came and went when I met his gaze and saw the strong emotion there. My desire to feed dwindled when reality weaseled its way in.

Oh. Oh wow. We'd just made each other come. On top of that . . .

My lips parted as shock, followed by horror, filled me. "I . . . I claimed you."

His only response was to caress my cheek and say, "You did."

A mix of mortification and confusion assaulted me, and I stammered, "I-I didn't mean to. It just happened. I didn't know what I was doing."

He continued to stroke my cheek, a contented look on his face. "An instinctual part of you did. That part knew exactly what it was doing."

I blinked at him. "You should have stopped me."

He studied me a moment before truthfully saying, "I didn't want to."

Oh crap. Oh crap, oh crap, oh crap. What had I done? What had *we* done?

A line had been crossed, one we couldn't ignore or erase. This hadn't been a simple kiss or harmless flirtation. We'd pleasured each other to completion. I'd *marked* him. My scent now lay beneath his skin. I'd basically placed a sign around his neck that said, *"Back off. He's mine."*

At a loss for words, I simply stared at him. Beseeched him with my eyes for help. Once again, I didn't know what to *do*.

"Don't worry, shortcake. I won't take this as a profession of your undying love for me. It'll be our little secret," he said, giving me a clear out. *Saving* me, once again. With a wink, he started to stand. When my legs refused to let him go, he chuckled, and I rushed to set him free.

He was glowing, practically his own *sun*, as he reached down to pull me up. I accepted his help, cringing when my legs wobbled unsteadily like a newborn calf. The sight only made him glow brighter. Of course it did. He was a *guy*, after all. A cocky, hot-blooded male beyond pleased with himself for making a girl come so hard that she could barely stand afterward.

Okay, I supposed that was a feat worth being proud of.

CHAPTER 23

KADE

She was jittery, casting me furtive glances every few seconds. I'd expected her to bolt from the safehouse the minute I started to clean up the mess she'd made of the living room, but she hadn't. Instead, she'd stayed to help me, righting chairs and sweeping up broken bits of glass. All the while, I struggled to keep a stupid grin off my face.

I knew she was conflicted, clearly still in denial about her actions. So I kept silent while we cleaned up, letting her process what had happened. Truth be told, I needed time to process it all as well.

I'd dreamed of having her bite me. Of having her scent buried beneath my skin. Now that it had happened, I felt intoxicated in the purest sense of the word. I half expected to leave my body any second now. The high that still thrummed through my entire being was like nothing I'd ever felt before. It went beyond the physical. I'd been bitten before during moments of passion, but never claimed.

Most vampires knew how sacred the act was, specially reserved and given to their chosen mate. But Isla . . . she was young and relatively inexperienced. She didn't know what her venom could do to me. How it would affect me not just physically, but emotionally.

When it had gushed through my body, my need for her had increased tenfold. I knew she wanted me in the physical sense of the word, but a union solely based on carnal lust rarely lasted long term. I needed more than sex with her. I needed *all* of her. But when her venom had hit my bloodstream, I would have given her anything. If sex was all she wanted from me, then that was enough. Or so I'd told myself as her venom stole my willpower. As it tore down every last barrier and made me a slave to passion.

I'd never lost control like that before. Not as a vampire. Never completely thrown away my convictions to revel in a moment of pleasure. I'd acted like a hormone-crazed teenager, grinding my cock against her in a lust-filled haze.

She was more to me than that. *Much* more. I'd spent my life seeking meaningless pleasure, unable to commit to more than that. Not *wanting* to. I wasn't going to do that with Isla. She was the end of the road for me. My days of wandering were over.

Which was why I currently fought back a smile, despite the weak moment I'd just given in to. She hadn't run away. She hadn't run from me. She was here, helping me clean up, casting me look after look. She might only want meaningless sex, but her claim on me said otherwise. There was still hope. Hope that she would someday return my feelings. Maybe not today or tomorrow, or even a year from now, but I could wait.

I could wait for an eternity if I had to.

CHAPTER 24

ISLA

"Take a break, shortcake. Here, put these on."

My fast reflexes kicked in and I caught what Kade threw in my direction, despite wanting to bat it away instead. I glanced at the leather gloves and froze, shooting him a suspicious look. "Why?"

"Because your time here is for healing, not tiring out your brain by trying to solve a case without proper resources. Besides, you work too much. You're sorely in need of a hobby."

I wrinkled my nose at him. "I have hobbies."

He crossed his arms over his chest. "Name one."

"Shopping. Mostly online these days, but that still counts. I also like to binge-watch movies and shows."

"What kind?"

"Pretty much everything. Fantasy. Crime and suspense. Romantic comedies."

"Which rom-com is your favorite?"

Caught off guard by his interest, nerves tumbled in my stomach.

When I didn't respond, he said, "What's that one where she returns home, only to discover that her heart still belongs there? Oh, yeah. *Sweet Home Alabama.*"

My heart did a weird little flutter. To cover it up, I huffed a laugh and said, "Yeah, that's a good one."

Except that it was *more* than good. I'd always loved that movie.

"I like when she finally realizes that the guy she left behind was the one for her all along," Kade continued, staring at me a little too intently. "All those years, he hadn't stopped loving her, and neither had she."

Oh, boy. I shot up from my seat, knocking the chair clean over. "Maybe I do need a break," I breathlessly said, stooping to pick up the chair. "It's not like I'm going to look any less guilty while I'm here anyway."

"Isla. You didn't kill that guy."

I set the chair down a little too forcefully. "But I was with him. And I *did* drain Saanvi."

"You *fed* on her. You didn't drain her."

I whirled toward him. "But I *could* have. I . . . I wanted to."

Sympathy sparked in his eyes at my admission. "What triggered you? What made you attack her?"

I looked down at the gloves in my hands. "I'm not sure. Everything happened so fast. She cut herself on some glass and then I just . . . blacked out. Next thing I knew, I was feeding from her arm."

He was silent for a beat. Then, "Have you blacked out before?"

"Not that I know of. Well, except for when I got drunk at the bar and woke up the next day with no memory of killing a guy."

I glanced up to find him rubbing the back of his neck, his brow deeply furrowed.

"It doesn't make sense."

I frowned in confusion at his muttered words. "What doesn't?"

He looked up at me. "Even when Loch has his Lochness Monster moments, he always remembers what he's done afterward. Same goes for vampires who go feral. As for getting blood drunk, Everett used to do it all the time in his younger years. He never once blacked out or forgot what he did."

"Maybe I suppressed the memories because they were too

traumatizing for me to face. Maybe I didn't black out at all. Maybe I *chose* to forget."

"Maybe," he said, his brow still furrowed. "What about that bartender guy? Did you try to attack him too? Is that why he pulled a gun on you?"

The need to defend myself surged up, so I responded a little too harshly, "No, I didn't touch him. Everything was fine until—"

Something dawned on me then. Something that sent ice slithering through my veins.

"Until what?" Kade said, eyeing me closely.

It was time to tell him. He needed to know. Trying to solve this case by myself had only made matters worse. Maybe he would have a fresh perspective.

"Until I got a phone call from an unknown number."

He frowned. "You mentioned a phone stalker earlier. Is that who called you?"

"Yes. They . . . they threatened to send the security footage to my dad if I didn't cooperate."

Kade's eyes widened. "What did he want you to do?"

"Well, I don't actually know if it's a *he*. The voice was scratchy and distorted, like they were using a voice changer."

"Isla, answer the question."

I worried my lip, then blurted, "They wanted me to drain the bartender."

Kade swore.

"But I *didn't*. I refused. Just like I refused when they told me to drain Saanvi."

"They told you to drain *Saanvi?*" Kade exploded, loud enough that all the hair on my arms raised.

"Yes," I evenly said, trying to calm him down. It didn't work. His eyes flashed dangerously the moment I added, "In a twisted way, I think they were trying to help me hide evidence of the murder."

"That's bull. They were trying to blackmail and *scare* you. What happened when you refused them?"

"The bartender got a phone call. The message was cryptic. Something about opening a drawer and using it on yourself. Next thing I knew, the bartender was pulling out a gun and aiming it at his head. I stopped him, but . . . he ended up dead anyway."

"And then you received that message on your car smeared with his blood."

"It was a warning from my phone stalker. That they could easily expose me as the murderer if I continued to not cooperate."

Kade swore again. "I'm guessing they were responsible for your apartment break-in as well?"

"Maybe. Probably. Reminding me that they knew about Gunner Landry's murder by dousing my apartment in vinegar."

Kade shoved a hand through his hair, his expression troubled. "And Saanvi?"

"I got a call right after she told me about the DNA evidence. When they asked to speak with her, I didn't think much of it at the time. I was in too much shock. But now, I realize that's when everything went wrong again. Just like with the bartender, Saanvi stopped what she was doing and randomly tried to hurt herself. And *that* is what's bothering me. Neither of them seemed like the type to injure themselves. The fact that it happened *twice*, right when my phone stalker told me to drain them, can't be a coincidence. Right?"

After a long moment, Kade quietly said, "No. I don't think it's a coincidence at all. I think you were set up. The stalker isn't trying to help you, that much is clear. In fact, I'm pretty sure they were trying to pin more evidence on you."

A swallow got stuck in my throat. "They said they wanted me to act on my true nature. And if I didn't, we would become enemies."

A muscle thrummed in Kade's jaw. "Well, they've just made one more enemy, and when I find them . . ."

I shivered at the low growl, at the scary look on his face. I wasn't used to seeing this side of him. I was equally nervous and thrilled at the dark promise in his eyes.

"Look," I said, finding it odd that I was trying to calm *him* for a change. "I'd love nothing more than to hunt the phone creeper down, but we can't do that right now. You're right. I'm here to heal, not to solve a case without proper resources. We can discuss this at a later time, okay?"

He looked ready to argue, then abruptly blew out a sigh and gave his head a hard shake. "Sorry. Yes. We'll discuss this later."

"Good," I said, relaxing when the intensity in his eyes slowly faded. I waved the leather gloves at him. "So, what exactly are these for anyway?"

He blinked and focused on the gloves. "Put them on and I'll show you."

When I hesitated, he lifted a brow in challenge. I huffed and tugged them on. "They're too big."

"Not important right now," he said, turning to grab something propped against the wall. The second he did, I shook my head and backed away. At my retreat, his eyes narrowed. "Are you going to keep running from your fears or face them, Isla?"

Well, if *that* wasn't a loaded question. At the double—possibly triple—meaning behind it, I bristled. "Hey, it wasn't my idea to come to this island. I was going to take responsibility for my actions and allow the SCA to lock me up, remember?"

"Yes, but coming here wasn't running. You're facing your

bloodlust so you can better deal with the murder evidence against you."

"See? I'm not running then."

"But you still believe you're guilty," he said, slowly stepping toward me. "You still fear the worst about yourself." He reached out a gloved hand to grasp one of mine, raising it palm up. "You still fear a sword that has protected me far more than it's hurt me. And," he quietly added, placing Betty on my outstretched palm, "you're still afraid of falling for me. Of giving your heart what it's wanted for years."

My breath came in short spurts, and not just because I was holding a deadly silver weapon. He'd called me out. The gloves were off now, so to speak. All the cards were on the table, and he was asking me to make my move. To face my greatest known fears. I didn't know what was more terrifying. The thought of facing my fears, or the fact that he so obviously knew of them.

We stayed like that for a frozen moment of time, his hand on mine and mine on the sword. I waited for the silver to burn me, waited for the pain to hit so I could use it as an excuse to run. To convince myself that avoiding my problems was safer. *Smarter.* But the pain never came. And Kade continued to stare at me, patiently waiting for me to make my decision.

But he didn't push. Didn't command me. I was in control here. He was giving me the freedom to make my own choice.

At the realization, something in me thawed. All on their own, my fingers closed around Betty, firmly gripping her hilt. "I'm going to face them," I said, gratified when my voice barely shook.

He grinned so wide that my breath caught. "Then prove it," he said, a challenge once again flashing in his eyes. "Start by learning how to wield Betty."

I raised my chin a notch. "Fine. Show me how and I'll do it."

"Gladly," he said, his voice little more than a silken purr. "But maybe we should take this outside. No need for you to destroy the rest of the house."

I stuck my tongue out at him and he laughed, making a smile tug at my lips.

He trained me for hours, teaching me more about swords than I ever cared to know. But I listened with rapt attention, enthralled by the passionate way he spoke about the subject. It wasn't just a hobby for him. Skilled swordsmanship was an important part of being Loch's drothen, of keeping him safe against threats.

I remembered a comment he made to Kenna the day he'd briefly lost his arm: *"I need both arms. I'm no good otherwise."*

I could tell he still believed that. Still thought his physical strength was the most important thing about him. But he was so much more than a glorified bodyguard. He needed to know that, to realize it for himself, but I couldn't seem to get the words out. I might have learned how to safely hold Betty over the course of a few hours, but opening up to Kade and sharing my deepest thoughts was going to take time. *Lots* of it.

At least I was here. At least I was outside, allowing him to teach me. To draw close to me without pulling away. And every time he did draw close, I wanted him to stay there. To touch me a little while longer. To share his warmth with me, the closest thing I'd felt to sunshine in years.

By the end of the session, I tiredly trekked back inside the safehouse with two new truths burning inside my mind: Kade was an excellent teacher, and, despite my fear . . .

I was undeniably, irrevocably falling for him.

I couldn't sleep again.

Not because of bloodthirst this time, but because of guilt. This was the second night in a row that Kade had taken up a post near the front door, insisting he was fine there. He barely showed it, but I knew he was exhausted.

He was always putting my needs above his own. Always being the one to sacrifice.

Well, it was *my* turn now.

When I got out of bed this time, I wasn't as careful. I wanted him to know I was coming. Wanted him to think I wasn't the least bit terrified of what I was doing. But I was. I was scared out of my ever-loving mind.

The moment I opened the bedroom door, I saw him propped against the front entrance again. But this time, he wasn't asleep. His eyes roved over my body, taking in my tiny white pajama shorts and fuschia tank top. Probably not the best choice of outfit right now, but there was no time to change.

"What's wrong?" he said, straightening from his slumped position. When it took him longer than usual to become alert, some of my fear faded. He needed this, and I finally had the power to give it without hurting him.

I knew what I wanted this time. I knew what I wanted with him.

"Nothing," I assured, stepping into the hallway. "I just can't sleep knowing you're not getting any."

His expression softened. "Isla, I'm—"

"No, you're not okay. It's been *days* since you've had any sleep. I want you to come to bed."

He went absolutely still. "With you?" he quietly asked.

"Yes," I said, feeling my pulse quicken. But there was no slowing it. I was very deliberately crossing a line, even though it scared me to death.

When he slowly stood from the chair, I curled my toes into the rough floorboards, forcing myself to stay put. Each step he took toward me felt like a lifetime. By the time he stopped in front of me, a slight tremor shook my hands.

"The last time we did this, it didn't end so well," he said, the deep rumble of his voice causing my stomach to flip.

Remembering how he'd worshiped my breasts with his mouth, my nipples hardened, pushing against my thin top. His gaze dipped, as if he too were remembering.

"I know," I whispered, "but I think I'm ready this time. Ready for more." His gaze snapped back to mine. We stared at each other, both equally stunned by the admission.

"You think?" he questioned, easing into my personal space so that I had to tip my head back. "I need you to be sure about this, Isla. I'm not playing games here."

My swallow got stuck in my throat. "I'm not either. I can't promise you forever, Kade. Not right now," I truthfully told him. "But this is me giving you what I have. If it's not enough, I'll understand. I know you probably want more than I'm ready for."

"And what, exactly, are you ready for?" he slowly said, watching me closely.

Oh, gods. He wasn't going to make this easy. I couldn't blame him though. He wanted to make sure that *I* was sure.

Understanding his need, I blurted, "I've thought about that kiss too. Every single day. And I think . . . I *know* I'm ready to kiss you again."

Heat simmered in his gaze. "You want to kiss me?"

"Yes," I said, the word a breathless whisper.

He watched me for a long time, like he was trying to see my

feelings through my eyes. And maybe he could. Because he finally said two little words. Two words that made my heart thunder uncontrollably. "Show me."

I glanced at his mouth and my heart pounded even harder.

"Show me, Isla," he repeated, standing so close that his warmth seeped through my clothes. But he didn't touch me. He was waiting for *me* to touch *him*.

Tension crackled between the scant inches separating our bodies. The air grew charged, pricking at my skin like tiny bolts of electricity. I continued to stare at his full lips, trying to drum up some courage. The same courage that had prompted me to kiss him five years ago.

It's only a kiss, I tried to reason with myself. *Not a soul-binding vow.*

I could kiss him without permanently tying myself to him. I could show him that I wanted more without declaring a lifelong commitment. I hadn't made any promises yet. He understood that one kiss didn't necessarily mean forever.

Right?

I could barely breathe now, second-guessing my decision to face him. Yes, I wanted more with him. Yes, I was falling. But what if I fell so hard that I hit the ground? What if I couldn't get up again? What if I *lost* who I was?

It would be so easy to get lost in him. I'd always known that. And that's what I feared most. Giving up everything for him. Letting him steal my heart and soul. Becoming his *slave*.

And then I really would be nothing. There would be nothing left for *me*.

But it's just a kiss, I insisted, slowly leaning toward him. *You can't lose yourself to a kiss.*

And I truly did want to kiss him. I'd missed the feel of his warm lips on mine. Missed the thrill it gave me. Missed his taste. Missed being close.

So I stopped thinking. Stopped giving myself a million reasons why I shouldn't do this.

And I rose up on tiptoe and kissed him.

The second my lips touched his, the charge building between us exploded. A jolt of heat raced through me, and I pulled back with a startled gasp. My wide eyes locked with his, growing wider still when I saw his irises ablaze with blue fire.

He hungrily watched me touch my tingling lips, then quietly rasped, "More."

My breath caught. I should have known a swift kiss wouldn't be enough. But it wasn't enough for me either, so I raised my trembling hand to his face, lightly running my fingertips over his short stubble. Then rose up once again and pressed my lips to his. He didn't move a muscle as I cupped his cheek and more fully kissed him, patiently allowing me to explore the contours of his mouth. A thrill raced up my spine when he ever so slightly parted his lips so that our mouths could lock together like two puzzle pieces.

All too soon, I pulled back again to catch my breath, lightheaded from his taste and scent. This close to him, my senses felt scrambled. I wasn't fully in control, which scared me. At the same time, it excited me.

I wanted to get lost in him. Wanted to fully immerse myself so that my feelings became his and his became mine.

And maybe—just maybe—that wouldn't be a bad thing. Maybe getting lost in him for a time didn't mean I'd be losing myself. Maybe I was finally ready to give up a little control, to trust that Kade would keep me safe, like he had when I'd gone feral.

"How was that?" I breathlessly said and dropped my hand, even though I still yearned for more.

He caught my wrist and raised it back up, guiding my arm around his neck. "I've been waiting a long time for you to do that again," he huskily replied. "But that wasn't nearly enough. Now it's *my* turn."

And there went my ability to function on my own. My knees weakened and I swayed toward him. That was all the invitation he needed. In a flash, his mouth crashed down onto mine. At the powerful jolt the contact gave me, my legs completely gave out. Before I could fall, he wrapped an arm around my waist and lifted me, bringing me up to his level.

My other arm went around his neck and I clung tightly to him as he began to feast on my mouth. Good goddess, I was way over my head with this man. He'd been holding back the first time we'd kissed. This kiss was pure, life-giving *energy*. Every time he brought our lips together, my skin buzzed like a livewire.

Overwhelmed by the powerful sensations, I started to whimper. I had no control over the sounds. No control over the way my body began to melt against his. He was thoroughly wrecking me in the best way possible and all I could do was hold on.

When his tongue slid past my lips and swept over mine, pleasure shot straight to my core. Gods, not only did he look like the sun, he *tasted* like it too. I whimpered again, boldly coiling my tongue around his to capture more of his taste. He groaned into my mouth, then thrust his tongue in deep. Like *really* deep. I lost track of where our mouths ended and began. They were one in that moment, fused together so that our tongues could dance.

With each stroke of his tongue, I felt myself surrender bit by bit. There was no way I couldn't. He'd so thoroughly possessed my mouth that it was his now. His to do with as he pleased.

He growled when my body went pliant against his. Not a single inch of me resisted him. He backed me against the wall and lifted my legs, securing them around his waist. As his hard erection pressed against my aching core, more energy shot through me, lighting me up like a firework.

When I breathlessly moaned, he dug his fingers into my hair and tugged my head back. His mouth abruptly left mine, burning a path over my jaw and down my neck. He sucked at the skin, hard enough to leave a mark. I shuddered, arching my neck back even more to give him better access.

The submissive move drove him wild and his mouth turned rough, kissing and sucking at my neck hard enough to leave bruises. Instead of cringing away from the pain, I reveled in it, enjoying the spikes of pleasure it gave me. But when he suddenly clamped down on my neck—not with his mouth, but with his *teeth*—I sucked in a sharp hiss.

"Kade."

At the panic in my voice, he immediately pulled back. "Was I too rough?" he said, his voice equally panicked.

"Yes. *No.* I liked it. A lot, actually." I struggled to catch my breath, to slow my erratic heartbeats. He was equally winded, his chest heaving as he waited for me to finish. I knew I couldn't lie. At the same time, telling him the full truth was too hard. So I settled on saying, "I just wasn't expecting the . . . the bite."

Technically, it hadn't even been a bite. No blood was drawn, and he hadn't used his fangs.

I was suddenly embarrassed. *Mortified.* Here I was, a *vampire*, scared of being bitten. What an oxymoron. "I'm sorry," I hurriedly said, no longer able to look him in the eye. "Let's just forget it."

His fingers released my hair and gently tapped underneath my chin, drawing my gaze back up to his. "You can talk to me, you know.

I won't judge you."

Ah crap, I could feel myself giving in. It was the gentle tone of his voice, the caring behind the words that made me blurt, "Ever since I was drained, I've been scared of being bitten."

The compassion in his eyes immediately made mine burn with unshed tears. "Because it hurt?"

"Yes. And because I couldn't move. I was completely at the mercy of a creature far stronger than I was." I looked away again before whispering, "I don't want to be that helpless ever again."

Heaving a sigh, he leaned forward and gently kissed my forehead. "I'm sorry you've been living with that fear. I had no idea."

"It's okay," I said, closing my eyes as his lips lingered on my skin. "It's not exactly something I want to share with the class. I struggle to fit into the vampire world enough as it is."

"You're allowed an adjustment period, shortcake. As long as you need."

I nodded. His words were comforting, even if I still felt like a freak.

He pulled back again to study me, and this time, I didn't look away. It was his acceptance of my flaws that gave me the courage to face him. I'd been so confident in my skin as a human and wasn't used to this level of insecurity as a vampire. But somehow, Kade always saw through it to the person I still was deep down inside. He kept reminding me, kept encouraging me to see the good.

Because of that, I fell for him a little more.

CHAPTER 25

ISLA

I was swimming in Kade's sun-kissed citrus scent. It was soothing, wrapping me in a deliciously warm embrace. I sighed contentedly, burrowing deeper into his scent. Hugging it. Cuddling it.

Wait. That didn't make sense.

I blinked my eyes open. The first thing I saw was skin. Lots of taut, golden skin stretched over gorgeous muscle. My cheek was resting on said skin. On a perfectly chiseled pec, to be exact. I couldn't see the rest of myself, but it was toasty warm. I was pretty sure my shirt had ridden up, because my stomach was exceptionally hot and pressed against something hard and flat.

Kade's stomach, most likely.

My legs felt weird, contorted as if they'd tried to form a pretzel shape. Except that they weren't alone. They were super hot too, tangled together with what I assumed were Kade's legs. I could feel one of his thighs firmly wedged between mine. It was also tightly pressed to my core, which literally felt like it was on fire.

As for my hands . . .

One of them *definitely* wasn't where I put it last night. It was hot and sweaty and—

Down Kade's pants.

Oh my gods!

I shot fully awake and scrambled to extricate myself. The second I did, Kade's hands halted my movements.

"Don't leave," he sleepily groaned. "I like you here."

With my *hand* down his pants? At least I wasn't holding his dick. But I had to be close. My hand was *super* warm.

"I didn't mean to," I blurted, because this hadn't been my plan at all when I'd asked him to come to bed with me. We'd gone to sleep on separate sides of the bed, but sometime during the night, my subconscious had decided to cuddle with him. And feel him up, apparently.

A chuckle vibrated his chest, one that I felt through every inch of me. "It's okay, shortcake. I'm a cuddler too."

Gah. That didn't make this any better! Especially since his reassurance made me want to forget my embarrassment and keep cuddling him. But cuddling could quickly lead to other things, and with the way I was currently feeling, it would. Plus, his dick was literally *inches* from my fingers. If I didn't pull away soon, I was going to accidentally touch it. And then I'd want to touch it some more. And maybe put it in my—

"Isla."

I craned my neck to look up at him. "Hmm?"

"I can smell your arousal. And with your hand in my pants, I'm having a hard time not responding. So if you don't want this to turn into sex, we should probably stop cuddling."

Alrighty, then. So we were thinking the same thing. Which meant that he was horny too. Which meant that his dick was probably rock hard, and I really *really* wanted to see it. Okay, I seriously needed to stop thinking about his dick.

Forcing my hand to retreat, I stayed silent for a lengthy moment to clear my mind. "Maybe," I haltingly began. "Maybe we should take things slow."

The second I said the words, I wanted to kick myself, especially since I was still horny as hell. I was an Andrews. Andrews lived in the fast lane. We didn't know the meaning of slow. Every instinct wailed at me to take back the words, to shove my hand down his pants again and grab what I wanted. Knowing he would willingly *give* me what I wanted only made things ten times worse.

I was used to getting what I wanted. My dad and brother had spoiled me rotten after my mom had died. Which was why fighting my blood cravings was extra hard for me. And why being stuck on this island had caused a mental breakdown.

I wasn't accustomed to enduring pain. To denying myself. To *sacrifice*. Not willingly anyway.

But with Kade . . .

I didn't want to screw this up, whatever this was. I was growing more than a little attached to him, and I didn't think the sire bond had anything to do with it. I was still scared, still terrified that I'd lose who I was. But at the same time, he made me feel good about myself. He didn't see me as a killer or a half-feral monster.

He saw *me*, Isla Andrews.

And he somehow loved who I was, flaws and all.

I couldn't jeopardize that by diving headfirst into sex with him. I needed to carefully think things through and not let lust cloud my judgment. He deserved that. Deserved to be treated with the same respect he'd given me. It wouldn't be easy, but I needed to listen to my heart for once, not my crazy libido. I needed . . .

I needed to take things slow.

"Is that okay?" I asked him, suddenly nervous that I'd pushed his patience too far. He'd already waited five years for me. The poor guy must have some seriously blue balls by now.

He abruptly rolled us over, trapping me beneath him. "Take all the time you need, shortcake. I can go slow," he murmured, then captured my lips in a deep, toe-curling kiss.

My stomach went crazy with butterflies. He found my hands and threaded his fingers through mine, pushing them into the mattress either side of my head. I gripped his fingers tightly as he continued to slowly shower me with mind-drugging kisses, full and sensual ones that robbed me of air. I whimpered when he pulled back a little too far. He chuckled and rewarded me with another breath-stealing kiss.

Just when my head started to grow fuzzy, along with my recent decision, he broke the kiss. As I struggled to catch my breath, he whispered, "How was that?"

I opened my mouth to reply, but only a breathless whimper emerged.

A slow and wicked grin curled the corners of his mouth. "I'll take that as your approval." Kissing me one final time, he rolled off the bed and stood.

I immediately wanted to whimper again, sad that I was no longer cocooned in his warmth. At the same time, I was happy to see that he no longer looked ready to keel over from exhaustion. Sharing a bed with him had been a good decision. Finally finding my voice, I said, "Where are you going?"

"To take a very cold shower," he said over his shoulder. Halfway across the room, he dropped his pants, then continued toward the door as if nothing had happened. As if he wasn't now fully *nude*.

"*Kade*," I squeaked, and covered my eyes. Then uncovered them. No way was I missing this strip show! Seriously though. I could bounce a billion quarters off that perfectly sculpted backside. I wanted to try. Starting right now. Okay, *focus*. I needed to set some ground rules, or taking things slow was going to be impossible. "You can't just walk around naked."

He grabbed the doorknob before glancing back at me with an

innocent expression. "Why not?"

"Because I'm way too horny to see you like that," I openly admitted, huffing when he barked a laugh. "Kade, I'm being serious. This is already hard enough, and without my vibrator, I can't relieve all this pressure."

At the sudden shift in his expression, my eyes narrowed.

"You took it, didn't you?" At his silence, I scrambled out of bed and shrieked, "Kade Carmichael, why did you take my vibrator?"

Still holding the doorknob, he at least had the courtesy to look guilty. But the last thing I expected him to admit was, "Because I was jealous."

My jaw dropped. "You were jealous of a vibrator?"

He shrugged. "It could give you what I couldn't."

All I could do was gape. Good goddess, he was serious. It shouldn't, but his confession made me super wet. I pressed my aching thighs together. "Where is it now?" I finally managed to say, my voice huskier than normal.

His eyes brightened at the sound. "I broke it."

I should be angry at the confession, but I was too turned on.

"You're torturing me," I whispered, leaning against the bed as my legs turned to jelly.

Unsuccessfully hiding a smirk, he opened the door then. But before he left, he looked back and said one last thing. Something that nearly made me orgasm on the spot.

"When you're ready for more, Isla, just say the word. I'll give you all the relief you'll ever need."

A pattern started to form over the following days.

I'd wake up snuggled against Kade, my body hot and horny for him. We'd kiss a little. Or a *lot*. But kept our hands to ourselves. Mostly. It was getting harder not to touch him. Even harder not asking him to touch me. But taking things slow let me learn and appreciate things about him I might have missed if we were constantly boning.

Like the fact that he had impressive restraint. He woke up every morning with a painfully swollen cock and never once tried to seduce me. As much as I wanted him to, I respected him more and more for not pushing me.

He was also extremely thoughtful, asking me if I needed anything before starting his day. After my feral experience, I'd decided not to deny myself his blood. So I always asked for that, feeding from his arm and not his neck, per my request.

He also shared personal things about himself while we cuddled in bed, like how he hated green olives and secretly enjoyed listening to Taylor Swift. I shared things with him too, like how I had an irrational fear of lobsters—which was dumb, since Maine was literally the seafood capital. We swapped stories about our childhoods, and I found out he used to have a pony named Pumpkin. He roared with laughter when I told him about my short emo phase, confessing that I used to have a tongue ring. He didn't seem disgusted by that *at all*, not surprisingly.

One morning, I woke up to him staring at me, a faint smile on his face.

"What?" I'd groggily said. "Was I drooling?"

Instead of answering, he'd tucked some hair behind my ear and said, "You never changed your nickname."

I'd stretched, blinking the sleep from my eyes before admitting, "It grew on me. Kind of like you."

When I'd glanced over again, his pleased smile had been so

adorable that I'd grabbed his face and peppered kisses all over it. He'd eagerly responded in kind, showering me with kisses until the need for *other* things became too hard to ignore. We'd gotten really good at taking cold showers. *Separately*, of course.

With each passing day, I felt more and more like my old self. I would always crave blood, but I felt less like its slave now. My need for it had grown manageable. As long as I didn't deprive myself for too long, I was pretty sure I could once again control my bloodlust.

I was in no hurry to test my newfound confidence though. For once in my life, I was actually content to remain exactly where I was. The island wasn't paradise by any means, but spending these last several days with Kade—getting to know him on a deeper level and exploring my feelings for him—had calmed my usual need to remain perpetually in motion.

During the day when I was sequestered indoors, he'd scout the island's perimeter and practice with Betty. I'd spy on him on occasion, shamelessly peeping through the curtains while he swung the silver sword like a Norse god. I could have easily spent my days watching him until the sun set and it was *my* turn to train, but I'd decided to try my hand at cooking. With how busy my private investigator work had kept me over the years, I barely knew how to boil an egg. But Kade's comment about hobbies had made me realize how narrow-minded I'd been.

There was more to life than work, and I was slowly yet surely beginning to see that for myself. I knew hardships still awaited us the moment we left this island. I knew sword training and cooking would become side pursuits once I faced the real world and its many problems again. But I wouldn't get lost in my work like I had before.

If I somehow didn't end up in a supernatural prison after this, then I intended to live my life more fully. No more hiding from my problems by burying myself in work. No more making excuses about why I couldn't pursue the life my human self had always wanted.

Kade had been right. I'd been given a second chance at life. I shouldn't waste it with what-ifs. Time for me to face my future head on, no matter how scared I was.

It was on the seventh day when I had a culinary breakthrough. We hadn't brought many food supplies with us, but there just happened to be enough of the ingredients I needed. With the help of a really old cookbook I'd found tucked in a cupboard, I'd managed to bake something that tasted halfway decent. It wasn't even burnt.

Best of all, I knew it was Kade's favorite.

Nerves fluttered in my stomach as I waited for the sun to set. He usually stayed out until then, giving me space to work in the kitchen alone. Probably so the sexual tension between us didn't reach a boiling point. See? Extremely thoughtful.

When I finally heard his heavy footfalls just outside the front door, my heart jumped with nervous excitement. I'd never done something like this before. Never made something for a guy I liked. My heart nearly stopped at my inward admission. Then started up again with a jolt when the truth of the words rang true.

I liked Kade. A *lot*. Not just as a friend either. This thing between us was growing, blossoming into something more. And I liked it. I *really* liked it. What's more, it no longer filled me with paralyzing fear. Somewhere along the way, I'd let go of the terror. Maybe because I didn't feel lost with him. I was still me. Still myself. He hadn't tried to control me in the slightest. I was my own person, a person I was starting to like again.

And I had him to thank. Through his unwavering patience, he'd led me back to myself, and that made me fall for him all the more. So much more that I was finally ready for the next step in our relationship.

Not only had I baked him his favorite dish, but I'd primped in front of the bathroom mirror for two hours, carefully applying my makeup and brushing my hair until it fell in soft waves.

After learning one night that his favorite color was blue, I'd carefully chosen my outfit for the day. The color of my top perfectly matched my eyes, sheer at the sleeves and cut low to reveal a healthy amount of cleavage. My skirt was frilly and white, falling to mid thigh. I hadn't worn it in years and was surprised to find it packed among my things.

Probably by accident when I'd hurriedly grabbed some stuff from my ransacked apartment. I was glad for it though. The outfit made me feel pretty and fresh and ready to pursue Kade more fully.

As the safehouse door started to open, I smoothed a hand down my skirt and straightened my top. A slight tremble shook my hands as I waited for him to see me, to notice what I'd made for him. I probably looked like one of those old-fashioned housewives who greeted their man with a home-cooked meal the second he came through the door, but I didn't even care.

He'd opened my eyes in so many ways. The least I could do was show him how much that meant to me.

The second I saw him, my face lit up and my stomach went crazy. Okay, I'd fallen for him a little harder than I'd thought. At the sight of me, he froze in the doorway to stare, clearly surprised. I let him look his fill, feeling an actual *blush* rise to my cheeks as he did. After a long moment, he said, "What's the occasion?"

I shrugged, unsuccessfully hiding a smile. "Just wanted to look nice for a change."

He slowly looked me up and down again before saying, "You always look nice, Isla, but I do enjoy seeing you in that outfit, so thank you."

At his praise, I blushed harder. "You're welcome," I said with a little curtsy, then stepped aside to reveal the fruits of my labor. "Also, ta-da! I made you a cheesecake."

I'd never seen him look more stunned. His throat worked as he silently took in the slightly lopsided confection. My nerves eventually got the best of me and I started blathering. "It's not *amazing* or anything. We didn't have strawberries and a few other ingredients, so I had to improvise. I'm sure you've had much much better, but . . ."

I stopped when he quietly closed the door and approached. His Adam's apple continued to bob, as if he were having a hard time swallowing. I expected his gaze to be on the cake—it was his favorite food group, after all—but it fixed on me and stayed there.

Which allowed me a clear view of his expression, and the emotions brewing in his sky blue eyes. At the unmistakable love there, a lump formed in my throat. I tipped my head back as he halted in front of me and simply stared. Stared and stared before drawing in a ragged breath and whispering, "It's perfect."

Then he collapsed.

CHAPTER 26

ISLA

My body felt made out of ice as I watched him fall.

Internally, I screamed as he hit the floor with a jarring thud. Outwardly, my body remained frozen solid. It was too shocking. Too unbelievable to see such a strong man go down so hard. I'd seen it once before when his arm had been ripped off. I'd frozen then too. I couldn't wrap my head around a weak and vulnerable Kade.

It couldn't be real. Nothing knocked Kade Carmichael down.

But here he was again, fallen at my feet, shaking uncontrollably.

The sight of him trembling was what snapped me out of it. He was in *pain*.

Gasping his name, I landed on my knees beside him. "What's wrong? What is it?"

When he groaned and struggled to push himself up, I helped him into a sitting position. He slumped against the kitchen cabinets, propping his arms on his bent knees. "It's been too long," he finally rasped.

"What has?"

"Since I last had blood."

I drew a blank, sputtering, "Well, where's your supply? I'll get you some."

He barked a humorless laugh, then groaned again. "There is no supply, Isla."

"Because you drank it all?"

"Because I never *brought* any."

Panic tightened my chest. "But . . . but that doesn't make any sense. I thought you hid your supply while I wasn't looking. I never asked because I didn't want to be tempted into looking for it. What were you *thinking* coming here without blood, Kade?"

"I was thinking," he heaved out, slowly lifting his head to meet my eyes, "that I didn't want to tempt you. That I would survive the same way you are." Oh no. The blood drained from my face. "I was thinking that I'd feed on you, the same way you've been feeding on me."

My eyes were wide as I stared at him, as I tried to come to terms with what he was saying. All this time, I hadn't bothered to ask. All this time, he'd been starving, silently bearing his misery while helping me get better. All this time, I'd been the most selfish person possible, focusing on myself without noticing how much pain he was in.

"Oh, Kade," I whispered, unable to hide my tears. "I'm so sorry."

He shook his head. "There's no need to be sorry. I knew this might happen when I agreed to come here."

I clenched my hands into fists, suddenly angry. "*Seriously?* And how did you plan to survive?"

"Isla, I'm fine," he said, softening his voice, which only made me angrier. "I was blessed with exceptionally high stamina. I can survive on this island much longer than this. I just overdid it with my training today."

"But you haven't fed in over a *week*," I snapped, jumping to my feet so I could glare down at him. "I can't imagine how much pain you're in right now."

He searched my face before saying, "I'm good with pain, Isla. It's one of my strengths. Even so, I'd endure much more for you."

I stiffened as I finally realized why he hadn't told me about this

224

earlier. "It's me. You haven't asked to feed on me because I'm afraid of being bitten." When he looked away, I knew I was right.

Feeling like I was about to explode, I lurched forward and yanked open a kitchen drawer.

"Isla, what are you—?"

I grabbed the sharpest knife I could find and aimed the tip at my wrist.

"*Isla.*"

"Let me *do* this, Kade," I yelled, digging the blade in. At the sharp bite of pain, I hissed and yanked the knife back. Furious at myself, I brought the knife down again, only to cringe away before it could cut me. After several more tries, I screamed and threw the knife across the room.

"Isla, you don't have to—"

"*Shut up*, Kade. You're drinking my blood," I shouted, grabbing another knife. "Here." I thrust the knife at him. "You do it."

"Isla," he said, shaking his head again.

"So help me, Kade," I growled, crouching so I could force the knife into his hand. "Think of *yourself*, for once. Think of your own needs."

He snorted. "I have. Why do you think I'm on this island with you? I've been thinking about myself a *lot* lately."

"And I've made you pay dearly for it, but that ends now."

His gaze sharpened. "What are you saying?"

"I'm saying that I want you to take what you've earned," I replied, working to gentle my voice. "I'm saying that I think . . . I think it's safe for me to fall for you now."

Every inch of him froze. He thoroughly searched my face, checking for any signs of hesitation, of *doubt*, before slowly saying, "You think?"

I shook my head, smiling a little. "I know."

He was silent for several moments, still as a statue as he continued to stare at me. Finally, he set the knife on the floor and whispered, "Then come here, shortcake. I need to feed."

My heart wildly thundered, both with fear and excitement as it became clear what his intentions were. He didn't want to cut me. He wanted to *bite* me.

Deep down, I knew that vampires craved being bitten. That a bite for them didn't hurt like it did for humans. That it was the ultimate pleasurable experience, even without venom. I was still scared of how vulnerable it would make me, but the thought of Kade biting me right now didn't make me want to run. He could have forced me so many times into letting him bite me. He had the ability. I wouldn't have been able to stop him.

Yet, he'd suffered in silence instead, putting my needs before his own once again. And so I decided then that if anyone was going to bite me, I wanted Kade to do it. I knew I could trust him to be gentle.

And, most importantly, I didn't have anything to fear from him.

At the startling realization, all the air fled my lungs. He seemed to sense that I'd come to a realization, because he offered me his hand. I readily took it, letting him guide me forward and onto his lap. When I was straddling his hips, he reached up and stroked my cheek, maintaining eye contact.

I slowly started to relax against him as his fingers continued to stroke my jaw, then my hair, gently drawing it over my shoulder. As his fingers gradually slipped to my neck, I shivered. He paused, then carefully grasped my nape and eased me toward him. As his head dipped toward my exposed neck, I grabbed his shoulders and dug my nails in.

"Easy, shortcake," he breathed, his warm breath skittering across my sensitive skin. "I won't hurt you."

I knew that, but my instincts were still going crazy. When he trailed his nose up my neck, I sucked in a surprised hiss. A second later, his lips found my skin, pressing soft kisses there. The moment I started to relax again, I felt the gentle scrape of a fang. My eyes flew wide and I went stiff as a board. But before I could panic, his fangs swiftly sank into my neck.

A scream stuck in my throat as memory after memory of the horrific time I'd been bitten and drained battered my mind.

And then it was over.

Euphoria quickly replaced the pain and I moaned, arching my body into Kade's. Taking that as a good sign, he sank his fangs in deeper and took his first pull from my neck. The feeling of his mouth sucking my skin, sucking my *blood*, sent more pleasure barreling through me and my eyes rolled back.

Good goddess, why had I been so afraid of this? It was pure ecstasy.

At the first taste of me, Kade groaned, shuddering violently. His reaction only fueled mine, and I gave myself fully to the moment. As if sensing my surrender, he held me to him tightly, so tightly that I couldn't tell where I ended and he began. I melted into the embrace, panting as he began to feed in earnest. Every pull sent spikes of bliss shooting through me, driving me so high that I forgot how to breathe.

Drinking blood often gave me a wicked high, but I'd never experienced anything like *this*. I felt like energy itself, lighter than air and charged with electricity. Nothing could touch me, because I was invincible. Every molecule in my body buzzed, and I instinctively sought to ease some of the growing pressure.

With my skirt bunched around my waist, the only thing separating my core from Kade's hard shaft was his jeans and my silk panties. I pressed against him and immediately cried out, nearly coming on the spot. My body was beyond sensitive, every nerve ending raw and hyperaware. I saw stars as he palmed my butt and squeezed, grinding himself more fully against me.

Then something unexpected happened. Even *more* euphoria blasted through me, so intense that I shot skyhigh and shattered. My body shook as I climaxed prematurely, swift and *hard*.

Kade immediately retracted his fangs and pulled back, holding my head as I continued to ride the orgasm. It went on and on, pumping through my body like . . .

Like venom.

The second I realized what Kade had done, an image pierced my brain. A memory. But not a memory that I remembered. It was of me on the back of a motorcycle, clinging to the man driving the bike. A skull with fiery eyes and the name Highway Demons was etched onto the back of his leather jacket.

As the memory faded, I gasped and jerked my eyes open.

"I'm so sorry, Isla," Kade was saying as I fought to catch my breath. "My instincts got the better of me and I—No, there's no excuse for this. You're not mine to claim and I never should have—"

"Do it again," I panted, grabbing onto his shirt.

When he just gaped at me in shock, I shook him a little.

"Do it *again*, Kade. I need your venom."

"Isla, what are you—?"

"Gods, we don't have *time* for this. I need to remember, Kade. Your venom helps me remember."

"Remember *what*, Isla?" he demanded, taken aback by my frantic urgency.

"The night of the murder!" I yelled, shaking him once more. "Please. Please help me remember. Please *bite* me. I need to know. I *need* to."

At my desperate plea, he blew out a sigh and did as I asked. As his fangs sank into my neck again, I didn't even flinch, too focused on dredging up another lost memory.

"Your venom, Kade," I groaned, feeling the effects of the bite steal over me. "I need your venom."

He immediately pumped his venom inside me, making my eyes roll back once more. Another memory hit. This time, I was inside a vaguely familiar room. A man stood before me, but not just any man. It was Gunner Landry, my murder case victim.

And he was *alive*.

Suddenly, a dark figure blurred toward him and struck. Gunner remained motionless as the figure viciously bit into his neck and began to feed. While the vampire ravenously drank, I couldn't see their face. Their identity eluded me as I stood like a statue and watched Gunner Landry grow weaker and weaker. When his eyes glazed over and he went limp, the dark figure picked him up and dropped him on the bed.

The *motel* bed.

We were at the crime scene, and I was firsthand witnessing the *murder*.

I was suddenly moving, heading toward the bed as Gunner's attacker smeared a little blood over the bite wound on his neck. The twin punctures immediately sealed shut. Next, he whipped out a handkerchief and, with a gloved hand, carefully rubbed the freshly healed skin clean.

Then he stepped back and I was moving again, bending over Gunner to position my mouth at his neck. For a split second, I hesitated. And in that split second, I realized one thing with absolute clarity.

Gunner Landry's heart wasn't beating.

He was already dead.

But my fangs dropped and I bit him anyway. I tried to feed, only managing to taste the last dredges of his blood. When I pulled away, the dark figure was gone. Without a sound, I left the room and closed the door shut behind me.

I released a strangled cry as my vision cleared. As the safehouse kitchen came into focus. Kade immediately retracted his fangs again and pulled away to give me a concerned look.

"Please tell me what's going on," he said, cupping my face when I struggled to breathe.

"It wasn't," I began, my voice trembling with emotion. "It wasn't *me*. I didn't kill him. Kade, it was someone else. Another vampire drained Gunner Landry. I'm not . . . I'm not a murderer," I finished with a whisper.

And then, I started to cry.

CHAPTER 27

KADE

It was like a part of Isla had been dead before.

But the moment she'd said the words, "I'm not a murderer," she came fully alive. I couldn't stop staring at the difference it made in her. She'd always been vibrant and animated, both as a human and vampire, but I hadn't realized how *subdued* she'd been the last couple of weeks.

She was talking a mile a minute now, wildly gesturing with her hands as she told me about the missing memories. I'd never once thought she was capable of murder, but news of her innocence still flooded me with relief. She hadn't even finished speaking before I shot to my feet, pulling her with.

As I fished a phone from my jeans, she paused to ogle it. "You've had a *phone* this entire time?"

"Just a satellite phone. How else were we going to get home?" I told her with a wink, quickly dialing Loch's number.

He answered on the second ring.

"Is it safe to talk?" I said by way of a greeting.

"Yes."

"We need to be picked up. Tonight, if possible."

"Be there in a couple hours."

When I ended the call, Isla was looking up at me with wide eyes.

"We're leaving?" she whispered, the words filled with disbelief. Something else too. Fear, maybe.

I set the phone down and snaked an arm around her waist, pulling her soft curves against me. I paused to inhale her scent, now diluted with mine from my accidental claiming. She didn't seem to mind having my scent beneath her skin, but we hadn't been able to properly talk about it yet—or process the fact that we'd *both* unintentionally claimed each other. Still, possessiveness rumbled in my chest when I smelled the claim, and I fitted her more fully against me.

"You're ready," I quietly assured her, reaching up to tuck a lock of blonde and pink hair behind her ear. "Your bloodlust is under control, and it's time we cleared your name."

"But I still don't know who the killer is. Without an identity, I have no proof of my innocence. You should bite me again. I'm still missing memories."

My gaze hungrily latched onto her neck when she tugged her hair to the side. Swallowing roughly, I forced myself to say, "We should hold off on that for a while. I've already given you way too much venom."

I internally groaned as she said, "I don't mind."

"Vampires can become addicted to venom the same way humans can, Isla. I don't want you to feel controlled by me."

She looked startled for a moment. Then, without explanation, she rose up on tiptoe and kissed my chin.

It was my turn to look startled. "What was that for?"

"You always say what I need to hear. I just wanted to express how much that means to me."

I felt my mouth stretch into a lopsided grin. "Then I should talk more often so you can keep expressing yourself."

She huffed a laugh, then sighed and said, "Guess we should start packing."

At the sadness in her voice, I frowned. "I thought you'd be happy to leave this place."

"I am, but life is so much simpler here. And . . ." Her gaze dropped. After a lengthy inhale, she blurted, "I don't want things to change between us. I don't want us to go our separate ways again."

My heart soared at her open admission. I knew we'd grown closer over the past couple of weeks, but her words were proof that she had feelings for me. The realization made me want to whoop loudly and kiss her senseless.

But she needed reassurance right now. Comfort. And I readily offered both, bending to kiss her forehead and whisper, "I'm not going anywhere, shortcake. You're stuck with me for as long as you want me."

The second Loch, Isla, and I walked through the castle's front doors, Kenna, Silver, and Everett were there to greet us. I kept my hand firmly wrapped around Isla's, in case the sight of Kenna triggered any lingering feral behavior. I listened to her breathing, relieved when it remained even.

"Welcome back," Kenna said, looking even more pregnant than the last time I saw her. I glanced at her swollen belly, gratified when I caught the trilling *thump-thump* of twin heartbeats. We still didn't know their genders or what manner of supernatural they were, but they were both healthy and strong. Kenna was faring well with the pregnancy, even thriving. It helped that she was doted upon hand and foot by three protective males, not to mention her parents and the king.

When I felt a pang in my chest, I looked back up at her face. Curiosity flitted through our bond as she subtly glanced between me and Isla, her eyebrows raised in question. When I slowly grinned, hope thrummed through the bond. I watched her silver eyes brighten, quickly filling with tears as I tugged Isla into my arms. Isla willingly melted into the embrace, tilting her face up toward mine.

My grin turned wicked. Winking at Kenna, I threaded my fingers into Isla's hair and brought my mouth down on hers. She sucked in a surprised gasp, but didn't resist as I passionately kissed her in front of everyone. When I eventually broke the kiss, I was pleased at how uneven her breaths had become. I glanced at Kenna again to see her grinning from ear to ear.

"*Finally*," she said, so loud that I threw back my head and roared with laughter.

CHAPTER 28

ISLA

I squirmed in my seat. Not because everyone in the king's office now knew that Kade and I had claimed each other, but because Kade was misbehaving.

This was supposed to be a *serious* meeting. Even the king was in attendance. At least my dad and brother weren't here. They'd definitely know something fishy was going on. Especially Noah. I'd spent the last hour retelling the group everything I'd already told Kade about my phone stalker. Now, we were discussing how Kade's venom had unlocked my repressed memories. Except that Kade had taken over speaking halfway through because I couldn't anymore.

Literally couldn't.

I'd completely lost the ability to talk when he'd placed his hand on my bare leg. The huge meeting table we were gathered around hid the move, but I was struggling to keep my face neutral. Every few seconds, his fingers would slowly inch higher up my leg. They were now beneath my white skirt, lightly tickling my upper thigh.

As he spoke, I squirmed again, which only shifted his fingers higher. I would have batted them away, but they felt too good. Plus, the barely-hidden PDA was intoxicating. I never thought I'd enjoy public touching like this, but I did. A *lot*.

"I wonder if the sire bond has something to do with it," Kade was saying, lazily stroking the skin of my inner thigh now. My core clenched at the contact, at how close he was to touching *there*. The spot that yearned for his touch the most.

I perked up at his words, wondering if he was right. How else could his venom have affected me so much?

Across from us, Loch leaned forward and said, "It's possible. A strong bond can break through mostly anything. McKenna was able to resist Troy's thrall long enough to mindspeak with me that time he kidnapped her. A sire bond isn't equal to a soulmate bond, but the same principles apply. The closer the two individuals become, the more powerful their bond becomes."

"Like our drothen bond," Kade said, continuing to sweep his fingers over my inner thigh.

"Exactly. We can share each other's strengths and feel each other's emotions far better than we could a century ago."

"The question is," Everett said from beside his younger brother, "how come Isla can't see the killer's face? Does the sire bond need to be stronger before she can fully regain her memories?"

Kade's fingers stilled.

"That makes sense," Loch replied without missing a beat. "Her subconscious could still be repressing memories she doesn't want to remember. A stronger bond could override that."

"But what does that mean?" Kenna spoke from Loch's other side, flicking a glance between me and Kade. "How can they strengthen their bond?"

Everett loudly cleared his throat, as if covering up a laugh. Even the king chuckled softly. A faint smile tugged at Loch's mouth before he said, "A close, intimate connection always works best."

Kenna's eyes widened, as did mine. "How close?" she had the guts to ask when I couldn't.

"He means sex," Kade said for all the world to hear. And with a straight *face*, no less.

"What are you doing?"

"Finishing what I started," he purred, gently nipping at my earlobe. Tingles erupted over my skin, traveling all the way down my body. I sucked in a quiet gasp, then another as his fingers slid higher and higher and higher. My heart started pounding like crazy, my anticipation building. I'd ached for his touch for so long, and now, I was finally ready. Every inch of me wanted this. Not simply for the pleasure it would give me, but for the deeper connection I'd feel with him. I yearned for that closeness, a closeness I'd never expected us to have.

But here we were, and there was no place I'd rather be. Pressed against a piano with Kade pressed against me. Our hearts thundering fiercely as we crossed new lines and, one-by-one, tore down the barriers between us.

Just before his fingers could reach my aching center, a sharp knock dispelled the moment.

"Kade, I need to speak with Isla," Loch's voice came through the door.

A long sigh fled Kade's nose. "Can it wait a few minutes?" he called back. Despite the need still pulsing through me, I struggled to hide a smirk.

"No, it's important."

With a quiet groan, Kade pulled his hand from my skirt and straightened. "Come in."

As the doors swung open, I scrambled to find my composure, adjusting my top and skirt before pushing off the piano. Loch strode in and immediately paused to audibly inhale.

Ah crap.

"Sorry for the intrusion," he said after a beat, a slight smile tugging at his mouth. "But I have a few questions for Isla that can't wait."

My lips suddenly unfroze, and I was blathering before I could stop myself. "But we're not soulmates. How can having sex strengthen a sire bond? You and Loch didn't need to have sex to strengthen your drothen bond."

Kade finally broke, loudly guffawing. His fingers resumed stroking my skin. "When anything supernaturally binds two souls, intention is what truly matters. Loch and I were never romantically interested in each other. We see each other as brothers, so our bond is platonic. You and I, on the other hand," he said, sliding his fingers up so high that they grazed the edge of my panties, "aren't exactly platonic."

At the swift jolt of pleasure the contact brought, I sucked in a quiet gasp. Desire flooded my body, soaking my panties with arousal. When the four large males in the room abruptly shifted in their seats, I threw Kenna a panicked look. By the way her lips were firmly pressed together, unsuccessfully hiding a smile, I knew that our secret PDA wasn't so secret anymore.

"Let's discuss living arrangements for Isla until she's able to identify the killer," King Ambrose said as if nothing had happened. "As you all know, Bill and Noah Andrews aren't here on account of the SCA's close monitorization. That doesn't mean Sanctum Isle isn't being closely watched though. Any whisper of Isla's presence here could mean harsh scrutiny for us all. They still want her brought in for questioning, not to mention face justice for an alleged murder and attempted murder of a fellow colleague. Until her full memories are restored, we have no proof to contradict their claims."

"She stays here in the castle," Loch spoke again, his tone brooking no argument. "We can keep the SCA in the dark a little while longer."

"What about her bloodlust?" Everett said, bringing up the elephant in the room. "We haven't tested her control yet."

"Kade can watch me," I chimed in, drawing surprised looks. I too was surprised at how readily I made the suggestion, but it made sense. My need for independence shouldn't jeopardize everyone's safety.

Besides, this situation wasn't permanent. I was determined to regain all of my memories and get my life back in order. Yes, I'd made several mistakes that would have to be answered for, but I hadn't actually *killed* anyone. Even if the SCA never employed me again, I was at least going to clear my name of murder, pick up the pieces, and start fresh.

"I can agree to that," Kade said, studying me closely. "Under one condition."

"And what's that?" the king said.

"No one pressures Isla into having sex with me."

Oh. My. Gods.

Mortified, all I could do was speechlessly gape at him.

"Deal," the king casually said, as if Kade had simply mentioned the weather. "We'll hold off the SCA for as long as we can, but be aware that the clock is ticking. The sooner Isla identifies the killer, the sooner we can lock them up and repair the alliance."

Which basically boiled down to: *Hurry up and have sex, you two, so we can get on with our lives.*

The meeting adjourned soon after that, thankfully with no more talk about sex. The second we were free of the king's office, I grabbed Kade's hand and dragged him after me. I was dying to chat with my best friend, but we'd have to catch up later. A certain *bonehead* needed a piece of my mind first.

Not wanting to be overheard, I marched all the way down the long hall. At the end was a music room with a grand piano gracing its center. I yanked Kade inside and firmly shut the double doors.

Whirling, I wasted no time lighting into him.

"*Seriously*, Kade?" I whisper-yelled, poking at his chest. "You think someone's going to *pressure* me into having sex with you? I'll have sex when I *want* to have sex. Not a moment sooner. And what was with all the touching? The *king* was in there, for heaven's sake!"

Grinning unapologetically, he grabbed my finger to tug me closer. "Admit it. You thought it was hot."

I yanked my finger back. "That's not the point. *Focus* here, Kade." When his arm snaked toward my waist, I spun out of his reach, ending up behind him. He turned to face me, challenge dancing in his eyes. "Look, the touching in public thing might have turned me on a little, but—"

"A little?" Kade interrupted, easing into my personal space again.

"But it was still *embarrassing*," I finished, retreating a step. Then another.

He pursued me across the room, still grinning like a fiend. "I didn't see you blushing. In fact, all I saw was how speechless it made you."

My butt smacked into the side of the piano, and Kade lunged before I could change directions, trapping me against it. My breath caught as he pressed into me, one hand gripping my waist while the other splayed on top of the piano.

"I wasn't speechless," I breathlessly argued, gripping the edge of the piano instead of shoving him away. "I was perfectly capable of—aahh!"

I cried out as his hand abruptly left my waist and slid beneath my skirt.

"What's wrong, shortcake?" he crooned, bending to whisper in my ear, "Cat got your tongue?"

As his fingers slowly inched up my thigh, I managed to gasp,

"It's fine," Kade smoothly said, seemingly unaffected by what almost happened between us. Until he slid behind me and leaned against the piano, snaking an arm around my middle to pull me against him. Right away, I felt his rock hard length press into my backside, which only made my heart start pounding again. He quietly chuckled at my reaction before saying to Loch, "Where's Kenna?"

"Getting ready for bed. The pregnancy has been tiring her out a lot lately. She wants to see you first thing tomorrow though," he said, directing his attention to me. "I tried to caution her but she's done keeping her distance. Can I trust you around her?"

I swallowed, barely able to hold his intense gaze. I didn't know how Kenna managed it. "Yes," I said, relieved when the word actually felt true. "But I understand if you don't want to leave her alone with me."

"I don't want to leave her alone with anyone," he honestly replied, "but you're her best friend and she trusts you. If I try to keep you two apart, she'll only sneak in to see you behind my back."

Kade and I snorted in unison.

"You both can keep an eye on us. I don't mind."

He nodded his thanks, then quietly closed the doors. "During our meeting earlier, you said something that got me thinking." He paused for a moment, then plowed ahead. "What was the last thing you remember before blacking out the first time?"

Caught off guard by the probing question, I froze, drawing a blank.

"No detail is too small, Isla," he encouraged. "Anything you can remember will be helpful."

I hesitated another beat, trying to recall exactly what I'd been doing before my memories went on the fritz. When it came to me, heat rose to my face. Oh, this wasn't good. Loch should have asked to speak with me alone. Not that it mattered in the long run. He would eventually tell Kade anyway.

Clearing my suddenly dry throat, I forced myself to spit out, "I was in the bathroom at Mike's Tavern with a guy." Kade's entire body stiffened. *Crap.* "We were . . . fooling around a bit. Mostly kissing. I'd had too much to drink. But before he could go too far, I stopped him."

Loch scrutinized my face closely, making me want to squirm. "What happened after that? Did he say anything?"

"Only that he understood when I said we were going too fast. Oh, and he gave me his number, but I told him the next day that I only wanted to be friends."

Kade's hand on my stomach slowly curled into a fist. Loch noticed the move, but didn't comment, choosing instead to say, "What happened when you left the bathroom?"

"I . . ." I paused to gather my memories of that night, new and old. After a long moment, my eyes flew wide. "I-I don't remember."

Loch's gaze hardened. "Was the guy you were with a vampire?"

"I . . . yes. Why?"

"What did he look like?"

"Tall, athletic build. Pale skin. Reddish black hair. Light brown eyes that almost look gold."

"What was his name?"

Alarmed at his brusque tone, I stammered, "S-Samuel. Samuel Quinn."

Kade's arm tightened around me when Loch went rigid. "What's wrong, Lochie?"

He shook his head, his expression one of stunned disbelief. "I haven't heard that name in a long time."

I blinked in surprise. "You know him?"

"I know *of* him. No one's seen or heard from him in nearly five centuries."

My jaw dropped.

Kade swore. "So what are you saying, Loch? What does this guy have to do with Isla blacking out?"

"If my theory is right, I don't think she blacked out at all."

"Then what happened?" I whispered, dread souring my gut when Loch pinned me with a severe look.

"I think you were allured by an Ancient."

CHAPTER 29

KADE

At Loch's words, something flooded my body. An emotion I rarely felt.

Rage.

Isla was understandably confused, asking what allure and Ancients were. I, on the other hand, was trying not to lose it. When my body began to uncontrollably shake, I stepped away from the piano and her, not wanting to freak her out. While Loch started to explain about a history few actually knew about, I worked on dragging in air. On cooling the heat surging through my veins.

"Ancients are Venturi who have become something more. They get that way from honing their skills over the course of several centuries."

"Several?" Isla squeaked, her eyes round like saucers.

Loch nodded. "They are the oldest of our kind, so old that we have no known record of their origins. Some say that Ancients don't come into their power until well over their four-thousandth year. But there have been so few of them recorded in history that we can't know for certain. Most vampires don't live that long. Cause of death varies, but living past a couple thousand years is rare."

"Wow. Okay," Isla said, casting me a worried look. "So there are a few *really* old vampires still in existence. What kind of skills do they have, exactly?"

"Superior senses and strength, more so than the most powerful

Venturi. A tolerance to silver. Exceptionally potent venom. And, most notably, the ability to allure."

"What's allure?"

"The ability to thrall vampires," I finally spoke, my voice little more than a guttural growl.

Even from here, I could see the blood leach from her face. As fear sparked in her eyes, I trembled harder, the urge to comfort her overwhelming. But I still felt seconds away from exploding. I didn't want her to see that. To give her one more reason to be afraid.

"They can also allure remotely," Loch added. "The ability is stronger than distance, and even vampire blood."

At the news, Isla weakly sank onto the piano bench. I held still by sheer force of will as she whispered, "The phone calls."

Loch nodded. "That's what tipped me off. You said both the bartender and Saanvi reacted the same way after receiving a phone call. That couldn't have been a coincidence. Then you blacked out twice and supposedly lost control, attacking two humans. To my knowledge, vampires don't black out. Even when they lose control, they're aware of their actions. Repressing the memories to protect yourself makes sense, but why would Kade's venom unlock them? No, it's more likely that the sire bond, triggered by his venom, partially broke through the allure placed upon you."

Isla swallowed several times, her hands noticeably trembling. "If . . . if all of this is true, then . . . then my phone stalker is probably Samuel Quinn. And that would probably also make him . . ."

"The killer," Loch finished for her, the beginnings of compassion stirring in his dark gaze.

When it became clear she was too overwhelmed to speak, I said, "But why her? Why would an elusive, nearly *mythical* Ancient target Isla like this?"

Loch shook his head. "I'm not sure. I only have second-hand knowledge of the tumultuous relationship Lord Samuel Quinn had with my grandfather. All I know is that they had a serious falling out shortly before my grandfather's death. I need to speak with my father about this."

Isla suddenly shot to her feet. "Excuse me," she said, throwing a hand over her mouth. "I think . . . I think I'm going to be sick."

She zoomed across the room at top speed and wrenched open the door, fleeing into the hallway.

The second she vanished from sight, the rage boiling inside me erupted. With a roar, I grabbed the piano and launched it across the room. A deafening *clang*, followed by the shattering of glass, echoed off the walls as the heavy instrument collided with a gilded mirror. Both crashed to the floor in pieces.

After several moments of heavy breathing, I calmed down enough to inspect the damage and grunt, "Sorry."

"Don't worry about it. I've broken far more stuff than you ever will," Loch said, ambling up beside me. We stood in silence, eyeing the wreckage together. "You okay?"

"He touched her. *Touched*. Her."

"I know how awful that feels. I'm sorry."

I blew out a weary sigh. After another moment of silence, I said, "I told her I loved her."

He raised a brow, not looking all that surprised. "How did she respond?"

I rubbed at the back of my neck. "She's getting there."

"I saw," he said, amusement trickling through our bond. I laughed, despite the rage still lingering in my veins. After a moment, he sobered again. "We're here for you. Both of you. Whatever you need, just ask."

I smiled at him, feeling it wobble a bit. "Thanks, Lochie."

"We're drothen, Kade. Your happiness is mine, as is your pain. We'll learn everything we can about this Ancient before finding a way to take him down."

I wordlessly clasped his shoulder, letting him feel through our bond how grateful I was of his support. He clasped my shoulder in return, nodding his encouragement when I broke away and headed for the door.

He already knew without words where I was going. Knew how powerful the pull was to pursue the desires of his heart.

And now, it was my turn.

CHAPTER 30

ISLA

My legs instinctively carried me to Kade's bedroom.

He found me minutes later, still heaving my guts out into his toilet.

I'd never felt more vulnerable. More *violated*. Even the time I'd been drained and killed couldn't compare to this.

I trembled as another wave of nausea hit me.

Fingers were suddenly in my hair, gently pulling the tresses back. In my peripheral, I saw Kade crouch beside me, offering me his comfort. The vulnerable position should have sent me running, but I was done running from him. Done hiding. Done keeping secrets. As his other hand rubbed my back, the cramps in my stomach gradually eased.

When I could finally speak again, I choked out, "He made me his *slave*."

"I know, baby. I'm so sorry," Kade whispered, his voice heavy with remorse as he continued to stroke my back.

"I had no clue. None. He could have done anything to me. *Anything*. And I wouldn't have put up a fight."

His hand began to tremble. "He'll pay for hurting you, Isla. I'll make sure of it."

"How long will the allure last? Does it ever fade away?"

"Eventually. Compulsion is different than spelled magic. It will wear off over time, although allure lasts much longer than thrall."

Bile threatened to surge up my throat again when I realized how close I'd come to having sex with Samuel. He'd wanted to *bite* me. What if . . . what if he'd taken advantage of me after I'd told him no and allured me to forget about it?

Oh, gods.

I heaved again, helplessly clinging to the toilet. "I'm such a clueless idiot."

"No, you're not," Kade said, helping me to my feet when I weakly tried to stand. "You couldn't have known. I knew Ancients existed and still didn't put the pieces together."

"But I'm an investigator. It's my *job* to figure stuff out. I should have known something supernatural caused me to lose my memories. And I wouldn't drain and *kill* someone, no matter how thirsty I was. I just wouldn't."

"I know you wouldn't. And anyone who truly knows you wouldn't think that either." Still supporting me, he flushed the toilet, then reached for a toothbrush. When he loaded it with toothpaste and said, "Open," I let him place it in my mouth.

I fell silent for a moment, taking the toothbrush from him to clean my teeth. When I leaned over the sink to spit, he once again held my hair back. Rinsing out my mouth, I put the toothbrush away and dared to glance at my reflection.

I looked like a ghost.

Tearing my gaze away, I focused on my trembling hands gripping the counter's edge. While I struggled not to fall apart, Kade continued to lend me his quiet support. It suddenly hit me that I would have fallen apart a long time ago if it weren't for his steadfast strength. I'd grown to depend on it the last couple of weeks. To *need* it.

Still looking at my hands, I blurted, "Why do you love me?"

His fingers in my hair stilled. I kept my gaze downward, too nervous to meet his eyes. I didn't know where the question came from, but I was suddenly desperate for the answer. He could have said any number of things. Could have said he loved my body, or my sass, or my quirky sense of humor. He didn't say any of those things. Instead, he said, "Because you make me happy."

All the air fled my lungs. Happy. *Happy*. Of all the things he could have said, that one meant the most to me. Here I was, a complete *wreck*, and he said I made him happy.

"Kade?" I whispered, not bothering to hide the tremor in my voice.

"Yes?"

"I want you."

Slowly, I lifted my eyes to his reflection. He looked stunned at my admission, drawing in a sharp breath. My hands began to shake again, but for a different reason this time.

"I know this is literally the worst time to finally admit my feelings, but after what we just learned, I can't wait a moment longer. The truth is, I've wanted you ever since I woke up in your arms as a new vampire. You told me I was going to be okay, and I wholeheartedly believed you. Then the sire bond kicked in and I let fear control me. I panicked. I thought a bond with you would mean losing myself. I thought you'd strip away my free will and make me your puppet. I thought you'd break my heart into a million pieces.

"But I still wanted you, and that hurt. It hurt so bad that I couldn't stand being near you. So I left. I left and tried to leave you in my past, but I couldn't. Every time I thought about you, old feelings would rise up. I'd try to drink them away, but that never worked.

"That's why I ended up calling you. Even though I can't remember doing it, I know it wasn't an accident. Somehow, I knew I was in trouble, and the first person I thought to call for help was you.

Because I knew I could count on you. Despite the sire bond, you've always been there for me. I was scared of the power it gave you over me, but I'm not anymore. Our bond isn't toxic, Kade. I was wrong about that. It's only toxic if abused, and I know now that you would never use it to hurt me."

He'd been silent the entire time I spoke, patiently letting me pour my heart out. But when I paused to take a breath, he grasped my shoulders and eased me around to face him. A lump formed in my throat when I fully took in the emotion simmering in his eyes. They shone brightly, as if tears were only a second away from filling them.

"Is that it?" he softly said, reaching up to touch my cheek.

"No," I admitted. "There's a lot I've been keeping bottled up. But I don't want to keep it in anymore. I could have lost *everything* when that Ancient decided to allure me, and I don't want to take a single second for granted anymore. Time is fleeting, just like you said, and I'm done wasting it. I know the timing is awful right now, but I don't want to wait any longer. I want to be with you, like *really* be with you. In every way possible. Because I'm pretty sure you're the only one for me, and—"

"Pretty sure?" he said, his half smile slightly trembling.

"I *know* you are. Why else would I constantly be thinking about you, day after month after *year?* Gods, I'm *obsessed.* The sire bond can't be the reason. It wouldn't make me yearn for your scent and taste. Wouldn't make me melt at the sound of your infectious laughter. It wouldn't make me crave your warmth and strength. I just . . . I just *want* you, okay? I might even—"

I gasped as he swept forward. As he captured my mouth in a searing kiss. His arms came around me. Lifting me. Cradling me to him.

He showered my lips with his undivided attention. Full kisses that made me feel warm and safe.

And *loved*. So very loved.

Tears slid down my face, coating our mouths. Mingling with our kisses.

"You won't lose yourself with me, Isla," he said against my lips. "I won't let you."

"I know," I whispered, touching his face. It was wet with tears. *His* tears.

"I'll protect your mind, heart, and soul. With every breath I take."

My chin wobbled. "I know."

"Whenever you need me, I'll be there. *Always*. My strength is yours to wield and command."

More tears fell. When he raised a hand to brush them away, I breathed his name. He pulled away enough to look at me, to see the deep desire in my eyes as I said, "Love me. Please love me."

He heaved a shuddering breath. Then another. "It would be my greatest honor to love you, Isla Andrews."

My smile trembled. "Then show me."

"*Finally*," he said, and I huffed a quiet laugh.

He kissed me again. Sweetly. Tenderly. As if I were the most precious thing in the world to him.

I thought I would float away, overwhelmed by the emotions soaring through me. Thought I would combust with desire for him.

When he lifted me into his arms, I melted against him, knowing I was safe wherever he went. He carried me to his bed and carefully laid me on the mattress, before stepping back to remove his shirt. All the air whooshed from my lungs. I couldn't help my reaction. He was just so . . . so . . .

"You're prettier than Thor," my mouth decided to blurt, dispelling the sweet moment.

He blinked in astonishment. Blinked again. Then busted out laughing.

I covered my face with a groan, mortified by how dumb I'd sounded.

When his laughter died down, I peeked at him through my fingers. A megawatt grin was still stretched across his face, and it was so mesmerizing that I lowered my hands to stare at him. "Well, you're prettier than Thor too, so I guess we're even," he said, climbing onto the mattress to hover above me.

I continued to stare up at him, unabashedly drinking in his beauty. Every line was flawless, exuding a masculinity that took my breath away. After thoroughly examining his face, I let my eyes travel down the thick column of his throat. They paused on the spot where I'd bitten him. Where I'd marked him with my scent. Since that day, I hadn't claimed him again, but I suddenly wanted to. Wanted to fill him with my venom, letting everyone know that he was *mine*.

I smiled.

"What?" he said, sweeping his thumb across my bottom lip.

Instead of answering right away, I snaked an arm around his neck and pulled. He fell, and I rolled with the movement, coming out on top. As he blinked up at me in surprise, I straddled his waist and tugged off my shirt. When I placed my hands on his chest and leaned forward, his gaze lowered to my breasts. They were on full display, barely covered by a thin layer of blue satin.

"I want to claim you again," I said, smiling wider when he shot me a look of pure want. "I didn't know what I was doing the first time I did it, but I do now."

He audibly swallowed, his throat bobbing. "I'm yours to claim whenever you wish."

My heart pulsed with happiness at that. An energy that could only be described as giddiness rushed through my body and I bent to kiss him. He eagerly kissed me back, gripping my waist to draw me closer. The move brought our naked skin flush together, and we both moaned at the contact.

As I pressed my chest to his, a growl rumbled deep in his throat. In an instant, his hand flashed up and undid my bra clasp. I gasped into his mouth when I felt him remove it, leaving our upper halves completely bare. At the feel of his skin on mine, my nipples hardened.

He abruptly rose into a sitting position, breaking our kiss to lean forward and suck one of my nipples into his mouth. At the sharp pleasure, my eyes rolled back and I cried out, bucking my hips against him. Releasing another low growl, he pushed me down onto his hard erection and held me there while his mouth continued to explore my breasts. Every. Last. Inch.

I didn't want him to stop. Didn't want to move a muscle as my world became one of ecstasy. But my need to reclaim him was too strong. So I took control once more, pleased when he willingly relinquished the reins. As I fisted his hair and tipped his head back, my fangs dropped. They throbbed while I opened my mouth and aimed for his neck, sinking them in deep. When they were positioned inside him as far as they would go, they seemed to sigh. To whisper their gratitude. Their *relief*.

I hadn't even thought to be afraid. It felt good to bite him now. More than good. I *craved* it. And his reaction to being bitten only excited me more. He groaned, loud and guttural, grinding me even harder against his erection. I rewarded him with a generous stream of my venom, gratified when he shuddered against me. As he slowly began to rock me against him, I took a long pull from his neck. He shuddered again and rocked me faster.

Bliss stole through my limbs, but I suddenly needed more. More pleasure. More *Kade*. I shoved my hands between us and frantically tugged at his jeans until the button popped free. He jerked, but didn't stop me from yanking his zipper, then his boxers down. When I felt his erection spring free, my greedy fingers wrapped around the thick base.

"Isla," he grunted, sucking in a hiss as I tried to make my fingertips touch. Startled when they couldn't, I retracted my fangs from his neck to look down at his dick.

"Holy goddess," I whispered, taking my time ogling him. "You're so much bigger up close."

He huffed a breathless laugh, then moaned as I slowly ran my hand up his length. My thumb swept over the soft tip and it swelled to twice its size.

"Holy goddess," I said again. "You're never going to fit."

"Oh, I'll fit, baby," he breathed, reaching his own hand between us. "As long as you're wet for me."

Oh, I was. But apparently he wanted to check for himself. As his fingers brushed my center through my panties, I gasped and bucked my hips again, reacting to the swift rush of pleasure. He did it again, drawing a moan from me.

"Oh, you're more than ready," he crooned in approval, leaning forward to nuzzle my neck.

"But I haven't . . ." I said, pausing when he deeply inhaled my scent. "Had any . . ." Another pause as he kissed the spot. *His* spot. The spot where he'd claimed me. "In a really long—AAHH!"

I cried out as he suddenly pushed aside my underwear and plunged a finger inside me. My walls immediately clenched around the digit. Before I could get over the shock of having his finger inside me, he did it again, adding a second digit. I released his erection to grab his shoulders, groaning as energy charged through me.

"Good girl," he purred, rewarding me by pressing his thumb to my clit. I cried out again and arched into his hand, shaking uncontrollably. "That's it, baby. Show me how much you want this. Show me how good I make you feel. Now, let's prepare you for my cock. Deep breath."

I'd barely taken a breath when he slid a *third* finger inside me. And they were *huge*. I dug my nails into his skin as my walls stretched to the point of pain. But I didn't complain or pull away, too enthralled by what he was doing.

His movements were experienced, yet he paid attention to my body, making sure he didn't push me too far. His consideration blew away any fear that I might have had, giving me confidence that I was in good hands. Literally.

He patiently waited for me to adjust to the third finger, then slowly eased them out. My breath came in ragged pants as I waited for his cock to replace the fingers. This was it. Kade and I were going to have sex. Our sire bond would strengthen and the last of my missing memories would be restored.

But that wasn't why I wanted this. *He* was what I wanted. Just him. Just Kade.

"I want you inside me," I blurted, trembling with need. "*Now*, Kade."

He pulled away to look at me, and I opened my eyes to meet his hungry gaze. Despite how much he clearly wanted to have sex with me, he touched my cheek and whispered, "Are you absolutely sure?"

Right then and there, my heart officially became his.

It warmed under his consideration, fluttering like crazy.

I smiled at him, whispering back, "More sure than I've ever been about anything."

His returning smile was devastatingly beautiful. With desire burning hotly in his gaze, he slowly lifted me and eased me on top of him. He watched me the entire time, making sure I was okay. Pausing when I flinched or tensed. Gradually, he pushed inside of me, filling me more and more and more. I thought for sure my body couldn't hold him, but somehow, I took all of him. Every. Last. Inch.

We were both struggling to breathe by the time he was fully inside of me. He held still, letting me adjust again, watching as I fought to catch my breath.

And then he looked deep into my eyes and said, "You're perfect."

That's when I completely fell. Head over heels. No stops. No brakes. So hard that all I could do was trust. Trust that he was waiting at the bottom to catch me.

As he started to move inside of me, I almost couldn't stand it. The deep intimacy. The connection. The *oneness*. I couldn't believe I was sharing this moment with Kade. I thought I'd had my life all figured out, but I'd been so wrong. I couldn't imagine living it now without him. He was a part of me. A *vital* part. And I never wanted to be separated from him again.

While we found a rhythm, learning how our bodies responded to each other, I held on tight. When our pleasure built and built, eventually catapulting us over the edge together, I clung to him. And even afterward, as we lay spent in each other's arms, I refused to let go.

I was *never* letting go. Ever again.

CHAPTER 31

ISLA

The second I woke the next morning, Kade's lips were on mine.

I sucked in a surprised breath, inhaling his sun-kissed scent as I did. Warmth immediately flooded my body and I moaned, twining my arms around his neck. In no time, our naked bodies were tangled together, rolling and twisting in the sheets.

When his hard erection pressed against my core, I moaned again and dug my nails into his back. He wasted no time thrusting against me, leaving my core aching and wet within seconds. At this pace, I was going to come swiftly, but neither of us slowed down.

It was like our bodies had taken over, desperate to make up for lost time. We'd spent five years mutually pining for each other, and now that we'd torn down the last barrier between us, we couldn't stop touching. This was our fourth time having sex in a matter of hours. I didn't even think it was possible for guys to have sex this frequently. Or maybe only Kade could. Because Kade and his penis were the stuff of legends.

Was I already addicted to having sex with him? One million times *yes*.

The guy had the stamina of a lion.

His hands dug into my hair as he relentlessly rocked. I scraped my fingernails up and down his back, drawing a groan from him. All the while, our mouths ravenously fed on each other, kissing and sucking and licking.

When pleasure filled every inch of me, almost more than I could bear, he lifted his hips a few inches, then drove his cock deep inside me. Shocked by the swift move, my claws shot out and gouged into his back. He simply chuckled against my mouth and began thrusting inside me.

My human self would have been too sore for more sex. But I had long since healed, my body primed and more than willing to be stretched by him again. I greedily answered his thrusts, rolling my hips up to meet him. He growled approvingly at my eagerness, slamming into me even harder.

My orgasm built quickly, leaving me gasping and trembling beneath him.

"Not yet, baby," he commanded against my lips, increasing the punishing pace.

In my efforts to hold off the orgasm, I started to whimper. He swallowed the sounds, mercilessly thrusting his tongue inside me.

Too much. Too *much*.

When I stiffened all over, unable to hold on a second longer, he grunted, "Now, baby. *Now.*"

I gave in to the release, screaming as I came. He groaned as his own orgasm hit him hard. Shuddering, he pulsed inside of me, expelling his release. We continued to kiss, slower now as we rode the high, prolonging the bliss with soft thrusts. When we finally came down, our bodies were slick with sweat and completely satiated.

"You're heaven, shortcake," Kade eventually said, breaking the kiss to peer down at me. "Have I mentioned that yet?"

I managed to open my eyes and give him a blissed-out smile. "Maybe. But I don't mind hearing it again."

He grinned at that. "How about every morning?"

I blinked slowly. "You mean every morning after we have sex?"

His grin widened. "Exactly."

Okay, wow, I was down with that. *More* than down. Being woken up like this every morning sounded like heaven to me.

I opened my mouth to tell him just that, but paused, a sudden bout of uncertainty filling me.

At my troubled expression, Kade's brow furrowed in concern. "What's wrong? Is sex every morning too much for you?"

"I . . . gods, no. It's just . . ." I blew out a breath, forcing myself to look him in the eye as I said, "I kind of feel like I pressured you into having sex with me. I didn't even ask if you were okay with it. I just *assumed*. And now that we know about the allure still in my system, I'm worried that you'll think I had sex for the wrong reasons. And then . . . maybe you'll regret what we did."

He studied me thoughtfully for a moment, then gently swept his thumb across my cheek. "You didn't pressure me, shortcake. I've waited over a hundred years to share a closeness like this with the woman I love. I couldn't possibly regret it."

When he leaned down and softly kissed me, my heart all but exploded. It was on the tip of my tongue. The very tip to tell him how I *really* felt about him, but someone chose that moment to disturb our intimate bubble.

"Kade. My father wants to speak with you two."

At the sound of Loch's voice through the door, I felt Kade smile against my mouth. Before I could stop him, he called, "Be out in a few minutes. We need to clean up first."

When I huffed at his thinly-veiled innuendo, he rocked his hips into mine, needlessly reminding me of where his dick still was.

"Hey, I only spoke the truth," he said in hushed tones, giving me an innocent look.

I rolled my eyes. "Yeah, and now everyone's going to know we had sex."

He grinned at me wickedly. "Oh, they're gonna know that with or without my confirmation. Even after we clean up, they'll still smell it on us."

He laughed when I covered my face with my hands and groaned.

Twenty minutes later, we emerged from the bedroom freshly showered and . . . still smelling faintly of sex. I'd scrubbed and scrubbed, but the scent still lingered. A part of me had known this would happen, but I hadn't cared at the moment.

Well, I did now. Meeting up with the king still smelling like sex was going to be super awkward. At least he wasn't a prude. He had fourteen *wives*, after all.

"You smell amazing," Kade whispered in my ear, as if he could sense my discomfort. "The perfect mixture of salty, sweet, and *me*." When I looked up and found a self-satisfied smirk plastered across his face, I couldn't even be annoyed. I was just so . . . so—

"Fates, I couldn't be more happy for you two right now," a feminine voice carried to us from down the hall. We glanced over to find Kenna standing in the middle of the hallway, tears welling in her eyes as she stared at us. As usual, Loch and Silver flanked her, a fact she didn't seem to mind in the least. They watched with affection as she sniffled and dabbed at her eyes. "Sorry. Pregnancy hormones. I've been extra weepy lately."

"Aaww, little Kenna," Kade said, striding forward to hug her.

"Careful," Loch warned, a word he'd been uttering a *lot* lately. But he didn't stop his drothen from sweeping Kenna into a bear hug.

"Oh, that's *strong*," Kenna said in surprise when Kade set her back down. As if embarrassed by her outburst, she flushed a scarlet red. "Sorry. The pregnancy makes my nose extra sensitive too. I-I didn't mean to—"

"It's perfectly okay," Kade drawled, casting a quick look over his shoulder to wink at me. "Getting laid four times in one night is hard to hide. Not to mention a fresh claiming."

Oh. My. Gods.

I was going to kill him.

Kenna's eyes widened, her blush deepening. Loch chuckled quietly, not the least bit shocked. Silver sniffed and twitched her whiskers as if to say, *What a highly inappropriate conversation this is.*

Everett chose that moment to amble down the hall toward us. At the odd looks on everyone's faces, he frowned and said, "What's going on?" He suddenly paused, inhaled, then rolled his eyes. "Never mind. It's about time, you two."

Giving up, I threw my hands into the air and blurted, "Fine. Kade and I had wild, passionate sex last night. Multiple times. I *finally* admitted my feelings and we're officially a thing now. So go ahead. Get the comments out of your system. I know you've been dying to for years."

Every single one of them turned to me and stared. Then started to laugh. Even the fox yipped her laughter. It wasn't long before I joined in, realizing how ridiculous I'd sounded.

When Loch suddenly motioned me forward, silently asking me to *join* their little group, my laughter faded. Kenna gave me an encouraging nod. When I hesitated, my heart fluttering with uncertainty, Kade held out his hand toward me. I focused on the hand, on the strength it represented. And chose to lean on it, letting it help me face the challenge before me.

My approach was cautiously slow, but the people I cared about continued to urge me forward. Still nervous about my bloodlust, I tried not to breathe in Kenna's scent too deeply. My senses stirred awake at the smell of her blood, but relief stole through me when I remained firmly in control.

Reaching their position, I slid my hand into Kade's, relaxing further at the warm, steady contact. But apparently my best friend wasn't content to simply have me near again. My eyes widened as she waddled forward and wrapped her arms around me. I went poker straight, expecting Loch to rip her away from me any second now. But he didn't. No one did.

And that's when I started to cry.

Kenna hugged me harder, offering comfort as I sobbed uncontrollably. Still holding my hand, Kade squeezed my fingers, further supporting me. Overwhelmed by the love surrounding me, I continued to cry, letting the tears wash away the fear and stress of the last couple of weeks.

"I'm so glad you're okay," Kenna finally whispered when my sobs lessened. "I was so worried."

I hiccuped in response, unable to speak.

"I know about the Ancient, and I'm so sorry for what he did to you." At the sorrow in her voice, I released a shuddering exhale. She knew how it felt to be controlled by a sadistic prick. To have her memories tampered with and her free will stolen. I clung to her tightly, soaking up her empathy.

"He won't go unpunished," Everett spoke up. "We've already started making plans to find and capture him."

I lifted my head to take in the determined expressions of the three males surrounding us. Sniffing back more tears, I said, "I want to help. I need to clear my name and stop him from hurting anyone else."

All three of them nodded.

"We were counting on that," Loch said. "Do you still have the phone number Samuel gave you?"

"Yes. It's saved in my contacts."

"Good. I know just how to draw him out of hiding. But first, you need to hear what my father knows about him. It might explain why he targeted you specifically."

Minutes later, we were all gathered around the table, this time in the dining room. With one glaring change. I was smack in the middle of Kade's lap, by no doing of my own. He'd simply grabbed and plonked me down before I could claim a chair, settling his arms across my middle when I'd squirmed. If I didn't know any better, I'd think he was being a little possessive. I thought that would bother me. Make me feel smothered.

But it didn't. In fact, it kind of turned me on.

The king had included my dad in the meeting, but only on speaker through a secure line. He couldn't see me perched on Kade's lap, which I was grateful for. He still didn't know about us, and I wanted to keep it that way. For now. Just until I—

"Well, I see you two wasted no time having sex. Have the last of your memories been restored, then?" King Ambrose said, giving me a slightly amused look.

I choked on the mouthful of blood I'd just sipped from my mug, nearly spewing it across the table. Kade's laughter rumbled through me, and I sharply elbowed him in the ribs. He retaliated by pressing an open-mouthed kiss just below my ear, making my toes curl.

"Not yet," I began. But before I could finish, a voice came loud and clear through the speaker.

"Called it. I hope you two used protection. Although, I suppose it doesn't matter, since female vampires are barren and human diseases don't affect you."

I slammed my mug on the table hard enough that half the contents sloshed out. "Noah Bartholemew Andrews," I snapped, then, "Dad, why is he on this call? I thought you were on a secure line."

"He is. We're all at the house," Noah butted in again before my dad could speak. "He thought Tess and I should be a part of this meeting. King Ambrose agreed, considering our close connection with you. Plus, Dad ordered fresh bagels from Mama Jo's. You know they're my weakness."

"Tess?" Kenna said in surprise from across the table. "I'm so glad you decided to join us."

"Of course, Kenna Joy. If Bill says his daughter is innocent, then I believe him," her ex-guardian replied through the speaker. "How are you and the babies today?"

"Great. Except that they kicked me in the ribs most of the night."

Tess chuckled at that. "And your parents? Were they able to buy that beach house?"

"Yes, they were. They still plan to move soon after the babies are born."

"Good for them. They'll still be close enough to visit you and the babies frequently, but have a little place of their own."

"Exactly."

A throat loudly cleared through the speaker.

"Apologies, Bill," Tess said.

"It's fine," my dad replied. "But maybe we can save pleasantries until the end. We have a lot to discuss."

"Indeed we do," King Ambrose said, leaning forward in his seat. "I've called you all here today so I can shed some light on the Ancient known as Samuel Quinn. Back when my father was king, the council didn't exist. He only had a royal advisor, a Lord Samuel Quinn, his most trusted ally and best friend.

"When I was born, my father was already a thousand years old. Shortly after my fiftieth year, he planned to step down and crown his only heir as king. He wished to retire and enjoy the simpler things in life. When Lord Quinn found out his intentions to crown me king, he was furious.

"Apparently, he and my father had agreed centuries before that if my father were to ever abdicate the throne, he would let his most trusted advisor rule in his stead. I never learned the details as to why he chose me instead. Maybe he simply thought the kingdom would be better off under D'angelo rule, as I do. Regardless, Lord Quinn wouldn't accept it and tried to take the throne by force."

King Ambrose paused, a faraway look entering his eyes, as if he were recalling the memory. "He nearly won. His strength was unparalleled, even then. He almost made my father rip out his own heart with a few words from his silver tongue. I'd never trusted the devil, though, so when he attacked, I was ready. Several of the Venturi that make up my council today helped me defeat him.

"But I made one huge mistake. Instead of killing him, I banished him from the kingdom. I thought the public shame would be enough to send him into hiding for good. He'd always been arrogantly proud, and the defeat should have quelled him. Then, one year later, my father killed himself. Or, at least, that's what I was made to believe. But I know it was Samuel, even if I never found proof that it was him. Ever since then, he's remained in the shadows. I haven't heard a whisper of his name in nearly five centuries . . . until now."

"So how come you didn't lock him up?" Everett said after a beat of weighty silence. He didn't add, *Like you did with Troy*, but we all knew he was thinking it.

"Simple," the king replied, easing back against his seat. "A cell reinforced with silver can't contain him. I doubt any prison could."

Everett released a soft whistle.

"Why do you think he came out of hiding after all these years?"

Loch questioned.

"My only guess is that, after the one hundred year curse was broken, he crawled out of whatever hole he's been hiding in to investigate. The world has changed a lot in the last five centuries. Information is easier to come by. He might have even caught wind of my recent weakened state and decided to vie for the throne again."

"Well, he'll have to get through *me* first," Everett said with a low growl.

A small smile twitched the king's lips. "You're a brave and strong Venturi, my son, but you cannot compete with his Ancient power. No one can. The only option is to band together and overwhelm him. Strength in numbers."

"Why do you think he went after Isla?" Kade spoke up, the question making my spine tingle with nervous energy.

The king studied me for a moment before saying, "I think he's looking for a chink in my armor. Brute force didn't work for him last time, so maybe he's now trying to cut me down from the inside. It's no coincidence that he ran into Isla when he did. He was probably following her for weeks. Maybe even months.

"I also think he targeted her specifically for her close connection with not only the royal vampire family, but with the SCA. She's in a delicate situation, riding the line between the human and vampire worlds. She alone can influence human's opinions of vampires with just a few words. Her actions are forever under close scrutiny, and showing her predatory nature in a dangerous way could threaten the fragile alliance we currently have with them. Lord Quinn must realize that if he exploits this balance, vampires will become vulnerable once again, as will I and my heirs."

Tension radiated through Kade. "Do you think he knows where she is right now?"

"Possibly. But I heavily doubt he'd step onto Sanctum Isle soil to find out for certain. He's arrogant, but not a fool. No, he'll bide his time before making his next move. At his age, time holds little meaning for him."

Silence descended. Dreadful, ear-piercing silence.

Guilt and shame ate at my stomach. Samuel had so easily used me as his *puppet*, pulling my strings to tear down what little trust the SCA and vampires had for each other. I'd almost single-handedly broken the alliance. Maybe still would, if I couldn't clear my name. Unable to bear the silence a moment longer, I said, "I'm sorry for being the weak link. I never meant to cause so much trouble."

Kade stirred beneath me, as if prepared to offer me words of comfort, but it was the king who said, "You're not the weak link, Isla. He chose wrong in targeting you, and we're going to prove it."

CHAPTER 32

ISLA

"No. I changed my mind. You aren't doing this."

At Kade's vehement words, I blinked up at him in surprise. I'd just slammed the trunk of his Mustang shut, securing the last of my things inside. We'd carried them out shortly after the sun set for the evening, making sure I had plenty of nighttime hours at my disposal. My eyes widened when he was suddenly beside me, yanking the trunk back open. "Kade," I protested as he began unloading my stuff. "*Kade.*"

"We'll find another way."

"We went over this already. There *is* no other way. How else are we going to draw Samuel out of hiding?"

"I can't believe Loch suggested using you as bait," he growled, continuing to remove my stuff with unnecessary force.

"It's a good plan," I argued, grabbing my stuff and shoving it back into the trunk. "Don't be mad at him. He's only trying to help."

"I'm not mad at him. I'm mad at the *dick* who put us in this situation," he growled again, grabbing all my belongings at once and dropping them onto the ground.

I stomped my foot in exasperation. "Save your anger for later, Kade. We don't have time for this."

When I bent to pick up the haphazard pile, he grabbed me and trapped my body against the car with his. "What I don't have time for is putting my *mate* in harm's way," he said in a deep rumble, securing both arms around me.

At the unexpected word, my heart did a weird little flutter. "Mate?" I whispered.

"Yes, *mate*. We are bonded in every way that counts. That makes you my mate."

"Oh," I breathed, a riot of butterflies tumbling in my stomach. I supposed for a supernatural, sex and claiming meant that the couple were now mates. Not exactly husband and wife, but still intimately tied together.

He searched my face for a moment. "Do you *want* to be my mate?"

Good goddess, what a question to ask when I should be focused on the mission right now. Our timing had never been that great, though. We continued to blunder our way forward, making mistakes and scrambling to fix them as we went.

At the slightest bit of uncertainty in his gaze, as if he worried that I'd reject him again, I placed both hands on his face. "Yes, Kade, I very much want to be your mate."

Slowly, he closed his eyes and released a shuddering breath. "Say it again," he whispered.

"I want to be your mate."

"One more time."

"I want to be your mate," I obediently repeated, biting my lip when he graced me with the most beautiful smile.

"Oh, Isla," he abruptly groaned, dropping his forehead to mine. "I've wanted this for so long. Now that I finally have you, I'm not ready to let you go."

My own eyes fluttered shut as I soaked up his warmth one last time. "You won't have to. I'll only be a little ways ahead. Once I make the call, you can easily track me if I'm forced to switch locations.

With both my dad and brother able to cast cloaking spells, you can be feet away and he won't even know until it's too late."

"I'm not so sure about that. He's lived this long for a reason. At the first suspicion of a trap, who knows what he'll do. He could go after you, and I don't want that bastard anywhere *near* you."

"I won't let him touch me."

"If he does, I swear I'll kill him."

I shivered at the dark threat in Kade's voice. Fear for me and my safety dictated his words, but I knew he meant them. Knew that he'd risk his very life to save mine. And that, more than anything, was what terrified me. He'd done it before and had been seriously injured. The thought of him confronting an *Ancient* filled me with paralyzing fear.

But I couldn't let fear rule my life. Samuel needed to be stopped, and we had to be the ones to do it. More innocent people would get hurt if we didn't, and leaving them to their fate went against every ethical code I possessed.

So, after a few quiet moments, I pulled back to look at him. "I can't keep living in hiding. I can't let others pay for my actions, even if those actions weren't my choice. And I won't be a fugitive any longer, not when I have the ability to make things right with the SCA."

His throat bobbed. "But your memories haven't been fully restored yet. He could use that against you somehow. And if he tries to allure you again, what if our bond isn't strong enough to fight it?"

"He won't get that chance. The second he reveals himself, you'll all be there to capture him. He can't fight all of you at once."

He tightened his grip on me, but I could tell my words were starting to sink in. "Are you sure I can't claim you again?"

I shook my head. "Everett was right. Your scent would be too strong. Too fresh. Samuel might get suspicious and run before we can corner him."

He blew out a long sigh. "This is it then. There's no talking you out of this."

I rose up on tiptoe and pressed a soft kiss to his lips. "It'll be over before we know it."

Before I could pull away, he cupped the back of my head and crushed our mouths together. The kiss was desperate, filled with all the fear and uncertainty he still felt. I tried to remain calm for him, but my own fear leaked through.

It would be idiotic *not* to be afraid of facing a powerful foe capable of controlling your every move. And if he didn't buy my damsel in distress act, I could seriously be putting myself in grave danger.

It was another twenty minutes before Kade finally let me go. As I started the Mustang and put it in drive, I told myself not to look back. Warned myself that doing so would make me lose my nerve. But I did. I looked in the rearview mirror and nearly lost the ability to breathe.

They were all there. My family and dearest friends.

Both my dad and Noah had portalled in a few short hours ago, ready to lend their support when they heard Loch's plan. With their warlock magic, they could stealth-tail me, hiding an entire car from sight if need be. Loch and Everett were all geared up, bristling with weapons. Tess would meet up with them after they crossed the bridge to the mainland. Kenna was staying behind, along with Silver and the king. Even though my best friend had wickedly powerful Syphon magic, no one was willing to risk her pregnancy.

And standing at the forefront of the group was Kade. The man who had pursued and won my heart. My *mate*. His caramel-colored hair was a bright beacon against the dark night, shining like a halo. Like a *sun*. As I stared at his reflection, I realized then that he'd truly become my very own sun. He'd touched my life with his warmth, making me feel stronger and undeniably loved. He'd chased my darkness away with his unwavering brightness, giving me the willpower to do better. To *be* better.

A better version of myself.

Tears blurred my vision, obstructing my view of him. Inhaling a fortifying breath, I blinked the tears away and refocused on the road before me. With the people I held most dear at my back, I squared my shoulders and eased the car forward. I'd been wrong. Seeing them all there, ready to support me, made me feel anything but weak.

Yes, the road ahead was dangerous, but I wouldn't be alone. And that knowledge gave me the strength to carry on with the plan.

I waited until I'd crossed the bridge to the mainland before seeking a spot to pull over. The success of our plan was hinged on one very important phone call. I'd never taken acting lessons, but I was no stranger to playing up my emotions. Plus, ad-libbing was an Andrews family trait. There was no room for error, and I had no intention of failing.

The spot I chose was remote, a stretch of tree-lined road just outside of a small, seaside town. I killed the engine and glanced around, noting the empty darkness. But I wasn't alone. Somewhere not too far away was a vehicle full of powerful supernaturals. Reminding myself of their presence, I grabbed my phone and tapped the screen.

Since the night I'd left Saanvi's apartment, I hadn't received any new texts or phone calls from my stalker, aka Samuel. It was like he'd forgotten about me. Or given up trying to use me.

Only one way to find out.

Blowing out a shaky breath, I searched my contacts list with trembling fingers and found the number he'd given me. Not allowing myself time to chicken out, I pressed the call button and raised the phone to my ear.

He answered on the third ring, his accented voice distinct as he said, "Hello?"

My throat closed as doubt suddenly assailed me. What if it wasn't him? What if he was another Samuel Quinn and not an Ancient at all? The name was common enough. Since my full memories hadn't been restored yet, I had no actual proof that he'd been the one to drain Gunner Landry. And my phone stalker's voice hadn't been accented. What if . . .

What if we were trying to capture the wrong person?

Gods, why did I have to question everything *now*? I couldn't play my part convincingly if I was getting cold feet.

When a beat of silence passed, Samuel pressed, "Who is this?"

Nope, I couldn't back out now. Everyone was counting on me to see this through. And if he *was* the Ancient, I would never forgive myself for letting him slip through my fingers. Time to suck it up and deal.

"Samuel?" I said, not even needing to fake the tremor in my voice. "It's me, Isla. Isla Andrews. You remember, right? That time at Mike's Tavern when we had drinks together?"

"Yes, I remember. I haven't seen you around in awhile. How are you?"

Oh, he was good. *Really* good. Unless he was actually being genuine. Unless he wasn't the Ancient after all.

STOP. Get a grip!

Shoving my plaguing doubts aside, I replied, "Not good, actually. It's why I'm calling. My thirst got out of control and I . . . I drained and killed a human. Then I almost did it again, so I ran. I-I thought King Ambrose would protect me, but I overheard him tell his sons

274

that he wants to turn me over to the SCA. Th-that I'm too much of a liability. So I packed my bags and ran again, but I'm out of places to hide. My apartment's been ransacked, and my dad and brother aren't speaking to me."

I drew in a shuddering breath, recalling the nightmare I'd had where everyone I loved hated me. Tears filled my eyes and I choked out, "I just . . . I have no one else to turn to. I'm all alone and scared and . . . Oh gods, I'm so sorry. I sound pathetic and shouldn't have called. This isn't your problem. I mean, you barely *know* me. I don't want you caught up in all this. I'll just hang up now. Sorry again for—"

"Isla, wait."

I held my breath.

"Where are you? I'll come get you."

My heart started to thunder. "Really? Are you sure?"

"Hey, it's why I gave you my number in the first place, remember? I'm always willing to rescue a lady in distress, and you definitely sound distressed."

It's working, it's working, it's working.

Sniffling loudly, I said, "Thank you so much. Seriously. I owe you *big* time."

Ego-stroking? *Check.*

"Don't mention it. I've been in a few tough scrapes myself over the years. I'll make sure you're safely hidden."

When I'd relayed my location to him and hung up, my entire body was shaking. Every last inch of me yearned to bolt from the car and run to Kade. To let him envelope me in his arms where it was safe. But I couldn't. Samuel could arrive in less than half an hour if he was still in Rosewood. Maybe even sooner if he'd chosen a spot closer to Sanctum Isle to wait for me in hopes that I'd emerge.

The thought of him being minutes away sent fear coursing

through me. I'd have to mask that fear somehow before he arrived. He'd sense it and know something was wrong. The road was practically deserted this time of night, but every time a car passed, adrenaline shot through me.

I hadn't brought any weapons, wanting to appear as innocent as possible. I'd already have to explain why a male's scent was on me. That wasn't going to look good, especially after I'd told him that I didn't date vampires. My only hope was that backup would arrive before he could become suspicious.

A little over half an hour later, a sleek black sports car drove past. My adrenaline spiked when it slowed and eased into a U-turn, rolling to a stop several yards behind me. This was it. Sink or swim time. Inhaling a few calming breaths, I grabbed my phone and popped the trunk. Even though I had no intention of loading my things into his vehicle, he needed proof of my girl-on-the-run act.

The second I saw him open his door and step from the car, I did the same. Before he could speak, I rushed to say, "The car isn't mine. I need to ditch it before the owner finds out I took it. I hope you don't mind that I have a few belongings with me."

"Not at all," he smoothly replied, buttoning his dark blazer. I felt like a frightened deer as his headlights illuminated my every movement toward the trunk. When I reached for the lid, he stepped toward me. "Here, let me help you."

My heart galloped inside my chest as he approached. There was no slowing it, nor stopping the wind from teasing my hair and blowing my scent his way. He froze and so did I, my hand on the trunk lid starting to tremble.

"You've recently been claimed," he said, and I shivered at the slight edge to his voice.

Opening my mouth, I stuck as close to the truth as possible, knowing he'd already seen me and Kade pressed up against this very vehicle in the motel parking lot not too long ago. "Just yesterday, actually. We've known each other for years, and I finally gave in to his advances. But . . . it was a mistake. He only ended up betraying me too."

Wow, that hurt to say, even if it wasn't true. I hoped Kade couldn't hear this conversation from wherever he was hiding, but there was a good chance he could.

The hard look in Samuel's golden eyes softened a little. "I know how it feels to be betrayed by someone you thought never would. I no longer easily trust because of it, but . . . I think I can trust you, Isla. I hope you'll come to feel the same way about me."

I forced a smile onto my face, wondering how long I could keep up this charade. The others should be in position by now. As he took another step toward me, I tensed, desperately trying not to reveal my fear. He was only a few yards away now. Any closer and I wouldn't be able to escape if he lunged for me.

There was suddenly movement all around us. In a flash, Noah, Loch, and Everett appeared on one side. On the other, my dad, Tess, and Kade emerged. Each held a deadly ball of magic or silver weapon, all of them directed at Samuel.

"*Freeze*," my dad barked, the magic at his fingertips growing brighter.

Samuel didn't even react to the sudden onslaught. Without taking his eyes off me, he softly tsked and said, "I see you're not a lady in distress after all. Clever girl."

My lips curled back in a silent snarl as I dropped the act. "I didn't mean a word I said, and neither did you. I know who you are. I know what you *did* to me. You're going to pay for killing those humans and trying to *frame* me."

He slowly shook his head, giving me a pitying look. "Oh, Isla. So young and naive. Did you really think I wouldn't realize this was a trap? I've been alive for a long, long time, after all. You should have stayed in hiding. What happens next is on you."

Before I could fully digest his words, the roar of engines and squeal of tires filled the air. Cars from both directions skidded to a stop beside us. Doors popped open and several masked figures in black clothing emerged. I lost sight of Kade as they raised their weapons and pointed them directly at . . .

Me.

CHAPTER 33

ISLA

"This is the SCA," one of the masked figures barked. "Isla Andrews, you're under arrest for murder. Don't move or we'll shoot."

"Stand down," both my dad and Tess shouted, pushing through the operatives to reach me.

"No, *you* stand down," the same female operative ordered, clearly the one in charge here. "Both you and Tess Walker have been suspended, effective immediately."

"On what grounds?" Tess countered, still shouldering her way through.

"For aiding and abetting a dangerous supernatural fugitive. Now step aside so we can—"

"But I'm not the *killer*," I interrupted, pointing a finger at Samuel. "*He* is. We were just about to—"

"Thank God you're here, officers. Sh-she *attacked* me," Samuel frantically said, startling me into silence. He took a stumbling step toward them, his hands and neck covered in blood. "I-I stopped, thinking she needed help, and then . . . and then she bit my *neck*. I think she has *fangs*."

I gawked in disbelief at his helpless victim act, then threw a wild-eyed stare at the operatives. "Don't listen to him. He's a lying *psychopath*. Can't you see that he's a vampire? He's trying to frame me again for an action I didn't commit. You have to see that. He's a—"

"Don't move!" one of the operatives yelled at me, even though my feet were firmly planted on the asphalt. I vaguely recognized him, which only made this worse.

"I'm not!" I snapped back, starting to lose my patience.

"Hands in the air."

"But—"

"*DO IT!*"

The second I did, he strode toward me with purpose. When I saw what was in his hands, fear paralyzed me.

"No, please," I whispered, cringing as he roughly grabbed one of my arms.

"Don't resist and we won't shoot you," he commanded, yanking my arm down to slap a cuff around my wrist. My skin immediately began to burn and I cried out in pain.

The air suddenly filled with an earth-shattering roar.

"You're hurting her!" Kade bellowed, loud enough that my ears rang. I looked up in time to see an operative go airborne as Kade knocked them aside, trying to get to me. When he plowed through two more operatives, weapons started to train on *him*.

I screamed as a gun discharged and Kade roared in agony. He only paused for a second to note the round bloodstain spreading across his stomach, then shoved another operative aside.

"Stop, Kade, *stop!*" I cried, tears streaming down my face as another weapon discharged. He grunted at the impact, glancing down to see an arrow shaft protruding from between his ribs. I stared in horror as more blood saturated his shirt.

Everything slowed to a crawl, then. Casting a desperate look around me, I searched for help. My dad and Tess were fruitlessly shouting at operatives to stop shooting. Loch was halfway across the road, aiming for his injured best friend. Everett was holding back a furious Noah, who looked two seconds away from blasting his magic at the operative closest to him.

And in the middle of it all stood Samuel, a smug grin on his face.

When my gaze locked with his, he sketched a low bow and slowly started to retreat. There was nothing, *nothing* I could do as he leisurely strolled toward his car, completely forgotten about amidst the chaos. I blinked as his door clicked shut, sealing him inside. Blinked again as he pulled away from the curb.

The second he was gone, I snapped back to myself. To the reality before me. There was only one thing I could do. One thing that could stop anyone else from getting hurt.

Tipping my head back, I screamed, "I SURRENDER!" at the top of my lungs.

The chaos ground to a halt. Everyone turned to look at me.

My skin continued to sizzle and burn from the silver cuff, but I held my other arm out to the operative and again said, "I surrender. Go ahead and cuff me. I won't put up a fight."

At a nod from the woman operative in charge, he secured the other cuff on my wrist. At the added pain, my legs nearly gave out.

"Everyone, clear the area," the lead operative ordered, waving her weapon at my dad and Tess to step aside. "Miss Andrews is under SCA custody. Any attempt to interfere will be seen as a threat, and we won't give you the courtesy of warning shots next time."

When the operative beside me grabbed my arm and forced me into motion, I didn't resist. Didn't do anything but focus on placing one foot in front of the other, on gritting my teeth and enduring the pain. It was the only thing I could do. The only thing that would stop the bloodshed and leave my family and friends alive.

"*Isla*," Kade roared, and the sound of his agony split me wide open.

I tried to look behind me, to find him in the crowd, but the operative relentlessly dragged me forward.

"ISLA!" Kade thundered again, and I desperately craned my neck around. Just before I was shoved inside an SUV, I caught a glimpse of him. He was still fighting. Still fighting to get to me. Loch struggled to hold him back, to prevent his best friend from getting shot again.

Blood filled my mouth as I bit my tongue to stifle a sob. I wanted him to think that I was strong. That I could handle whatever awful fate the SCA had in store for me. But I knew the act was more for me than for him, because he knew. Without a doubt, he knew how utterly terrified I was. Still, I put on a brave face when our eyes connected, letting him see in that brief moment how determined I was.

I was defeated, but this wasn't going to be my end.

I wouldn't let this destroy me.

I'd never been inside one of the SCA's high security prisons before. Never had a need or desire to.

Because of the large amount of supernaturals residing in and around Maine, their biggest prison was also here. It was located deep within the heart of Maine's thick pine forests, just north of Moosehead Lake. I'd always heard it was super high tech, making it nearly impossible for the prisoners to escape, be they vampire, werewolf, witch, or warlock.

Vampires had always been the biggest threat to humans though. Therefore, the prison cells were mainly designed for them.

The three hour ride to the prison was pure agony. They wouldn't remove my silver cuffs, no matter how many times I assured them I wouldn't try to escape. I couldn't really blame them though. I was much faster and stronger than a human, and they all thought I was feral, or close to it. But the pain. The *pain*. I'd given up trying to look or sound brave hours ago. My head was slumped forward, swaying with the motions of the SUV. I'd shed so many tears that my cheeks were now stiff with salt.

When the vehicle finally rolled to a bumpy stop, I was too weak to stop my head from whacking against the window. Doors opened and I nearly fell out when mine abruptly swung wide.

"Out," the male operative who'd cuffed me said, reaching for my arm again. I let him half drag me from the SUV, hissing in pain when my cuffs shifted. My legs were almost too weak to carry me, but the operative bore most of my weight, hauling me toward what looked like a concrete bunker. A few bright spotlights lit up the otherwise pitch black night. It was probably around one or two in the morning. The cold air did nothing to soothe the blistering heat eating away at my wrists.

Entering the prison was a blur of glaring fluorescent lights, shuffling combat boots, and weapons shifting my direction. Voices blared over walkie-talkies, issuing orders and updating statuses. Apparently, I was a hot ticket item. Or maybe they did this with all the new prisoners. Either way, everyone was in a tizzy as I stumbled inside.

"Process her, then take her to B Wing Seclusion," the female operative who'd led my arrest said. "Make sure she doesn't have a phone."

A few hallways later, the male operative led me into a small room and finally let go. "Remove all your personal effects, then put on that clothing over there," he said with a nod at a bench along the wall.

I blinked when he took up a post in front of the open door. "What, no privacy?"

He didn't reply, his stare only hardening.

Okay, then. I wasn't exactly shy about my body, but still. Awkwardly, I removed my shoes, pants, and phone, hoping I at least got to keep my underwear. "Um . . . I can't get my shirt off with these on," I muttered, holding up my wrists.

His lip curled, but he strode forward and grabbed one of my arms. "Try to escape and you won't make it fifty feet before a bullet takes you down. And don't bother trying to thrall me. You know we take precautions," he stiffly warned, unlocking one cuff. The relief was instantaneous. Fresh tears filled my eyes as the silver torture device fell away, allowing my raw skin to rapidly heal. He kept the other cuff on, but the pain was more manageable now.

Turning away from him, I tugged off my shirt and reached for the prison jumpsuit on the bench. Didn't think I'd ever be wearing one of *these*. At least it was blue and not ghastly orange. After I buttoned it up and donned a white pair of socks and shoes, I turned toward him again.

"I'll get my phone back after this, right?"

A muscle feathered in his jaw as he ground his teeth together. *Yikes.* Wrong thing to say, apparently. Instead of answering, he grabbed my arm again and slammed my free wrist back into the cuff. I sucked in a hiss as the freshly healed skin began to burn up once more. Swallowing a whimper, I let him guide me from the room and down a hall. At the end was a solid, reinforced door. Probably coated in silver.

The operative nodded at a guard stationed beside the door, who turned to unlock it for us. Once past the door, two rows of cells awaited us. My sensitive hearing picked up movement behind several of the doors, but there were no windows to see inside. Instead of stopping at one of the cells, he led me down the hallway and took a left, where more cells awaited us. At the end was a guarded stairwell, and it only went one direction.

Down.

Panic tightened my chest. By the time we reached the bottom, I could barely breathe. We were clearly underground now. I could feel it, *smell* it in the air. After passing through one more guarded door, we arrived at a patch of isolated cells. There were only six in total, and I couldn't detect any movement beyond the doors.

At the second to last one, the operative finally stopped and looked up at a security camera. A few seconds later, the door unlocked and he pushed it open. When he nodded for me to enter, I did. As I caught sight of the interior, I whirled around in a panic. The operative was already closing the door.

"Wait. *Wait*," I cried, rushing forward. The door slammed shut and I made the mistake of touching it. Smoke rose up from my fingertips as they immediately melted at the contact. I jerked them away and screamed, "My cuffs! You forgot to remove my *cuffs*."

I heard him pause. Heard him blow out an agitated sigh.

"Please," I begged, not even caring how broken I sounded. "Please don't leave me like this."

I waited for what felt like an eternity, but he eventually started to move again. I muffled a sob as I heard the door click open. Shuffling back to give him room, I beseechingly held out my wrists. Hatred brewed in his eyes as he marched forward and grabbed my arm.

While he unlocked my left wrist, I whispered, "I didn't do it. I didn't kill anyone. I'm being set up."

He paused, staring daggers at my wrist. After a long moment, he yanked the cuff off and got to work on the second. "Saanvi is one of the kindest people I know. You betrayed her, Isla. You betrayed *us*. I guess that's what we get for trusting blood-sucking monsters. I hope you rot in here."

With that, he swiveled on his heel and stormed from the cell, taking the cuffs with him.

I thought I was alone. Thought I was the only soul down in this barren hellhole.

There weren't any windows, only a single lightbulb. A narrow cot was bolted against one wall, but there was no sink or toilet. Just a metal bedpan. The four walls were completely solid. Chiseling out an escape route through a pipe or vent wasn't an option.

I hadn't heard a single sound other than my panicked breaths for a solid hour.

Then, suddenly, I heard a voice. One that I hadn't heard in nearly five years. It scraped across my flesh like a dull razor, mercilessly scouring my sensitive skin.

"Isla Andrews, as I live and breathe. You must have been a very naughty girl to be placed down here with *me*."

At Troy's spiteful drawl, every last hair on my body stood on end.

I slowly rose from the cot on unsteady legs, instinctively crouching in a defensive stance. My eyes locked on the far wall, on the location of his voice. He was in the cell beside me. Troy D'angelo, the vampire who'd ordered my death sentence, was only a few feet away from me. Only a wall separated us. One flimsy *wall*.

"I know what you're thinking," he went on, clearly not expecting me to respond. "'Oh no, the evil D'angelo brother is here. Run. *Hide*.' Don't worry, Isla. I can't get to you through this wall. Not that I would if I could. My beef was never with you directly. You just happened to make excellent bait."

My lip curled back at that.

After a beat of silence, he said, "So, how is everyone? How are my father and brothers? How is the illustrious Syphon, savior of our people?"

At my refusal to answer, he clicked his tongue in disapproval.

"Come now, Isla. I've been down here alone for five long years. Haven't I been punished enough?"

"It'll never be enough," I hissed, squeezing my hands into fists.

"Ah, she *speaks*. What a sweet, sweet sound. I think that's what I miss the most. The pleasures of female company. That and fresh warm blood from the vein."

My mouth dried. I tried not to think about his words. Tried to block the sound of his voice. But he was relentless. He went on and on and on, as if making up for five years of silence.

"They starve you in here, you know. Not enough to be accused of inhumane treatment, but I never get enough blood. It's like they're trying to purge out the vampire in me. The *evil*. Don't they realize exorcism is for demons? I was born this way. Depriving me of blood will only make me crave it all the more. Right, Isla? I remember how you struggled. I bet that's why you're in here. Did you finally snap? I don't blame you. Vampires were meant to feed directly from the source, and you were deprived of that, poor thing."

"*Shut up*, Troy!" I finally shouted, slapping my hands over my ears. "The last thing I want to hear is your incessant *yammering*."

My outburst only seemed to fuel him *more*.

"Just think, Isla. If you all hadn't tried to stop me, you could be feeding to your heart's content. No one would look at you as if you were a monster. Humans would be your playthings, not your *jailers*. Oh, how the righteous have fallen. Guess that makes you the villain too. It's poetic justice, really. Knowing you're as trapped as me is almost enough to make me come."

My butt hit the hard floor as I curled into a tight ball and began to hum. To rock. To do *anything* that would drown out the torment of his voice. I couldn't think of a worse punishment than this. I'd prefer being tortured with *silver* than have to listen to Troy's voice a moment longer.

But there was no changing my fate. I was stuck down here with the vampire who'd destroyed my human life. Who'd drained my best friend. Who'd betrayed his own family. Who'd hurt Kade. Even more, I could already feel my sanity slipping. The tenuous control I had over myself might not last if I was forced to remain here much longer.

And, if I went feral, they might *never* let me out.

CHAPTER 34

KADE

My soul felt torn to shreds.

Every cell in my body yanked at me to follow after Isla. The need to protect her stole my sanity, making it nearly impossible to obey Loch when he ordered me to stay.

For the first time in my life, a part of me resented our drothen bond. I was being forced to choose duty over love. Before Isla, I'd never struggled to put my drothen responsibilities first. But now, the desires of my heart outweighed my need to serve.

If Loch and I didn't have such a strong bond, if I hadn't felt his deep sympathy, I would have left him. Would have sacrificed the very thing that had given me new purpose for the woman I desperately loved.

"We aren't deserting her, Kade," Loch said as I paced the castle's foyer.

I'd refused to go any farther, not even to change my torn, bloody shirt. The arrow and bullet hadn't slowed me down. I'd ripped them out, barely feeling the pain over all the adrenaline pumping through my system. The itch to hop back into my car was overwhelming. I couldn't stand being several hours in the wrong direction from Isla. My only consolation was that I knew where the SCA had taken her. Knew, because I'd helped escort Troy to that very prison five years ago.

My mate. *My mate.* Was trapped with that sadistic monster. I'd never felt more desperate, more *helpless* in my entire life.

"Her dad, brother, and Tess are there right this very second, doing everything they can to convince the SCA of her innocence," Loch went on, trying to calm *me* for once. "As soon as we come up with a new plan to capture Samuel, we'll join them."

"And who's to say that plan won't fail too?" I unfairly shot back. Grimacing, I threw Kenna an apologetic look. Loch could take my ire, but she'd never seen me so . . . unhinged. She smiled at me sadly, but didn't offer any other form of comfort. Which was good. I didn't deserve anything more. Her best friend was in prison because of my failure to keep her safe.

"It won't fail," the king said, striding into the foyer with Everett at his side. "The first plan was too transparent. Lord Quinn is too distrustful to fall for such a trap. I suspected this would be the outcome."

I stopped dead in my tracks to glare at him. "You knew? You knew and didn't *tell* us?"

"*Suspected*," he corrected, pausing to assess my barely restrained fury. "I suggest you remember yourself, drothen. I know Isla means a great deal to you, but—"

"She's my *mate*," I snapped, ignoring the shrieking bells in my head warning me to back down. "She's mine to protect. *Mine*. She needs me and I'm stuck here against my wishes. So unless someone has a plan to get her out, I'm leaving. I don't care what punishment I receive for it."

At my outburst, Kenna muffled a gasp, both hands pressed over her mouth. No one else made a sound. I knew I'd crossed a dangerous line. Knew that my words were akin to treason. But I wouldn't take them back. Couldn't. I'd already wasted too much time following protocol. If the king ordered me thrown into a dungeon cell for my insubordination, I'd escape before his guards could touch me.

No one was going to separate me from my mate. *No one.* I'd fight tooth and nail to free her from that prison. *Alone,* if I had to.

After a long moment, King Ambrose frowned in disapproval and said, "You forget yourself, Kade. Need I remind you of the *oath* binding you to my son? The safety of this family always comes first. You have sworn to eternally obey and protect at the very cost of your life. A drothen's sole duty is to—"

"Remain unfailingly loyal at all times," Loch intervened, stepping toward me. "Kade hasn't forgotten himself. He's fought bravely by my side for over a century and never once put his needs above my own. He's become a brother to me in every sense of the word. But there is no denying fate when it brings you true love," he said with a soft glance at Kenna. "I know that more than anyone. Kade has found his mate, and that makes her family. So he hasn't abandoned his duty. Quite the opposite, in fact. He's trying to uphold his oath, and we've done nothing but stand in his way."

The king stared at his son thoughtfully. I wanted to do the same, but didn't dare take my eyes off Ambrose. Eventually, he sighed and turned to me once more. "If that's the way my son feels, then so be it. Kenna became a part of our family, and so shall Isla. She falls under your sacred drothen duties, and therefore has become your top priority. But before you go rushing off to save her, I'd like to share my plan—if that's okay with you."

At the wry twist of his lips, I bowed my head, showing him the respect he deserved. "Apologies, my king. Thank you for allowing Isla to be a part of this family. I will gladly accept any help you have to offer."

"Better," he said with no small amount of amusement. "First, I should warn you all. You're not going to like this plan. But here's why it's going to work..."

King Ambrose was right.

I *hated* this plan.

We all did.

Everett had begun yelling the moment his father had finished speaking, demanding we find a better solution. Loch had remained silent, his face set like granite. Kenna had worried her lip while she tilted her head in concentration, either having a silent conversation with Loch or her familiar.

"I've already contacted the council about the plan," Ambrose said when Everett paused to take a breath. "I wanted to be prepared in case it came to this. They'll make the proper arrangements if everything goes sideways."

"You mean set me on the throne if you're *killed*," Everett snapped, hints of fear overlying his harsh tone.

The king's expression softened. "I must protect the alliance we made before it breaks. Cooperation with the SCA will ensure our race's survival in a world that is forever changing. Our kingdom is relying on us, son. This is what it means to rule. Sacrifices must be made—"

"Yeah, but not your *life*," Everett argued. His face suddenly crumpled. "I'm not ready."

"Yes, you are," Ambrose said, clasping his son's shoulder. "I was much younger than you when the crown was placed upon my head. Besides, you have your brother. Together, you'll protect the D'angelo bloodline and keep our kingdom from falling into the wrong hands. I have faith in you both."

"You're not going to die, Father," Loch finally spoke. "Not if I have anything to say about it."

"That's the thing," Ambrose said, giving both his sons a stern look. "I think both of you should remain here."

His suggestion was met with deafening protests. After a few minutes, he raised his hands in surrender.

"Fine. I should have known better. But he can't know you're there. One hint of your presence could jeopardize the whole plan."

"He won't," Loch and Everett said in unison.

Nodding, the king finally turned to me. "Are you ready?"

I dipped my head. "Yes, my king."

"Good. Then make the call."

CHAPTER 35

ISLA

Several hours passed before I finally succumbed to a restless sleep riddled with nightmares.

Troy's voice dominated my subconscious, whispering to me again and again to embrace my darker side, to give in to my instinctual cravings and prey on innocent humans.

"Listen to me, Isla," he crooned in my ear. "Do exactly as I say."

I nodded, suddenly giving in. Suddenly *listening* to him.

No, no, no, I screamed at myself, but it was like I couldn't hear. The only sound that registered was Troy's voice.

"I want you to thrall that man over there into leaving the bar with you. Flirt with him. Make him believe he's going to get lucky. Suggest he take you to a motel room. Once you're there, I will arrive with further instructions."

I nodded again, then did exactly what he said. Within minutes, I was stumbling from the bar with Gunner Landry's arm draped over my shoulders. I giggled like a schoolgirl, batting my lashes up at him. His free hand reached down and grabbed my butt, and I didn't even flinch.

Minutes later, we were pulling into a motel parking lot. While he went inside the lobby to secure a room, Troy's voice was suddenly whispering in my ear again. Except that it had an accent this time. British. *Familiar.* It wasn't Troy's voice after all. It was . . .

Samuel Quinn's.

"When you're inside the room, thrall him to stand still and not make a sound. I will knock, and you will let me in. When I'm finished with him, you will bite him and feed. Then, you will leave and walk home. The minute you're inside your apartment, forget everything that happened from the moment you left the tavern's bathroom."

I followed his instructions to the letter, walking all the way home to promptly pass out on the couch.

The dream shifted, and I was suddenly standing in Saanvi's apartment with my phone pressed to my ear. "Let me speak with her," Samuel said.

I did. Seconds later, she grabbed the glass and cut her wrist. I tried to scramble away, but Samuel told me to drain her. When I refused, he said, "Listen very carefully, Isla. This is exactly what is going to happen. You're going to grab Saanvi's arm and feed on her. When you're finished, forget my instructions. You fed on her because you lost control, not because I told you to."

The second I ended the call, I grabbed Saanvi's arm and began to feed. She didn't struggle or utter a sound, as if she'd been commanded not to. A face suddenly materialized behind my closed lids. Not Troy's. Not Samuel's.

Kade's.

He was sad as he watched me feed on my innocent victim. "Stop, Isla," he pleaded. "This isn't you. You're not a killer."

"Help me," I whimpered, still clutching Saanvi's arm.

"Help yourself. You can do this, Isla. *Fight.*"

"I . . . I'm *trying*. But I—"

"Isla, wake up. *Wake up.*"

I awoke with a gasp, sitting straight up in bed. Except that I wasn't in bed. I was on the floor. Not in Saanvi's apartment, but in a prison cell.

"Do you always whimper when you sleep?" Troy's annoying drawl filtered through the wall. "If so, I'll have to put in a request for earplugs. I need my beauty sleep."

Ignoring him, I replayed the dream I'd just had. The more I recalled the details, the clearer it became that the dream was actually the last of my blocked memories. It worked then. Our strengthened bond had broken through the allure. I was finally free of Samuel.

But I was still a prisoner.

I glanced around the cell, my swift moment of relief fading. I had no idea what time it was, but I'd been in here long enough for my throat to start burning. Did they really starve vampires down here? Also, I desperately needed to *pee*. I flicked a glance up at the corner where a security camera blinked at me. Sure, I could easily jump up and rip it from the wall, but I didn't exactly want to know what the punishment would be for doing that.

Swallowing my humble pie, I quickly relieved myself in the bedpan, grateful when Troy didn't utter a word. Just as I shuffled over to the cot to sit—what else was I supposed to do?—a sound from outside my cell had me standing alert.

A door clanged shut, followed by the stomp of boots. As they neared my cell, I crept toward the door on silent feet, stopping just shy of touching it. A part of me couldn't help but unrealistically hope that they'd stop, unlock my door, and declare me innocent. Instead, the boots swiftly moved past my cell and stopped in front of Troy's.

"Finally," I heard him say as something plastic scraped across the concrete floor. "Did you guys forget I was down here again? I'm a prince, you know. I'm still waiting for those magazines you promised. The ones with all the pretty naked ladies. Unless you want to send Isla over here naked. I'd be okay with that. I've been dying to see those curves of hers. The curvier, the better, am I right?"

"Shut up and drink your blood, *parasite*," a male guard said, which only made Troy laugh like a lunatic. A boot kicked the door before the guard stomped off in the direction he'd come.

"Wait," I said as he marched right past my cell, but he didn't stop. A door slammed in the distance, then all fell silent.

"Aaww, did they forget about you?" Troy crooned with fake sympathy. "Best get used to it. I'd share my blood with you if I could. For a favor, of course. I'm a virile male with needs, after all."

Despite how hungry I was, my stomach soured at his vulgar suggestion. "You're disgusting."

"I like to think of myself as pragmatic. I know what I want and take it. Those who deny themselves are simply weak and pathetic."

I clenched my jaw to keep from verbally sparring with him. It's what he *wanted*, and I wouldn't give him that. Besides, he would never listen to reason anyway. The guy was a self-obsessed narcissist.

Another few hours crawled by, then a few more . . . and a few more. Based on how starved I was, it was probably late evening. I hadn't expected my friends and family to get me out, especially this soon, but being alone down here with Troy as my only company was demoralizing. Even though I *knew* I wasn't guilty of murder, being stuck in this cell made me feel like I was.

The mental stress was almost worse than the physical. Doubts assaulted me. What-ifs. What if I never got out of here? What if the people who cared about me eventually gave up trying to prove my innocence? What if Kade got tired of waiting and found someone else to love?

That one hurt the most.

The very thought made me tightly curl up on the floor again. As determined as I was to get out of here, I didn't know how to make that happen. We still didn't have any proof that Samuel killed Gunner

Landry and allured me into feeding on Saanvi. And now that he knew we were onto him, he could be halfway across the world, for all we knew.

My future was looking bleaker and bleaker. And if the SCA truly thought I was guilty, then the future for all vampires was in jeopardy.

I needed to *fix* this. But how?

"Someone's coming," Troy suddenly droned. "I'll put in a good word for you this time. I'm not a heartless monster, after all. And, who knows. Maybe they'll let me out early for good behavior."

I didn't even bother responding. Troy D'angelo was *never* getting out of that cell. He'd hurt way too many people. His very existence threatened the delicate balance between the human and supernatural worlds.

It hurt knowing the SCA thought I was exactly like Troy. That my very existence could destroy the world as we knew it. I understood their fear, but at the same time, I hated it. Hated how unfair this situation was. Hated how *helpless* I was.

Once again, I had no control over what happened to me, and I was getting sick of it. *Sick.*

As a door down the hall unlocked, I rose from my curled up position, prepared to make myself heard this time. I wasn't guilty, and I'd make sure everyone within hearing distance knew that. I'd tell them every day for as long as it took. Even if they kept me in here forever, I wouldn't stop. Wouldn't stop trying to clear my name. To get my life back.

I was going to *fight*. Because I had so much to live for.

I recalled Kade's face as he made love to me, and my resolve hardened all the more. No way was I giving that up. Giving *him* up. I'd finally admitted how much he meant to me, and I wanted to spend the rest of my very long life showing him just how much.

And I still needed to tell him. To confess how deep my feelings went.

I *needed* him to know. That, after all this time, I—

My cell door unlocked. Shocked, I nearly jumped out of my skin. As it swung open, revealing the male operative who'd cuffed me a day ago, every inch of me froze. Something was wrong. The hair on my neck stood on end as he stared at me with wide eyes. He was trembling from head to toe, a look of pure terror on his face.

Before I could question him, a voice spoke. One that spread ice through my veins. "You may speak now. Tell Isla what you came here to say."

The operative continued to shake as he stuttered out, "Y-you are free to go."

"And?" the voice prodded.

"And I'm s-sorry for locking you up."

"Good. Now knock yourself out."

I stifled a gasp when he suddenly grabbed the doorframe and bashed his head against it. Blood streamed down his forehead, but he did it again and again, until his eyes rolled back and he crumpled to the floor.

As soon as his body fell, a tall figure slid forward and took his place in the doorway.

"Hello, Isla," Samuel Quinn said, that same smug smile still on his face. "Looks like you could use some rescuing for real this time."

I stared and stared, too dumbstruck to respond. When I flicked a glance at the unconscious operative, Samuel made a small sound of disgust.

"Sorry about the mess. I really only brought him down here to apologize. It was petty of me to call the SCA on you. I truly am sorry for that, but I don't like being double-crossed, Isla. I'm over it now, though. Here. I'll prove it to you." He stepped aside and gestured me forward. "You're free to go."

I stared at the opening, still rooted to the spot. "What's the catch?" I finally said, narrowing my eyes suspiciously.

"Ah, you don't trust me," he replied with a soft tsking sound. "Would it help if I said that this wasn't even my idea?"

I frowned. "Then whose idea was it?"

"Someone who must care about you a *great* deal. Now, come along. I ordered a guard to shut off the cameras, but we only have a small window before outside communications become suspicious." When I noticeably bristled, he sighed and added, "I have no intention of controlling you again, Isla. As long as you cooperate, I won't have a need to. When we're safely out of here, you can go wherever you wish."

"But why? Why are you helping me?" I couldn't help but ask. This was too good to be true. Depending on what his plan was, leaving with him could be worse than staying in this cell.

"It suits my interests," he cryptically replied with a shrug.

My frown deepened. "Let me guess. You have an interest in *framing* me again, this time for escaping prison?"

He slowly smiled. "You really are a clever one. It really is a shame that I'm not your type."

"Indeed. I draw the line at mind-controlling sociopaths."

His lips twitched into a slight frown. "None of this was personal, Isla."

"Of *course* it was," I hissed, digging my nails into my palms. "You *used* me to get to the king. How is that not personal?"

"Hey," Troy abruptly interjected. "What are you talking about? Who's trying to get to my father?"

Samuel's head suddenly snapped in the direction of Troy's cell.

"Who are you?"

"Prince Troy D'angelo, favored son of King Ambrose. Who are you?"

Stupid, *stupid* Troy!

"Pay no attention to him," I hurriedly said, taking a step toward Samuel. "He's delusional."

Samuel held up a gloved hand to stop me, then stepped in the direction of Troy's cell. When my door was clear, I slipped forward on silent feet and peered into the hallway. Samuel was staring at Troy's cell door, curiosity stamped across his face.

No, no, no, this was *not* good. What was worse than one psychopath on the loose? *Two* psychopaths. And if they decided to team up, it would be that much harder to stop them.

Hopping over the unconscious operative, I cautiously approached Samuel, saying, "You really don't want to do that. Troy isn't someone you can trust. He—"

I froze in horrified shock when Samuel suddenly grabbed the handle and wrenched the reinforced door open like it was a flimsy piece of plywood. As the vampire of my nightmares slowly emerged from his cell, my legs started to shake. Troy saw me and threw a wicked grin my way. Vengeance sparked in his hazel eyes, making my limbs quake harder.

Samuel noted the exchange with a slight frown before saying to Troy, "I've heard stories about you. Is it true that you tried to start a war by exposing our true forms to humans?"

Troy smirked at him. "You heard right."

"Do you think yourself clever, boy?"

Troy's smirk dimmed. "I have my moments. Who are you anyway, and how did you bust through this door so easily?"

"Let's just say I'm an old friend of the family."

"Well, *friend*, it's been nice catching up, but I have places to be. Anywhere but here, actually. So, thanks for springing me, but—"

Lightning fast, Samuel's hand shot out and gripped Troy by the throat. "You're an idiot, just like your grandfather," he lightly growled. "He once thought exposing ourselves to humans was a clever idea too. Do you think yourself a god? You are *nothing*. You're a mere speck of dust on a vast timeline. What arrogance you possess to think you can change how the world turns. When I've taken my rightful place on the throne, then and only then can true change take place."

Troy struggled to break free, but for all his strength, his efforts were futile. I was too shell-shocked to do anything but gawk at the scene. When Samuel finally let Troy go with a shove, he turned from him dismissively, as if he truly was nothing. Rage contorted Troy's features. With a roar, he lunged at Samuel. I scrambled back, nearly stumbling over the inert operative as Troy crashed into Samuel in a tangle of powerful limbs.

The fight lasted seconds.

Samuel flipped Troy over his shoulder and slammed him to the ground. The cement shuddered and cracked under the force, fissuring up and down the hallway. When Troy tried to rise, Samuel froze him in his tracks with a single word. "Stop."

Troy immediately obeyed. He gaped up at Samuel, disbelief stamped across his face. "What . . . what are you?"

"A powerful being that isn't to be trifled with. Soon, your entire family will be reminded of that fact."

Something flashed in Troy's eyes then. Something that looked a lot like fear. His lips pulled back in a quivering snarl. "Don't touch my family."

Samuel slowly crouched beside him. "You mean the family who put you in here? Who *betrayed* you? Why would you even care?"

Troy's lips thinned.

"*Answer* me," Samuel commanded.

"Because I still love them," Troy spat, trembling in fury.

"Ah. That's unfortunate," Samuel impassively said. "Because it's time for the D'angelo line to end, and you won't have the opportunity to say goodbye."

It only took Troy a second to register the words, then he was roaring. Cursing and screaming. But he didn't move from his spot on the ground, still trapped under the allure. My heart pounded out of control as I reeled from Samuel's words. Before I could so much as take a breath, Samuel was speaking again. Uttering a command that finally had me reacting.

Four words. That was all he had to say. *Four words.*

"Tear out your heart."

I screamed. Screamed and screamed as Troy's claws shot out and gouged deeply into his chest. He threw back his head and roared, the sound of fury quickly turning to one of fear and pain. Awful sucking and tearing noises cleaved the air as he literally wrenched his own heart from his chest. My throat sealed shut, cutting off my screams. I stared, my mouth open in frozen horror, as Troy lifted his own heart into the air.

He'd stopped screaming, but his heart . . .

Oh gods, his heart was still beating.

I looked at his face and found his eyes open. They were glazing. Glazing over in death. But not before they fixed on me.

Protect my family, they seemed to plead. *Keep them safe.*

The moment only lasted a split second, but I nodded. With tears streaming down my face, I promised my greatest enemy his dying wish.

As the last of his breath left him, he seemed to sigh in relief. His hand dropped, still holding his now unbeating heart.

CHAPTER 36

ISLA

I was no stranger to death.

But Troy's death . . .

It would haunt me for the rest of my days.

I thought I couldn't hate anyone more than I had hated him, but I was wrong. Samuel Quinn was the epitome of everything I hated. Predator of the weak. User. Exploiter. *Murderer*.

Troy had been evil, but he'd somehow still retained the capacity to love his family. But as far as I could tell, Samuel only loved one person.

Himself.

As he led me through the prison's maze of hallways, I tried to bottle my rage and focus on the here and now. He hadn't allured me or even touched me yet, and I planned to keep it that way. Despite how terrified I was of him, I didn't stray from his side, keeping one step behind him at all times. If he thought I was cowed by the brutal act of violence I'd just witnessed, then maybe I could get the drop on him somehow.

No way was I letting him get away this time. Now that I knew he intended to kill off the D'angelos one-by-one before assuming the vampire throne, I'd never been more determined in my entire life to bring the bad guy down. He might have superior strength and mind control on his side, but I had my own strengths. Ones I planned to use at the first available opportunity.

"You're awfully quiet," Samuel finally spoke, nearly making me jump.

As we passed yet another unconscious guard, I replied, "Not much to say. I'm just a pawn in your diabolical game, after all. My opinion doesn't matter."

"Isla," he softly chastised, making me bristle. "You forget that breaking you out of here wasn't my idea."

"Right. And killing Troy wasn't your idea either."

"No, actually. At least, not until he posed a problem. I'm a reasonable man, Isla. I never wanted there to be bloodshed. I'm saddened that it came to this."

Movement down the hall interrupted our conversation. Faster than I could blink, Samuel shoved me to the side as a spray of bullets zipped toward us. I covered my head as one bit into the cement wall inches from my face. With a growl, Samuel streaked toward the lone operative. *Fast.* Faster than I'd ever seen a vampire move before.

The operative didn't even have a chance to cry out before he was on the ground, his neck twisted at an odd angle.

My heart hammered as Samuel stared down at his most recent kill and, without a speck of emotion, said, "He must have slipped past my control. We should hurry in case he called for backup."

When he moved away from the dead operative to peer around the corner, I swallowed the fear rising in my throat and swiftly joined him. Except that, at the last second, I paused at the fallen operative and crouched as if to check for signs of life. I only had a split second. *Less* than a second. To make my move.

Angling my body so that Samuel couldn't see my left hand, I reached up with my right and felt the operative's neck for a pulse. There wasn't one, of course, but I kept up the ruse until I found what I was looking for. The feel of cool metal against my fingertips set my heart to pounding. I almost sobbed with relief. Sliding the phone from the operative's pocket, I quickly palmed it.

To hide my reaction, I pursed my lips before shooting a glare at Samuel. I nearly choked on my tongue when I found his eyes already on me. Narrowed suspiciously.

In one smooth motion, I jumped to my feet and bit out, "Why did you have to kill him? Why couldn't you have just knocked him out like the rest?"

He studied me for a moment, long enough that my palms began to sweat. "You really do care about humans," he finally said, still looking at me oddly.

"Of course I do," I said with heat. "The second I don't, I become nothing more than a monster."

He seemed unfazed by my not-so-subtle jab, staring at me a moment more before motioning me to rejoin him. When I did, he resumed walking down the hall. "To answer your question, I killed him because he shot at you. He threatened my plans, and I don't take kindly to that."

"Why do you care if I get shot? It's not like I'm much use to you anymore. The SCA already believes I'm the murderer. Since the cameras are down, they'll have no choice but to blame this mess on me. Whether I'm dead or not doesn't matter. The damage will further convince the SCA that vampires can't be trusted, and they'll dispel the alliance. Tensions will rise once again and hostility will turn to bloodshed. The vampire kingdom will look to their king for protection, and that's where you come in, I presume."

He glanced at me with a raised brow. "You've done your homework, I see. And yes, that is the gist of it. Except that, unlike Troy, I want to limit the casualties. A change in rulership rarely happens without some form of contention, but I'm only seeking what was promised to me. I have no desire for war with humans, or to rule over them. I simply want what I'm owed, and if I have to kill a few people to make that happen, then so be it. As for keeping you alive, I made a deal, and I *never* back out of a promise."

"How chivalrous," I deadpanned. "You must be so proud of yourself."

"I am, actually. I waited for my due time to take the throne, but Ambrose stole what was rightfully mine. I've patiently allowed him to be king for nearly five centuries, which is far more than he deserves. Blood doesn't make you a ruler. *Power* does. And soon, the entire vampire kingdom will see just how misplaced their faith has been."

"And then you'll just *kill* Ambrose in cold blood, along with his family, because they *threaten* your plans."

"That's an unpleasant way of putting it, but yes. What with the recent curse they incurred upon the kingdom and this latest tiff with the SCA, their reign has never been more questioned. The king's own son led a revolution against him, nearly starting a global war. Vampires respect strength above all else, and the king has appeared weak countless times. Once I show them just how weak Ambrose really is, no one will question my decision to take his place."

"And his sons?" *And Kenna? The babies?*

"Are a liability. No trace of the D'angelo bloodline must remain for me to secure the throne."

I wanted to scream. To rage. To attack him with my fangs and claws. Instead, I channeled all of my investigator skills into this moment, keeping him talking so he wouldn't notice how furious I was. "What about the whole 'killing them only if they pose a problem' speech?"

Samuel paused to open a door for me before saying, "I did my homework too, Isla. The eldest two sons are loyal to a fault. They won't allow me to rule in their father's stead, so they must be eliminated. I'm guessing they set a trap for me the moment we step foot outside this prison, the little fools. If they try to interfere with my plans today, I'll make sure they never do again. Your lover's sob story was convincing, but everyone knows in the game of chess that the king is the most important piece. Once captured, the game is over, and I very much doubt they're ready to admit defeat."

I almost blew my cover then. Almost demanded he tell me what he meant. What he planned to do. Fear for my family and friends, fear for *Kade*, nearly got the best of me. I didn't know what to expect when we left this prison, but apparently Samuel did. And I couldn't warn them. Couldn't do anything but keep Samuel talking.

Something was bothering me though, and as we neared the front entrance of the prison, I slowed to ask, "Why are you telling me all this?"

He slowed as well, coming to a complete stop in the middle of the lobby. Several operatives lay sprawled where they'd fallen, hopefully only unconscious. A few remained upright, blank expressions on their faces, as if they were in a trance.

"Because I meant what I said that first day we met in the tavern," Samuel replied, turning to face me. "I'd like us to be friends. Even more, if you'll allow it. I enjoy your company, Isla, and I've had no one to truly talk to in a long time. I know we've had a rocky start, but I'd like to make it up to you. Give me a second chance. Come away with me today and you'll want for nothing."

When I didn't respond, when I didn't do anything but stare at him, he took that as an encouraging sign. As he eased into my personal space, my lungs seized with panic. Instead of retreating though, all I did was slowly inch my left hand behind my back. He didn't notice the subtle move. His focus was solely on my face, on the way I desperately tried not to show my fear.

He stopped so close that the tip of his shoe brushed mine. My limbs began to shake, but I held still, held still as he reached up and gently grazed his knuckles over my cheek. Every instinct screamed at me to shove his hand away and *run*. But I didn't. I fought off a shiver of revulsion and allowed him to trail his fingers over my skin. Fingers that had so callously killed a man mere moments ago. All the while, I held eye contact, facing my new greatest fear.

My new greatest *enemy*.

Unexpectedly, he dropped his hand and said, "You still pine after the male who claimed you." When my eyes widened, he added, "I saw your reaction when he got shot the other day. It's okay, Isla. You can tell me the truth. I won't force it from you."

Swallowing my panic, I whispered, "Yes."

He nodded. "I thought as much. Which means killing him would turn you against me." My throat closed again. I knew he could hear my thundering heartbeats, knew he could sense my panic and fear. Yet his expression remained soft, as if he were trying to calm a spooked horse. Clearing his throat, he said, "If you promise not to betray me this time, I'll promise not to harm him. I will even let you keep him, so long as he remains under my control. But if you come with me today, you will be *mine*, Isla. Mine to claim, not his. Agree to this and I won't touch him."

Stunned by his words, I could barely breathe, let alone think.

Before I could fully process what he was asking me to do, a deep growl came from the entrance. "Try to claim her and I'll tear your throat out."

We both whirled to find a powerfully built man framing the entrance doors. A look akin to death burned in his piercing blue eyes. My heart thundered anew, but for a completely different reason this time.

He was here. Kade was *here.*

My feet moved toward him all on their own, the instinct to be near him a pull I couldn't ignore. Samuel intercepted my path in one swift move, nearly causing me to ruin everything. I ground to a halt, tucking my precious cargo further up my shirtsleeve. I did it so quickly that I didn't think he'd catch it, but Kade's gaze flicked to my left hand. Only for a second. Then narrowed on Samuel once more.

"Ah, the besotted lover has arrived, right on schedule," Samuel said, a hard edge clipping his words. "Isla and I were trying to have a *private* conversation though, so if you don't mind waiting outside a moment longer. There's a good chap."

"She's *mine*, you sorry ballsack," Kade said, his voice dangerously low. "A deal's a deal. I deliver my end and you deliver yours. Now hand her over."

"I see no evidence that you delivered on your promise," Samuel countered, slowly reaching for me. "So unless I see proof . . ."

"Ambrose is in my car," Kade bit out, staring daggers at Samuel's encroaching hand. "He's been bound and drugged with silver. We only have minutes before his sons arrive, so I suggest you take your end of the deal and keep your filthy hands off my mate."

Wait, the *king* was here? What was going *on?*

"Careful, boy," Samuel hissed, "or I'll rip out your tongue and feed it to you."

Kade widened his stance even more and flicked his fingers in a taunting "come hither" gesture. "Come on then. I'd like to see you try."

Samuel tensed, as if prepared to do just that.

An image suddenly slammed into me. Of Troy's fight with Samuel that had only lasted seconds. That had ended with him broken and bleeding on the ground, his heart ripped from his chest by his own hand.

The image suddenly changed and it was *Kade* on the ground, staring up at me as that beautiful light left his eyes.

A roaring filled my ears, louder and louder until it burst from me in a single word.

"NO!"

Without a single thought other than Kade's safety, I lunged for Samuel. When I latched onto his arm, he actually stopped in his tracks. Kade, on the other hand, bared his fangs at the sight of me touching the powerful Ancient. He violently trembled with barely restrained fury, his chest heaving as he fought to control himself. Forcing my gaze to Samuel, I looked up at him beseechingly and said, "Please don't hurt him. You promised."

At that, his eyes dropped to mine. As he studied me, I already knew what he would find. Acceptance. *Submission.* Victory filled his golden gaze. I could practically *taste* it. A smile that could be construed as charming tilted his lips, but I knew better. "I thought you drew the line at mind-controlling sociopaths?"

"I want my life back," was all I said with a shrug.

Apparently, the right thing to say. "Something we have in common," he replied with a nod of approval. "Tell your boy toy to stand down, and I won't touch a hair on his pretty head."

It wasn't a command. In fact, he hadn't allured me once since breaking me out of my cell. Whether he thought he could win me over or simply believed I wasn't a threat didn't matter. All that mattered was playing along, even if it hurt Kade. Even if he never forgave me. Even if it meant doing exactly to him what I most feared done to me.

At least he would still be *alive.* And that was all I cared about right now.

"Control him," I said to Samuel, all while looking Kade dead in the eye. The shock, the *disbelief* on Kade's face, was almost enough to undo me. I silently pleaded with him to understand. To trust me. This was the only way. Before I could start crying and tip off Samuel, I switched my attention back to him. "Controlling Kade is the only way to keep him safe from what happens next. Please, Samuel. Allure him to follow your command so we can take him with us."

"Isla, *no.* Whatever you're doing, *stop*," Kade growled, but the sound gave me a smidgeon of hope. Because it wasn't laced with a command. He wasn't using his ability on me.

"Please, Samuel," I said again. "If you want a second chance with me, then please let me bring Kade."

I could tell he didn't fully buy my sudden devotion to him. He would be stupid to, and I knew he wasn't dumb. I'd already duped him once. Still, his pride and arrogance couldn't help but be enamored at the prospect of gaining me as a consolation prize. The thought disgusted me, but I would stomach it for as long as it took.

I saw the moment when he gave in. His eyes both softened and flashed in warning as he dipped his head and said, "As you wish, my lady."

Kade's thunderous roar cleaved the air, and my heart broke at the agonized sound.

Before he could so much as take a step, Samuel snapped his fingers at him and said, "You. Come here."

Just like that. Just. Like. That. Kade's spine snapped straight and he obediently strode toward us.

A part of me died right then. Seeing him so utterly helpless, *powerless*, was devastating. And it was all my fault. I'd taken away his strength. His *purpose*. Everything that made Kade Carmichael who he was had been stripped away in a second.

He was nothing now but a slave.

CHAPTER 37

ISLA

I knew they were close by, my friends and family.

Just out of sight. Hidden by magic. Waiting.

Kade never would have come here without them. Never would have willingly given up his own king, even to rescue me.

He was too good. Too loyal to betray his family.

But they'd obviously orchestrated a desperate plan, offering up the one thing Samuel wanted most.

King Ambrose.

I still couldn't believe he was here. Still couldn't believe they'd used him as a bargaining chip to free me. But this wasn't just about me. This was about *all* of them. About securing their futures. Their *children's* futures. No one wanted Samuel to take over the vampire kingdom. And maybe this was the only way they could ensure he didn't.

By placing their king out in the open. By making him look *vulnerable*.

It was a lure Samuel couldn't resist.

But they hadn't accounted for one thing. Samuel's interest in me. It went beyond using me to get to the king. And that interest changed everything.

I could make sure he didn't kill the king. Even more, I could make sure he didn't kill Kade or Loch or Everett or Kenna or the babies.

I just needed a little time. A little more time to see my own plan to fruition.

My promise to Troy was what fueled me now. Was what made me ruin their plans and take matters into my own hands.

There was no room for doubt or what-ifs. No room for panic or fear.

I was going to do this or die trying. This was my chance to save everyone I loved, and I'd taken that chance without a backward glance.

I knew they were still there though, my friends and family. Puzzling over the unexpected twist. Watching as Samuel led me toward his car. As Kade followed in our wake with a barely conscious Ambrose slumped over his shoulder.

For all they knew, we were now under Samuel's allure. I wasn't exactly struggling to get away. Still, I prayed they wouldn't try to intervene. Prayed they would wait. Just a little while longer.

Please, I silently begged them. *Please wait. Don't try to save us.*

The timing wasn't right. Not yet.

I knew my plan would work. Knew that I could fix everything. *Everything*. If they would just wait.

My plan was daring, and definitely dangerous. But it could incriminate Samuel for good so that he never hurt another soul ever again.

If they would just wait.

Samuel brought us to a gated, high security compound just outside of Rosewood. The well-manicured property covered several acres, all the way to the ocean. As we pulled up to the front gates, I noticed a pair of guards. One of them looked vaguely familiar.

"I started recruiting months ago in preparation for this," Samuel said from the driver's seat beside me, no doubt sensing my confusion. "Most of the guards are Feltore I found in clubs and bars. They're completely under my control. They respond only to me and have orders to attack anyone who sets foot on this property. Don't worry though. They'll be receiving new orders not to touch anyone in this vehicle, unless I say otherwise."

I could tell he wanted me to be both impressed and cowed by his explanation. All I felt was bone-chilling dread. For some reason, I'd expected him to live alone. Maybe because he was so distrustful. But, for all I knew, he had an army of vampires in there. An army that had no choice but to obey him.

Okay, don't panic, I silently berated myself. *Your plan can still work. None of these vampires have to get hurt.*

But avoiding *all* casualties might be impossible now.

I didn't comment, flicking a glance at the side mirror to make sure Kade was okay. Samuel had ordered him into the back seat to guard a still barely conscious Ambrose. But not before commanding him into silence. He hadn't spoken a word for the entire three hour trip.

I knew he was silently taking in every single thing Samuel said though. His eyes were currently narrowed, fixed on the back of Samuel's head. But they suddenly shifted, as if he could feel my gaze on him. When his eyes found mine in the mirror, my chest tightened painfully.

I'm so sorry, I tried to silently tell him. *I'm going to fix this. I promise.*

I forced myself to look away again, afraid of his response. Afraid that, instead of understanding, I'd find hatred instead.

When the guards opened the gates and the car rolled forward, I tamped down my worry over Kade and went into investigator mode. The road was a straight shot to a three-story mansion beyond. The structure was white with black trim, colonial in design, with thick pillars supporting the wide front. Off to the side was a smaller building. A carriage house, maybe.

I assumed that's where his puppet soldiers slept. I kept a close eye out for them. It was in the middle of the night, of course, the only time Feltore could be outdoors. This was the perfect time to get a rough estimate of their numbers. To distract Samuel from my fixation on his guards, I said, "The house is beautiful. How long have you had it?"

"Oh, not long. I've been in London up until recently. It was a good place to lay low after I was exiled. Vampires tend to stay away from heavily populated areas as a rule. It suited my needs though. When the curse broke, I headed this way and eventually settled into this place. Only temporarily though. The owners are actually still here. They've been rather *gracious* hosts."

My mouth dried. That could only mean one thing. He'd kept the human owners around to use as his in-home food source. The king kept humans in his castle—even his *wives* were human—but they weren't thralled to be there. None of them were forced against their will.

That's what made Ambrose a great ruler and would make Samuel a terrible one. Soon, everyone else would know that too, vampire and human alike. I'd make sure of it, as soon as I had a moment alone. One single moment was all I needed. But reaching that moment without getting caught was going to be harder than I thought.

When we pulled up to the house, another pair of guards swept forward to open our doors. Samuel immediately exited the car to relay his new orders, gesturing at us while he did. Judging by how one of the guards was eyeballing us, I knew we weren't getting inside that house just yet.

In my line of work, I knew the drill. Distrustful bad guys always checked their *guests* for hidden weapons and communication devices. He seemed confident that we hadn't been followed, but I doubted he'd take any chances with us in his house.

So, as discreetly as I could, I tugged my precious cargo from my sleeve and bent over as if to tie my shoe. Lickity split, I shoved the phone down my jumpsuit and into my sports bra, then quickly straightened. It wasn't a perfect fit, but my ample cleavage nestled the thin device between my breasts, keeping it from shifting around.

"Isla," Samuel suddenly said, nearly making me jump out of my skin. Had he seen? My eyes were wider than they should be when I peered up at him. Clearly misunderstanding my deer-in-headlights look, he said, "No need to worry. My security has been informed of your presence. You can safely step out of the car now."

I did, relieved when my boobs kept the phone firmly in place. Soon, Kade joined me, ordered by Samuel to remove the king. Ambrose still had thick silver chains wrapped around his arms and legs. I winced when they shifted and I saw how raw his wrists were. Instead of slinging him over his shoulder again, Kade slid an arm around Ambrose for support and propped him up as best he could. The king's head lolled forward, his usually impeccable clothing in disarray.

Still wearing the gloves he'd worn in the prison, Samuel slowly stepped toward him and, one-by-one, tugged his fingers from the gloves. When his hands were bare, he made a show of reaching out and touching the silver chains. His skin barely sizzled from the contact. After a moment, he gripped the chains with both hands and said, "Guess you don't need these anymore." With a sharp yank, he ripped the chains off the king's arms.

Ambrose let out a weak groan, but was otherwise still.

I dug my nails into my palms as Samuel swiftly crouched and did the same to the king's leg shackles. Straightening, he dusted imaginary dirt off his dark suit jacket before fixing his gaze on Ambrose's face. When Ambrose was still too weak to lift his head, Samuel shot out a hand and grabbed a chunk of the king's hair, wrenching his head back.

My hands shook as I forced myself to remain still. I swiftly glanced at Kade and found his jaw set like stone. If looks could kill, Samuel would be dead ten times over. I wanted to reassure Kade somehow, but all I could do was watch and wait. I was risking the most with this moment. After nearly five years of working as a private investigator, I knew how the scumbags of the earth thought. But they weren't always predictable. Sometimes, they're emotions controlled their actions, making them do things prematurely.

I could only hope that Samuel's very long existence had made him a master of self control. He'd want to draw this out, not end the king quickly. Ambrose had said he'd publicly shamed Samuel before banishing him. I could only guess that Samuel wanted to do the very same thing to Ambrose. Revenge was predictable that way.

Killing him right now, with so few witnesses, wouldn't be very satisfactory. No, he would wait. He would wait until the moment was right. When he had the attention of the entire vampire kingdom.

Sure enough, Samuel started to taunt his rival. Not with bodily harm, but with vicious words. Bringing him down low. Lower than he already was.

"It's been a long time, Ambrose. Time hasn't treated you well, I see. I expected you to grow stronger, not *weaker*. I was surprised when I heard a rumor that something had happened to you. That your sons were trying to hide how pathetic their father had become. You should have passed the mantle to one of your sons while you had the chance. I would have much rather challenged a young, able-bodied male than an ailing failure like you. The fight won't even last seconds, kind of like the one I had earlier today with your youngest son."

Oh no. Please, no. Not like this.

But Samuel was relentless, smiling when Ambrose finally cracked his eyes open. "Yes, that's right. I had an unexpected run-in with your prodigal son. I have to say, I wasn't impressed. If all your sons are like him, then I'll have no trouble killing them too."

"No," Ambrose rasped, weakly reaching for Samuel. "You lie."

Samuel shoved his arm back down. "I don't lie, Ambrose. That was always *your* thing. Your *father's* thing. Backstabbers. Betrayers. I made sure your weak spawn got exactly what he deserved. You should thank me, really," he said, slipping a hand inside his jacket. "Leaving him to rot in a cell for eternity is cruel. Having him tear out his own heart is much more merciful, don't you think?"

When he pulled out something round and bloody—Troy's heart—the king cried out. Cried out in pure anguish. A tear slid past my control. Then another, and another. Samuel didn't notice, too fixated on the king's pain.

But Kade did. His own eyes shone with tears as we shared a glance. *Did you see it happen?* he seemed to ask.

I nodded, my lips trembling.

Sorrow and compassion lined his face.

I had to look away before I broke down too. As awful as this moment was, I had to remain strong. Falling into Kade's sympathy would only leave me vulnerable. They were counting on me. They *all* were. I'd failed countless times over the past couple of weeks, but this

321

was one time I refused to. The stakes were too high.

I waited for the torture to stop, certain that Samuel couldn't tear down the king anymore than he already had. I was wrong. While Ambrose still wept over the death of his son, Samuel dropped the heart and kicked it aside like a discarded piece of trash. Then, faster than I could blink, he tore the clothing from the king's body, stripping him bare.

I almost couldn't stand it. Couldn't stand seeing a once so powerful man naked and wholly vulnerable before his spiteful enemy.

"Remember when you did this to *me?*" Samuel hissed in Ambrose's face, still gripping his hair. "You stripped me of my honor, my *dignity*, in front of the entire court. You made me look like a fool in front of them all. I had to walk *naked* from the castle. Had to roam the streets of Sanctum Isle in search of clothing, only to be turned away again and again. You turned everyone against me. *Everyone.* All because you felt threatened by my superior power. Well, how do you like that power *now?*" he finished with a roar.

I jumped when Samuel abruptly whirled and slammed a fist into the hood of his car. The metal caved in, leaving a fist-sized crater behind. Jerking his hand out, he slowly straightened and adjusted his clothing as if to collect himself. After a moment, he turned again and pointed at Kade. "You. Strip." He pointed at one of his guards next, saying, "Check every inch of his clothing. Make sure he isn't carrying anything that could lead his friends here."

As Kade began to obey his command, Samuel set his sights on me. When I went rigid, some of the coldness in his eyes dissipated. "Apologies, Isla, but I must search you too. I'm not prepared for unexpected visitors just yet."

My heart skipped several beats as he approached, clearly intending to search me himself. If he asked me to strip naked too, this was all over. My plan would miserably fail. I frantically racked my brain for an alternative, but came up empty. All I could do was stand there and pretend I had nothing to hide.

"I get it," I abruptly said, startling myself at my sudden bravado. "I mean, the SCA already confiscated all my stuff, but you're welcome to frisk me if it'll make you feel better."

Oh. My. Gods.

Balls of steel. Yep. I had balls of steel.

I followed up my suggestive words by raising both arms and spreading my legs.

Please take the bait, please take the bait.

Oh, he took it. Hook, line, and sinker.

His eyes noticeably brightened at my submissive move, a small smile curving his lips as he stopped before me. I wanted to squeeze my eyes shut and block out his face, but I didn't. I held his gaze, silently giving him permission to feel me up. That was all the invitation he needed. Starting with my hands, he slowly ran his fingers up my wrists and arms. I didn't move a muscle. Encouraged, he cupped my neck and slid his fingers into my hair. I sucked in a quiet breath, as if I was enjoying his touch, when all I really felt like doing was biting his fingers off.

Reacting to the sound, hunger bled into his eyes. His touch turned sensual. More invasive. He trailed his fingers down my throat and collarbone, then ran them over the sides of my breasts and rib cage. When he squeezed my waist, I drew in a gasp. Lower and lower his hands went, skimming over my thighs and legs. Then they reversed course, sliding up the *inside* of my legs.

Crouching before me, he stared up at my face and gripped my thighs, nudging them wider. I didn't dare look at Kade. One glimpse of his expression would break me. I was already filled with self-loathing for allowing this cruel monster to touch me. I couldn't bear Kade's pain too.

Samuel's thumbs boldly swept up my inner thighs, all the way to my apex. Even with clothing on, I could feel the firm pressure of his fingers as they pressed against my center. I wanted to sob. To scream. To lash out and scratch his lust-filled eyes from their sockets. Instead, I sucked in another breath.

After a lingering moment, his hands rounded my pelvis and firmly gripped my rear. With a short squeeze, he stood, bringing his greedy hands with. They roved over my stomach, higher and higher until his thumbs grazed the underswell of my breasts.

I abruptly dropped my arms. "There. Satisfied?"

His fingers paused. At the expectant look on my face, he cleared his throat and let his hands fall to his sides. "Yes. I appreciate your cooperation."

That's a good boy. I mean, what else could he say? Excuse me, but I haven't finished groping your boobs?

When he stepped back, my knees weakened with abject relief.

But I made a mistake then. I looked over at Kade.

Stripped naked, he stood trembling, exposed for all to see. But instead of shame or vulnerability in his eyes, there was nothing but deep hatred. For a split second, I thought the powerful emotion was directed at me. But as Samuel turned to speak with one of his guards, Kade's eyes followed him.

He curled his hands into tight fists, and his trembling increased.

CHAPTER 38

ISLA

I was getting desperate.

I'd thought Samuel would simply lock us up for the evening and start fresh in the morning. It was late, after all. Sometime after midnight.

But he'd decided to play *host* to his unwilling guests. He took us on a grand tour of the estate, making sure we saw every single room. The king could barely stand. Kade still lended him his support, but Samuel had sadistically forced them both to roam the halls naked. I was still in my prison jumpsuit, which he suddenly seemed to notice.

"If you'd like to change, I can lead you to your room," he said to me. I bristled at the word "room." He said it like I truly was a welcome guest here. Or worse, a permanent resident. Had he planned for this? Planned for *me* to come here with him?

Turning to him, I shoved down my disgust and replied, "Thank you, I'd like that."

"Would you like me to send one of the home owners to your room as well? You look parched."

The burning discomfort in my throat increased tenfold at his offer. I swallowed the painful lump and managed to rasp, "No, thank you. I'd just like to retire for the evening, if that's okay."

It hurt. It hurt to play nice with him when everyone else in this house was his prisoner. But I didn't fool myself into believing he trusted me. He still hadn't allured me, but I knew this was a test. One false move and he'd have me under his control faster than I could blink.

Before we reached the room, Samuel stopped Ambrose in his tracks with a few words. "Don't move from this spot until I return."

I was surprised when he didn't order Kade to watch over him, instead beckoning him to continue following us. I found out why a few minutes later. As Samuel opened a heavy oak door leading into a sizable bedroom, he snapped his fingers at Kade and said, "You are to remain in this room until I fetch you. You will not speak and you will not bite Miss Andrews. That is all."

My eyes nearly bugged out as Samuel waved Kade inside, then stepped aside for *me* to enter.

Noticing my expression, Samuel chuckled. "Come now, Isla. I promised to make it up to you if you gave me a second chance. This is the first step in repairing the damage between us. We'll have all the time in the world to get better acquainted once I'm king, but tonight, I think you'll be most comfortable with him. Go to your lover. Do with him as you wish. I won't stop you."

When I hesitated, he gave me an encouraging smile. Was the dude *serious* right now? Was he *gifting* me a night with Kade in hopes that I'd soften toward him? That I'd eventually have *sex* with him?

The guy couldn't be any more of an arrogant *dick*.

Still, I murmured my thanks like a good girl and scooted inside the room, trying my best not to look too eager. Not eager for the reasons he was probably thinking in that sicko brain of his, but because he was finally leaving me *alone*. I could finally. *Finally*. Execute my plan.

The moment he shut the door, I got to work. First things first: make sure there were no cameras. Listening devices would be harder to find, but I didn't need to speak for this next part. No sooner had I started my search than hands were on my shoulders. Startled, my eyes shot up to meet Kade's. He opened his mouth, but nothing came out. He tried again, then grunted in frustration.

Grabbing my hand, he flipped it over and began writing on my palm. *What?*

I met his eyes again and froze at the desperation I found there. Shame immediately filled me. I'd done this to him. Left him powerless and in the dark. Left him with no choice but to trust me. Raising a finger to my lips, I gestured around the room before taking his hand in mine. *Not alone*, I wrote, hoping he'd understand.

Nodding, he threaded his fingers through mine and strode toward what looked like an attached bathroom. Closing us inside, he immediately turned on the shower and tugged me into the stall with him. Before the cold water could hit me, he backed me into the corner, using his large body as a buffer. As a *shield*. I was safely hidden from any possible cameras now.

Kade, you big beautiful genius, I wanted to say, but didn't. Better to keep quiet. Even with the water running, any words I said might get picked up.

As Kade splayed his hands on the tiles either side of me, cocooning me as best he could, I finally revealed my precious cargo to him. At the sight of a phone sliding from my bra, Kade's eyes rounded like saucers. I smirked and pointed at my boobs, mouthing, "*Best assets.*"

A look of awe crossed his face. I wanted to bask in his expression, pretending that everything was okay between us. But I couldn't waste these precious seconds, no matter how badly I wanted to fix the terrible hurt I'd caused him. Dropping my gaze to the phone, I held the device closely to my chest and turned it on.

The first thing I saw was the "low battery" icon flashing.

My lungs seized in panic and I nearly dropped the phone as my hands began to shake. Fingers were suddenly on my face, cupping my cheeks. My fear-filled eyes flew back up to Kade's, only to find his expression calm.

"*Breathe*," he mouthed, gently sweeping his thumbs across my cheekbones. Their steady warmth and quiet strength started to soothe my frayed nerves. In a matter of seconds, I felt panic's tight grip begin to loosen.

Inhaling a trembling breath, I gave him a grateful smile and got back to work. Thankfully, I knew exactly what needed to be done. First, send Samuel's confession video to my dad. I knew I could count on him to check his messages, even in the middle of the night. He'd know what to do with it. The video was all the evidence we needed to clear my name and convict Samuel of murder. More importantly, it would spur the SCA into action. He'd attacked their prison and confessed his plans to kill the D'angelo family and crown himself king, after all. They'd want him found and captured immediately.

My fingers flew over the screen as I executed my plan, sealing Samuel's fate one letter at a time. When the video was sent, my knees weakened. Continuing to lend me his strength, Kade pressed his legs against mine to keep me upright.

There was only five percent battery left as I frantically typed up a message to go along with the video. I used short sentences, paraphrasing what had happened to us and where we were now. I quickly described the gated compound and explained how the guards were under Samuel's control. How Kade and the king were too, but I wasn't. I then admitted to Samuel's obsession with me and how I planned to exploit it. I could keep Kade and Ambrose alive until help arrived, but it needed to come soon.

I didn't want to give myself to Samuel, to sacrifice all that I was for him, but I would. To keep Kade and the king safe, I would give up everything.

I left that last part out though. It was my *dad*, after all. He didn't need to know that I was willing to whore myself out to a monster to keep him from killing anyone else. I prayed it wouldn't come to that. Prayed that help would reach us in time.

At the last second, I added that Troy was dead. They needed to know. To understand just how powerful Samuel was.

When I finally hit send, I couldn't quite stifle a relieved sob. "I did it," I breathed, fighting with the emotions overwhelming me. The most vital part of my plan had been accomplished. Kade responded by pressing a kiss to my forehead, his hands still warming my face. I immediately melted at the contact, squeezing my eyes shut. But only for a moment.

Forcing myself to pull away, I tipped my head back to look at him. "*I'm so sorry,*" I silently mouthed, allowing him to see my shame and guilt. About ruining their plans, about forcing him to come here, about the king's current state, about letting Samuel touch me. Tears filled my eyes. "*Do you hate me?*"

"*Never,*" he immediately mouthed back, then pointed at himself. "*I. Follow. You.*"

My chin wobbled. "*I. Will. Fix. This.*"

"*I know.*"

A quiet sob escaped me. Reaching up with my free hand, I slowly slid my finger down his chest, directly over his heart. "*I.*" A heart shape came next. "*Love.*" Then, "*You.*"

I watched as he received my message. As he inhaled a ragged breath. Then another. Tears shone in his eyes, making mine spill over. He cupped my hand and pressed it to his thundering heart.

I love you too, his eyes clearly said, making me cry harder.

When he lowered his head to kiss me, softly caressing my lips with his, I sighed against his mouth, "Forever. You're my forever too."

In response, he slid his fingers into my hair and kissed me passionately. My toes curled in my shoes before pushing up so that I could eagerly return the kiss. In no time, our mouths grew greedy. Desperate. So did our hands. As my fingers began exploring the hard contours of his chest and stomach, Kade started unbuttoning my jumpsuit. The air thickened with warmth, both from the water and our rapidly heating bodies. The glass walls fogged, concealing our frantic movements.

When Kade pushed the jumpsuit off my shoulders, I helped him slide the material down my arms and body. Toeing off my shoes, I kicked the bunched clothing aside, only for him to tug on my panties next.

Gasping, I pulled my mouth back to breathe, "Samuel."

At the mention of his name, a growl rumbled in Kade's chest. I pulled back even more, surprised when Kade shook his head and mouthed, "*I. Don't. Care.*"

Good gods, that shouldn't make me wet, but it did. Kade's nostrils flared as he scented my arousal. With another growl, he hooked his fingers into my underwear and tore it from my body. The primal move sent bolts of excitement shooting up my legs. Reacting to my excitement, he reached between my thighs and slid his fingers through my wet center. At the rush of pleasure, I threw my head back against the tiles and moaned.

We were really doing this then. Essentially saying "screw it" in our need to comfort each other, to *love* each other. Screw anyone listening or watching. No one could control this moment. No one could *take* it from us.

This moment. This *precious* moment. Was ours.

While his fingers continued to stroke me, Kade gripped the nape of my neck and ran his hot tongue up the length of my throat.

I trembled uncontrollably, nearly losing my hold on the phone. As if suddenly remembering it, he paused to take it from me. I whimpered at the loss of his fingers, and he chuckled. Faster than I could blink, he removed my bra and wrapped it around the phone before setting the bundle on my discarded shoes.

And then he was kneeling before me. Looking up at my face as he grasped my thighs and eased them apart.

My eyes widened as his intentions became clear. Good goddess, he wasn't messing around. He didn't only want to say screw it. He wanted to say screw *you* to Samuel by claiming me in every way he could.

Sure enough, he reached up and ran a finger over my stomach, forming the letter *M*. Without taking my eyes off his, I felt him shape a word down the length of my torso. A word that made me shiver from head to toe.

MINE.

Expelling a breath, I nodded and whispered, "Yours. Only yours."

Heat brightened the blue of his eyes, making my core tighten painfully with need. Sliding my fingers into his hair, I gripped the ends and guided his head to where I desperately wanted it to be. My core spasmed when he released a pleased growl and wasted no time taking me.

As his tongue darted out and licked all the way up my aching center, I saw stars. My back arched and I cried out from the sharp jolt of pleasure. He rewarded my reaction with a mindblowing tongue swirl that made me lose all sense of time and place. All I could do was hold on as he feverishly licked and sucked, leaving me a panting, trembling mess above him.

His tongue felt so good that bliss rapidly stole through my limbs. I whimpered his name as a powerful orgasm started to build. My body grew limp and he gripped my thighs to hold me up, licking me faster. *Harder.* A shockwave of ecstasy abruptly shot through me and I screamed his name, shaking violently as I climaxed against his tongue.

Oh, but he wasn't done.

No sooner had the orgasm hit me than he was on his feet, whirling me around to face the wall. In one swift move, he aligned his erection with my entrance and slammed into me. I cried out from the pleasure pain, digging my nails into the tiles as he began to thrust, deep and *fast.* His fingers wrapped around the base of my throat, lightly squeezing. I could barely catch my breath, overwhelmed by the powerful way he claimed my body.

But I loved it. Loved the dominance. The roughness. The possessiveness. With anyone else, I would have hated it. Hated how little control I had. But with him, I surrendered to the moment. Willingly submitting, because he was my protection. My safe place. My *home.*

As he buried his face against my neck, breathing heavily, my body sang. Despite our dire circumstances, I'd never felt more free. If this was to be our last moment together, then I would cherish it forever. Because it was perfect, both breathtakingly vulnerable and painfully honest.

Nothing was hidden.

It was just him and me, expressing our love in a way that words never could.

And whatever happened after this precious fleeting moment of time, we would face it, knowing that our love was stronger than even the greatest of fear.

CHAPTER 39

KADE

I claimed her all night long.

Not with my bite and venom, but in every other way possible.

She claimed me in return.

First my cock, sucking and licking the length until I expelled my release with a roar. My body might be imprisoned in this room, but I made full use of what little freedom I had to thoroughly love my mate. Our bond burned stronger and stronger with each intimate act, an invisible fiery thread that tied us closer and closer together.

With one final lick, she crawled up my body and latched onto my neck, feeding like a ravenous animal. I cradled her to me, rolling us over in bed to shield her naked body with mine. I knew we were being watched, and I didn't care. That didn't mean I wanted my mate's body exposed to *him* longer than necessary, though.

I knew Samuel wanted her. Knew that my having sex with her all night long wouldn't stop him from pursuing her. He didn't care that she was mine.

The sick freak only cared that he could *take* her from me whenever he wished.

When he'd put his hands on her earlier, I'd sworn an oath right then and there to tear him limb from limb. After I was finished, I'd set his mutilated body on fire and make him watch it burn. I didn't know when or how, but I would do it. His blood was mine. *That* I knew.

I could still feel the effects of his allure making me stay in this room. Forcing me into silence. Forbidding me from biting Isla. But as she released her venom inside me, *claiming* me, I felt his hold ever so slightly loosen.

That's it, baby, I silently encouraged my mate. *Claim me. Strengthen our bond. Only then can I be set free.*

I didn't shower the next morning, despite Isla's warning that Samuel might react poorly to the powerful scent of sex on my body.

I didn't care.

He saw me as little more than a kept man. A sex toy for Isla until he could claim her for himself. He didn't see me as a threat, only a mild inconvenience.

At least he'd ordered the female homeowner to deliver me my clothes about an hour ago. Probably so he didn't have to stare at my dick any longer—which was no doubt bigger than his.

The bedroom's closet had been generously stocked with feminine clothing though. Shirts, pants, dresses, shoes, even undergarments that were exactly Isla's size. If I didn't want him dead before, I did now. The whack job had been planning for this. For Isla to stay here with him.

He hadn't simply wanted to get his hands on Ambrose. He'd been hoping that Isla would eventually warm up to him. *Willingly*. Her genuine acceptance of him seemed to be important. So much so that he was willing to tolerate my presence.

For now.

As for Ambrose, my sensitive hearing had picked up on his location hours ago. I worried for his safety, but he wasn't as weak as his appearance suggested. Even though his idea hadn't gone according to plan, there was still hope that he'd survive this. Especially if Samuel's current fixation with Isla continued to distract him from completing his end goal.

Isla seemed to sense this as well. She'd chosen a rather evocative white dress to wear for the day, one that plunged both in front and back. There were cutouts at the waist that revealed even more skin, and the tight hemline barely covered her shapely rear. She looked sinfully sensual, and it took all of my restraint not to rip the dress off and toss her on the bed for another round of rough sex.

But our night of lovemaking was over, and I could hear footsteps approaching. *His* footsteps. A growl stuck in my throat and I once again tested my freedom. Words failed me, confirming that I was still under his control. But not for long. My veins were racing with Isla's venom, fit to exploding. She'd injected so much in her attempt to free me that I was still high on her bite.

If I wasn't careful, the invincible feeling gushing through me could be my downfall. Once I broke free of his allure, I only had seconds to incapacitate him. He mustn't suspect anything before then, or the game was over. Not just for me, but maybe for Isla too. I couldn't let that happen, so I did my best to school my expression. To make myself look like the mind-controlled puppet Samuel wanted me to be.

His footsteps slowed as he reached our room. A knock at the door needlessly announced his presence. It was all an act. A part he played to win over my mate. Isla's back went ramrod straight at the sound. She threw me a look over her shoulder. A desperate one. A *terrified* one. I curled my hands into fists, forcing myself to hold still when all I wanted to do was pull her into the safety of my arms.

Infusing as much calm into my expression as I could, I nodded once, encouraging her to open the door. I watched, relieved when the fear slowly bled from her gaze. She nodded back and swept toward the door, her high-heeled shoes clicking against the floorboards.

That's my girl.

As she opened the door to Samuel, the first thing I saw was his pleased expression. He didn't bother with subtlety, boldly raking his gaze down her body. Another growl pushed at my throat.

"I take it the accommodations were to your liking?" he said by way of a greeting, clearly including *me* in that comment as he flicked me a dismissive glance.

"Yes, thank you," she evenly replied, not even a hint of fear in her voice.

"I'm glad to hear it. And, might I say, you look absolutely gorgeous in that dress."

She smiled prettily. "Whoever picked it out has good taste. And it fits me perfectly."

"I hoped it would," he replied with a devilish smirk, one that made me want to rip off his lips and shove them down his throat. He held out his arm to her, his head slightly tilted to the side in invitation. "Shall we?"

Her shoulders tensed, but she took his arm with barely a hint of hesitation before saying, "We shall."

When he swept her from the room and firmly shut the door, not even bothering to look at me, my calm facade evaporated like smoke.

I rushed toward the door, determined to follow them. But when I grabbed the handle, my hand refused to turn it. I tried over and over, becoming more and more desperate with each passing second. But it was no use. I was stuck in here.

Stuck while my mate was in the clutches of a monster determined to seduce her.

CHAPTER 40

ISLA

I tried not to panic, but it was almost impossible as Samuel took me farther and farther away from Kade.

I knew what he was trying to do the minute he offered me his arm.

I knew the signs. Saw the looks he cast at me. With the king now firmly under his thumb, he was apparently taking a little break to *woo* me.

What the cocky bastard didn't know was that I *wanted* him to. I'd just thought Kade would be present while he did. Not that I wanted to subject Kade to more pain, but without him here, I was struggling to remain calm.

When we passed underneath a window at the end of the hallway, a ray of late morning sun hit me. I gasped as my skin immediately began to sizzle from the exposure. Samuel whirled me away from the window, blocking the sun's deadly rays with his body.

"Apologies, Isla," he said, reaching up to touch my collarbone where the sun had struck. As his fingers feathered over my rapidly healing skin, I forced myself not to flinch away. "I'll have the windows treated immediately."

I smiled my thanks, even as I fought off a repulsed shiver when his fingers slid a little too low. They lingered near the top swell of my left breast before falling away.

"I sometimes forget how fragile Feltore can be," he said, tucking my arm through his again. "It's something I intend to fix when I become king."

My smile froze as I blinked up at him. "What do you mean?"

"My blood has become very powerful, Isla," he explained, turning to lead us down the stairs. "Its healing properties surpass that of Venturi, making it possible to cure Feltore of their sun aversion. I would use it to strengthen our kingdom, if given the chance. That's all I've ever wanted for our people. Unity. Strength. I'm really not the bad guy everyone makes me out to be, you know," he finished with a chuckle.

My mind reeled at his words. I could be cured? I could go out in the *sun* again?

"I've upset you."

Startled, I looked up to find him watching me. Watching my *reaction*. The blood slowly drained from my face. Had he planned this? Had he intentionally forced me into the sun so he could look like the *hero?* Gods, I was such an idiot. I'd actually *fallen* for his little speech. Swallowing, I quickly shook my head. "No, not at all. You just caught me by surprise."

His expression softened. "I could change our world for the better, Isla. I could change *your* world. I know you want your old life back, but if you'll let me, I can make your wildest dreams come true. Why settle for less," he quietly said, reaching up to touch my cheek, "when you can have more?"

Samuel said all the right things. *Did* all the right things.

The guy knew how to wax and wane poetic, that was for sure. A small traitorous part of me was intrigued by some of the promises he offered, but they came at too steep of a price. I desperately wanted to feel the sun's warmth on my face again without burning to a crisp, but not at the cost of everything I held dear.

Still, I pretended to fall under his sway, spending hours in his company as if I enjoyed every moment. Before I knew it, evening was fast approaching.

"You must be starving," Samuel abruptly said, standing from the living room couch where we'd been chatting. Correction: *he'd* been chatting. Just in time too. His hand had been inching *way* too close to my bare thigh. As he helped me to my feet, he added, "I hope you don't mind, but I have a little dinner entertainment planned for this evening."

"Oh?"

"I've been trying to figure out the best way to spread the word of my challenge for the throne. Times have drastically changed, and a meeting in the town square is sadly a thing of the past. Our people now span across the globe, and news of my intentions must travel fast if I am to remain uncontested during the trying days to come. As I said earlier, I don't want bloodshed or war. Only what was promised to me. Once the kingdom sees that I hold them no ill will for past wrongs, they should accept me soon enough."

"But most of them love King Ambrose," I dared to say, hoping I wasn't overstepping. "Killing him and his family could incite a riot."

He didn't look angry at all by my words. More like sympathetic. "You are a newly turned vampire and still fairly ignorant of our ways, Isla," he said, making me want to spit on him. "In vampire politics, strength will always supersede adoration. Despite their love for the D'angelo family, our people will understand why I have to eliminate them to secure my place. Once they see for themselves how frail Ambrose has become, they won't fight my decision to take the throne."

"And how do you plan to do that?" I asked, trying to keep my voice neutral.

His eyes brightened almost gleefully as he said, "I think showing you would be best. Despite the learning curve, I'm in awe at the power of social media these days."

Dread clutched my throat. Oh, this was bad. I could feel it in my bones. A being as old and power-hungry as Samuel should *not* have access to social media.

I couldn't prepare myself though. Wasn't ready for what he had to show me.

As we left the living room, he led me straight to the dining room. And inside the room, sitting *naked* at the table, was . . .

The king.

He just sat there. *Sat.* No chains bound him. Only sat, clearly under Samuel's allure.

Perched on the table in front of him was a phone attached to a tripod. Nausea swirled in my gut. I had to do something. *Say* something. Anything that would stop Samuel from doing something that couldn't be undone.

"You know that terrorists use this method to scare their enemies, right?" I blurted, trying to keep my tone light. "They send public videos of them torturing their prisoners or forcing them to say things, using the footage as blackmail. Is that your big plan?"

Okay, I was definitely crossing a line here. A *dangerous* one. Instead of pricking his pride and making him rethink his strategy, I could end up awakening an angry *beast*.

I struggled to breathe as he turned to me with a calculated look. This was it. I was going to die now. I'd opened my mouth and blabbered for the last time.

But instead of going all homicidal monster on me, Samuel laughed. *Laughed.* A genuine sound of amusement. "Oh, Isla," he said, raising his hand again to stroke my cheek. "This is why I picked you. Your passion is a breath of fresh air. You will make an excellent queen someday."

Say *what* now?

All the air left me in a whoosh. "W-wait," I stuttered, trying to catch my breath. "*Queen?* I—that's impossible. First off, I'm a Feltore. I'd have to be Venturi to be queen, and—"

He stopped my rambling with a soft *shhh*, placing his finger over my lips. "That law is of the past. I seek *change*, Isla. Our kingdom has been without a queen for far too long. A queen will bring *stability* to the uncertain times ahead. With you by my side, Venturi and Feltore will unite as never before, allowing a new era to be born. I would have you as my queen, Isla," he huskily whispered, sliding an arm around my waist to draw me close.

"Say yes," he implored, lowering his head so that his lips were nearly touching mine. "Help me secure our kingdom's future. Help me *strengthen* it. Together, we will be unstoppable."

This wasn't happening. This wasn't *happening.*

But what was I supposed to say? *Eat crow, loser. No one wants to be your figurehead queen.* Yeah, that wouldn't go over too well.

So I nodded. *Nodded.* Because I was playing this part until the bitter end, apparently. I didn't know what other choice I had. If I rejected him, he'd probably kill me, then publicly shame and execute the king next. After that, he'd definitely kill Kade. And I couldn't . . . I couldn't allow that to happen. I had to keep fighting the only way I could. I had to—

Rising up on tiptoe, I kissed Samuel.

He seemed startled at first, stiffening as I pressed my lips to his.

But when I slid my fingers into his hair and kissed him harder, he swiftly responded. With a low growl, he backed me up against the nearest wall and crushed my mouth with his. A scream built in my chest, but I shoved it down and returned his hungry kisses, allowing his tongue entrance when he thrust it past my lips.

I nearly gagged. Gagged on his scent and taste. It wasn't my mate's. It wasn't my *mate's*. I inwardly howled in sorrow and shame, all while I let my enemy possess my mouth.

I knew what was coming next, but I couldn't prepare for it. Couldn't tell my body how to respond when he started to touch me. His hands were greedy, roving over my curves as if he owned them. I felt my body start to shy away, to reject his unwanted touch.

It only wanted *him*. Kade. My *mate*.

Not this slimy creep who simply wanted me for my body. For *power*.

When I tried to break the kiss, desperate for air, for *space*, he grew even more persistent. He slipped a hand beneath the hem of my dress and reached between my legs.

"Stop," I cried, wrenching my mouth from his. "Stop. Please stop."

I can't do this, I can't do this, I can't do this.

I thought he wouldn't listen. Thought he'd force himself on me, overcome with lust. But, surprisingly, he stopped.

Before I could breathe a sigh of relief, he pulled back to search my face. My heart started to pound when he frowned at whatever he saw. "What's wrong?"

"I . . . nothing. Sorry, I just . . . I need a minute."

A muscle feathered in his jaw. "Is this how it's going to be with us? You pull away every time I get too close?"

My eyes widened. "What? No. It's just . . . it happened really fast, and I—"

His hand suddenly shot up and gripped my face. Not hard, but firmly enough that fear pumped through me. His frown deepened further at my reaction. "Why, Isla? Why can't you give yourself to me?"

When I didn't respond, not knowing how to, his expression changed. I wanted to scream, to rip my face away, to *run*. But it was too late.

I felt my control melt away as he peered into my eyes and spoke words infused with allure. "Tell me the *truth*, Isla."

"B-because," I stammered, my teeth chattering. "Because I only want Kade. We're bonded. He's my chosen mate, and I . . . I love him."

He hissed in displeasure, his upper lip quivering.

I thought for sure he would kill me then. I officially was of no more use to him. But I underestimated his obsession with me. Oh boy, did I ever.

"I will make it easy for you then," he said, still gripping my face as he pinned my lower half against the wall with his. "My venom is highly potent. One bite and any bond you might have will be severed. All you will want, all you will *crave*, is me."

"No, please. Don't bite me, Samuel," I whispered, starting to struggle against his grip. When I tried to shove him away, he grabbed both my wrists in a punishing grip.

"I didn't want it to be like this between us," he said, digging his fingers into my face as he pushed it back to expose my neck. "I wanted you to *choose* me. But if this is the only way I can have you, then so be it."

"No. *No!*" I screamed when his fangs appeared, flashing toward my neck.

As they punctured my skin, a phone buzzed. Samuel paused. The phone buzzed again and he sighed, retracting his fangs. I shuddered with relief, not bothering to hide my tears. Samuel ignored them as he let go of my face to pull out his phone.

"What?" he impatiently said.

I held my breath so I could clearly hear the voice on the other end. It was hurried. Frantic.

The words were music to my ears.

More tears sprung to my eyes. Tears of *relief*.

They had come. By the sounds of it, they'd *all* come.

Samuel must have read something on my face. Must have seen the *victory*. Thunderclouds darkened his golden gaze and, with a deafening roar, he threw his phone across the room. He suddenly slammed me onto the dining room table. The violent action knocked the wind out of me and I wheezed as he loomed over me, his expression pure rage.

Before I could drag air into my lungs, he gripped my throat and squeezed. "You *betrayed* me," he thundered, his eyes flashing with murderous intent. Gone was the softness. The patience. Even the lust had vanished. Nothing remained but the *true* Samuel Quinn, powerful Ancient and sadistic sociopath.

My claws shot out and dug into his arm, frantically trying to loosen his hold on me. To reward my efforts, he gripped my throat with *both* hands, squeezing so hard that darkness clouded my vision.

"I gave you a second chance," he continued to rage, but his voice was already growing distant as I wavered on the edge of consciousness. "I *trusted* you. I would have given *everything* to you. I . . ."

I could no longer hear him. Could no longer see the hatred on his face. My efforts to break free were futile against his superior strength. My body went limp as he continued to choke the life out of me. It wouldn't kill me, but I was helpless if he decided to find a more creative way to destroy me next. Maybe he would just squeeze and squeeze until my head popped off.

My body suddenly trembled, as if a great shockwave of sound had charged through me. Samuel's hands abruptly fell away. My crushed throat immediately began to open, to *heal*. Air leaked in and I gasped, desperate for more. Gulping lungful after lungful, I curled onto my side, shaking uncontrollably. I coughed, struggling to open my eyes. To see. To *hear*.

Another shockwave trembled through me, but this time, I knew what it was. A roar. A deafening roar of *fury*. And not just any roar. *Kade's* roar.

My heart soared at the sound, even as I weakly tried to stand. Seconds later, my vision finally returned. The first thing I saw was *him*. My mate. Slamming Samuel against the wall again and again. Pounding a fist into his face. He was still roaring, using every ounce of his strength to keep Samuel in place.

Blood spurted from Samuel's mouth and several gashes on his face. He looked stunned to see Kade. To realize that he'd broken through his allure. But only for a moment. Anger replaced his shock and he fought back, shoving Kade so hard that he flew across the room and nearly crashed through the opposite wall.

Forcing my trembling limbs to move, I staggered toward Kade and helped pull him from the wreckage. The second he was free, his arms came around me, pressing me tightly to his side. I clung to him with all my might, allowing fresh tears to fall.

"It's over, Samuel," I said, my voice a quiet rasp. "Give up. You're surrounded. There's no way to escape this time."

I focused on the Ancient, on his red hot fury at seeing me in Kade's arms. In that moment of tense silence, I could hear them now. Hear the shouts and fighting beyond the walls. Some even sounded close enough to be *inside*. The chaos was everywhere. Dozens of people, both vampire and human alike, had come to take Samuel down.

After a moment more, he laughed. Not like before. This sound was cold. *Cruel.* "Oh, I'm not defeated. It's impossible to defeat me," he said, wiping the blood from his mouth. "Even five hundred years ago, Ambrose knew I'd be back someday. It's why he so desperately wanted heirs. He *knew* I would challenge him again. Knew that I would win this time. That I would finish what I started. And this time, there's nothing anyone can do to stop me."

A door burst open in the next room, distracting us. And, in that split moment of distraction, Samuel made his move.

"Rip your heart out," he commanded.

Terror gripped me. I waited for the pull to obey him. But it never came. Kade didn't move either. The only one moving was . . .

I looked over just in time to see Ambrose place a hand over his chest. Over his *heart.* Faster than I could blink, his claws shot out and sank deeply into his flesh.

"No!" I screamed, whirling to stop him. Kade moved too, but we were too slow. We wouldn't make it in time.

There was suddenly an explosion of movement across the room. A figure soared through the air and crashed into Ambrose, taking him to the floor. As they rolled, I caught sight of a familiar face. Everett. He grappled with his father for control, wrenching his claws from his chest.

"Go!" he shouted, and I turned around just in time to see Samuel disappear into the next room.

"*Samuel,*" I shrieked, surging after him. Kade followed closely at my heels as I raced after the Ancient. He was moving *fast.* Faster than I could keep up. I kicked off my heels as Kade passed me and barrelled toward the door Samuel had just slipped through.

Before we could stop him, Samuel charged outside. Kade followed, but I frantically skidded to a stop just before the setting sun's rays could touch my bare feet. Cursing, I hovered just inside the entrance and helplessly watched as Kade pursued Samuel without me.

He wasn't alone though.

There were vampires and SCA operatives everywhere. Some of the Feltore guards under Samuel's control had donned protective clothing that allowed them to endure the waning sun. They attacked the operatives with ferocity, unable to do otherwise. I could tell the operatives tried to incapacitate them with nonlethal shots, clearly having gotten my message. Tess was using her crossbow, the silver-tipped arrows slowing them down, one by one.

Not too far away, I saw a brilliant blast of magic, then another, as my dad and Noah pushed back the mind-controlled Feltore. Even from here, I could hear them shouting spells, temporarily freezing their targets in place.

A blur of dark movement, of *shadows* caught my eye, and I shouted, "Loch!" Still moving, he whipped his head toward me. I frantically pointed in the direction that Kade and Samuel had gone. He nodded once before putting on a fresh burst of speed.

I lost sight of Kade then. Samuel too. They were too far away, heading toward the ocean. Toward Samuel's greatest chance at escape. Gritting my teeth, I thrust a hand out the door, then immediately yanked it back as painful blisters spread across my skin. Whirling, I backtracked inside. Only for a moment. Only to grab a blanket draped across the living room couch.

Steeling my spine, I threw the blanket over my head and dashed out the door.

CHAPTER 41

KADE

I didn't catch up with him.

He was too fast. Faster than any vampire I'd ever seen.

He would have escaped. Would have dived into the ocean and evaded my pursuit, only to wreak havoc another day. But he slowed. He *purposely* slowed, allowing me to catch up.

And I knew why.

He wanted to fight me. He wanted to *end* me.

I didn't slow. I plowed right into him, taking him to the ground. Right away, he let his strength be known. Unlike earlier when I'd caught him off guard, he was fully ready for me this time. His claws shot out and raked across my chest, cutting deep enough to sap the air from my lungs. Pushing through the pain, I brought my arm back and punched him square in the nose. The cartilage snapped and blood spurted. Seconds later, the injury healed.

We grappled for the top position, raining viscous blows on each other. I knew he was physically stronger than me. Knew that he could best me if this lasted much longer. But I fought with all the desperation, with all the pent-up fury I'd amassed while he'd held me prisoner. I didn't give him an inch. There wasn't an ounce of mercy in my blows.

All I saw before me was a walking dead man who'd made the terrible mistake of hurting my mate. It would be the last mistake he ever made.

"You're a fool, thinking you can best me," Samuel hissed, digging his claws into my back. I grunted as he wrenched them out again, taking chunks of flesh with. "You're nothing but a slab of meat. A *lackey*."

I blocked his next strike, feeling my muscles begin to shake. "She *hates* you," was all I said, knowing it was the best way to distract him.

He bared his fangs and snarled. I threw him into a headlock to get the upper hand, but my strength slipped and he got loose. I was suddenly flat on my back, partially dazed from the powerful blow he'd delivered to my temple. He straddled me, bearing down on his arm pressed against my throat.

"I'm still going to have her," he breathed in my ear. "Once she's addicted to my venom, I'm going to take her. Over. And over. And over. She will be my plaything to do with as I please. And she'll let me, fueled by the need for more of my venom."

With a thunderous roar, I shoved him off me and shot to my feet. He whirled and faced me, a taunting leer pulling at his lips.

"Kade!" a familiar voice shouted. Just as Samuel lunged at me, something sleek and silver whistled through the air toward me. Instinctively, my hand shot up and caught the hilt now tightly wrapped in leather. Without a moment's hesitation, I swung Betty around and caught Samuel across the chest.

As he reeled back with a hiss, I threw my drothen a grateful look and called, "Thanks, Lochie."

"Need some backup?"

"I could use a little. Sammy here won't take the hint that no one likes him."

Samuel growled at the nickname. I grinned like a fiend and twirled Betty, gratified when he flicked a nervous glance at the sword.

That's right, dirtbag, I inwardly purred. *Get a good long look. She's going to be severing your limbs soon.*

I saw the moment he realized his predicament. Saw and knew what he'd do next. Sure enough, he opened his mouth. But before he could entrap us with his allure, I bellowed, drowning out the sound of his voice. In the next instant, we attacked. As Betty sliced toward Samuel's neck, a shot fired. Samuel stumbled back when his leg took the hit, barely able to evade my whistling blade.

We kept him on the move, taking turns wearing him down. Not giving him a chance to speak. To escape. Hope rose in my chest as he slowed. He was purely on the defensive now, dodging bullets and swords swipes. But some of the blows hit home, knocking him down bit by bit. Sweat poured down my face and neck. Fatigue shook my arms.

I'd never fought against a foe this powerful before, but I thought for sure we had him. It was only a matter of time now before he fell.

A feral gleam unexpectedly entered his gaze. He flicked a glance over my shoulder as if he'd spotted something. The quickest of looks. It threw me off, just enough for him to grab my blade with both hands. Blood gushed from his nearly severed fingers but, with a roar, he yanked the sword from my grasp and sent it sailing.

Stunned by the desperate move, I didn't react in time.

"Stop," he ordered, casting his allure at both me and Loch. In my peripheral, I saw Loch freeze. My own limbs deadened, rooting me to the spot. I inwardly fought and screamed, just like I had earlier today. Through sheer force of will, I'd broken through his control, my strengthened bond with Isla the catalyst.

As I fought to break free now, a rush of strength surged through my body. It was from the drothen bond this time. Loch was sharing his powerful Venturi strength with me. I fought harder.

Samuel paused a second, allowing his fingers to heal. Then he approached. His eyes weren't on me though. They were once again over my shoulder. When he reached me, he dipped his chin as if in greeting. "Isla," he said, then yanked me around.

My eyes widened in horror as they spotted my mate, standing several yards off with a blanket draped over her. The sun hadn't quite set. Angry red blisters covered her bare feet and legs where the blanket couldn't protect them. She was clearly in pain but stood unwaveringly strong, staring Samuel down with determination.

"Don't hurt them," she said, loud and clear.

"Or what?" Samuel harshly bit out from behind me, still angry at her betrayal.

"Or nothing. Let them go and you can have me. Do whatever you want with me. Torture me. Inject me with your venom. I don't care. I won't fight you."

"Isla, no—"

Samuel's fingers bit into my throat and squeezed, cutting off my words.

"I can't trust you anymore, Isla," Samuel replied. "I need more than words now."

"Fine. Tell me what to do and I'll do it."

I renewed my inner struggle to break free of his control.

"Okay," Samuel said after a moment. "I want you to stab your lover through the heart."

Even with the blanket shadowing her features, I could see the blood drain from her face. "That's not . . . Samuel, no. I can't do that."

"You make it sound like I was giving you a *choice*, Isla," he hissed, tightening his hold on my throat. "Take up his sword and stab him through the heart. That's an *order*."

At his growled words, she cried out. Cried out in anguish and fear. But she obeyed, her legs woodenly carrying her to where Betty

351

lay. Crouching, she picked up the sword with trembling fingers and approached. Tears poured down her face. When our eyes connected, she started to sob.

"I'm so sorry. I'm so sorry, Kade," she choked out, but still kept coming.

"It's okay," I strained to say past Samuel's rigid hold on my neck. "It's okay, baby. Just look at me. Look at my face."

She did, even as she stopped and raised the sword. Even as she placed the tip to my chest, directly over my heart.

"I have one last thing to say to you," I said over her sobs, making sure to hold eye contact. "One very *important* thing."

My fingers twitched as the blade bit into my skin.

"What?" she whimpered, trying and failing to stop the sword's forward momentum. Blood trickled down my chest. "What is it?"

Drawing in a lungful of air, I looked her dead in the eye and expelled words. Words bursting with sire command. "*Don't listen to him.*"

Her lips parted in shock. Shock as my words, as my *intentions* sank in.

Samuel barked a laugh. "Really? No last profession of love? How utterly pathetic—"

He suddenly made a noise. A terrible, awful choking noise as Isla lifted the sword and plunged it through his throat. Blood splattered the side of my face, but I was already moving. Already whirling around to grab him. My movements were slow as I continued to fight off his control, but they were fast enough. Yanking the sword from his throat, I brought it down on his right arm.

He screamed as the blade cleanly severed his limb. Screamed again as I did the same to his other arm. He fell to his knees, gasping for air. I raised the sword again, this time aiming for his neck.

"Wait," Isla said. I paused to glance at her, surprised at how calm she looked. Blood had spurted everywhere. Her white dress was soaked with it. And yet, she crouched before Samuel. She looked him right in the eye and said, "Let's see how powerful you are without a tongue."

And then my mate, my beautifully strong mate, reached inside the Ancient's mouth and ripped out his tongue.

CHAPTER 42

ISLA

I watched Samuel's body burn until it was nothing but ash.

By that time, the sun had set, taking the last of my pain with it. My family and friends were gathered around the clearing, the crackle of dying flames and pounding ocean waves the only sounds. The second Samuel had died, the power of his allure had begun to fade. The Feltore under his control had stopped fighting. Loch could move again, and the king had been set free.

They'd all joined us to watch Samuel's demise, human and vampire alike. Many things had been destroyed during his short reign of terror, but I was certain we could rebuild again. With the truth burning before us, we had everything we needed to repair the damage done to the alliance. It wouldn't be easy, but nothing worth fighting for ever was.

I tipped my head back and glanced up at Kade. His handsome face glowed in the flickering flames, making his blue eyes appear brighter. He looked down at me and tightened his arms around my middle, tucking me more firmly against him. I smiled and whispered, "We're a pretty good team, partner."

His answering smile was more radiant than the sun. "That we are, shortcake," he said, kissing my forehead. "That we are."

EPILOGUE
1 Month Later

ISLA

The castle was in a tizzy.

"The babies are coming, the *babies* are coming!" could be heard up and down the halls for the past several hours, the staff and even Ambrose's wives scurrying about as they made final preparations.

Kenna had wanted a homebirth, so she was currently in bed, screaming her lungs out. I cringed as another contraction hit and her cries reached my ears.

I paused in my pacing to eye her bedroom door. "Maybe I should—"

"Nope."

I cast a glare at Kade leaning against the wall not far away. "But she could need—"

"Loch's with her. So is the doctor. She has everything she needs right now."

I fisted my hands and began to pace again. Kenna's parents gave me sympathetic smiles as I stormed past. Even Silver blinked at me serenely, her bushy tail loosely curled around her paws. Why was everyone handling this better than me? Why were they all so *calm?* My best friend was basically pushing two *footballs* through her vagina.

How could *that* not freak everyone out?

Farther down the hallway, the king was doing some pacing of his own. Okay, maybe I wasn't the only anxious one after all.

When I strode back up the hall, Kade snagged my waist and whirled me into his arms. "Kade," I protested, but he sealed his lips over mine, effectively distracting me. I didn't *want* to be distracted though. I wanted to remain alert in case Kenna needed me. I wanted to . . .

Good goddess, he was doing that thing again. That thing with his mouth that he *knew* I couldn't resist. Unmindful of our audience, he kept doing it, ever so slowly coaxing my mouth open. When his tongue swept inside, there was no stopping my moan.

A throat cleared behind me. I tried to pull away, but Kade's mouth wasn't finished with mine yet. "Go away, Everett," he murmured against my lips. "We're busy."

"How can you make out with"—Kenna let out a bloodcurdling scream—"*that* going on?" Everett incredulously said.

Even Kade flinched this time. With one final sweep of his lips, he finally broke the kiss.

Now that I was officially turned on, I didn't want him to stop. I rose up on tiptoe to reinitiate the kiss when another cry reached my ears.

A *baby's* cry.

"Thank the mother," Kade sighed, finally revealing his frayed nerves as he grabbed my hand and strode across the hall. Not even bothering to knock, he burst inside the room, dragging me with. At the sight of a pink squirming infant in the doctor's arms, Kade stopped dead in his tracks.

"A boy?" I heard Loch whisper, awe in his voice as he slowly approached his child. Tears filled my eyes when the doctor nodded and placed the baby boy in his father's arms. Loch's expression went soft, softer than I'd ever seen it before. Kade's fingers squeezed mine as he witnessed the tender moment. I glanced up to find his own eyes bright with tears.

Kenna cried out again. Loch was beside her in an instant, protectively cradling his newborn son, all while comforting his wife. After another gut-wrenching scream, another baby slid into the world.

"Kade," Loch quietly said as the second baby let out a loud wail.

Kade jumped, his eyes flying wide when his drothen gestured for him to take the second child. He hesitated as if afraid, and I gently nudged him forward.

"You can do this," I whispered, and he gratefully squeezed my fingers one last time before letting go.

As he approached the squalling infant, I couldn't help but smile. He looked so *huge* next to the tiny thing. So huge and utterly terrified. The doctor wrapped a blanket around the baby and placed it in Kade's waiting arms. He flicked a panicked glance at me, only looking down again when I smiled reassuringly.

"Kade," Kenna tiredly breathed, and he immediately turned to her.

At her questioning look, his face split into a megawatt grin. "It's a girl."

All three of them shared a look, no doubt sensing each other's emotions through the bonds that tied them together. It was so beautiful that I pressed a hand over my mouth to keep a sob from escaping.

Despite the trials we'd endured over the years, each one of them brought us to this precious moment in time. We'd mourned losses, yet we'd gained so much. And as more family members poured into the room, drawn to the miracle of new beginnings, I thanked the stars for blessing me with this second chance at life.

I'd always struggle in some shape or form with who I was. I was still figuring things out. Still mending fences and facing my fears. And maybe that was life. Maybe my job was to live in the moment and simply do my best with the time given to me.

I might not know what awaited me in my future, or how long that might even be. But I would live each fleeting moment to the fullest, surrounded by the people I loved.

ALSO BY BECKY MOYNIHAN

A TOUCH OF VAMPIRE
Shadow Touched
Curse Touched
Fate Touched
Sun Touched (spin-off standalone)

THE ELITE TRIALS
Reactive
Adaptive
Immersive

GENESIS CRYSTAL SAGA
Dawn till Dusk
Fall of Night
Stars till Sun

ACKNOWLEDGMENTS

Okay, can we just acknowledge how perfect Kade is? Like, I know I'm married, but can I still have Kade, please?? To everyone who encouraged me to write his story, thank you!! I loved giving him his well-deserved HEA. And Isla too, of course. That girl was a challenge to write considering how opposite our personalities are. I admire her spunk and humor so much! Her courage is #goals. Although I don't have any current plans to write more books in this series, I can always be persuaded to write more if there's an interest, hehe. So go ahead and persuade me!

As always, I must thank my beta readers—Kate, Morgan, and Melissa—for their loyal dedication. You give me the confidence to share my stories with the rest of the world!

To my ARC readers, I live for your excitement and reviews! I know many authors don't read their reviews, but I absolutely love knowing what my readers think of my stories. It seriously keeps me writing! Thank you for loving on this series and sharing it with others!

To my readers, I can't thank you enough for obsessing over these characters with me. I adore chatting with each and every one of you about them! Your enthusiasm makes my heart happy!!

BECKY MOYNIHAN is a bestselling, award-winning author of YA/NA Fantasy & Science Fiction. Her debut series is The Elite Trials, a YA dystopian romance. Her newest series, A Touch of Vampire, is a steamy paranormal vampire romance. She's also co-written the Genesis Crystal Saga, an urban fantasy romance series.

To stay up to date on new releases, sign up for her monthly newsletter: www.beckymoynihan.com/newsletter